H A R M
N O N E

A Rowan Gant Investigation

A Novel of Suspense and Magick
By

M. R. Sellars

E. M. A. Mysteries

HARM NONE: A Rowan Gant Investigation
A WillowTree Press / E.M.A. Mysteries Book

PRINTING HISTORY
WillowTree Press First Edition / June 2000
Second Printing / June 2001
Fifth Printing / November 2004

ISBN: 0-9678221-0-6

Cover design by Johnathan Minton, Copyright © 2000
Author photo by K. J. Epps, Copyright © 2004

PRINTED IN THE UNITED STATES
by
TCS Printing
North Kansas City, Missouri

Books By M. R. Sellars

<u>The Rowan Gant Investigations</u>

HARM NONE
NEVER BURN A WITCH
PERFECT TRUST
THE LAW OF THREE
CRONE'S MOON

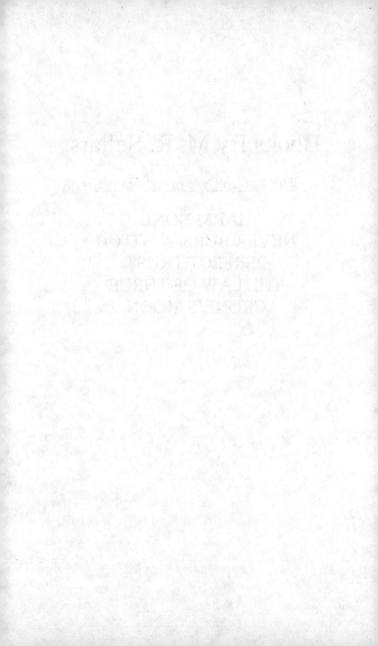

Praise for Harm None:

"Hooray for M.R. Sellars, the master of Pagan fiction! HARM NONE is a tale so real, so complex, and so terrifying, that it won't just keep you on the edge of your seat until the very last word - it's guaranteed to leave you breathless and begging for more."

— Dorothy Morrison
Author of *Everyday Magic* and *The Craft*

"HARM NONE is a superbly suspenseful thriller... highly recommended."
— Midwest Book Review

"...Sellars is a wonderful surprise all around...A good murder mystery has mystery, it has action, it has its dark sides, it has plot twists, and it has entertainment value. You can find all of that in this book."

— Boudica
The Wiccan - Pagan Times

"Fans of *Hamilton* and *Lackey* will want to religiously follow the exploits of Mr. Rowan Gant."

— Harriet Klausner
Literary Reviewer

"HARM NONE is a gripping, carefully plotted mystery that will keep pages turning right to the end."

— P.J. Nunn
Senior Mystery Reviewer,
The Charlotte Austin Review

"HARM NONE is one of the most remarkable books I've read this year. I bow to M.R. Sellars' superior story telling ability!"

— Elizabeth Henze
Murder on the Internet Express

"Fans of Mercedes Lackey's defunct *Diana Tregarde* Mysteries rejoice— a new witch is in town! Wonderful characterization from a first-person view, chilling suspense, and a baffling mystery make this first Rowan Gant mystery top-notch."

— Melanie C. Duncan,
The BookDragon Review

ACKNOWLEDGEMENTS

I would be sorely remiss if I didn't take a moment to thank at least a few of the individuals who were there to act as my sounding boards and as my moral support staff throughout the writing and editing of this novel—

Officer Scott Ruddle, SLPD without whom Detective Benjamin Storm would be just another one dimensional psuedo-cop; Jacquelyn Busch Hunt, Attorney, for the legal advice and mighty strokes of her blue pencil; Roxanne and Sharon for reading, re-reading, and then reading some more; and of course, my wife Kat, who put up with me throughout it all.

ACKNOWLEDGMENTS

For my parents.
Thank you for teaching me
that the true value of the
written word is priceless.

AUTHOR'S NOTE:

While the city of St. Louis and its various notable landmarks are certainly real, many names have been changed and liberties taken with some of the details in this book. They are fabrications. They are pieces of fiction within fiction to create an illusion of reality to be experienced and enjoyed.

In short, I made them up because it helped me make the story more entertaining, or in some cases, just because I wanted to.

Note also that this book is a first-person narrative. You are seeing this story through the eyes of Rowan Gant. The words you are reading are his thoughts. In first person writing, the narrative should match the dialogue of the character telling the story. Since Rowan, (and anyone else that I know of for that matter,) does not speak in perfect, unblemished English throughout his dialogue, he will not do so throughout his narrative. Therefore, you will notice that some grammatical anomalies have been retained (under protest from editors) in order to support this illusion of reality.

Let me repeat something—I DID IT ON PURPOSE. Do NOT send me an email complaining about my grammar. It is a rude thing to do, and it does nothing more than waste your valuable time. If you find a typo, that is a different story. Even editors miss a few now and then.

Finally, this book is not intended as a primer for WitchCraft, Wicca, or any Pagan path. However, please note that the rituals, spells, and explanations of these religious/magickal practices are accurate. Some of my explanations may not fit your particular tradition, but you should remember that your explanations might not fit mine either.

And, yes, some of the magick is "over the top." But, like I said in the first paragraph, this is fiction...

Eight words ye wiccan rede fulfill,
AN IT HARM NONE, DO WHAT YE WILL.

Final Verse
The Wiccan Rede
Lady Gwen Thompson
Original Printing— "Green Egg #69"

PROLOGUE

"Be it known to all that the circle is now to be drawn," stated the slight, robed figure as she raised her arms upward to the sky. Her dainty hands held tight to the leather bound handle of a dirk, its brightly polished blade reflecting the light of the full moon high above. "Let no one be here but of their own free will. Blessed be."

"So mote it be" came a solemn chant in unison from the coven members gathered around her.

The air was still in the large, semi-wooded Saint Louis backyard as the Priestess slowly and purposefully drew the ceremonial knife, her athamè, through the air above her, scribing a five-pointed star, starting and ending with the top point. With the imaginary Pentacle drawn, she fluidly lowered the dirk and brought her arms to rest outstretched before her and pointing to the East.

"R.J.," she said to the young man directly before her. "Would you please light the circle candles?"

The young man gave a perceptible nod and pulled back the hood of his robe to reveal his mane of long black hair. Turning, he struck the end of a wooden fireplace match, bringing it to life, and as the flame settled to evenness, merged it with the wick of a yellow votive candle resting in a homemade stand.

"At the East, I bring light and air to our circle," spoke the strawberry-blonde priestess from the center of the group. "All hail the Watchtower of the East, element of air. May it watch over us in our circle. Blessed be."

"Blessed be," chanted the gathering around her.

The young man worked his way to the South, and touched the burning match to a red votive.

"At the South, I bring light and fire to our circle" came the priestess as she made a clockwise quarter turn. "All hail the Watchtower of the South, element of fire. May it watch over our circle. Blessed be."

"Blessed be." The chant in unison came stronger.

Evenly, the young woman turned to the West as the young man brought a blue candle alight.

"At the West, I bring light and water to our circle. All hail the Watchtower of the West, element of water. May it watch over our circle. Blessed be."

"Blessed be!" Stronger still the chorus echoed.

"At the North, I bring light and earth to our circle," the priestess melodically spoke as she turned. The young man applied the fire to a green candle fixed securely in its holder. "All hail the Watchtower of the North, element of earth. May it watch over our circle. Blessed be."

"Blessed be!" The coven's chant lifted skyward, harmonious and strong.

The Priestess kissed the blade of the athamè and lifted it upward, scribing the Pentacle in the air once more.

"All hail the four towers, and all hail the God and Goddess. We welcome and invite Pan and Diana to join us in this rite we hold in their honor. Blessed be, so mote it be!"

"Blessed be, so mote it be!" chimed the coven.

At this point, the dark-haired man had returned to his original position in the circle, and the members had joined hands, interlocking their fingers, left palm up, right palm down.

"Ariel," his gaze leveled on the priestess, "may I ask that you lead us in the weave."

The young woman gave a nod and after once again kissing the blade of the athamè, laid it reverently on the altar before her.

"Weave, weave," she began the melodious chant, "weave us together. Weave us together, together with love."

The remaining members of the coven joined in and they sang the verse twice more. When the last note had drifted away on the still air, no sound was left but for the midsummer song of the crickets.

"The circle is cast," Ariel finally said. "You may release hands and we shall remain as one."

The group released their grasps on one another and while remaining alert and attentive to their priestess, began to relax.

"Our circles are a happy time," she continued, her strawberry-blonde hair drifting lazily about on a sudden breeze as she turned around the circle, bringing her eyes to bear on each member's face. "A time for us to rejoice in our kinship with nature...with the Mother Goddess Diana...and with Pan the Hunter. Our circles are meant for exchanging knowledge. Tonight..." Ariel caught her breath and looked down at the ground. She paused for what seemed an eternity to all present as a single teardrop began its slow journey down her cheek. Sadness welled in her voice as she began once again to speak. "Tonight, we come together to make a decision; a decision that will affect the direction and future of this coven. We have all discussed this over and over, so I will spare you the details."

The members of the coven lowered their gazes to the ground as she once again paused and angrily wiped away another tear that had escaped her eye. They knew how much she hated losing control of her emotions, and they felt a great empathy for her. They remained quiet and kept their gazes averted as she struggled for her composure. However, one member among the group refused to grant her the reprieve. He stared at the back of Ariel's head, unblinking, with cold grey eyes. His face remained expressionless, and to the coven, that cold countenance was the most frightening thing of all.

"Let it be done," stated the young dark-haired man known as R.J. in a compassionate attempt to assume her painful burden.

He stepped forward to the altar and lifted a pewter goblet from its weathered surface. One by one, R.J. stepped before each member of the coven and held the goblet out to them, and one by one, each member deposited a single stone. When he came before the expressionless, grey-eyed man, he waited. The man continued to stare, as if looking straight through him to remain fixed upon Ariel.

"Go on, Devon," R.J. said, "you still have a vote."

Momentarily, the expressionless man's eyes unglazed, and he focused his glare on R.J.

"I don't recognize this vote" was all he said, and once again he seemed to stare icily through to Ariel.

R.J. fought back his desire to tell Devon just where he could get off. This was going to be over soon enough, and he knew there was no need for an altercation now. He continued around the circle and came finally to rest in the center.

Standing at the altar opposite Ariel, R.J. held out the goblet and let a stone fall into it from his own palm, silently casting his vote. Slowly, Ariel lifted her hand to its rim and dropped in her stone. It rattled and clinked in the tense silence of the circle, then fell still. She brought her gaze up to meet R.J.'s, drew a deep breath, and then gave a slightly perceptible nod. R.J. tilted the goblet down to the altar and poured the stones out upon its surface. The pebbles glittered, as if winking back at them in the candlelight, each of their polished surfaces obsidian black.

Ariel turned and faced Devon, summoning every bit of strength in her being and borrowing from her fellow coven members as much as she could.

"You know the most basic law of The Craft is to harm none." She stared at him coolly as anger seeped in to replace sadness. "You have violated that law, Devon."

He continued to stare back at her, pupils large in his irises like puddles of ink in dirty grey ice. The circle candles flickered as a mild breeze began to blow.

"So I sacrificed a dog," Devon answered her frostily. "You little wimps are just afraid to take the next step. You'll never be anything but a bunch of wannabees."

Ariel continued, ignoring his comment. "For your disregard for life and the most basic of Wiccan laws, you are hereby banished from this coven. Your punishment is that which you bring upon your own self, as anything you may do will return to you threefold. May the God and Goddess take mercy upon you."

"So Mote It Be," the members of the circle solemnly chimed.

Devon looked slowly around the circle, resting his cold gaze for a moment upon each member of the coven; finally, leveling it once again on Ariel's face.

"You're going to wish you never did this, Ariel," he said. "Fuck you... Fuck all of you."

Three weeks later...

CHAPTER 1

Blue-white wisps curled upward from the lit end of a tight roll of tobacco that was hooked under my index finger. I took a lazy puff and rolled the spicy smoke around on my tongue before blowing it outward into an evenly spreading cloud that wafted about on the warm breeze. Then, with a lazy stretch, I rested my forearm across my knee and contemplated the slowly growing ash on the end of the cigar.

It had been more than six months since my last cigarette, so my wife, Felicity, was none too excited when I decided to revive my old habit of cigar smoking. As I am not one to do things halfway, these weren't the greenish, dried out logs you pick up at the local stop'n'grab. Not at all. My humidor was filled with rich, Maduro-wrapped symbols of masculinity available only from a good tobacco shop. Inevitably, with such quality there comes a price, and said price served simply to provide Felicity with yet another reason to harbor disdain for the habit.

Of course, with any marriage—well, good ones anyway—there is a generous amount of compromise. The "compromise" that had been reached in ours was something on the order of a matter-of-fact statement from my headstrong wife of, "If you're going to smoke those things anyway, you're going to do it outside!" After eight years with this auburn-haired, second generation Irish-American dynamo on a five-foot-four frame, I had learned to cut my losses and run; for as much as she hated to admit it, Felicity fit neatly into the stereotype of the tempestuous, Irish redhead. Though her singsong accent was normally faint—unless she was tired, angry, or had been in close proximity to her relatives, whereupon it became very pronounced—her stubbornness and temper were with her 24/7.

In this particular instance, however, the fact that there was no way she was about to let me in the door with a lit cigar was only one of a trio of reasons I had for being parked on the cement stairs of our modest, suburban Saint Louis home this warm, late summer's evening. The second and most important reason for smoking outside was that we had only recently discovered that Felicity was six weeks pregnant. The third—I was waiting for someone.

Earlier in the day, I had received a phone call from my long time cohort, Ben Storm, a detective with the Saint Louis City police department. Since he had a tendency to work somewhat bizarre hours, I was pleasantly surprised when he suggested that he drop by this evening for an impromptu drink to congratulate us on our impending family addition. I was more than agreeable to the idea; unfortunately, the tone of his voice told me there was an underlying, less social reason for the visit. His inflection only confirmed a suspicion that had been nagging at me for nearly two days now.

Late Wednesday night I had received a short, cryptic call from a distracted and extremely official sounding version of my friend. He had been seeking information about the meaning of a religious symbol known as a Pentacle. Though I knew he was perfectly aware of my religious practices, I was mildly amazed he had equated me with the emblem. In keeping with his official demeanor that night, as soon as I finished giving him the requested details, he abruptly ended the call with curt politeness.

When we spoke again today, I was sure I had detected a definite note of that same distraction in his voice. I hoped that I was wrong but deep inside felt that I wasn't. However, on the chance that I might have misinterpreted the tenor of his speech, I had kept the observation to myself, mentioning it neither to him nor Felicity.

"I take it Ben hasn't gotten here yet." I heard the half question, half statement from my wife through the screen door behind me.

"Nope," I replied and took another lazy draw from my cigar. "But you know how Ben is. If he says six in the evening, he really means eight."

"Ever since his promotion, we're lucky to see him at all," she expressed. "Are Allison and Ben Junior coming?"

"I doubt it. He said something about Al taking the little guy out shopping for clothes."

"Well..." She pushed the screen door open a bit to allow one of our cats to exit the confines of the house. "I'm going to go upstairs and pay some bills. Let me know when he gets here. I don't want to miss this little celebration. Remember, I'm the one who's pregnant."

"I doubt that you'll let me forget it," I answered, looking back at her with a grin. "I'll call you when he shows up."

She smiled in return and left me to my cigar and quiet contemplation of the tree-lined street, as well as my attempts to dull the secret, foreboding sensation with a tumbler of single malt scotch on the rocks. Ten minutes short of an hour later, not only had I still not managed to shake the feeling, but it grew even stronger as a tired-looking Chevrolet van rolled into my driveway. The engine knocked and complained as the driver switched it off, and then it sputtered into silence. After a moment, the door opened with a labored screech, and the occupant extricated himself from the seat.

Ben Storm was a Native American, six-foot-six with jet-black hair and the finely angular features one associated with the boilerplate portrayal of feather-adorned natives from TV Westerns. He kept himself in excellent physical condition and made a very imposing figure both in and out of uniform. When he had been a street cop, I often joked that he was the last person I would want to see coming down a dark alley at me if I had done something wrong. He always made it a point to bet that he would be the first person I would want to see coming down that alley were I in trouble. I never hesitated to agree.

Just over a year ago, fate dealt him a winning hand. He had been promoted to Detective and was assigned to homicide investigations. This was a radical, though welcome, change from knocking down the doors of crack houses, which had been his previous assignment. Now, at times, his work schedule had become less structured and was often expanded with overtime. However, that time was more often spent interviewing suspects and gathering evidence than dodging bullets sprayed from an illegally modified, Tech Nine machine pistol in the hands of a fifteen-year-old gangbanger.

I knew for a certainty that his wife was happy to have him out of the direct line of fire. Felicity and I had made no secret of the fact that we were just as relieved.

The van door made a loud groan of protest as he pushed it shut, then he turned and strode up my sidewalk with a brown paper bag tucked casually under his arm.

"I can't believe you're still driving that old piece of crap," I called to him and motioned toward the decrepit looking Chevy.

He was halfway up the flagstone walkway when he stopped, looked back at the vehicle for a moment, then turned back to me. "What?" he answered, feigning insult, then with a shrug continued walking. "It still runs."

He climbed the stairs and parked himself on the edge of the porch then stretched and let out an exhausted sigh.

"Ya'know," he finally said as he set the paper bag

carefully on the first step. "Bein' a copper is a menial job... It's kinda like bein' the secretary for all the chaos out there in the world...But anyway…" He reached into his jacket and pulled out two cigars then handed one to me. "Congrats on the kid ya' silly 'effin white man."

"Thanks, Chief." I took the cigar and gave it a close look. "Dominican, eh? Been hanging around the tobacconist playing Wooden Indian again?" I grinned.

"Yeah, blow it out your ass," he laughed. "One of the coppers I helped with a case owed me one and finally paid up." Reaching into the bag he pulled out a bottle of *Glenlivet* and a bottle of de-alcoholized white zinfandel. "So where's the little woman?"

"Upstairs doing that bill paying thing," I answered, sliding the cigar beneath my nose with a flourish and sniffing the spicy, Spanish cedar veneer that encased it. "She's gonna just love you for this," I continued, waving the expensive smoke at him. "I'm supposed to call her down when you get here, and I suppose that would be about now."

"I'll get 'er," he told me as he stood up and took a stride to the door. "I need a glass and some ice anyway. You good?"

"I could go for a couple of cubes. Just fill the ice bucket and bring it out if you want."

"Everything still in the usual place?" he asked as he opened the door.

"Yeah, same as always."

I could hear him calling up the stairs to Felicity as the screen door swung shut; something pseudo-official sounding about having the place surrounded and that all tiny red-headed women should come out with their hands up. His call was answered by my wife bounding down the stairs followed closely by our English setter and Australian cattle dog vociferously making their individual presences known.

A few short minutes later he returned, ladened with the ice bucket, a fresh glass, and Felicity in tow.

"So, before you even get started with your cop stories," my wife began, perching herself on the ledge near the stairs, "how are Allison and Ben Junior?"

Ben extracted the cork from the bottle of white zinfandel and filled the wine glass she held forth.

"Good," he answered. "Pretty good. Al said ta' tell you guys 'hey' and sorry she couldn't make it. The little guy told me to make sure I said 'hi' to the dogs."

"We really need to find some time to get together for a barbecue or something," I stated as he planted himself back on the edge of the porch and went about the task of opening the Scotch.

"Yeah," Ben returned. "Why don't ya' tell that to the bad guys. I could use a little time off." He poured himself a drink and topped mine off before sticking his cigar between his lips and setting it alight with a wooden match. "Ahhhhh," he exclaimed, blowing out a stream of pungent smoke. "I've been so damn busy lately, I really haven't had a chance to enjoy a cigar... Ya'know, I think this is the first time I've had anything lit in my mouth in a month."

"Like you really need it," Felicity admonished. "Allison and I get you two to quit cigarettes, and the next thing we know you're sucking on some other burning carcinogen."

"Boys will be boys," I told her.

"Yeah," Ben chimed in. "What he said."

The friendly chatter eased my mind for the time being, but I still felt a nag in the back of my skull. Sitting here, I knew that just as I had suspected, my friend was without a doubt its undeniable source.

Later in the evening, we called out for pizza and moved our celebration indoors. After putting the dogs through their paces for a handful of the crusts, Felicity said her goodnights and went off to bed, for she had an early outing with her nature photography club the next morning.

Ben had grown quieter as the evening wore on, leaning more heavily on the Scotch than I can ever recall him doing before. After I finished clearing the dishes from the table, he refilled our glasses from the near-depleted bottle of *Glenlivet*, and then we ventured out to the back deck.

My friend dropped his large frame heavily into a chair and went about trimming the end from a fresh cigar as I lit the citronella-oil-filled tiki torches that rimmed the deck. Mosquitoes had been bad this summer, and these seemed to stave them off fairly well while providing an unobtrusive light. After bringing the last torch to life, I took my seat opposite Ben at the patio table and proceeded to work on my own after-dinner smoke. I could literally feel his introspection building to a point of release and knew that the worry clouding the back of my mind would soon be summoned forward.

"You'n Felicity are still into that Wicca thing, right?" Ben queried after an extended silence.

"If you mean have we converted to Catholicism or something, no we haven't," I answered. "We aren't connected with a coven right now, but we still practice. Once you're a Witch, you usually stay a Witch." I lit my cigar and then took a sip of my Scotch. "Why do you ask?"

"Just curious," he replied hesitantly.

I knew there was more to the question than mere curiosity, but I also knew better than to press this particular subject with Ben, for that would only serve to make him feel ill at ease. He had always been willing to accept that Felicity and I practiced what was considered by most to be a nontraditional religion but usually showed a clear desire to leave it in the background. Out of sight, out of mind. As with most things that didn't fit with the majority view, the masses, including Ben, were entirely off base in their misconceptions regarding Wicca, WitchCraft and almost any other alternative religion for that matter.

I had once attempted to explain to him that Wicca and WitchCraft, or simply "The Craft" as we often call it, involved no pointed hats, bubbling cauldrons, or flying brooms. To the knowledge of any practitioner of the religion, it never did truly include such things. I told him that Wicca was simply an Earth religion, and as for deities, ours were the Earth and the Moon: Diana and Pan, respectively. There was no evil intent, and in fact, our most basic and all-important covenant was to "Harm None." We viewed our religion as a way of life through which we did our best to live in harmony with nature, and through study and meditation, we attempted to learn control over the natural energies that inherently reside within all of us. I further explained that in doing this, we sometimes developed abilities that some would consider psychic in nature, such as an uncanny sixth sense or the ability to heal others and ourselves: We think of these as learned talents, nothing more, and nothing less. I even added that I knew of no incident where anyone had been turned into a frog, except in fairy tales. The simple fact was that even if that were possible, no self-respecting Witch would consider it.

Even after I had answered his several pointed questions, he still clung to his misconceptions, and so, out of respect for him, I made sure to steer clear of the subject entirely.

Now, for the second time in less than a week, Ben was asking me about a part of my life he normally avoided. I wasn't about to push, so I was more than willing to bide my time and wait for him to get around to what he wanted. I could feel his preoccupation thick in the darkness around us, so I was certain my wait would be a short one.

"So… You remember when I called you 'bout that five-pointed star a couple days back?" he finally asked.

"You mean the difference between a Pentacle, and a Pentagram?" I returned. "Yeah, I remember."

"That's it," he affirmed. "Would ya' mind tellin' me the difference on that again?"

"No problem. A Pentacle is basically just what you said, a five-pointed star surrounded by a circle. It's a very common symbol in the Wiccan religion. When it's upright," I scribed the symbol in the air with my finger, "with only one point at the top, it represents man and the spirit as it rules over the four elements. That's when it's called a Pentacle. If on the other hand you turn it one hundred-eighty degrees, and two of the points are at the top," I spun my finger in a circle, "it's called a Pentagram and represents the spirit's union with material elements." I relaxed back into my chair. "Some however, place an improper, albeit widely accepted, meaning on the Pentagram. They claim it represents Satan, evil, black magick, etcetera."

"So, if it's right side up or whatever, it doesn't mean anything evil?" he posed.

"It actually depends on who drew it, and the significance THEY placed on it, but it's really nothing more than a symbol. Inherently, neither of them mean anything evil," I answered. "In my religion anyway."

Ben stared thoughtfully out into the night, absently fingering the rim of his Scotch glass and quietly puffing on his cigar. I didn't disturb him. Instead I watched the orange glow on the end of the cigar each time he puffed and waited patiently for the next question.

"What about colors?" he asked. "Do ya' color it in or somethin'? You know, like a rainbow?"

"Sometimes you'll find a different color at each of the four corners," I answered. "Yellow in the upper left, blue in the upper right, red in the lower right, and green in the lower left. They represent the elements of Air, Water, Fire, and Earth. On occasion the top point will be white, representing Akasha, or the spirit."

"Would they be pastels?" he queried.

"Well, I suppose if you wanted to be artistic about it they could," I laughed. "But they don't have to be. Just yellow, blue, red, green, and white." I could feel his tension congealing around us and knew that something about a Pentacle was really bothering him. I was just about to break my own rules and press for the problem when he elected to reveal it on his own.

"So listen, Rowan," he began. "I've got this case I'm workin' on, and ta' be honest, it's really got me screwed up. It's not normal...there's somethin' real strange about it."

"Something to do with a Pentacle, I assume?" I asked, already knowing it to be true.

"Yeah," he continued. "The theology expert the department called in can't seem to make up his mind. His theory changes every time we try to talk to 'im. A couple of the old timers on the force say the whole thing reminds them of a Satan-worship-slash-cult-murder they worked a few years back. That's why I called you Wednesday night."

"I'm not sure I follow."

"I was almost ready ta' agree with 'em about the cult stuff, but somethin' kept eatin' at me," he explained. "I'm sittin' at my desk thinkin', 'where have I seen this star thing before?' All of a sudden it hits me..." Ben pointed at me and waved his hand about. "Hangin' around YOUR neck."

The fact that he had been able to match me with the symbol suddenly made sense. The quarter-sized pendant I wore was for all intents and purposes a part of me, for I almost never took it off; much as one who wears a Crucifix or the medallion of a patron saint. For the most part, it remained hidden behind the fabric of my shirt, and I had honestly never given any thought to the fact that he might have noticed it, but obviously, he had. Of course, what good is a cop if he's not observant?

"So you called me to find out if I was in a cult or something?" I posed.

"Hell no, I knew better than that. I called ya' because I figured ya' just might know a little more about what it means than the wingnut the department hired." He let out a frustrated sigh. "Now the problem is I'm even more confused."

"Why's that?"

"Well, if this star is a good thing, I don't get why it was at the scene."

"If I'm following you, you're talking about a murder, correct?" I asked.

"Yeah," he answered and took a long swallow of his drink. "Murder... Sacrifice... Something..."

"And you're sure what you found was a Pentacle, and not a Pentagram?"

"It had five points, and it was right side up," he explained. "So yeah, it was a Pentacle I guess."

"So what does your expert have to say?"

"Well, the latest theory from that Einstein is that it's a ritual sacrifice from a Satanic African cult called Santeria."

I puzzled over the information wordlessly for a moment, staring deliberately into my own drink as I formed a response. "I realize that I haven't seen the evidence myself, but based on what you've said, I would seriously doubt that."

"Why?"

"To begin with, a Pentacle isn't a Santerian symbol, but

that's only a minor part of it. Santeria is an Afro-Cuban religion, not a cult, and it has nothing to do with Satan worship. Their sacrifices are normally small animals such as chickens, not human beings. In most cases, the animal is cooked and eaten as a part of the ritual. Truth is, they treat their dinner with more respect than you or I do.

"Another thing you might want to take into account is the fact that the actual Satanic religion doesn't endorse human blood sacrifice either. My guess would be that your expert has some pre-conceived notions and is misinterpreting the facts."

"How do you know all this stuff?" Ben looked at me with an expression of mild surprise, his cigar held frozen several inches before his face.

"I read a lot," I told him. "Wicca and WitchCraft get compared to everything under the sun. Good, bad, and otherwise. I just like to keep up with what I'm being accused of."

"Makes sense." Thoughtful silence followed his measured reply, leaving us with the trilling night song of countless crickets.

I realized my explanation had, unintentionally, served only to add more confusion to his current discomposed thoughts. I could also feel his aura of internal conflict as he debated over his next question. In the interest of addressing both of the complications, I voiced my own query, "So...Are you looking for help?"

"I shouldn't drag you into it," he answered after a long pause.

"You aren't dragging me anywhere, Ben," I told him. "If what happened is actually some kind of cult sacrifice, it could mean something bigger than just one homicide. Besides, the fact that you found a Wiccan symbol bothers me just as much as it does you. Like I've told you before, our most basic rule is to 'Harm None'. Even if it has nothing to do with the religion, if I can help you track down whoever did it, then let me."

Ben ran one hand through his hair and smoothed it back, a gesture I had come to equate with his being lost in thought. I had known this man for more years than I cared to remember and had seen him through good and bad. He was a consummate professional, without a doubt. Still, I knew that all the training and even all the experience in the world could never prepare someone for every scenario he may encounter in this line of work.

I was constantly amazed by my friend's ability to remain detached and objective in an investigation, but tonight was different. I had never seen him so disturbed by a case. Ever. I could tell from his troubled demeanor that this one must be beyond what even a seasoned veteran considered bad.

"I've got some pictures with me," he finally spoke after what seemed a lifetime. "Do ya' think you can give me an idea of what some of the stuff might mean?"

"I'll be happy to give it a try," I told him.

"You haven't seen this stuff yet," he replied. "It's bad, Rowan."

"I understand."

"No you don't," he sighed. "When I say bad, I mean it's fuckin' sick."

I had just turned on the overhead light in the dining room and seated myself at the table when Ben returned from his van with his briefcase. He peeled off his sport coat and threw it over the back of a chair then sat down. With a quick snap, he released the latches on the case and retrieved a large manila envelope bearing a case number and the word EVIDENCE printed in bright red block letters. I could see sweat already forming on his brow, and his hands trembled slightly as he handed me the packet.

"Man," he said. "I really hate ta' do this to ya'. This shit is enough to give ya' nightmares. It has me."

"Like I said," I took the envelope, "you aren't doing anything to me. I offered to help."

I unwrapped the string that held the package shut and folded back the flap. Tilting it, I slid out a healthy stack of eight-by-ten photographs, some color, some black and white. I began thumbing through the pictures slowly, studying each one carefully and giving Ben my general impression of the images.

The first photo was of a crudely painted Pentacle on a wall. Sections were shaded in pastel yellow, blue, and green. The outline of the symbol was a deep, rusted red, and a portion of it was smeared with the same color.

"Now I see why you were asking about the pastels," I stated. "But the red looks a little strange. Not really a pastel."

"It's the victim's blood," Ben volunteered matter-of-factly, his voice almost a whisper.

"Oh," I replied. I couldn't think of anything else to say.

The second picture showed the Pentacle at more of a distance, revealing a mound of black and a mound of white on the floor. The following picture, a close-up of the mounds, showed them to be candles that had burned until they extinguished themselves, leaving behind hardened puddles of wax.

"Obviously a ritual of some sort," I told him. "I'm not sure for what."

I thumbed through more pictures of the candles and wall from various angles. The black and white images were much easier to tolerate, though knowing that the Pentacle had been inscribed in blood made me imagine I could still see the glaring red within the crisp black and grey tones. Eventually, I came to a picture of another wall. In the same dripping crimson strokes as the Pentacle were the words "All Is Forgiven."

"The consultant still can't manage to explain that," Ben told me, indicating the pictured words. "He says it probably has somethin' ta' do with blood sacrifice rituals. Says he thinks it might..."

"No," I interrupted him, holding up a hand, "those words have nothing to do with a blood sacrifice ritual."

"Whaddaya mean?" he queried, sitting up a little straighter and focusing his attention.

"Your *expert* is apparently pretty full of misinformation. I'm not saying that there wasn't a sacrifice ritual performed mind you, but just because the victim's blood was used, that doesn't make it so," I detailed. "The Pentacle and the inscription are components of a spell."

"You mean a hocus-pocus-poof-you're-a-frog kinda spell?"

"No. That's a fairy-tale misconception. While spells sometimes do involve what can be called magick, they are primarily something like a prayer. This particular spell is a separate ritual unto itself, and if I'm right, then I'm willing to bet your killer performed it because of the murder, not as a part of it."

"I still don't get it," Ben told me, both eager and frustrated.

"Just a second..." I got up from the table and went across the room to the bookshelves. "I just want to verify something real quick to make sure I'm right." I scanned the shelves reserved for our Wiccan and alternative religious literature and quickly found what I was after. "Here it is..."

I pulled the book from the shelf and leafed quickly through it as I strode back across the room and once again took a seat at the table.

"What is that?" Ben asked as I continued rapidly turning and perusing the pages.

"A grimoire," I told him. "Kind of like a recipe book for Witches." I stopped leafing through the book, and my eyes followed my finger down the text while I quietly mumbled to myself. Eventually I came to rest halfway down the page. "Yes, it's a variation of an Expiation spell."

"A what?" Ben's still confused voice reached my ears as I handed him the spellbook and quickly leafed back through the pictures I had already seen. According to the grimoire, a piece of the spell appeared to be missing. I felt sure it was there but that I simply hadn't noticed it.

"An Expiation spell," I repeated. "A ritual to rid yourself of guilt and regrets—a way of asking forgiveness from yourself. I'm not finding it..." I stated hurriedly. "Was there a cup or goblet there? It would have had wine in it. Or maybe water." Only silence met my ears. "Ben?" I queried again, looking up.

He was staring at me across the table, face ashen, the spellbook held loosely in his hands.

"Are you okay?" I asked, growing mildly concerned.

"Yeah, we found a wine glass all right," he said quietly. "But, it wasn't filled with wine."

The look on his face told me that which I needed but didn't want to know.

"It was filled with blood wasn't it?"

"Yeah," he replied. "We think the bastard drank her blood."

The two of us shared a wordless stare as we were simultaneously bludgeoned by the revolting possibility he had just voiced. I swallowed hard and slowly forced my eyes back down to the permanent visual records of the abomination. Five photographs later, it was my turn for the greyish pallor to overtake my face. The glossy color image before me showed a bed with the nude body of a petite young woman draped across it. Her mouth was frozen in the oval shape of an agonized scream, her dull eyes staring horrifically into space. The wall next to the bed was spattered wildly with blood. Her throat had been cut, and her long, strawberry-blonde hair was matted into the sheets, which flowed to the floor like a crimson waterfall. From the ragged incision at her throat to a point just below her waist, and from shoulder to shoulder, she was nothing but bare exposed muscle. She had been skinned.

As if that weren't enough, there was something else that made me hold my breath a beat longer. That something was the fact that her face held more than just a passing familiarity to me.

"An invocation rite," I stated flatly, fighting back insistent waves of nausea.

"What's that?" Ben asked.

"A ritual used to call forth someone or something from another plane of existence."

"You mean like a spirit or somethin'?"

"Yeah," I answered, "it's the 'or something' that bothers me."

"How can ya tell that's what it is?" Ben pressed. "All the symbols were with that Expiation thing."

"The flaying," I answered. "Skinning and mutilation are considered parts of a ritual sacrifice for invocation in some old religions. Have you gotten a report from the coroner?"

"No, not yet...Why?"

"Whoever did this..." I caught my breath and started again. "Whoever did this probably skinned her alive. The sonofabitch performed two rituals. One to invoke who knows what, and one to forgive himself for doing it."

"Jeezus," Ben whispered.

"I need to see this crime scene, Ben," I told him, still staring at the two-dimensional horror.

"I don't know, Rowan..." he began to protest.

"No, Ben," I shot back, "I'm serious. I don't know for sure what this guy is up to yet, but you've already told me that your expert can't find his way around the block. If this bastard is really trying to do what I think he is, then I doubt if he's going to stop here. If I'm physically on the scene, maybe I can find something that will help." Without realizing it, I had stood up from my seat and had begun pacing. "Besides," I stopped, looked down at the picture for a moment and then back to Ben's face, "I know the victim."

"You know 'er?" He stared back at me incredulously.

"Her name's Ariel Tanner," I stated quietly and then turned away as if having the photographs behind me would make them magically disappear. I took a deep breath before adding, "She's a... was... a Witch."

"How did you know her?"

"I was her teacher. I instructed her in The Craft."

I could hear him scribbling quickly, making notes like a good cop was supposed to do. I had started him on the road to solving one of his mysteries, but an entirely new one was unfolding before me. A new one that my instincts were telling me would need to be solved very quickly.

"Shit," Ben muttered as he made his decision. "Okay. I'll pick you up in the mornin'."

"I'll be here."

CHAPTER 2

I didn't have any of the nightmares Ben warned me of—of course, you have to go to sleep in order to have nightmares. I was still sitting at the dining room table, absently studying the pattern of the sponge-painted walls when Felicity awoke and wandered in.

"Aye, it's four A.M.," she said with a yawn as she hooked her arm around my neck and fell into my lap. The fact that she wasn't fully awake was allowing a hint of her Celtic brogue to show through. "How late were you and Ben drinking, then?" She reached out to the table and picked up my coffee cup then took a swallow. "Yech, needs sugar."

I wrapped an arm about her waist and held her close. I had never been any good at breaking bad news to people, and I wasn't really looking forward to doing it now. I let my head rest against her chest and took in the sweet scent of her long auburn curls. I felt comfortable and safe against her, and I held her even tighter. A foreboding deep inside told me that this was the last time I was going to feel this way for a while, so I allowed it to linger as long as I could.

"Row," she asked, resting her cheek against my head. "What's wrong?"

Her drowsy voice threw back my thin security blanket of denial and exposed me once again to the frigid reality I had come to accept only a few hours before. I took in a deep breath and let it out in a slow sigh, and then reluctantly, I spoke, "Remember Ariel Tanner?"

"Of course," she replied. "What about her? Is everything okay?" She pulled away, remaining in my lap, and bringing a hand beneath my bearded chin, raised my face to meet her concerned gaze.

"She was murdered," I told her. "Ben is the investigating officer."

"Oh no..." she whispered, her voice trailing off, and then hugged me tightly. "When did it happen? How?"

"A couple of days ago. As for the how...well, it wasn't pretty. It looks like it might have been a ritual murder."

"A ritual murder!" she gasped. "You mean as in someone sacrificed her?"

"That's how it appears." I continued, "In the crime scene pictures Ben showed me, anyway."

Her voice suddenly took on a sharp, almost angry tone, "Why would he show pictures to you, then? Has he lost his mind?"

"Now don't go off the deep end." I helped her gently from my lap and stood up. "He had no idea that I knew her, and he was showing me the pictures because I offered to help. It seems his expert wasn't having much luck deciphering the symbols left at the scene." Picking up my coffee cup, I went into the kitchen to freshen it, Felicity trailing along behind.

"I see." She calmed and held out a cup she had retrieved from the cabinet. She stopped me when I had filled it just over halfway. "Were you able to figure anything out for him?"

I leaned against the counter and took a sip of hot java. "Well, whoever committed the crime performed a ritual flaying, I would assume in order to invoke something. What's interesting though, is that there were also blatant signs of what I'm pretty sure was supposed to be an Expiation spell."

"Expiation spell," she repeated while stirring sugar into her cup. "So do you think that the killer felt remorse and was trying to get rid of the guilt then?"

I nodded. "That's my best guess for now. I'll know more

in a few hours."

"What happens in a few hours?" she queried, her bright, green eyes peering at me over the rim of her cup as she took a drink.

"I'm going to look at the crime scene with Ben."

"You're what?!" Her eyes grew large and she nearly dropped her mug. "What in the name of the Mother Goddess are you doing that for?"

"Calm down, sweetheart." I held up my hand defensively. "You know as well as I do that if this creep is for real, he's likely to do something like this again sooner or later. Probably sooner."

"Aye, so let the police handle it," she shot back. "It's their job, not yours."

"I intend to," I told her. "But you also know that if he's leaving behind blatant occult symbology, the media and the cops will end up on a real 'Witch' hunt. If they knew what they were looking at to begin with, then Ben wouldn't have asked for my advice."

"Well." She calmed significantly as the logic took hold. "You're right about that."

"I just want to make sure they get the real bad guy and not pin it on some poor unsuspecting kid just because he has long hair and a copy of *Buckland's Complete Book of WitchCraft* on his bookshelf."

"I agree," she surrendered.

"Besides," I said, turning and attempting to look out into the darkness through the sliding doors but seeing only my ragged reflection staring back at me, "if this cretin actually has a background in The Craft..."

"...It's going to take a Witch to catch a Witch gone bad," Felicity finished the sentence for me. "And that Witch is going to be you."

"It might have to be," I told her.

"Aye, that's what scares me," she replied.

I convinced Felicity to go ahead on her planned outing with her nature photography club but only after promising to call her if something of consequence happened. She made a great show of placing her cell phone prominently in a pocket of her photo vest and reminding me of the number before loading her equipment and setting out. I had showered and tied my long brown hair back in a ponytail after she left and was making a futile attempt to relax on the front porch swing when Ben pulled into the driveway.

"Hey, paleface," he greeted me as he climbed the stairs.

I held up my hand in a classic TV Indian greeting. "How, Tonto."

"However I can get it." He motioned to the coffee cup in my hand. "Got any more of that? I'm havin' a hell of a time wakin' up this mornin'."

"Yeah, sure," I replied, getting up and opening the door. "Same here. It's the only thing standing between me and sleep right now."

Ben took a seat in the living room and was promptly accosted by a large, green-eyed, black cat that elected to take up residence in his lap. Dickens, as we called him, loved having visitors, especially men, and was quick to claim them for his own. I headed for the kitchen while he settled in, then quickly returned with a steaming cup of black coffee and handed it to Ben.

"I gotta be honest with ya', Rowan," he began, scratching the purring lump of fur beneath its chin. "I was thinkin' on the way over, and I'm not so sure about you goin' to the scene and all."

"What's the problem?" I asked. "Is it because I'm a civilian?"

"No, not at all," he answered. "Civilian consultants ain't that unusual. What I'm worried about is the fact that you knew the victim."

"I see," I nodded. "So you think I might be too close to this whole thing."

"It crossed my mind," he answered and then took a sip from his cup.

I had seated myself across from him in my favorite chair, an antique rocker. Gazing thoughtfully into space, I gently nudged it into motion. I had been told more than once by my parents that as a child, whenever I was lost in thought, I would rock, rocking chair or not. I still did.

"I'm not going to lie to you Ben," I finally said. "It does get to me that Ariel is the victim, and yes, she was a good friend even though we hadn't seen one another for over a year." I stopped the chair and leaned forward. "On the other hand, I have knowledge that might help to catch whoever did this. I think I demonstrated that last night."

"I'll give ya' that," he replied. "But what do you think you're gonna find at the scene that wasn't in the photos?"

"Hopefully something that will tell me if this guy is for real or just trying to make it look that way."

"And that somethin' would be?"

"I won't know until I see it...or feel it," I explained. "What I'm looking for might not be visible to the naked eye."

"You mean like some kinda *psychic* thing? You know I don't believe in that stuff."

"I know, but I do, and if it gives you a solid lead, what does it matter?"

"Okay, tell me this." He skipped past answering my question and proceeded into another of his own. "You ain't lookin' for revenge or somethin' are you?"

"No. Not at all," I answered with unabashed honesty. "There's no need. What goes around comes around. He'll get what's coming to him whether I help you or not…Eventually."

"Yeah, well that's a pretty idealistic sentiment."

"It comes with the religion."

Ben grunted and stared thoughtfully into the depths of the mug held between his large hands. After a short period of suggestive silence, he looked up at me with deadly serious eyes. "Mind if I ask where ya' were Wednesday evenin'?"

I was taken aback by the question and what it implied. At first I was hurt and then angry. It took less than a second for the anger to be replaced by understanding. I knew the victim, and I knew The Craft. The symbols and words in the pictures were no great mysteries to me. I was sure that Ben didn't truly suspect me of the crime, but if he was going to bring me into this investigation, someone was bound to ask the question. He was correct to assume that I would prefer it came from him.

"Felicity and I had dinner with my dad," I answered. "We went over to his place around four-thirty and left from there."

"Where'd you eat?"

"Union Station," I told him. "There's a restaurant down there with a fantastic mixed grill. Before you ask," I added, "we got home around nine-thirty."

"Your old man can verify this, right?"

"The phone's right there." I pointed at the bookshelves. "His number is on the speed dial. I'm sure the receipt is upstairs if you want a copy of that too."

"I'm sorry, man." He looked back down at his drink. "You know I had ta' ask…"

"...Or somebody else would," I finished the sentence for him. "It's all right. I was a little miffed at first, but I understand."

"Okay," he answered, then drained the coffee from his cup and set it on the table before him. "Let's go do this."

Ariel Tanner had lived on the first floor of a four-family flat on a street called Shenandoah within the city limits of Saint Louis. From my house in the suburbs, it took the better part of thirty minutes to reach it even though the Saturday morning traffic was light. The morning sun was already climbing in the sky when we rolled into the alleyway behind the flat and Ben pulled the Chevy into something resembling a parking space.

"This is it," he told me, switching off the knocking engine and pushing open his complaining door.

I climbed out as well, and we stood in the small patch of grass that served as a backyard, quietly studying the rear entrance of the building. A short flight of wooden stairs led up to a whitewashed exterior door. The porch light, fitted with a dim yellow bulb, still burned in the crisp shadows caused by a small overhang jutting from the brick wall to cover the landing.

"The apartment next to hers," Ben told me, "and the one directly above are currently unoccupied." He pointed to each of the windows. "The other upstairs apartment belongs to a forty-year-old woman who's stone deaf. Besides, she wasn't even home."

A ghostly flash of noise battered my eardrums for a moment. The briefness and ethereal quality of the mechanical rumble told me it was only in my head, but I knew immediately what it meant.

"And the air conditioner was running," I stated. "No one could hear her over the noise if she screamed."

"Yeah," Ben paused and looked at me sideways. "The other neighbors didn't hear a thing." We started walking toward the stairs. "Anyway, the outer doors automatically lock, and there were no visible signs of forced entry, so we assume she either knew the killer and let 'im in, or he had a key or somethin' of that sort."

"Locksmith, maybe," I offered as we climbed the stairs and came to rest on the landing.

"We're checking into that," Ben replied. "The upstairs neighbor was the one that found 'er when she was comin' in later that evenin'. Her door was propped open, and the neighbor thought it was a little strange."

"Deliberately propped open?"

"Looked that way."

"Odd…" I mused aloud. "That would seem to indicate that whoever did this wanted the body found quickly."

Taking out a key that had been provided to the police by the landlord, he opened the exterior door, and we stepped into what could be referred to as a small, shared mud room. To either side, there was a door, each with a large, sectioned pane of glass. Peering through the left window, one could see that the apartment was empty. Through the right, the small kitchen appeared lived in. Shiny copper pots and pans hung from a ceiling rack in the center of the room, and there was a can of vegetarian chili sitting on the counter in front of a small microwave—a last meal that was never eaten. Ben took a small lock blade from his pocket, opened it and cut the Police Crime Scene seal on the door. Stowing the knife and using another key, he unlocked the door.

"Uhhh, Ben." I reached out and grabbed his arm as he started to push the door open. "I'd better warn you about something."

"Warn me 'bout what?" He turned to face me.

"This..." I started. "This might get a little weird, for lack of a better word."

"Are you talkin' about that hocus-pocus shit again?" he asked, still holding the doorknob.

"One," I shot back. "Yes, if that's what you want to call it. Two, it's not shit."

"Okay, okay," he answered, knowing that he'd raised my ire. "Sorry. But I already told ya' I don't really believe in all that stuff." He slipped his hand up to smooth his hair and let out a resigned sigh. "Okay, look, I'll give it a try your way, but don't expect too much from me. I operate in a world where physical evidence is what makes the case."

"Fair enough. For the sake of argument though, you might want to take notes. Also, if I *zone out* on you, don't touch me. That would break my concentration."

"Okay," he answered and pushed the door open. "Whatever you say."

I knew he was still unconvinced, but I also knew I could trust him to do as I asked. In any event, as soon as the door swung open, there was no turning back.

The first thing I felt was the hair on the back of my neck as it stood on end then was rapidly followed by every other hair on my body mimicking the action. My skin began to burn as if I were baking under a sun lamp. Proceeding forward, I stepped through the entrance, followed closely by Ben. I scarcely heard the faint click of the door as he pressed it shut.

"Be careful of that crap they used to dust for prints, it'll stain..."

I held up a hand to cut him off and walked quietly through the kitchen, working my way to the counter. I began to consciously control my breathing, slowly and deeply in through my nose and out through my mouth. I relaxed and imagined a spire of light, white and pure, running from the soles of my feet to the center of the Earth. In a matter of moments, I was "grounded," and I cleared my mind, allowing it to become a blank, unblemished slate. I slipped easily into a shallow trance, and when I felt relaxed, centered, and in control, I reached out to touch the unopened can of chili on the counter. When my hand made contact, I invited the last few moments of Ariel Tanner's life to play themselves out upon the empty screen I had created.

My vision tunneled, and colors bled away, running like paint being poured from a can. I could hear the melodious humming of a female voice, pretty and distinct. I looked around to see where it originated, only to realize that it was coming from within me as I assumed Ariel's role. A part of me struggled to remain earthbound, and I knew that the humming was occurring only inside my head. My conscious self would have to narrate what I was seeing for Ben.

"I, Ariel, am humming," I told him. "I'm happy and I'm getting ready to fix myself something for dinner."

"Whaddaya mean 'you, Ariel'?" Ben was perplexed. "What are ya' talkin' about?"

"Just listen," I instructed him.

What was that? A noise. Maybe there's someone at the door. I'd better check.

The scenario continued to project itself inside my mind, and I turned and walked to the door. I was vaguely aware of Ben quickly shuffling out of my path and following along behind me.

"There might be someone at this door," I continued talking aloud. "She heard a noise, and she's checking on it. She's opening the door."

That's funny, no one there. I was sure I heard something. I guess I just imagined it. Oh well, I need to eat soon. I just took my insulin twenty minutes ago.

"There's no one there." I went on, "She thinks she must have imagined the noise." I turned and walked back to the counter. "She's a diabetic, and she has to eat something because she just took her insulin."

"Yeah, we found it in the fridge," Ben told me hesitantly, and I didn't admonish him.

What?! What's going on? Who's there? STOP! Let me go! Don't do that! Get that away from my face! What's that smell? I'm gagging. Stop it!

I could feel her struggling as she was grabbed from behind, and I was forced to tense my own muscles to keep from lashing out in a mirrored response. A phantomlike, sickly sweet odor tickled my nostrils, urging me to drift off into sleep. I shook my head, fending off the woozy sensation. "Someone grabbed her from behind. She's struggling, but he's too strong. She smells something. He put something over her face. Chloroform or something..."

Dizzy. Sleepy. I'm falling. Falling.

"She's blacking out," I stated urgently.

Ouch! What was that? Something bit me on my arm. Did a mosquito get in here? No. It felt like a needle. Oh, I feel strange. What's happening to me? Why does my head feel like this. I'm dizzy. Why is the room getting so dark?

"Pain," I almost shouted. "Something on her arm. A bite? No, a needle. The bastard drugged her. Look at his face, Ariel! Dammit, look at his face!"

The sequence ended in a black fog, and I stumbled against the counter. I sensed Ben reaching for me uncertainly then pulling back, apparently remembering I had told him not to touch me if I tranced.

"I'm okay," I told him, regaining my balance and pulling off my glasses in order to rub my eyes. "He drugged her. Did the medical examiner check for drugs?"

"Should have. Tox screens are SOP," Ben answered. "I still don't have a report yet. You sure you're all right?"

"Yeah, I'm okay," I answered. "Let's keep going. Maybe she saw his face at some point."

"Look, Row," Ben started. "Uhhh... Are you tellin' me that you're actually seein' what Ariel Tanner saw the night she was murdered?"

"Believe it or not, Ben," I looked at him squarely in the face. "Yes. That's exactly what I'm telling you."

"Jeezus," he said, "I've seen some strange shit, but this..." his voice trailed off.

Though I had explained to Ben some of the more minor aspects of WitchCraft, this was the first time he had ever seen any of the abilities I had cultivated in my studies. Considering his feelings on the subject, I realized I was asking him to take a rather large leap of faith, but of all my non-practicing friends, I felt certain he could be the most open-minded even if he hadn't demonstrated it as yet. I flashed him an understanding smile to let him know that I understood what he must have been thinking at the moment and patted him lightly on the arm as I moved past into the wide hallway.

At the end, I could see where the passage opened into a combination living room/dining room area. To my left, there was a closet and bathroom, to my right, the doorway to Ariel's bedroom. I continued my measured breathing as I stepped lightly along the worn hardwood floor. Once again, my hairs began to pivot upward painfully and my skin to sear as I entered the actual scene of the murder.

Blood on the walls and sheets had turned a rusty brown where it had continued to dry. A tracing of Ariel's body was stretched out across the bed like a frozen caricature of the once vibrant young woman, the yellow lines clashing with the brownish red crust of dried blood. I moved slowly to the bed then grounded and centered. Once again, the color rapidly drained from the scene about me, and I felt myself being sucked into a dark tunnel.

Oh my head hurts. Why can't I see? It's dark. No, there's a light. I have to move toward it. My arms. Why can't I move my arms? I'm cold.

As before, the events of that night flooded into my brain caustically. I was experiencing her terror. Her pain.

Why am I on my bed? I'm cold. Where are my clothes? My arms hurt. My back hurts. What's that noise?!

"I'm...she's..." I started again, speaking from the trance I had fallen into. "...On the bed, my arms hurt and I can't move them. They're tied behind me...her. I'm..." I fought to maintain a separation between the experience and myself. "...She's nude. The air conditioner is on and it's blowing on her. She's cold. She hears a noise."

Who's there? Why can't I speak? I'm trying so hard but nothing is coming out. I'm so cold. I'm frightened. What's happening? That noise again. Someone is here. They're moving around. Why can't I remember anything? My head hurts.

"He's moving around, but she can't see him," I continued. "He must be out of her line of sight or maybe out of the room. I'm not sure."

A crash! Am I being robbed? Oh please, let whoever it is just take what they want and leave. Wait. Someone grabbed me when I was in the kitchen. Who was it? Oh why can't I remember? I'm cold. I'm scared.

"She heard a loud crash or something. From another room maybe," I spoke. "She thinks it might be a burglar, but she still can't see. She remembers being attacked in the kitchen. Whatever he drugged her with is still working on her. She's foggy. She's having trouble moving. Come on, Ariel," I continued out loud. "Fight it. Concentrate."

Maybe if I try to move forward. Ouch, that hurts. Just a little more. I'm so cold. Why is this happening to me? There, now I can see the door. Ohhhh, I'm feeling sick...hanging upside down...I can't. Oh my head hurts.

"She managed to move herself a little. Her head is hanging over the side of the bed now, upside down. It's making her nauseous."

Who is that? Why is this person in my house? Why is this person wearing a ceremonial robe? Pull the hood back. I can't see who you are. It's cold. No, don't go to that side of the bed, I can't see you. What are you doing? Am I going to be raped? Please, don't let him rape me.

"He came into the room," I continued. "He's wearing a ceremonial robe, and the hood is covering his face. He walked around to the other side of the bed. She can't see him. *NO, don't do that. I can't see you.*" I slipped for a moment, and Ariel blended into the voice of my conscious self. "She's afraid he's going to rape her."

What are you doing? He's touching me. What? What are you saying? You're sorry? Sorry about what. It's cold. My arms are killing me. Why are you doing this?

"He's speaking to her!" I exclaimed out loud. "He's telling her he's sorry. She doesn't understand. Concentrate, Ariel," I coached the vision. "Help me help you."

What are you talking about? Sorry? What are you sorry about? I don't understand. Tell me what you mean. Your voice sounds familiar, but I can't remember who you are. Ouch! What are you doing? Get off of me. Oh, why can't I scream? If I could just scream, someone would come to help me. It's cold. Get off of me. What is that in your hand? What are you doing?!

"He's on the bed with her. On top of her." I relayed the vision to Ben. "His voice seems familiar to her, but she can't place it. He has something in his hand."

My athamè! What are you doing with my athamè? No! No, don't do that! STOP!

My head exploded. At least, that is how it felt as a desperate scream that only I could hear echoed forever inside my skull. My skin burst into a violent blaze, and starting at my throat, running the length of my chest then spreading rapidly outward, I felt as if every single nerve were raw and suddenly plunged into a vat of alcohol. I clawed at my own chest, fighting to push away the ethereal knife that was ripping my flesh.

"Dear Mother Goddess!" I cried. "The son-of-a-bitch is skinning her alive with her own athamè!"

I fell to my knees and continued to claw at the air in front of me. I was faintly aware of Ben's concerned voice screaming my name, but I couldn't respond. I was trapped in the vision. I could see nothing but dull red and black as I squeezed my eyes tightly shut, fighting to deny the searing pain. I could feel the blade of the athamè, at once steely cold and white hot, as it slid beneath my skin, separating the layer of nerve impregnated flesh from the rest of my body. I was certain I could hear thick tearing as my hide was peeled away, exposing muscle, nerves, and hot viscid blood. I screamed my own guttural wail of agony as I struggled to break free of this vision I knew could easily kill me. It seemed to last an eternity. It seemed to last only a second. Time no longer meant anything.

Why doesn't somebody make him stop?

"I can't Ariel. I can't," I sobbed.

Why? Why are you doing this? Where are you going? I hurt so bad! Why did you do this? I have to see you. Who are you? What are you doing with those candles? Why are you drawing a Pentacle on the wall? It's such a bright red? Where did you get that red? What are you writing? I hurt so bad.

"What the hell is he doing?" I whimpered aloud.

What are you doing with that wine glass? No. Don't come back over here. Go away. Go away. What are you doing?! NO!

Again blinding pain.

Again a scream, but unlike the other, cut short at its peak to become a faint gurgle followed by silence. He had cut her throat. Her slowly fading misery continued to play its sickening scenes inside my head. I saw, as she saw through dying eyes, her killer raising a wine goblet filled with blood. A goblet to be used for his own perverse distortion of an Expiation spell as he prepared to forgive himself for the unspeakable things he had just done.

I was just beginning to lose sight of consciousness when I was unceremoniously lurched back into the physical realm.

"Rowan! Talk ta' me! What's goin' on?!" Ben screamed frantically. He grabbed me by the front of my shirt and shook me so violently that his knuckles pounded into my chest. "ROWAN!"

"He was practicing," I sobbed, pressing the heels of my palms against my eyes, driving back the tears and fighting to bring my breathing back to normal. "The bastard was just practicing."

"What the hell are ya' talkin' about?!" Ben practically screamed. "Practicin' what?"

"Practicing the *art* of flaying," I spat, pulling my hands away from my eyes. "He didn't even try to perform an invocation ritual. He was just teaching himself how to skin someone alive."

"What the hell for?"

"To prepare," I answered, climbing to my feet and steadying myself against the wall. "He's trying to learn... Most likely so that he can actually perform the invocation sometime in the near future. Trust me, he's not going to stop here. This is only the beginning."

"This is fucked up, man," Ben stated wildly, turning in place, looking about the room as if some unseen creature was about to sneak up on him. "You saw all that?! You felt what she felt?!"

"Yes." I had begun to regain some composure. "That's exactly what I did. The fact that she was a Witch made it easier to do and..." I paused, "much more intense than I was expecting."

"Okay, look," Ben told me sternly. "I'm not entirely sure what I think about this, but I can damn sure tell you no one else at the department is gonna believe it, so this stays between you and me, got it?"

"Yeah, I got it," I answered. "Just let me help you get this S.O.B."

"If any of this stuff matches up with the coroner's report," he waved his notepad in front of me, "you better believe you're gonna help."

"Good," I told him. "Now let's get out of here. I need to get away from this before it sucks me in again."

I walked past Ben to the door and reached into my shirt pocket for my glasses. I looked back to see that he was following me then turned back to the doorway.

I turned back just in time to see a young man with long dark hair and the lamp he was swinging at me.

CHAPTER 3

I lifted my arm instinctively to guard my face, and the table lamp met it with violent force. The vase-like, imitation china base shattered and continued its arc, glancing against my forehead. The blow struck hard enough to stun, causing me to lose my balance and fall backward to the floor. A gash had been opened at my hairline, and blood immediately began to trickle down my face and into my right eye. I had deflected enough of the impact that I felt certain I wasn't seriously injured, but my ears were ringing, and I knew I was going to have one hell of a headache.

In the same moment I was falling to the floor, I saw Ben's large form flash in front of me as he took two large strides and slammed my attacker forcefully against the wall.

"You better get out of here," the near breathless young man croaked. "I called the cops. They'll be here any minute."

Ben held the young man against the wall, twisting one arm up behind his back while pressing him into the painted plaster. With his free hand, he ripped his badge from his belt and shoved the gold shield into the attacker's face.

"I AM the cops!" he shouted angrily. "Who the hell are you, and what're ya' doin' here?!"

"I'm sorry, man!" The young man now seemed a bit more frightened as the realization of what he had done set in. "I didn't know who you guys were. I came by to water Ariel's plants, and I heard voices. I thought you guys were burglars or something. Really, man, I'm sorry," he spoke frantically.

"You okay, Row?" Ben queried, looking back at me as I dragged myself from the floor and stood up shakily.

"A bit rattled," I answered. "I think I'm okay. There always have been four of you, right?"

Ben cracked a smile and turned back to the young man who was still held firmly in place against the wall.

"So we know why you're here," he continued. "But ya' still didn't tell us who ya' are."

"R.J.," he answered. "My name's R.J. Does Ariel know you're here? What's going on?"

I looked at Ben, then back at the gory sight of the bedroom. He immediately picked up on my cue and maintaining his grip on the young man, pulled him away from the wall and guided him out the door into the hallway. I followed along, stooping to pick up my glasses, which had been knocked from my hands, then exited the room, closing the door behind me. While Ben still held R.J. in the hall, I went into the bathroom and found a washcloth. After running it under cold water, I wiped the blood from my eye and forehead and then used it as a compress on the gash and the rapidly rising welt.

"What's going on man?" R.J. exclaimed as I came out of the washroom. "Why won't you tell me what's going on?"

Ben had him spread eagle against the wall and had apparently searched him while I was tending to my wound. He was studying what I assumed to be R.J.'s identification. He nodded to me and released his grip on R.J.'s shoulder. For the second time this morning, I was confronted with being the bearer of bad news. After a brief moment of indecision, I elected to treat it like removing a bandage and take a "get it over with quickly" approach.

"Ariel's dead, R.J.," I told him as he turned to face me, rubbing his shoulder where Ben's viselike grip had been. "She was murdered."

"She was what?!" he exclaimed. "No way, man, I don't believe you. She's visiting a friend in Chicago for a week.

She can't be dead."

"I haven't got any reason to lie to you about something like this," I replied.

"He's serious, man," Ben echoed as he returned the wallet to him.

R.J. stared at Ben, then at me. I could see in his eyes that the reality was sinking in, but he was still desperately fighting to deny it. Ben had relaxed his guard, and I was tending to my wound, so when the young man bolted for the bedroom door, neither of us were prepared to stop him. He rushed past me and flung open the door, bursting into the room. He only managed to travel three steps into the horror before freezing in place. Ben and I were immediately behind him as he stared at the blood-soaked bed like a frightened child. The stunned silence was finally broken as his head dropped and his shoulders began to heave. I led him gently from the room as he buried his face in his hands, sobbing uncontrollably.

In the small backyard of Ariel Tanner's flat, we waited for R.J. to calm down. I had the impression that Ben wasn't necessarily convinced that he wasn't putting on a performance for our benefit. Of course, Ben was suspicious of everyone, and that was one of the things that made him such a good cop.

Personally, I could feel the anguish exuding from the young man, and I seriously doubted that it was an act.

"When did this happen?" R.J. queried at last, wiping his reddened eyes with his shirtsleeve.

"Wednesday," Ben told him. "Sometime after six in the evening." He was holding a small notebook and ever vigilant, continued, "So, were you her boyfriend?"

"No," he sniffed. "Just a friend."

"You said you were here ta' water the plants. I assume Miz Tanner gave you a key?"

"Yeah."

"When would that have been?" Ben pressed as he scribbled more notes.

"Last Sunday. She was supposed to leave last night, and she asked me if I'd keep an eye on the place."

"And that's the last time you saw 'er?"

"Yeah."

Ben paused for a second as he turned to a fresh page, then tilted his head to look directly into R.J.'s face. "Mind tellin' me where you were Wednesday night?"

"I was..." He started to speak and then caught himself. He almost visibly pondered his answer for a split second before continuing, "I was out of town on a camping trip."

"Were you with anyone?"

"My dad. It was our annual fishing trip," R.J. answered, then his eyes grew wide with sudden realization. "Am I a suspect?!"

"It's just routine," Ben told him. "But I'd prefer it if ya' kept yourself available."

"How long did you know Ariel?" I asked him.

"A couple of years," he replied. "I was a member of..." he paused uneasily, "...a club she was in."

"You mean you were a member of her coven?" I questioned.

He stared back at me with a shocked, almost frightened, expression. He reached up to his chest and fingered a silver Pentacle hanging about his neck as if he had forgotten it was there.

"It's not what you cops think..." he started.

"Whoa," I stopped him and jerked my thumb over my

shoulder at Ben. "He's the only cop here. My name's Rowan Gant." I held my hand out to him. "I'm a Witch too."

"Rowan Gant," he repeated my name as he took my hand and shook it. "The Rowan Gant that Ariel studied with?"

"Yeah," I returned. "That's me. I'm just here as a consultant."

"Ariel talked about you and your wife all the time," he continued. "She even had a picture of all you guys together on a camping retreat you took."

I smiled slightly, remembering the trip well. Felicity and I had taken Ariel and a number of other Wiccan friends on a weeklong retreat to the Shawnee National Forest in southern Illinois just over two years ago. We had camped, studied nature, and become closer to Mother Earth as well as one another. We had ended that trip with a ritual circle on Summer Solstice, one of the religion's four Lesser Sabbats.

After what I had experienced in the apartment less than an hour before, the memories of that holiday were pleasant and very welcome.

"I'm glad it was a happy time for her," I told him.

"I thought she told me you were into computers or something like that," he said.

"I am."

"Then what are you consulting with the police about?" he queried.

"You probably didn't notice the walls in her bedroom," I started carefully. "There were some symbols left behind. Her death is apparently related to The Craft in some way."

"Devon!" he screamed suddenly. "I'll kill him! I'll kill the son-of-a-bitch!"

With that, he once again bolted past both Ben and me as he ran full speed up the small space between the buildings with my friend on his heels. Being shorter of stature and much wirier, R.J. was able to negotiate the cramped alleyway with slippery ease, quickly widening his lead and bursting out on to the street. I, with my throbbing skull, arrived in front of the building just in time to see Ben trying to yank open the door of a gold Trans Am.

R.J. gunned the engine, and the car jumped away from the curb, tires squealing against asphalt. Ben managed to follow alongside for a few steps before losing his grip on the handle, and choosing discretion over valor, back-peddled from the vehicle as it sped away.

"Are you all right?" I called to him as he jogged toward me.

"Yeah, I'm okay," he nodded. "Did ya' catch what he said?"

"He said he was going to kill someone named Devon," I replied. "I seem to have triggered it when I told him Ariel's death was somehow connected to The Craft."

"Well," he said walking toward the back of the house. "Let's get back to the van and get his plate number out over the air. I'm thinkin' maybe we need ta' find out who this Devon guy is."

Using the police radio in his van, Ben was able to get R.J.'s license plate number, as well as a description of the car and him, out to the on-duty patrols. We were just pulling into the parking lot of the medical examiner's office when a call blared over the tinny speaker stating that he had been picked up. Ben quickly instructed the arresting officer to bring him to the M.E.'s office where we would be waiting.

Ben was thumbing through his notes as we walked across the lot in the general direction of the entrance. After flipping back and forth between pages a trio of times, he settled on a particular scribble and glanced over at me.

"What's an at-tommy?" he queried as he searched his breast pocket for a writing implement.

"Athamè," I corrected. "It's a Witch's personal knife. It's used in rituals and the practice of The Craft. Why?"

He quickly added the words "Witches Knife" to the scrawled notation.

"When you were doing that thing, whatever it was, back at the apartment, you screamed something about the killer using Ariel's own Ath-Tommee," he still stumbled over the word, "to skin her."

"Yeah." The thought brought back unpleasant phantom pains in my chest. "That's what I saw."

"Whaddaya use it for?" he continued. "To sacrifice things or something?"

"No," I answered. "Not in the sense you mean. A Witch's athamè should never draw blood, and the only sacrifice a Witch makes is of him or herself."

"So ya' think Ariel Tanner was tortured and killed with her own Witch knife?" he voiced.

"Yes," I answered. "Which is something that made it even worse for her because an athamè is a very personal tool to a Wiccan practitioner. Hers was a dirk."

"Which is?"

"A European double-edged dagger about six inches long," I explained. "It's double-beveled and has a black handle."

"Is that somethin' you saw in your vision?"

"Yes. But I knew even before then. I gave it to her when she went out and started her own coven. It was a gift."

We entered the coroner's office and were greeted by a pleasant young woman at the reception desk who led us back to a room with stainless steel tables and tile floors: a room where the emptiness of death pervaded every sense to one who is aware. The young woman introduced us to Dr. Christine Sanders, the chief medical examiner who was also the M.E. working Ariel's case.

Despite my protestations, Ben pointed out my recent injury and asked if she might be able to take a look at it. After an effusive amount of concern, I was forced to be x-rayed and the gash stitched up. This was not something I expected from someone who spends her days with the dead, and I made the mistake of stating as much. She was quick to point out that she was in fact an M.D., so I elected not to argue.

Once my spur-of-the-moment medical treatment was finished, we gathered in Dr. Sanders' office. With its carpeting, mauve walls, and strategically placed paintings, it was a much more pleasant place to be than the chilled antiseptic realm of the autopsy suite.

"Ariel Tanner..." she began. "Just finished that one yesterday afternoon. You guys are lucky you caught me here," she added. "This is supposed to be my day off. I only came in to finish up some paperwork."

"I know the feelin', doc," Ben replied.

Dr. Sanders continued leafing through a thick file folder and finally came to rest on the page she sought. Her glasses hung loosely on a chain around her neck, giving her a stern look. Her demeanor, however, was much more pleasant than her outer appearance immediately suggested. She tossed back a shoulder-length shock of grey-flecked, brunette hair and slid the glasses onto her face, resting them lightly on the end of her nose.

"It appears that we are still waiting on some of the tox screen results," she told us. "But cause of death was due to an acute trauma to the neck resulting in massive blood loss. Judging from her histamine levels, the trauma to the chest..." She looked up over her glasses at me then to Ben.

"It's okay," he told her. "He's consulting on the case."

"...Then," she continued, "the trauma to the chest and excision of the dermis occurred antemortem."

"In English, doc," Ben said.

"She was skinned alive, Detective."

Jotting down quick notes, Ben continued, "Any idea what the killer mighta used ta' accomplish that?"

"Based on the size and shape of the wounds..." She looked back at the file and flipped over some more pages. "A short, beveled blade of some sort, but that's just a guess."

"One last question," he asked. "And it might seem a bit odd. Did ya' find any marks on her arms? Like a puncture wound?"

"Now that you mention it, yes we did," Dr. Sanders answered. "There was a puncture wound on her left arm, consistent with an injection. I assumed it was from a dose of insulin since she was a diabetic."

"We've got reason ta' believe she might have been drugged. Possibly with an injection," Ben told her after glancing quickly at me.

"We took a tissue sample," she submitted. "It's being screened with all the rest."

"Dr. Sanders?" the intercom on her desk blared.

"Yes, Cecilia?" she answered.

"Sorry to bother you," the disembodied voice continued issuing from the speaker. "But there is an officer here in the lobby to see Detective Storm."

"Thank you," Dr. Sanders said to the young woman at the other end then turned back to us. "Is there anything else I can do for you gentlemen?"

"I think that's it for now," Ben told her, standing and stowing his small notebook in a shirt pocket. "I'd appreciate hearin' from ya' as soon as the tox results are in." He handed her his card.

"No problem," she replied, clipping the card to the front of the file folder and then turning to me. "And you, sir… I recommend you go home and get some rest."

"You'll get no argument from me," I answered and shook her hand. "Thanks for the quick treatment."

"You're very welcome," she smiled. "It's nice to see one of my patients leave under his own power for a change."

Once outside the office, I turned to Ben as we headed down the intersecting maze of corridors toward the reception area. "So what do you think?"

"I think if that puncture wound turns up somethin' besides insulin that you're one spooky S.O.B." was all he said.

We were met in the lobby by a uniformed patrol officer and followed him outside to his vehicle. Ben sent him across the street for a cup of coffee, and we climbed into the back of the squad car on either side of R.J., leaving the doors partially open to avoid being locked in. His hands were cuffed behind him, and he appeared even more disheveled than earlier. He shot Ben a frightened look as we climbed in and then glanced at me as if asking for help. It was obvious that he had never been through an ordeal such as this.

"Would ya' mind tellin' me," Ben started, "just exactly why I shouldn't throw the book at ya'?"

"For what?" R.J. squeaked, trying unsuccessfully to appear tough.

"For pickin' your nose in public," Ben shot back sarcastically. "It doesn't really matter! Let's look at the facts. One. I'm tryin' to conduct a homicide investigation. Two. You show up at the scene and clock my consultant in the face with a table lamp. Three. You flee the scene screamin' that you're gonna kill some individual by the name of Devon. Killin' someone is a felony, ya'know." He paused for effect. "Now put yourself in my place. What am I supposed to think?"

R.J. hung his head and squirmed uncomfortably in his seat. I could feel his anguish, his fear...his sadness. Quite a bit had been thrust upon him within the last few hours, and I was sure that he was rapidly approaching critical mass. I only hoped that I would be able to defuse it without getting in the way of Ben's investigation.

"He wasn't even home," R.J. finally muttered.

"You mean Devon?" I queried.

"Yeah, Devon," he answered, nodding his head. "His neighbor said he hasn't been home for a couple of days."

"Who is this Devon character?" Ben asked, once again flipping open the cover of his ever-present notepad.

"He used to be a member of our coven," R.J. said, glancing quickly at Ben, then back at me, as if only I would understand. "Up until a few weeks ago."

"He didn't leave on very good terms I take it," I coached.

"We banished him. He had been straying from the path for a while, and he started talking about ritual magick a lot. It was like he was trying to get us involved too."

"Ritual magick isn't necessarily a bad thing."

"His idea of it was."

"Okay, go on," I told him, glancing up to look at Ben who met my gaze quietly and continued scribbling.

"We didn't know how long he had actually been practicing Black Arts, but he really got a big head about it." R.J. squirmed a little more against the biting handcuffs then continued. "He started bragging about an invocation rite and even showed us where he had done it."

"What did he sacrifice?" I asked, knowing what the ritual

implied.

"A dog," R.J. spat, showing a flash of disgust. "He said he got it from the pound. It made all of us sick, but Ariel took it the worst. She felt like she had failed or something."

"That's a Pisces for you," I told him. "I remember how she used to beat herself up over what she considered her own failings."

"It wasn't long after that when we held our Full Moon meeting. Devon was unanimously cast out of the coven." He looked back to Ben as if a sudden rush of anger had displaced his fear of his own current situation. "He told us we would regret it."

"So ya'think Devon is the one who did this to Ariel?" Ben interjected.

"It has to be," he replied. "He was mad at all of us but especially with Ariel. If what Rowan said is true about her murder being connected to The Craft..."

"What's his last name?" Ben cut him off.

"Johnston. Devon Johnston. He lives over in South City."

Ben wrote down the information as R.J. relayed it to him and then looked up from his notebook. I caught his eye and motioned for him to step out of the car with me. He nodded and shoved his door open wider.

"We'll be right back," I told R.J. as I pushed against my own door. "I know this hurts man. I know it's tearing you up inside... I'm feeling it too. Ground and center, you'll feel better."

He nodded, and even as I exited the car, he began to consciously slow his breathing just as he had been taught.

"What do you think?" I asked Ben over the roof of the vehicle, keeping my voice low.

He squinted and held up his notebook to shade his eyes. "I think there's somethin' he's not tellin' us," he answered me in his own quiet tone. "He was kinda hesitant when I asked him about where he was Wednesday night... Not ta' mention the fact that he has a key. What about you?"

"I picked up on that too, but honestly I think he's just a scared kid. What about his story on that Devon Johnston guy? If he actually did sacrifice an animal then a human could be the next logical progression."

"Yeah, I definitely wanna have a chat with Mister Johnston."

"If you're game," I submitted after a moments pause, "I'd like to try something."

"What's that?"

"I'd like to talk to the rest of the coven members." I continued, "Get an idea of their feelings about Devon. And," I added, "THEIR stories about what happened at that Full Moon meeting."

"You think the kid's makin' it up?" Ben asked. "You're startin' ta' sound like a copper."

"I don't really think that he's making it up, but I think his judgment may be a bit left of center," I answered. "Actually, what I do think is that he was in love with Ariel Tanner."

"Where the hell'd you come up with that?"

"Just a feeling."

"Well, I'd actually like to talk to them anyway, so I guess we can get their names from him and call them downtown," he suggested.

"No." I shook my head. "I think that might make them a little too uncomfortable, and they'd just clam up. Remember, you're dealing with a group of Witches here. We're already persecuted enough."

"You got a better idea?"

"I want to let R.J. make the calls and get them over to my place," I recited my idea. "A nice, informal atmosphere where we can talk Witch to Witch."

"I don't know..." Ben started.

"I want you there too," I added, stopping him before he could finish his objection. "I just don't want to spook these people. I'm pretty sure that I know their type a little better than you do. Remember, I'm one of them."

Ben paused then smoothed his hair back, letting his hand rest at the back of his neck, his telltale physical manifestation of intense thought. I knew that he was concerned about what he considered to be an unorthodox approach to the investigation, but it had lost its normalcy the moment he asked for my advice. I also knew that he was still skeptical about the entire concept of WitchCraft, even with what he had witnessed so far today.

"Okay," he finally told me. "When do ya' wanna do this?"

"Tonight if at all possible," I replied.

He nodded and then frowned. "Yeah. Sooner the better. Shit! Allison's gonna have my ass."

"So what's new about that?"

I opened the door to the patrol car and squatted down next to it. R.J. looked over at me, as the sound had apparently startled him.

"Do you think you can get in touch with all of the coven members pretty quickly?" I asked him.

"Sure. Why?"

"I want to get everyone together over at my place this evening if we can." I continued, "We really need to talk about what's happened, and the more information we can get, the quicker the cops can catch whoever killed Ariel."

"But..." R.J. started.

"I know, R.J.," I interrupted. "I know you think that Devon did it, and what he's getting himself into is some sick shit, I agree. But, right now there's no proof it was him. Believe me, they plan to pick him up and question him." He settled back in the seat as I talked. "We have to help the police, man. Not fight against them. Okay?"

"Okay," he nodded after a short silence and then hung his chin down to his chest.

"We're on," I told Ben as I stood up.

My friend nodded and stepped to the driver's door of the squad car. He opened it and reached in to the controls near the dash. He punched a button and the light bar atop the roof blinked to life. The pre-arranged signal quickly caught the eye of the officer belonging to the vehicle, and he was soon making his way back toward us from the coffee shop across the street.

After signaling the patrolman, Ben got in the back seat momentarily and unlocked the handcuffs that were restraining R.J.

"I'm gonna have the officer drop ya' off at your car," he told him. "You've got a real friend in Rowan here, so don't fuck it up and pull any shit this time."

R.J. nodded quietly and rubbed his wrists where the restraints had bit into his skin.

"Here." I held out a business card to him. "This is Detective Storm's card. My number and address are on the back. Tell them we'll have sandwiches and the like so they can eat there. Say we set everything up for about seven tonight? Sound good?"

"Okay," he nodded.

"Stay grounded." I smiled at him. "We'll work this out."

Ben returned the handcuffs to the patrolman and instructed him to return R.J. to his vehicle. We both thanked him for his time and watched them pull away before making the short trek across the parking lot to the van. It was coming up on noon, and I was starting to fade. Exhaustion, not only from the lack of sleep but from the mental trauma of channeling Ariel's murder, was taking its toll.

"You really think the kid's gonna show?" Ben asked me,

looking quickly each way then nosing the van out into the traffic.

"Yeah." I slumped in my seat. "He'll show. I'm sure of it."

"I hope you're right," he told me as we entered the flow and came to a halt at a signal that had just winked to crimson. "Ya'know, Rowan," he said after a pause, still looking straight ahead. "If I didn't know ya' better, I'd have ta' consider ya' a suspect."

"Because of everything I told you this morning at Ariel's apartment," I stated matter-of-factly.

"Yeah," he sighed. "Ya'know I'm gonna have ta' check out your alibi with your dad."

"I figured you would. In fact, I'd be disappointed if you didn't."

He looked quietly out his side window and then turned his eyes back to the front. It was apparent that he was wrestling with something other than my whereabouts Wednesday night. "Ya'know, I'm still kinda weirded out about this stuff," he finally admitted.

"I know."

He looked over at me. "For your own sake, keep this between us."

"I will," I told him.

The dull background noise of the city was sharpened momentarily as a horn blared to our rear, angrily alerting us to the fact that the traffic light had changed. Ben pushed the van into motion, and we rolled on through the intersection and down the street in the general direction of my suburb.

"Mind if I use this?" I asked, picking up his cell phone.

"Go ahead. Gotta call the little woman?"

"Yeah," I replied, punching in my number. "She should be home by now."

After a pair of trilling rings, the phone was answered by

my wife's tranquil voice. The evenly spaced, rattling noises in the background told me she was in the darkroom, probably processing the film she had shot on her outing. We exchanged greetings, and then I relayed a sketchy outline of the morning's events before filling her in on the plans for the evening. I had gingerly talked around the incident involving the table lamp and my forehead but knew that I had better warn her before she saw me. I had to pull the phone away from my ear quickly to protect my hearing as soon as I uttered the words x-ray and stitches. A moment or two later, I held out the handset to Ben.

"She wants to talk to you," I told him.

CHAPTER 4

Fortunately, Ben knew Felicity well, and as a cop, had dealt with distraught individuals a number of times before. He allowed her to decompress and simply listened as she vented her feelings regarding the circumstances of my injury. Just as fortuitous was the fact that Felicity was not one to hold a grudge and worked through her anger very quickly. By the time we pulled into the driveway of my Briarwood home, they had both apologized to one another, and the entire incident had somehow become my fault for having my face in the wrong place at the wrong time.

Ben dropped me off and headed, I assumed, to his own home in order to spend what little time he could with his family. He planned to return for the meeting somewhat earlier than the rest and had told me he was still trying to figure out how to make it up to his wife and son. Something told me he would be taking time out to visit my father along the way. After a quick wave, I ambled up the stairs to my front porch and was greeted by Emily, our calico cat, who leapt lithely down from the window ledge and began weaving herself about my legs, purring madly.

"Yes, I missed you too," I told her as I stooped to pick her up.

Emily continued her throaty trill as I allowed her to drape herself across my shoulder, then lifted the lid on the mailbox and retrieved the contents. There was the usual mix of bills and junk mail, as well as a yellow pickup slip for a package that had needed a signature—most likely one of my client's software in need of modification or repair. Felicity had probably been in the darkroom ever since returning from her photo expedition and had missed the postal carrier. I resigned myself to picking it up at the branch office on Monday since it was already after noon. Besides, my evening was already booked, so working was out of the question anyway.

I twisted my key in the deadbolt lock of the heavy, oak front door and pushed it open, following it inside then closing it behind me. I lifted the rumbling ball of fur from my shoulder and gently placed her on the arm of the couch then tossed the mail in the small wicker basket Felicity kept by the door for just such a purpose. Fatigue washed over me, and the sofa was all but screaming my name. I sat down and within moments became horizontal on the soft cushions. Emily remained perched on the arm, near motionless, her ears at full attention, as if she were a small furry gargoyle watching over me. Scarcely had I reclined that I heard my wife's footsteps as she came up from the basement and into the living room.

"I thought I heard you up here," she said softly, seating herself on the edge of the sofa next to me.

I looked up to see her lightly freckled face, framed by her auburn hair wrapped loosely in a *Gibson Girl* about her head. It never ceased to amaze me how this woman I had married could easily slide from hippie activist to china doll in the blink of an eye. Her bright green eyes stared back with concern as she reached out and lightly touched my forehead near the stitches.

"How are you feeling?"

"Physically or spiritually?" I asked, weakly smiling back at her.

"Both."

"Physically," I told her, "like I've been hit by a truck. Spiritually...drained, but still grounded."

"I wish you wouldn't do these things to yourself," she gently admonished, lightly placing her hand over the wound on my head. "A person can only take so much."

"I've got to be honest with you." I relaxed, feeling the healing energy she was directing through her hand. "I lost control today. When I channeled those last few moments of Ariel's life, I couldn't keep myself separated. She kept breaking through and taking over. I know it scared the hell out of Ben."

"Oh, Rowan," she whispered. "It scares the hell out of me too."

Felicity was filled with an inherent desire to make everything well and at the moment, she wore a deeply empathic grimace. I watched her close her eyes and felt her ground and center, directing a cool wash of energy over me that appeared in my mind as a soothing green light. Soon, my dull headache subsided, and the last knots of tension uncoiled from my neck and shoulders.

"Have you eaten?" she asked me.

"No," I answered. "Not yet."

"I'll go make you something." She leaned forward and lightly kissed me on the forehead. "You just relax."

I vaguely remember the smell of corned beef hash and eggs wafting into the room as I drifted into tortured sleep.

Screaming.

Screaming forever with no pause. Distorted noises. Sounds of ripping and tearing. The forever tortured banshee wail. I am in Ariel Tanner's apartment. The kitchen. I am standing in the kitchen. The room is bathed in a surreal wash of white. I shade my eyes against the stark brightness.

Silence.

Clear, unbroken silence.

My heart pounding. Thump thump, Thump thump, Thump thump. Louder. Fighting to escape from my chest. Blood rushing in my ears, pushing back the silence.

Fear.

Pure, unadulterated terror.

"Please come in," a voice.

I turn to face the direction of the voice. Ariel Tanner is standing before me, radiant and lovely in a white lace gown. She smiles at me.

"Rowan, how nice to see you." Her voice floats mellifluously, displacing the rushing in my ears. "It's been so long."

"Ariel?" I question.

She jerks spasmodically, and the smile flees her lips. Her eyes grow wide and she looks down. A spot of crimson appears on the high neck of the lace gown and begins growing. Spreading. Her mouth falls open in shock, and she looks back at me with questioning eyes. The vermilion stain waxes unceasingly, covering her chest.

"Why, Rowan?" she mouths. "Why?"

Darkness.

Falling. Wind rushing past. Faster, faster, faster...

An unearthly sound. A demonic chord growing stronger.

Impact.

I'm standing in Ariel Tanner's bedroom. Everything is cast in an eerie blue light. Her body is spread across the bed, her dead eyes staring at me. I walk toward her, and they follow me. The bloodstains appear black in the supernatural light. A sound at my back, slow and rhythmic, but unintelligible. I turn. A figure in a robe is there lighting candles.

"Who are you?" I ask, but my voice is drowned out by the muffled chant.

I take a step forward and the figure disappears. There is a sound like a crashing wave, recorded on tape and played in reverse. The murmur is behind me now. I turn again, and the robed figure is on the opposite side of the bed. The figure is pointing at me. The chant becomes louder, and though disjointed in its cadence, clear.

"All...Is...Forgiven. All...Is...Forgiven..."

"Why?" a voice drifts over the chant.

I look down to see Ariel's mutilated corpse. Her lifeless eyes glare back at me and her mouth slowly animates.

"Why, Rowan, why?"

An endless scream.

I awoke with a start, my hair and clothes drenched in a cold sweat. Felicity was once again sitting next to me on the edge of the sofa, deep concern creasing her brow and sad tears clouding her eyes.

"Are you okay?" I asked her, immediately worried by the expression on her face.

"Yes," she sniffed. "I'm all right. The question is are you going to be okay?"

"I don't know," I replied. "I think so."

"You kept saying 'Why, Rowan, why', over and over," she told me as she intertwined her fingers with mine, then wiped away a tear with her free hand. "All I could feel from you was fear, and I couldn't wake you."

"How long was I out of it?" I asked with a sigh.

"About half an hour," she returned. "What's going on? You've never done anything like this before."

"I don't know. Probably just a bad dream." I reached up and brushed a loose strand of hair from her face. "The things I've seen in the past twenty-four hours would give anyone nightmares."

"It's more than that," she told me. "You and I both know it."

I lightly caressed her cheek. "Never can fool you, can I?"

"This isn't going to stop until you find the killer, is it?"

I didn't answer. I didn't have to.

By some miracle, I actually slept. No dreams, no visions, no nightmares. It was only an hour, but at least it was peaceful. Upon waking, I re-heated and practically inhaled the meal Felicity had made for me earlier. I never realized corned beef hash and eggs could taste so good. After eating, I parked myself in my upstairs office with a solid stack of reference books. The Expiation spell had been readily recognizable to me, even considering the killer's sickening variations, but the rest of it was only vaguely familiar. I knew from past reading that flaying and vivisection of a live sacrificial victim were components of the invocation rites performed by ritual magicians of days long past. What I wasn't clear on was what he might be trying to invoke or why. I felt that if I could pin these facts down, I might have a clue about what he would do next. Whether or not this would be important to the police, I also didn't know, but it was important to me.

It became quickly obvious after only a few moments study that the healthy pile of books held none of the answers I sought. Reference material about The Craft didn't deal with the horrors I had only recently witnessed, and any other historical texts in my possession touched on it only briefly. Feeling this avenue now closed, I pushed the books off to the side of my desk and switched on my personal computer. A few keystrokes and mouse clicks later, I was logging in to my local Internet service provider and merging with the electronic fast lane of the information superhighway. I navigated through the various starting pages and came to rest at my objective, a database search screen. I began my quest for information by typing in the keywords HUMAN SACRIFICE and clicking on the SUBMIT icon. If my service provider happened to be randomly monitoring this line, I mused silently, they were probably thinking I was some kind of psychopath. The status lights on the modem flickered quickly, and the screen re-painted itself, displaying the online addresses of the various matching World Wide Web sites.

The majority of the web pages listed dealt with historical text and benign non-literal references such as those sacrifices one person makes for another. I was simultaneously pleased and demoralized by the listing of sites that purported to be reservoirs of information regarding active religions that encouraged the actual sacrificing of a human victim. Upon closer inspection, they were obviously no more than idle electronic chatter, but they contained information I felt might be useful. Still, I was violently disgusted by the fact that anyone would claim to subscribe to such beliefs. The world really didn't need any more sickos than it already had.

When all was said and done, I had conducted several searches of the "Web" using keywords ranging from BLOOD SACRIFICE to FLAYING. With each of these searches turning up a listing of site addresses, I easily investigated over one hundred web pages within a few hours. The information I gathered held references to historical events and dead religions, as well as fictional books and horror movies. All of it told me that I was on the right track in my belief that the killer was practicing for an invocation ritual, but it still didn't tell me who or what he was trying to invoke.

The digital clock resting in the corner of my monitor screen attested to the fact that the afternoon had slipped by virtually unnoticed. It was rapidly approaching time for our meeting with Ariel's coven, and I knew Ben would be arriving early. I logged off the network and shut down my computer after the printer spit out the last of the information I had sent to it. Much to my chagrin, I caught a glimpse of myself in a mirror as I made my way downstairs. My clothing was disheveled, my hair matted and stringy, and my face pallid and drawn. Overall, I looked like death warmed over. A glance at my watch told me I still had some time, so I decided to become acquainted with hot water and a bar of soap.

I was just climbing out of the shower when Felicity poked her head in the door and told me Ben had arrived. By the time I finished drying off and throwing on some clothes, the two of them were parked at the dining room table. I joined them and helped myself to a mug of hot ginger-mint tea.

"I did some research on invocation rites." I indicated the sheaf of papers I had brought down from my office. "Pretty general stuff. Not much help to be honest."

"I'll take your word on it," Ben nodded as he spoke. "So, Red Squaw here was tellin' me you had a hard time of it after I dropped ya' off this afternoon."

"Nightmare I guess," I told him. "I'll get over it."

"Uh-huh," he grunted, unconvinced. "By the way, I dropped in on your old man."

"I thought you might," I nodded. "How'd he handle it? Should I be expecting a call?"

"Prob'ly not. I didn't wanna get him all worked up, so I told him I was in the area and just stopped in to say hi."

"Were you able to find out what you needed?"

"Yeah. I managed ta' fit it into the conversation."

"Thanks. I appreciate it."

"Hey, no prob, white man."

During our conversation, Felicity had remained steadfastly silent. It suddenly dawned on me that she hadn't expressed any interest in the somewhat cryptic exchange, so I turned my attention to her side of the table. A familiar file folder lay open across an equally familiar envelope near the center. A thick stack of crime scene photographs were spread neatly before my wife. One of the glossy monstrosities was resting carefully between her fingers as she studied it intently. All the while, she absently chewed on her lower lip as she concentrated.

"What the hell are you doing?!" I sputtered, nearly choking on a mouthful of hot tea.

"Catching up," Felicity spoke without looking up from the pictures.

"Dammit Ben!" I turned to him. "Are you out of your mind?!"

"Hey!" He held his hands up defensively. "She told me you wanted her ta' look at 'em."

"It's not his fault, then," she stated, deftly laying the photo she was studying on to a stack then looking up at me. "That's what I told him."

"Well forget it," I exclaimed and started reaching for the grisly prints. "I don't want you looking at these things."

"NO!" Felicity angrily snapped, grabbing my wrist and forcing my hand away. "I didn't ask you what you wanted!"

"Wh-wh-what?" I stammered, surprised by her sudden outburst.

"I'm not letting you get away with it this time, Rowan," she stated, an emerald fire of determination blazing in her eyes as she held my gaze. "You're always trying to protect me. I know why you do it…" Her voice softened. "But I'm a grown woman, not a child. I saw what this experience did to you this afternoon, and I'm not going to sit on the sidelines and watch it tear you apart. I'm going to help."

"You don't know what you're getting yourself into," I pleaded.

"And you do?" she shot back. "You yourself admitted that Ariel ripped through your defenses and almost took over. We both know that something like that could kill you."

"Excuse me?" interjected Ben, who had remained quietly neutral until this point. "Whaddaya mean, kill 'im?"

"If a spiritual entity," Felicity explained, turning her attention to him, "manages to take control, especially in the case of something such as this, and plays out the last moments of its physical life, it will repeat the event with the channeling host."

"Are you tryin' to tell me that Ariel Tanner's spirit or somethin' would kill him?" Ben asked, still confused.

"Not on purpose," she continued. "But if she was in control of his physical body and re-experienced her death, the shock could kill him, yes." She returned her gaze to me. "You didn't bother to tell him that did you?"

"I didn't think I would need to worry about it," I answered sheepishly.

"Jeezus H. Christ!" Ben exclaimed. "This is fuckin' nuts! All I'm tryin' to do is solve a murder here, and I got some kinda weird ass *Twilight Zone* episode going on around me."

We both turned to look at him as he threw up his hands in exasperation and fell back in his chair. After a moment, he again leaned forward and rested his forearms on the table. He quietly looked from my face to Felicity's then down at the table.

"Listen," he said, "I've always figured you two for a coupl'a tree-huggin' agnostics or somethin', which I got no problem with. You know that. But, I don't really know much about this whole Wicca-slash-WitchCraft thing, and ta' be honest, I'm not sure if I wanna know any more." He paused as if trying to pick his words carefully. "I can't believe I'm sayin' this, but this mornin' I saw some stuff that I can't explain. Right now I'm willin' ta' accept it. But, I also saw my best friend rollin' around on a floor clawin' at his chest like he was havin' a coronary or some shit like that. Now," he pointed a finger at me and brought his gaze up to meet mine, "YOU start bein' straight up with me if there's some kinda risk involved." He then shifted his attention to Felicity. "And YOU. Watch his back or whatever you Witches do. Okay?"

"You can count on it," she told him, her face spreading into a smile.

"Yeah," I added, "you're right."

"Okay," he said, relaxing and settling back in his seat. "So R.J. and company are s'posed to be here in about half an hour. You palefaces wouldn't happen to have a slab of buffalo or somethin' around here would ya'? I'm starved."

CHAPTER 5

Ben had demolished a plate of sandwiches by the time the doorbell rang. At the sound, the dogs immediately shifted into territorial protection mode and yelped riotously. The cats, which had been entertaining themselves in a free-for-all wrestling match, scattered. Salinger, our Himalayan, was the only feline left to be seen, and he was perched well out of reach on the exposed rafters of the living room.

When Felicity and I remodeled our house, we had vaulted the ceiling in an effort to create a lofty, open feel. The cats had discovered the rafters and learned, to their great delight, that they afforded both a safe haven and a bird's eye view of everything that happened in the room. Salinger sat upon them now, intently studying the scene below. It was clear he thought something interesting was about to happen.

I answered the door as Ben assisted Felicity in setting out platters of freshly made sandwiches and honey cakes along with a large thermal carafe of iced chamomile tea, as it had inherent calmative properties. We wanted the surroundings to be as comfortable and hospitable as possible for this group.

To Wiccans, the death of a brother or sister of The Craft is supposed to be considered a graduation, an advancement to the next level of learning, and therefore treated not as a time of sorrow but as a time of celebration. I assumed the members of the group would be of roughly the same age as R.J. Because of this, I suspected that this was the first time any of them would be dealing with the crossing over of a fellow Witch. This fact, combined with the circumstances of Ariel's death, was likely to bring on grief as opposed to happiness.

Once the necessary questioning was finished this evening, Felicity and I would be taking it upon ourselves to offer counsel to this leaderless coven and help them along their path.

Swinging the door open, I was greeted by a small huddle on my front porch. Apparently, Ariel's coven believed in safety in numbers, and they had elected to descend upon us as a group. Turning, I commanded our two boisterous canines to sit. They immediately planted themselves where they stood, though Quigley, the Australian cattle dog, continued to whine quietly. With the commotion settled, I returned to the task at hand and pushed the screen door open with a smile.

"Rowan Gant?" a young brunette queried.

"That's me," I answered. "Come on in."

I held the door as the five of them filed in and proceeded to nervously mill about in my living room. I closed the door, turned to our guests, and noticed that there were no familiar faces.

"How many more of you should we be expecting?" I asked.

"This is it," replied the brunette guardedly. She had apparently been elected speaker for the group. "Except for R.J."

"I noticed he was missing," I returned, smiling. "Didn't he come with you?"

"No," she answered. "We aren't sure where he is. He called all of us and said to be here at seven tonight."

"Well," I proceeded, "I'm sure he's just running a little late." I held out my hand to her. "Since he's not here to do the introductions, I suppose we should do that ourselves. Obviously, you have me at a bit of a disadvantage..."

"Calliope," she said, taking my hand. "But everyone calls

me Cally."

"Nice to meet you."

Cally proceeded solemnly around the group, and I was introduced to Shari and Jennifer, two blonde young women who were obviously identical twins. Continuing, I met a tall, lanky young man with hair the color of a ripened tomato named Randy and finally, his wife, a statuesque woman with dark, penetrating eyes and coal black hair. Her name was Nancy. I led them through the archway into our dining room and repeated the introductions for Felicity and Ben.

"So where's the kid?" Ben asked, referring to R.J. as he surveyed the group.

"He seems to be running a little late," I told him, adding a sharp look to encourage a bit more tact.

"Why doesn't everyone have a seat and get comfortable," Felicity interjected, slicing surgically through the tension in the room then motioning to the serving platters on the table. "If anyone is hungry, please help yourself. That's what it's here for."

We had installed both leaves in the table, and it was more than large enough to accommodate the small gathering comfortably. There was a noticeable amount of distance kept by the group between themselves and us, especially Ben. I had a feeling that the brushed stainless, nine-millimeter pistol nestled under his arm in a shoulder holster played a role there, as he had draped his jacket over a chair, leaving the handgun exposed. He had done this purposely, I was sure, using it as an intimidation tactic on this youthful group.

It was apparent that the four young women had attempted to apply an appropriate amount of makeup to their faces in order to disguise the fact that they had been crying. It was also obvious, even to a casual observer, that Randy had shed a few tears as well.

"I'm not gonna stand on ceremony," Ben announced with a shrug, then reached out and grabbed a sandwich.

"Aye, do you have a hollow leg or something?" Felicity gave him an astonished look. "You just ate three sandwiches less than forty-five minutes ago!"

"Don't get decent food that often," he told her between bites. "I'm not home that much."

"Don't let Cochise over here scare you," I told the group. "Dig in. We need to wait for R.J. anyway."

Quietly, one by one, they helped themselves to the food before them. They ate mainly in silence; uttering only necessary polite phrases required whenever offered a drink, or more to eat. It was rapidly approaching eight P.M. when the doorbell finally sounded again. Felicity brought the dogs to rapt attention as they once again began to howl, and I excused myself from the table.

As expected, R.J. was on the opposite side of the door when I pulled it open. He smiled sheepishly and pulled open the screen door.

"We were starting to wonder about you," I told him quietly as he stepped inside.

"I'm sorry, man," he apologized and looked around nervously. "I saw Cally's van out front. Is everyone here?"

"Yeah," I answered, shutting the door. "We were just waiting on you. Everyone's in there."

I pointed to the dining room, and he advanced around the corner with a solemn expression and joined them at the table. Something definitely seemed different about R.J. since I had last seen him, and I wasn't sure whether it was good or bad. In any event, before he had ever exited the living room, my ears discerned a low growl followed by a throaty yowl and hiss. I turned and looking up at the rafters, saw Salinger glaring down at R.J., ears laid back and tail twitching. Animals being considered by some as good judges of character, I took note. Something about R.J. had set Salinger off. Fortunately, for the moment, I was the only one who noticed.

"Where ya' been, kid?" Ben was asking as I rounded the corner into the dining room.

"I had some stuff to do," R.J. answered as he took a seat next to Cally.

"You couldn't call?" Ben retorted.

"I was busy, okay?!" The young man spat indignantly. "It's not like I'm under arrest or something, or am I?"

"It can be arranged!" Ben challenged, starting to rise from his chair.

"All right, all right, all right," I intervened. My voice rose with each syllable, and I motioned him to sit back down. "Before this goes any further, let's all calm down. Now, R.J..." I looked over at him. "It would have been common courtesy for you to call and let us know you were running late." I turned to my simmering friend. "And Ben, no one here is under arrest to my knowledge, right?"

"Right," he answered grudgingly.

"Sorry I didn't call," R.J. muttered.

"I know everyone is on edge here." Felicity reinforced my intrusion into the dispute. "But going at each other like that isn't going to accomplish anything."

"Listen," Ben offered. "Maybe I was outta line jumpin' on R.J. like that, but I've just got this thing about bein' on time."

The group looked silently around at one another then back at him. They all seemed too tightly strung but quietly nodded in assent.

"Okay then," he proceeded. "We might as well get started then. I've already been through this with R.J., so I'll ask the rest of ya'. When was the last time you saw Ariel Tanner alive?"

"See, I told you," R.J. announced haughtily. "The cops are trying to blame it on us!"

"Do you intend to Mirandize us, Detective Storm," Cally interjected bluntly.

"Don't tell me, let me guess." Ben threw up his hands and rolled his eyes. "Law student."

Cally held her position at the table, but the look on her face showed that Ben had just exposed what she believed to be a trump card. It became immediately obvious why she had been picked as the speaker for the group. Now that he had knocked some of the wind from her sails, I hoped we could get on with what had brought us all together.

"I already told ya'," Ben explained. "Nobody here is bein' accused of anything. These are just routine questions. As for Miranda, since nobody is under arrest, there's no reason to read anyone their rights. We just wanna talk to ya' about Ariel Tanner and Devon Johnston. Okay?"

"There's no reason for any of you to be on the defensive," I added. "We're all on the same side. We just want to find whoever is responsible for Ariel's death."

Once again they cast timid glances between themselves. Finally, someone other than Cally spoke up.

"So this isn't just some shakedown 'cause of us being involved in The Craft?" Randy asked.

"No," I answered. "Not at all. Surely R.J. told you that Felicity and I are Witches. I was Ariel's teacher."

"Yes, he did…" Shari said.

"…But you're with the cops," Jennifer finished.

"So?" Ben interposed, "You got some kinda problem with cops?"

"It's usually the police that have a problem with us," stated Randy, still wearing a befuddled expression.

"Yeah," Shari agreed. "Ever since that one cop here in the county started giving lectures…"

"...About how WitchCraft is evil and the same thing as Satan worship. You know," Jennifer finished again.

"Are you two gonna do that all night?" Ben asked staring at the twins.

"Do what?" they asked simultaneously.

"Never mind," he shook his head. "And yeah, I know what you're talkin' about. I'll admit that there are quite a few coppers that don't understand what you guys are all about. Hell, I don't even understand it, but I can tell ya' this... Rowan has been my friend practically forever. Shit, I was his Best Man when he and Felicity got married. I know that Rowan isn't doin' anything *quote quote* evil." He held up his fingers and made invisible quote symbols in the air before him. "And if you guys are into the same thing he is, I've got no reason ta' believe that you are either."

"So are we all clear on where everybody stands?" I asked after an expectant pause.

"Yeah," Cally once again spoke, this time with a relaxed smile. "We're clear."

The rest of the group voiced and nodded their agreement, and the tension drained quickly from the room. I had expected a little rough going at first because of Ben's presence. The last thing that crossed my mind was that I would come under some kind of suspicion because of my relationship with the police, especially after the way R.J. had behaved toward me earlier in the day. I was painfully aware that the general public misunderstood Witches, but I never imagined that Witches would misunderstand one of their own.

As the group was settling in, I noticed Dickens, our black cat with the fondness for male visitors, lurking in the shadows. He silently padded forward to the chair R.J. was seated in and then reared back on his haunches as if he were about to climb into his lap. Suddenly, the hair along his back stood on end, and he puffed out like a furry black balloon. His ears laid back, and he dropped back down to all fours then skirted widely back around the chair to investigate Randy instead. "That's two of them who don't seem to like him," I thought to myself and wondered if Emily would make her opinion known.

"I'm glad that's taken care of," Felicity piped up. "Now can we get down to business?"

"Ben?" I looked over to him questioningly.

We had discussed this meeting earlier between ourselves and decided that he should take the lead. What we would reveal regarding the case so far was already public knowledge. There had been a leak at the department, and the local paper's headline for the day had read "SATANIC KILLER LOOSE IN CITY." The story that followed contained grotesque, sensationalized details of Ariel's death.

"As you already know," he started, "Ariel Tanner was murdered sometime this past Wednesday evening. There were no witnesses, and I'll spare ya' the details of her death, except ta' say that it was particularly gruesome, and whoever did it is one seriously sick bastard. I brought Rowan into the investigation as of Friday evening because of some symbols left at the scene. He was able to decipher what our *expert* couldn't and has helped pick out a few clues we might otherwise have missed. Any questions so far?"

"R.J. said you told him that the murder was connected with The Craft," stated Randy. "Do the symbols you mentioned have something to do with that?"

"Yes they do," I answered. "There was a Pentacle drawn on the wall, and it was shaded with the colors of the four towers, leading me to believe they were hailed."

"How do you know it just wasn't something that Ariel had done?" Cally posed.

"Because," I took a deep breath and continued, "the

Pentacle was drawn, and the Southern Tower shaded, with Ariel's blood."

Cally gasped and the rest of the group stared on at me as if I'd just slapped them. In a way, I guess I had.

"I'm sorry," I told them. "I really am. Believe me, it gets worse, so if you don't think you're up for hearing this..."

"No," Cally answered my hanging question quietly. "Go on. We have to know what happened."

"As long as you're sure." I looked on and continued only after they had all agreed. "In addition to the Pentacle, the words 'All Is Forgiven' were inscribed on the wall in the same manner. Also, a black candle and white candle had both been burned. A wine goblet was used, and," I choked slightly, "it appears that Ariel's blood was in it."

"What does it mean?" Shari asked. "What is this guy..."

"...Some kind of vampire?" Jennifer finished.

"I doubt it," I answered. "I expect it's just a sick twist he added to the spell."

"What spell?" Randy questioned.

"An Expiation spell," Felicity explained. "You might never have dealt with one before, but it is pretty basic. It's a ritual performed in order to rid yourself of guilt and regrets. Kind of a *self atonement* spell."

"So you think whoever did it regretted killing Ariel?" Cally queried.

"So it would seem," Felicity answered.

"That would mean you're looking for a Witch then, right?" asked Randy.

"Yes and no," I told him. "It's very likely that the killer practiced WitchCraft at some point in his life, and he's obviously familiar with the Wiccan religion to a degree. The Expiation spell shows that, even if he did warp it hideously by using Ariel's blood." I paused to let my words settle in. "Based on the fact that he, for one, broke the basic rule of

'Harm None,' and for two, went through the motions of a blood sacrifice, I would say he fancies himself a ritual magician. A mage of the Black Arts."

"And that," Ben sighed, "brings us back to why we asked you all to come here tonight. R.J. spoke with Rowan and me this mornin', and I'm sure he's told ya' all about it." He looked over at R.J. who dipped his head in an affirmative. "He gave us some information with regards to a Devon Johnston who was apparently hooked up with your group until recently."

"Have you found him yet?" R.J. asked

"Not yet," Ben answered, "but we're lookin'."

"I understand that Devon was starting to play around with Black Arts and the like," I stated. "Do any of you have any thoughts on that?"

With the exception of a few questions, thus far, Ben and I had done the majority of the talking. Now, placing that burden upon the group elicited only an uneasy silence. The atmosphere might have been cleared, but the undercurrent of tension was still circulating slowly around the table.

"What about you?" Ben urged, directing the question at Nancy. "You haven't said two words since ya' got here. You got an opinion on this guy?"

"I didn't know him that well," she answered, appearing clearly apprehensive at being singled out. "I'm kind of new to the coven...I don't really know."

"If you want my opinion," Cally spoke up, protectively redirecting our attention. "I don't think Devon could've done it."

"Why do you say that?" Felicity queried.

"He's a lot of talk, and no action."

"What about the invocation rite?" R.J. asked indignantly. "He sacrificed a dog. He showed it to all of us."

"A dog is one thing, R.J.," Cally retorted. "But a human

being? Besides, he wouldn't harm a hair on Ariel's head. He was crazy about her."

"Excuse me?" Ben chimed and gave her a look of great interest.

"That's right." She turned her attention to him. "The guy was madly in love with her. It just about destroyed him that she voted to cast him out of the coven."

"How do you know this?" I asked.

"He told me himself."

"When?" I urged.

"He called me the night after the coven meeting."

"Why did he call you?" Felicity asked. "I thought it was a unanimous vote, which would mean you voted him out as well."

"True," Cally answered. "But I guess he figured I would still talk to him. He's my cousin."

"Your cousin?" Ben interposed.

"Not a blood relation," she added quickly. "I'm adopted. I can't say that he's my favorite relative in the world, and what he did to that dog makes me ill, but I don't see him killing Ariel. He had it bad for her."

I noticed R.J.'s face was creased with a tight-lipped frown, and he appeared to be stewing. With every word that came out of her mouth, his temperature seemed to rise.

"Anyone else?" Ben asked. "What about you two?" He motioned to the twins, Shari and Jennifer.

"He was in love with Ariel all right…" Shari told us.

"…You didn't have to be a rocket scientist to figure it out," Jennifer chimed in.

"So you don't think he was capable of killing her?" I questioned.

"Maybe," Jennifer answered.

"I don't know," stated Shari.

"He was a little weird if you ask me," Randy spoke up.

"I'm askin' you," Ben told him. "You wanna elaborate on that?"

"I dunno," Randy proceeded nervously. "He just struck me as kinda odd. He didn't talk much, but he was really into the whole ritual thing, you know?"

"Go on," I prodded.

"Well," Randy continued, "I've been practicing for about six years now, and I don't know about you," he focused on Felicity then me, "but I was under the impression that Wicca is really about 'deeds not words' you know? Like, the ritual is just a tool and not the main focus of the religion."

"That's how we look at it," Felicity told him.

"Well, not Devon," he told us. "The ritual was *it* for him. If it wasn't exactly perfect, then as far as he was concerned it wasn't worth doing."

"Randy's right about that," Cally said. "He spent all kinds of time rehearsing rituals for Sabbats."

"He even got real upset with me at a circle once..." Shari intoned.

"...Because she didn't recite something exactly like he wrote it," Jennifer added.

"See!" R.J. finally burst. "You all agree that something was wrong with the guy. And Rowan just said that whoever did this was into rituals."

"You're just jealous, R.J." Jennifer spat.

"What have I got to be jealous of?!" He was practically out of his chair now.

"Come off it, R.J.," Shari told him. "Everyone knows you had the hots for Ariel too."

"Sure we do," Cally interjected. "You followed her around like a lost puppy."

"Shut up, Cally!" R.J. shouted.

"Or what?" she baited.

"Stop it all of you!" Felicity was on her feet. "This is

ridiculous. Your friend... Your sister in The Craft has been murdered, and you're sitting here arguing like school children! Rowan and I studied with Ariel. I know damn well she thought better of you, or she never would have stood in circle with you then!"

The room fell silent. Each member of the group looked self-consciously about the room as the gravity of Felicity's words set in. Chairs made shuffling noises as they shifted in their seats and shamefully realized she was correct.

"Okay," Ben inserted his voice into the silence. "Now that that is finished... Did Miz Tanner happen ta' mention to any of ya' that she may have a reason to fear for her life?"

Heads swiveled back and forth indicating the negative amidst soberly mumbled "No's" and "Not to me's."

"Out of curiosity," I queried, "do you have any other former members, and have you had trouble with any of them getting involved in things they shouldn't?"

"Not really," Cally expressed. "At least I don't think so."

"You haven't kicked anyone else out?" Ben posed.

"No," she replied.

"How about members leaving of their own accord?" Felicity interjected. "Has that happened recently?"

"There was Stacey and Roger," Shari piped up.

"And Will," Jennifer added. "But they all left a few months ago."

Ben noted the names with his quick scribbling. "Did they leave on good terms?"

"Pretty much so, I guess," Randy, answered. "Will moved to Florida for his job, or I'm sure he'd still be with us."

Nods of agreement circled the table at his comment.

"What about the other two?" I pressed. "Stacey and Roger was it?"

"Yeah," he answered. "They just stopped showing up."

"Ariel said Stacey was just a poser," Cally explained. "Once she found out that she wasn't going to learn how to cast a spell on her ex-boyfriend, she lost interest. We figured Roger was just there because of her, because as soon as she stopped coming, so did he."

There was nothing unusual about having a poser enter and leave a coven. Some individuals would attempt to embrace the Wiccan religion based entirely upon their misconceptions about it. When they discovered that The Craft was about a harmonious existence with nature and NOT about "casting spells upon your enemies," they would become almost instantly disenchanted. Just like the two individuals that had just been described, a poser would simply and harmlessly go away.

As if on cue, the end of Cally's statement was punctuated by a quiet, evenly spaced, electronic beep that became increasingly louder with each pulse.

"Can I use your phone?" Ben asked me, switching off his pager.

"Sure," I replied. "You want to use the one in the bedroom?"

"If you don't mind."

"You know where it is."

The tension had ebbed once again, and Felicity took her seat at the table once more. The group started muttering apologies to one another, and faces were starting to break back into weak smiles.

"Hey, Rowan," Ben called from the bedroom down the hall. "Can I talk to ya' for a minute?"

I excused myself and made my way back to where he was. We spoke in hushed tones, and he explained to me what the phone call had been all about. After listening attentively to what he had to say, I called for Felicity to come back and join us. I heard her excuse herself and tell the group she would only be gone a moment, then seconds later she entered the room and shut the door behind her.

"What's going on?" she whispered, leaning against the doorframe.

"Do you think you can take over here and get these kids to comprehend what it means for a Witch to cross over?" I asked her gravely. "I need to go with Ben."

"Why?" She bolted up from her relaxed position. "What's wrong?"

"That page was from my lieutenant," Ben answered. "The Major Case Squad is taking over the investigation... Rowan was right, it looks like this psycho hit again."

CHAPTER 6

A predicted weather system had been moving in throughout the afternoon and evening, and before Ben and I left for the crime scene, a warm, gentle rain had begun to fall. Felicity, though not happy about being left behind, realized the importance of looking after the spiritual well being of the group seated at our dining table and immediately shifted into a nurturing maternal mode. Six pairs of questioning eyes fell upon us as Ben donned his sport coat and announced that we were leaving.

"Who is it?" Cally asked.

"We don't know yet," he told her. "I just got the call."

"Where did it happen?" Randy intoned.

"The body was found in a park here in the county," Ben stated irritably. "That's all I know until we get there. You ready yet Rowan?" He gave me an anxious look.

"In a sec..." I answered.

Felicity was stuffing a small camera bag with various pieces of equipment and film I had requested. The fact that she made her living as a professional photographer afforded me the luxury of having a better than average camera on hand whenever the need arose.

"I thought you were a city cop," R.J. announced. "Why are you investigating a murder out here in the county?"

"Normally a muni would handle its own case load," Ben stated, noticing that I still wasn't prepared to leave. "But this crime got flagged 'cause of the similarity to the Tanner case. Ya'see, back in nineteen eighty-one, the Greater Saint Louis Major Case Squad was formed as a multi-jurisdictional task force. Pretty much it's a collective of departments around the Metro area that investigates highly publicized or related crimes. Ariel's murder was my case, and so now that they have been given jurisdiction over it, I've been temporarily re-assigned to head up the investigation. I go wherever the scene is."

"Here," Felicity was telling me. "You've got the *PZ-1* with a 28-to-80 and macro. It's loaded with high speed transparency, and I put fresh batteries in it and the *Sunpak*."

"Thanks," I said and kissed her on the cheek. "I don't know how long this is going to take."

"Don't worry," she answered. "I'll take care of everything here."

While waiting for me, Ben quickly jotted down everyone's phone numbers in order to contact them with any further questions and then handed out his business cards. We expressed hurried goodbyes to the overwhelmed group and hastily headed out into the dense melancholy of the stormy night. I pulled Felicity aside on the front porch as she saw us out, lagging for a moment behind Ben who had already ventured forth into the rain and was starting his van.

"Look, I don't know if you noticed or not," I stated, "but Salinger and Dickens seem to have some kind of problem with R.J."

"Don't worry," she answered. "I'm sure you're just being overly suspicious because of everything that's going on. It'll be okay."

"I just want you to be careful," I continued.

"I'll be fine," she admonished. "Now go, then. Ben's waiting."

I watched her wave to us then turn and go into the house as we backed out of the driveway. I wasn't sure that she was correct, but then, after all that I had been through, it was possible that I had become more suspicious than usual. Maybe Ben was rubbing off on me. In any case, I knew my wife well, and she would be just fine. I also knew that she had almost instant access to a loaded *Ruger* .357 magnum, for neither of us was naive enough to think that the rest of the world believed as we do. The very concept of "live and let live" seemed almost alien to the general populous anymore, and the headlines of the newspaper or a quick glance at the evening news gave testimony to that fact. At Ben's urging, for our own protection, Felicity and I had purchased the weapon and been rigorously trained in its proper use by him. If it came down to a matter of life or death, I was certain my wife wouldn't hesitate to pull the trigger.

"So," I asked Ben as we motored down the street, its shiny wetness reflecting the glare of the streetlights. "Exactly where are we headed?"

"Some park called Thayer," he answered. "You know where it is?"

"Yeah, it's not far from here. Hang a right at the next stop sign."

We arrived at the park and turned in to the main access road, following it past the ball field and darkened pavilions. Ben had placed a magnetic bubble light atop the van and plugged it into the cigarette lighter receptacle as we entered. The red light flickered eerily across the face of the uniformed officer at the gate and reflected brightly from his rain-slicked yellow poncho. Ben rolled down the window and held out his ID to the officer, who illuminated it with the bright beam of a three cell *Mag-Lite*.

"Evening, Detective," he said and brought the beam to bear on me. "Who's that with you?"

"Consultant," Ben answered him authoritatively.

The sodden officer nodded and pointed the long flashlight up the road. Its beam, though powerful, eventually dissipated into the murky darkness.

"Just over that rise, sir," he told Ben. "Then about two hundred yards. Evidence unit is all over the place, you can't miss it."

Ben thanked him and rolled up his window, pushing the van into motion up the slight grade. The wind and rain were beginning to pick up, and a few distant flashes in the western sky were testimony to a rapidly approaching thunderstorm.

"Look behind your seat," Ben was telling me as we topped the rise. "Should be some rain slickers back there."

I turned in the seat and rummaged about in the dark. My hand brushed against what felt like a gym bag, and I yanked it from beneath the seat and tugged on the zipper.

"In this bag back here?" I asked.

"Yeah, prob'ly."

I could feel the van slowing and pitching slightly to the left as Ben took a wide turn into a parking space and brought us to a halt. I quickly found the rain ponchos I sought and with them in hand, turned back around in my seat.

The spectacle outside the windshield was illuminated like a toppled-over Christmas tree stuck in overdrive. Red lights, blue lights, and white lights on emergency vehicles, even yellow caution lights on sawhorses blinked randomly in the night. The lack of sync in the pulses seemed to bring even more chaos to what appeared to be an already disordered scene.

Ben reached out and grabbed one of the slickers from my motionless hand, taking notice of my blank stare and mouth agape.

"Welcome to my world," he told me, then paused. "Sucks

don't it? Go ahead an' put your poncho on."

I broke from the short stupor and began pulling the yellow plastic rain gear over my head. The extra room in the cab of the van made me realize why Ben refused to get rid of the decrepit vehicle.

"How should I introduce ya'?" Ben asked, unlatching his door. "I doubt if they'll go for Good Witch of the East."

"How about, Alternative Religion Specialist," I replied.

"Sounds good ta' me."

A distant streak of lightning followed by a sharp crack and low rumble of thunder alerted us to the ever-increasing violence of the storm as we stepped out into the downpour. We walked across the parking area, past the flapping yellow tape that cordoned off the crime scene. I was concerned that important evidence might be washed away, but my fears were soon allayed when I noticed the core of the activity involved the cinder block building that housed a set of the park's restrooms.

"Ben Storm," my friend told another detective, displaying his badge as we approached him. "City Homicide Unit. I'm assigned to the MCS."

"Carl. Carl Deckert. County Police." The thickset, greying detective reached out and shook Ben's hand. "You the one investigating that Tanner homicide?"

"That's me," Ben answered.

"This your partner?" he queried, reaching out to shake my hand.

"Rowan Gant," I told him, returning the gesture.

"He's a specialist on alternative religions," Ben explained. "He's consulting for us on the symbols left at the Tanner crime scene."

Detective Deckert motioned to another officer who produced a partially sodden clipboard. Ben scrawled a signature on the damp paperwork and then indicated a spot for me to sign and record the time.

"Well," our stocky escort said as the three of us began walking toward the entrance to the restroom. "You've got plenty to consult about. Looks like a freakin' Satanic graffiti party in there."

"Have you ID'd the victim?" Ben questioned.

"Found a purse," Deckert continued. "Driver's license matches up to a Karen Barnes. Twenty-eight years old..."

A bright flash exploded in my eyes, momentarily blinding me. At first I thought a streak of lightning had hit nearby, but the telltale clap of thunder was never forthcoming. Instead I heard shouting, expletives, and what sounded to be a scuffle.

"What the..." Ben exclaimed.

"Shit!" Detective Deckert shouted. "How the hell did he get in here?!"

My vision began returning to normal, and what had sounded like a scuffle was revealed to be just that. Two uniformed officers were on either side of a struggling young man holding a camera affixed with a powerful flash unit.

"Get him outta here!" Deckert ordered the two officers. "And tighten up the perimeter!" he shouted after them as they dragged the photographer away. "Sorry about that. Freakin' media. Every damn one of 'em's got a police scanner. Sometimes they get to the scene before we do."

"You were sayin'?" Ben prodded.

"Oh, yeah," he continued. "Karen Barnes, twenty-eight years old. Lives about three blocks from here. Looks like she was out walking her dog. The son-of-a-bitch killed it too."

"Family been notified?" Ben asked.

"Got a car waiting for the husband. Neighbor said he was out of town on business. She was expecting him back tonight."

"Any kids?"

"No. Just her and the spouse."

"Well at least there's that."

We had paused at the entrance of the women's restroom on the side of the cinder block structure. Evidence technicians were exiting, carrying bulky cases containing the tools of their trade.

"Being a public restroom, there are prints everywhere," Deckert pointed out. "We didn't find anything real fresh except for some smudges. Looks like he was wearing gloves." He pulled a pair of packets from the pocket of his trench coat and handed one to each of us. "Speaking of which, you better put these on just to be safe."

I took the offered surgical gloves and with some work, managed to pull them over my damp hands as we entered the building.

I caught my breath and nearly stumbled as waves of ethereal pain washed over me. I quickly fought to disconnect myself from the supernatural plane associated with the scene and ground myself here in this reality. A sharp pain, followed by a frigid, tingling sensation consumed my body, then slowly subsided as I mentally slammed on the brakes, preventing my otherworldly senses from continuing down the path that beckoned them.

"You okay?" Ben whispered in my ear, grabbing my arm to steady me. "You aren't getting ready to flip out or do that channeling thing are you?"

"I'll be all right," I answered in a hushed tone. "I caught it before it happened."

"Good. Just try not to go all *Twilight Zone* on me with the rest of these guys around here."

A white sheet was arranged in the center of the room covering a section of the smooth, grey concrete floor. Beneath the shroud laid the lifeless body of another young woman. Patches of deep crimson diffused slowly through the sheet at various points where it contacted portions of the torso. A cloying odor, both sweet and musty, intermingled with the stench of the restroom, tingling my nostrils. The pungent scent was all too familiar.

"Sage and rose oil," I stated aloud.

"Come again?" Detective Deckert asked.

"That smell," I told him as he started taking notes. "It's sage and rose oil. Probably a little charcoal mixed in to help it burn. Did you find a pile of ash anywhere?"

"In the sink over there." He pointed. "That mean something?"

"He burned it to cleanse the room," I replied. "Sage is often used in incense for purification. You'll probably find salt in the North, South, East, and West positions of the room as well."

I stepped past him and peered in the sink at the pile of grey cinders. The floor in the area was littered with broken glass, silvered on the back. The mirror above the washbasin had been shattered.

"Evidence unit took the larger pieces of the mirror with them," he offered. "We don't know if the killer broke it or if vandals did it earlier."

"My guess would be that he did it," I told them, turning and finding Ben taking notes. "Probably before he performed the ritual."

"Why do ya' think that is?" Ben asked.

"If he was trying to invoke something..." I caught myself, remembering that Detective Deckert was in the room. "You know, if he thought he was attempting to conjure up a spirit," I explained. "Some legends have it that if a spirit witnesses its own reflection in a mirror, it will become mesmerized and therefore, trapped. I would guess he probably subscribes to that belief."

"So the wacko busted the mirror," Deckert's gruff voice interjected. "So his little ghost buddy wouldn't see himself?"

"It's one possibility," I replied carefully.

The wall opposite me was inscribed with a familiar-looking Pentacle. The symbol was drawn on the painted, cinder block wall, once again in blood and shaded with pastels. At the base of the wall, slags of hardened black and white wax were obvious remnants of extinguished candles. Nestled next to the solidified remains stood a simple wine glass, partially filled with coagulating red liquid. Between the symbol and the floor was once again lettered, All Is Forgiven.

"So," Deckert was asking Ben. "You think it's the same guy?"

"Oh yeah," I said as Ben turned to me. "It's the same guy all right. Only this time, he might not have been practicing."

"Whaddaya mean 'practicing'?" Deckert looked from Ben's face to mine and back with a puzzled expression.

Ben explained. "We've got reason to believe that the ritual this guy is performin' was never actually completed at the first scene. He was doin' like a dress rehearsal or somethin'."

"Holy shit!" the detective exclaimed. "This prick committed murder to rehearse a murder? Holy shit!"

"Tell me about it," Ben chimed.

"Well, if he did what he set out to do, then he probably won't kill any more, right?"

"I don't know for sure," I answered as I squatted next to the covered corpse and examined the floor. "He might not be finished yet."

"Finished doing what exactly?" Deckert questioned.

"Invoking whatever spirit he's after. He'll continue to perform the ritual until he has succeeded," I explained. "Or, at least, perceives that he has." I paused thoughtfully for a moment before speculating aloud, "He might kill again because maybe he wants to get caught."

"What makes ya' think that?" Ben asked.

"The Expiation spell." I motioned at the wall behind them. "I originally thought that it was an aberration at the first scene. Possibly because whoever killed Ariel Tanner might have known her. But this...it might have been the real thing for him. The actual ritual played to its conclusion, yet, he's still seeking atonement from himself. It doesn't make sense to perform an atonement ritual at the site of a sacrificial ritual.

"You see an Expiation spell is a private thing, very much like going to confession. By performing it at the scene, essentially he exposes himself. He may be seeking atonement from society as well. In short, kind of a sick cry for help. So it leads me to believe that either he wants to get caught, or he's not finished yet. Maybe even both."

"Jesus," Deckert said. "Where did you get all that from?"

"Trust me," I heard Ben say. "You don't wanna know."

"Let's just say I did a lot of research this afternoon," I told him as I stood and walked over to the rune-covered wall. "Anyway, it's just a theory."

I pulled out the camera and fired up the flash unit. The thyristor began charging with a low hum and then grew quickly to a quiet whine. Status lights began glowing on the unit's back, indicating its readiness.

"Crime Scene Unit already took pictures," Deckert told me as I placed the *PZ-1* to my eye and began tightly focusing on the Pentacle.

"I know," I replied absently. "But I'd like to take some of my own if it's okay."

"Hey," he answered. "Whatever makes you happy."

"Who found the body?" Ben inquired.

"Local kid," Deckert responded. "He was out walking his dog. Says when he walked it by here, it just went nuts. Broke away from him and ran in. Apparently, the door had been propped open."

"Animals can sense death," I stated aloud, still taking pictures of the scene before me. "He did the same thing with Ariel Tanner. The door was propped open. Could be he wanted the body found as soon as possible."

"You sure you ain't some kinda psychiatrist or something?" Deckert asked the back of my head.

"I've got a semester of college psych," I told him as I turned. "But that doesn't qualify me to practice the science, no."

"Well," he continued. "You sure sound like some kinda FBI shrink. It's like you're getting inside this asshole's head or something."

"Like I said, I'm just speculating," I replied.

Detective Deckert didn't realize how close to the truth he was with his last comment. My experiences channeling Ariel's death and the blatant evidence left at both scenes were all acting as catalysts to pull me in. The more I saw, and the more I sensed, the more I feared what would be waiting around the next corner.

"What time do ya' think the murder occurred?" Ben inquired.

"Based on the time the neighbor says she left for her walk," Deckert started, "and the time the kid found her, we're estimating somewhere between five-thirty and eight P.M."

"Between five-thirty and eight," Ben repeated, looking at me from the corner of his eye.

I knew what the glance implied. He had been suspicious of R.J. from the beginning, and I had to admit, his actions this evening coupled with his late arrival at the meeting hadn't helped. Salinger and Dickens voicing their feline distaste had even compelled me to wonder about what the young man was hiding.

"We might be able to pin it down a bit closer," Deckert intoned, "once your M.E. gets here."

"She's here."

A voice came from the doorway, and the three of us turned to face a bleary-eyed woman clad in faded denim. Dr. Christine Sanders pushed back the hood of her rain-soaked jacket and hefted a thick aluminum case from one hand to the other.

"Detectives." She nodded to them as she entered the room. "I thought I told you to get some rest, Mister Gant."

"And I thought this was your day off," I replied with a slight smile.

"Me too," she returned. "But that was before the captain of the Major Case Squad called me at the request of Detective Storm."

"You're familiar with the Tanner case," Ben stated matter-of-factly.

"Officially, I'm only here as a consultant," she informed him. "This is out of the city jurisdiction. You're just lucky the county coroner and I have an understanding."

"I know, Doc. I just want the best on this."

"Save the flattery for your wife, Storm," she told him with a weak grin. "You're still going to owe me big."

By now, Dr. Sanders was kneeling next to the body of the young woman and had thrown back the sheet that had been covering it. The injuries appeared very similar to those of Ariel Tanner. The skin had been peeled away from what I could see of the woman's chest, leaving behind raw, exposed muscle. Her eyes stared off blankly, and her face wore a grimace of excruciating pain and horror. Her arms were twisted behind her body, and though I couldn't see them, I was sure they were bound.

A departure from the similarity with Ariel's torture was the fact that Karen Barnes' mouth was covered with a wide strip of duct tape. It had been wrapped tightly around her head to keep it from coming loose. Her ankles were also secured in the same fashion, and the tape wrapped around the post of a stall to keep her legs in place.

"I'll have to do a swab," Dr. Sanders was telling us. "But if he's establishing a pattern, I doubt if she was raped. The Tanner woman wasn't."

"He didn't rape her," I said. "That would have soiled her. He wouldn't defile his sacrifice."

I moved around to get a better view of the body and was about to expand upon my statement when the angle that had been blocked by the doctor's kneeling form came into my line of sight. Directly beneath Karen Barnes' rib cage, a deep, ragged incision stretched horizontally across her flayed torso. The uneven gash puckered open like a bloody, toothless smile, exposing lacerated internal organs. Instantly I turned away and bolted for a stall, bile rising in my throat.

A few moments later, I heard Deckert asking from behind me, "Are you gonna be all right?"

I had just finished expelling the contents of my stomach into the toilet I was kneeling before. I spat and wiped my face then stood and flushed.

"Yeah," I answered weakly. "Sorry about that. I'm not as used to this stuff as you guys."

"Used to it, hell," he answered. "I came close to doing the same goddamned thing earlier."

I walked out of the stall, and Deckert patted me on the shoulder as I passed him. Dr. Sanders was cutting the body loose from the metal post, and the County Coroner had come in and was preparing a body bag. Ben was facing away from the morbid activity looking very green.

"Her heart has been removed. Can anyone here tell me if it was found?" Dr. Sanders asked as she and her peer rolled the body and slid the open, rubberized bag beneath it, then let it gently back down.

"You won't," I told them, wiping my mouth with the back of my hand. "He took it with him."

"What, like a souvenir or somethin'?" Ben asked.

"No," I replied. "As part of the ritual."

The violent bout of vomiting had shocked my system and broken my concentration, effectively weakening my defenses against otherworldly interference. Dizziness swarmed over me as the room began to spin. I was losing control. My ears filled with a rushing sound, and color melted liquidly from the images before me. I fell backwards down a dark tunnel, speeding inexorably away from an ever-diminishing point of light. When I at last jerked to an abrupt halt, I was floating above the room, looking down upon the recent past.

A hooded, cloaked figure.

A pretty, vital young woman bound nude on the floor.

A dirk. I know that dirk. It belonged to Ariel.

She wants to struggle but she can't. I can feel her trying to scream, but he's taped her mouth. Her head hurts. She remembers someone attacked her from behind.

What are you doing? Get away from me with that knife!

I can feel the silent scream, the searing pain as the knife bites into flesh, peeling back the skin.

"Stop it you bastard," I say to myself, struggling to break the connection.

"I'm sorry," he says to her.

Why is this happening? Our Father who art in heaven, hallowed be Thy name. Thy kingdom come...NO!

I see him press the knife, Ariel's athamè, into her solar plexus and draw it across carefully, making the ragged cut.

The pain is unbearable, indescribable.

He slowly removes a surgical glove.

He thrusts his hand into the incision. With a twisting motion, he wrenches it back out.

Still quivering.

Dripping.

Karen Barnes heart lay in his hand.

"Rowan," Ben's voice echoed in my ears. "Hey, Rowan." He was nudging me. Colors flashed back into the scene and kaleidoscoped wildly before finally settling to their proper shades and places.

"Yeah," I half whispered. "Yeah, I'm okay."

"You kinda spaced on us there," he told me.

"Just a second." A sudden realization hammered down upon me. "Dr. Sanders, don't you do something with Superglue and a black light to find fingerprints on skin?"

"Cyanoacrylate fuming," she corrected. "And it's a bit more than just a black light. But it really depends on the circumstances. Sometimes we use Ninhydrin. Fingerprints on skin are very short lived. Perspiration and other natural secretions destroy them rather quickly. Why?"

"He took off his glove before he removed her heart."

"How can you know that?" Detective Deckert asked me.

"Intuition. Inspiration. Divine perception. It doesn't matter," I spoke quickly. "Trust me on this. He took his glove off."

CHAPTER 7

With some colorfully worded urging from Ben, the medical examiner finally agreed to check the body for latent fingerprints. Still, neither she, nor Detective Deckert, seemed inclined to believe my claim about the glove, and I couldn't really blame them. I could provide no evidence to back up my statement, and they really had no idea who I was. I often thought that life would be much easier if I could just say, "Hey, I'm a card carrying Witch, see?" and show an ID badge. Of course, that would only work if the rest of the world were disposed to saying, "Oh, well, why didn't you say that in the first place?"

We spent a few additional minutes looking over the interior of the restroom, and I took several more pictures, including some of the body, shot in haste to avoid another bout of vomiting. Deckert pointed out the remains of Karen Barnes' Jack Russell terrier heaped in a corner. The animal's skull was crushed, apparently from having been repeatedly dashed against the cinder block wall. Grossly violent yet still a much more merciful death than faced by its owner. Dr. Sanders bagged the remains of the dog at Ben's request, and then we followed her back out into the stormy night. Detective Deckert and I tagged along behind as Ben drew up next to her.

"What are the chances of getting' some preliminaries back tonight, Doc?" Ben asked.

"You're kidding, right?"

"No," he answered bluntly. "Did I sound particularly funny to you?"

The rain had slowed momentarily, but the earlier downpour had flooded the low-lying sidewalk. The wheels on the gurney containing Karen Barnes' body made sadly mournful swishing noises as they rolled through the puddles.

"Who's going to authorize this?" Dr. Sanders stopped in her tracks and stared angrily back at Ben. "Remember, I'm only here in a consulting capacity."

"Look," Ben softened, "I'm sorry about the wisecrack. It's been a long day, and right now I'm not seein' the end of it."

"I know," she answered, calming. "Same here."

"Listen, no offense," he addressed the county coroner. "But do you have any problem with allowin' Doctor Sanders here do the autopsy?"

"None taken. It's unusual," he answered with a weary nod. "But it's okay with me. I don't suppose it would be a problem with the right paperwork."

"Submit whatever ya' need, and I'll sign off on it," he told him with a tired smile.

"Where can I reach you?" Doctor Sanders queried.

"Right now I'm not sure where I'll be. You can try to catch me at my office, and if you don't get an answer then beep me. The number's on my card."

"Okay."

Deckert and I had stopped behind them and allowed Ben to do the talking. We stood in the light rain and watched as Doctor Sanders and the county official loaded what was once a living, breathing human being into the back of the coroner's hearse. The hatch-like door slammed shut with a dull finality as if audibly marking the end of Karen Barnes' existence.

Farther in the distance, across the parking lot and behind the police barricades, a small city had grown. Microwave dishes and retractable towers were pointed skyward, extending from the roofs of numerous news vans. Bright lights shined surrealistically through the night, igniting the falling raindrops into fleeting fiery gems. Primped, pressed, and preened reporters staunchly clutching umbrellas faced cameramen and rehearsed their expressions of concern.

"Fuckin' vultures," Ben muttered.

He and Detective Deckert traded cards and set up a meeting time for the following morning, as they were both assigned to the Major Case Squad. We shook hands and parted, leaving Deckert to wrap up everything at the scene while Ben was to go get the ball rolling with the rest of the MCS. We had barely made it halfway to the van before we were ambushed.

"Detective Storm, Detective Storm, can I have a word with you."

A lithe, young beauty in a neatly fitted trench coat and high heels was sauntering quickly toward us. Her hair was fashionably coiffed and honey blonde, the exact shade of which I was certain could only be available from a bottle. The cameraman behind her suddenly switched on an intense spotlight and bathed us with its harsh glow. As we squinted against the glare, the woman stopped before us, effectively blocking our path.

"I'm here on the scene with Detective Benjamin Storm of the Saint Louis City homicide unit. Detective Storm, does the fact that you're here mean that the Major Case Squad has been called in?" she spoke rapidly into a microphone and then thrust it forward into Ben's face.

"Go away Brandee," Ben told her. "I'm not in the mood for this right now."

Ben started around her, but she quickly sidestepped, her high heels clicking on the pavement.

"Is it true that this homicide is related to Wednesday evening's murder of Ariel Tanner?" Again, the microphone bearing the stylized logo of her station shot forward.

"Talk to the public relations officer," Ben returned flatly.

"And you sir, your name is?" She shoved the microphone toward me.

Before I could get "no comment" past my lips, Ben reached out and removed the microphone easily from her dainty hand. With a quick snap, he disconnected the line cord and handed the device back to her.

She looked at him, dumbfounded for a moment, then angrily stamped her foot as her luminous, blue eyes grew large, clearly revealing an empty void behind them.

"I said," Ben, told her, as he brushed past, "go away Brandee."

We heard her wheel about as we continued across the lot to the van. She let out a frustrated shriek that was rapidly followed by the sound of the disconnected microphone as it roughly impacted the pavement near us and skittered by.

"I'm going to get this story, Storm!" she screamed after us. "You're not doing this to me again!"

By the time we climbed into the van, Brandee Street was berating her stony-faced cameraman, her arms flailing wildly as he simply stared at her.

"What'd she mean 'you're not doing this to me again'?" I asked Ben as he started the van. "And what the hell is she chewin' his ass for?"

"Brandee Street has never, I repeat, NEVER gotten a story from me," he answered, pulling his plastic poncho over his head. "As for ol' Ed out there, she probably just caught him addin' to his collection."

"His collection?" I puzzled, removing my own rain slicker. "You know that guy?"

"Hell yes, all the coppers know Ed. He's been a cameraman for years. As to the collection, he tapes reporters when they throw temper tantrums. He's got a whole library of 'em... calls hers 'Brandee Whines'."

"Seems like they would try to get him fired."

"Oh, they have," Ben, continued. "Ed's got a couple of things goin' for him though. First, he's the best cameraman in the state. Second, a real good union."

"Bet that pisses them off," I mused.

"Uh-huh. Drives 'em nuts. I'll have ta' give you a call next time Ed wants to get together for some beers and 'movies'."

"Count me in."

We pulled out of the parking space in silence. The windshield wipers tapped out an irregular swooshing tempo as they displaced the rain, only to have it return a second later. We slowly started past the news vans, enduring the bright lights that were quickly brought to bear on us. I was sure that Ben felt some extra heat coming from the savage glare Brandee Street was throwing at him as we hooked around her vehicle.

"So," Ben said as he nudged the van along, exiting the small city of reporters. "You went off into 'la la land' there for a minute." He shot me a quick glance then returned his eyes to the road. "That where you got that whole glove thing from?"

"Yeah," I replied. "That's what I saw him do. I don't know if it will do any good or not. He didn't take the glove off until just before he pulled her heart out."

"Shouldn't that have caused you some damage or somethin'?" he queried. "You know, like Felicity was talkin' about this afternoon."

"If I had experienced it directly," I explained. "Like I did with Ariel. This wasn't the same. I didn't get pulled into the experience. It was like I was just a spectator."

"So you didn't feel anything this time?"

"Well, yeah, I felt some of the pain. Just not directly."

We continued along quietly for a moment or two,

winding along the park access road and out to the main street.

"Did ya' see his face?" Ben asked.

"No," I answered. "I wish I had. I've never witnessed a past event like that before, and it came on me all of a sudden. I think when I got sick I let my guard down, and that's why it happened. How long was I blanked out anyway?"

"Around a minute, maybe two," Ben told me. "Deckert thought ya' were gonna puke again." He paused for a moment and merged with the main street traffic. "Did ya' see anything besides the glove thing?"

"Ariel's athamè," I told him. "He used it again." I hesitated. "A lot of fear... A lot of pain... She was trying to recite the Lord's Prayer to herself when the bastard pulled her heart out."

We rode the rest of the way to my house in silence. The storm was dying out now, and the rain had tapered to a gentle, patchy sprinkle as the tail end of the system moved through the area.

"I don't know what's gonna hit the news tomorrow, Rowan," Ben spoke as he came to a halt in my driveway. "But for now, this whole thing stays with us. You can tell Felicity, but I don't want those kids in there babblin' all over creation if ya' know what I mean."

"Yes," I answered, "I know exactly what you mean."

"Do you think you can meet with the MCS tomorrow?" he queried.

"What for?"

"I'd like you ta' fill them in on the symbol and inscription," he explained. "Along with some of the ideas you had tonight. I think it might give us some places to start."

"Are you sure?" I asked, mulling over the implications.

"I'm not some kind of 'FBI shrink' like Detective Deckert said."

"I know, but you're the closest thing we've got to an expert," Ben answered. "Yeah, I'm sure."

"Okay. Just say when."

"I'll call you in the mornin'. Go get some rest. And give the squaw a hug for me."

I watched as Ben backed out of the drive. The handset of his cell phone was pressed to his ear. Even at a distance, I could see his mouth moving rapidly and a sad look in his eyes. I knew then that he was talking to Allison—telling her yet again not to wait up for him.

"We saw you on the news."

I heard my wife's voice behind me and turned to face her. She had come out on the porch where I was standing.

"Did they get my good side?" I joked half-heartedly and then gave her a tired peck on the cheek.

"The cheek?" she pouted. "Don't you love me anymore?"

"Considering the gastric event I experienced, until I brush my teeth and get a swig of mouthwash..." I trailed off.

"It was bad, huh?" she asked, instantly understanding.

"Worse than Ariel," I told her. "But I can't tell you about it until we're alone."

"I understand."

We went into the house, and I headed directly for the bathroom where I could make myself a bit more presentable. When I returned to the dining room, the entire group was seated around the table talking. They were in a much more relaxed mood than before I left.

"So what happened?" R.J. immediately asked as I sat down.

"I can't tell you much," I answered, pouring myself a glass of tea. "Suffice it to say, there was another murder."

"Well," Cally intoned. "Was it the same killer or what?"

"We think so," I replied.

"We saw you on the news, Mr. Gant..." Shari stated.

"...But just from a distance," Jennifer continued.

"Rowan. Please." I nodded, remembering the glaring lights and sea of reporters at the scene. "So, what did they say?"

"They're calling him the Satanic Serial Killer," Randy intoned. "They said he killed this woman the same way he killed Ariel. Is that true?"

"I wish I could tell you guys," I answered, "but I can't. If the police are going to be able to trust me to help them with the investigation, then I have to follow their rules."

There was some grumbling, but with Cally's prodding, they all grudgingly agreed. She was a strong young woman and level headed for the most part. With a little further training in The Craft, I felt certain she would be able to pick up with the coven where Ariel had been prematurely forced to leave off.

"So how did things go around here after Ben and I left?" I questioned, looking about. "From the looks of things, I missed a circle...Any good discussions or revelations?"

Extinguished candles still sat in holders on the table: yellow, red, blue, green, and a white one in the center. Two small dishes, one containing salt, the other water, were positioned together with the white candle, and the last crumbs of a honey cake adorned a plate. A pewter goblet and Felicity's athamè completed the centerpiece. I could still feel the leftover energy that had been created by the casting of the circle and raising a cone. I was sorry I had missed it, especially since I could feel a trace of darkness in the energy. Something tainted was lingering in the background, and I feared it was coming from a particular individual in this room. If I had been present in the circle, I might have been able to pinpoint its source.

"We talked quite a bit about crossing over," Felicity chimed with a smile.

"Yeah," R.J. added. "It was pretty intense."

"Ariel never said anything about the crossing," Cally interjected. "We had all read about it, but...well, you know."

"Yes, I do," I answered. "I'm afraid I was probably a little lax in her teachings when it came to that. I had to deal with another particularly difficult crossing a few years back, so I have a tendency to avoid the subject sometimes."

"Who?" Cally asked.

"My mother," I answered.

"Your mother was a Witch?" Randy questioned.

"Yes, she was," I told them then fell quiet.

"So we held a simple death rite for Ariel tonight." Felicity broke the silence. "It went fairly well, except..."

"Ariel won't leave..." Shari interrupted.

"...She won't cross the bridge," Jennifer finished.

"That isn't unusual," I told them as I pondered what the twins had just said. "In the case of a violent death, one's spirit sometimes hangs around on this plane searching for closure."

"You mean Ariel's stuck here?" Randy exclaimed, emphatic concern in his eyes.

"Maybe for a while but probably not permanently," I comforted him. "We can try another rite once the killer is caught. Maybe that will allow her to move on."

I looked at my watch. It read midnight. I suddenly realized I was running on four hours sleep out of the past forty.

"I don't know about the rest of you," I stated with a shallow yawn. "But I'm beat, and I need to hit the sack."

The pendulum clock on the wall began to bong out its count of the hour as the hands finally came to rest on twelve. Cally looked at her own watch, and her eyes widened slightly.

"I'm sorry," she exclaimed. "I didn't realize it was this late."

"Nothing to apologize for," I assured her. "It's been a long day for all of us."

"Do you think," Randy queried as they all began gathering themselves to leave, "that maybe we could have circle with you and Felicity again sometime? You know, like a Full Moon meeting or something?"

"Certainly," I grinned.

"Of course." Felicity smiled. "We'd love to."

The group gathered their things, and then Cally, Nancy and the twins hugged both Felicity and myself. Randy hugged my wife and shook my hand. R.J. still seemed to remain somewhat aloof. He shook hands with both of us, and when I clasped my hand about his, I mentally probed for the streak of darkness I had felt earlier. He had been taught well, and his defenses came up, immediately blocking my psychic exploration. I was more experienced and could have easily broken through the ethereal wall separating us, but it was both inappropriate, and at this point in time, uncalled for. He looked back at me coolly, knowing full well what I had tried to do, and said nothing.

Once they were gone, Felicity sent the dogs out to take care of whatever they needed to do and then let them back in. I had just finished letting Emily out the front door to go on her nightly "mouse patrol" when the rambunctious canines scrambled past me and into our bedroom. My wife trailed along behind them, switching off lights as she went. We finished locking up the house and shutting off the remaining lights together then dragged ourselves off to bed as well.

The crisp, fresh sheets on our waterbed felt wonderful,

and I expelled a tired sigh as I stretched out. A tranquil hum issued from the slowly spinning ceiling fan above as it moved the cool air about the room. I heard the light switch in the bathroom, and Felicity emerged, having twisted her hair atop her head and donned an oversized t-shirt bearing the faded quip, "Photographers do it in a darkroom." After moving the bedroom light from dim to off, she gently slid into the bed next to me and rested her head on my shoulder.

"Do you want to talk about it now?"

Her voice drifted to me in the darkness. I shifted and slid my arm around, pulling her closer.

"It's the same guy," I told her. "No doubt in my mind. I don't think he was just practicing this time though, but I can't be sure. It looked like he performed a full ritual..." I paused. "Complete with removing the victim's heart."

I could feel her shudder against me. I wasn't sure how I felt about giving her the details, but I knew that if I didn't, she would get them from Ben as soon as I turned my back.

"Why in the park?" she asked.

"I don't know," I replied. "Based on what I've seen so far, I'm thinking he might want to be caught, but this was more than a little brazen if you ask me."

"From what I saw on the news," she lent, "those restrooms were the ones in the back of the park. They're pretty isolated."

"I know, but still, people walk their dogs back there. That's how the body was found. A kid walking his dog." I told her, "Dog went nuts when they passed by the restrooms. The door was propped open, and he broke loose and ran in."

"Poor kid," Felicity sighed. "I doubt if he was ready for that."

"Yeah, he was still talking to a police shrink when Ben and I left."

"Do you think the killer knew the victim?"

"We didn't find anything to indicate that," I answered. "So I'd be inclined to say no, but I'm sure they'll be checking into it."

"Did they find anything at the scene that might help?"

"Not much," I answered. "He hailed the towers and performed an Expiation spell again, presumably after the other ritual. He bound her wrists and ankles and gagged her with duct tape. They might get something off that. When I projected..."

I felt her tense against me, and I knew what she was thinking.

"...Don't worry, I didn't channel, I just projected. It wasn't the same as with Ariel..."

She relaxed, and I gave her a reassuring squeeze.

"When I projected, I saw him pull his glove off before he reached in for her heart." I couldn't believe how calmly I was relaying this story. I hoped that I wasn't becoming jaded to the atrocities I had witnessed lately. "I don't know if they'll get anything, but they're going to look for latent prints on the body."

"Maybe that will turn something up," she said.

"Maybe. Even if it does, unless he's on file from some previous offense or something, it won't be much help in finding him."

The waterbed rippled slightly, and we felt movement in the dark followed by a muted rumble growing closer by the second. Within moments, Salinger climbed onto my chest and curled up, purring interminably as Felicity scratched his ears.

"That reminds me," I said shifting slightly, recalling Salinger's earlier opinion of R.J. "How did the circle go for you? I noticed a little streak of dark in the residual energy when I sat down at the table."

"It was there during the circle too," she told me. "It really didn't seem to come from anyone though. It was more like it was just hanging around from something else. It wasn't terribly overwhelming or anything, so I just had everyone ground all their negative thoughts and energies. I figured it was probably their thoughts of seeking revenge and such."

"You could be right," I mused. "I suppose some of it could have been left hanging around. How did the cats act?"

"Nowhere to be found," she answered. "They were probably in here asleep on the bed."

"You know Ben really suspects R.J.," I told her. "Especially after the time of death for Karen Barnes was placed somewhere between five-thirty and eight P.M."

"Karen Barnes. They identified her pretty quickly."

"Her purse was at the scene."

"I know R.J. was late and all," she stated. "But I think Ben is on the wrong track. I would have felt something from him if he had done it. He wouldn't have been able to mask that while in the circle."

"Well," I intoned, "I tried to feel him out when he shook my hand, and he put up defenses immediately."

"You would have done the same if someone tried to check you out," she told me. "That doesn't make him guilty of anything."

"Yeah, you're right."

We laid wordlessly in the dark listening to the sound of the humming fan blend with the contented, throaty rumble of the lump of fur curled up on my chest.

"Is Ben going to call tomorrow?" Felicity finally asked.

"Yeah," I answered. "In the morning. He wants me to meet with the Major Case Squad. I might end up needing those slides."

"Then I guess I'll have to get up early and process them, so I can get them mounted," she stated and then gave me a light kiss. "Go to sleep dear. You have to be exhausted."

"I am." I patted her lightly on the rear as she rolled over. "I love you."

"I love you too."

I stared off into the darkness, the meter of the swirling fan blades setting up an audible, hypnotic rhythm. I was so tired I felt I could sleep forever, but at the same time, I was still coming down from the adrenalin pumping through my veins. I listened to the soft rhythm and started a mental exercise to relax. Clearing my mind, I allowed the stress of the past two days to pour out of me like water from a faucet. I closed my eyes and let the last thoughts in my head drift away.

Before long, my body was completely infused with a comfortable drifting sensation. Indigo darkness enveloped me broken only by a bright blue light in the distance. I reached for the light, and I was gone.

CHAPTER 8

Felicity allowed me to sleep in the next morning, and it was going on eight A.M. when I finally dragged myself from the bed and into the shower. I felt rested for the first time in what seemed like forever. Apparently, I had been too exhausted to have any nightmares, and about that, I wasn't going to complain.

My wife was seated at the dining room table when I was finally dressed and prepared to meet the day. A portable light box inhabited the surface of the table, and she was huddled over it with a loupe held to her eye. A stack of freshly mounted color slides occupied the space to her right, and she was inspecting them one by one as she arranged them on the illuminated panel before her.

"How did you sleep?" she asked without looking up.

"Better than I expected." I kissed the top of her head. "How'd the slides come out?"

"Technically, okay, though I can't say as that I really care for the subject matter," she returned. "But I wouldn't quit my day job if I were you."

"Always the critic," I told her. "You eat yet?

"No. These haven't exactly done wonders for my appetite." She dealt another handful of the transparencies onto the light box. "Besides, I was waiting for you."

"Well, isn't that sweet."

"Not really. It's your turn to cook."

"I should have known."

I was in the kitchen quickly sautéing onions when the phone rang. I picked up the receiver and tucked it between my ear and shoulder while I whisked eggs to a medium froth in a mixing bowl. "Hello?"

"Good mornin'" came a familiar, but rough voice. "I didn't wake you guys, did I?"

"No, we're awake, Ben," I told him. "I'm just now making breakfast."

"What are we havin'?" he asked.

"What do you mean we?" I laughed. "Are you on your way or something?"

"Actually," he replied, "I'm in the driveway."

"In that case, you're having a Denver omelet and hash browns."

I hung up the phone and retrieved the carton of eggs from the refrigerator then began cracking more of them into the bowl.

"Honey?" I called out. "Could you unlock the front door? Ben's in the driveway."

I was folding large chunks of chopped ham, peppers, onions, and shredded cheese into a fluffy omelet when a haggard, unkempt Ben Storm ambled into my kitchen and helped himself to a cup of coffee.

"Are you sure you're going to be able to do without doughnuts this morning?" I asked, sliding the finished omelet from the pan and preparing to make another.

"Yeah, yeah, yeah," he replied, seating himself at our breakfast nook. "Like I haven't heard the cop-slash-doughnut jokes before. You get any sleep last night?"

"Uh-huh," I grunted, pouring frothy eggs into the pan. "How about yourself?"

"Got a couple hours." He sipped his coffee. "Didn't get home till four this mornin'."

"How's Allison taking all this?" Felicity asked. She had been standing in the doorway and now took a seat opposite him.

"She's not happy about it," he answered. "But she's been through it before. It goes with the job."

"What about the little guy?" I asked, sliding plates containing omelets and hash browns before them.

"Not as good. He doesn't understand why I'm never home." Ben shoveled in a mouthful of food and sat chewing thoughtfully. "I think I'm gonna take a vacation when this is all over."

"Might be good for you," Felicity told him. "AND your family."

I finished filling my plate and joined them at the small bar. After moving some magazines, there was just enough room for the three of us.

"So," Ben asked between bites, "have ya' seen this mornin's paper?"

"I brought it in," Felicity answered, "but I haven't even unrolled it yet."

"You might wanna put it in a scrapbook... or the garbage, depends on how ya' look at it." He gestured at me with his fork. "You're all over the front page."

"Me?" I stopped a forkful of food halfway to my mouth and put it down. "What am I doing on the front page?"

"Remember the asshole with the camera that jumped out in front of us last night?" Ben was up and refilling his coffee cup. "Anyone need a warmup?"

Felicity held out her cup, and he topped it off.

"Anyway," he continued, returning to his plate, "he caught ya' like a deer in headlights."

By now, I had gone into the living room and returned with the rolled up newspaper. Taking my seat back at the nook, I slid off the string and unfurled it. My wife leaned over next to me in order to view the curiosity. Offset to the upper left of the front page was a large color photo of Ben, and Detective Deckert, and myself as we were walking toward the crime scene last evening. As Ben had said, the look of surprise on my face gave me the appearance of a stunned animal. Forty-eight point type below the masthead spelled out the headline, "Police Witch Hunt." The lead of the story read, "Saturday evening, Saint Louis Major Case Squad detectives brought Rowan Gant, a self-proclaimed witch, to Thayer Park, the scene of yet another grisly cult-like murder." The rest of the story went on to recount details of both Ariel's and Karen Barnes' murders and speculate about my involvement in the investigation.

"How the hell did they come up with this?" I exclaimed. "How'd they know I wasn't just some cop?"

"Sidebar, page five," Ben answered, placing his dishes in the sink. "Hey, you got any of those cake things left over from last night?"

Felicity directed him to the honey cakes as I rapidly flipped through the pages of the newspaper and found the accompanying article to which he had referred. Another photo of me, this time black and white, was staring back. This particular photo had been taken when I had addressed a group at a local Wiccan gathering two years ago. The article was a slightly reworked copy of the original interview I had given that reporter.

"Somebody at the paper had a good memory," Felicity intoned, peering over my shoulder.

"Yeah," Ben added, "I've already caught ten kinds of hell from the chief because of it."

"I'm sorry, Ben," I told him, folding the paper and tossing it disgustedly on the nearby counter. "I guess you won't be needing me at the meeting today then."

"Shit yes, I need you at the meetin'," he answered and sucked down a honey cake in one bite. "I said I caught ten kinds of hell. I didn't say he won."

"I should have known," I said as I gathered the rest of the dishes and started washing them.

Felicity rolled her eyes at Ben as he devoured the

remaining cakes, then she grabbed a towel and began drying the freshly washed plates.

The dining room table had seemed to become our *command center* over the past few days, and once again, we gathered around it to look over the slides and discuss the upcoming meeting with the rest of the Major Case Squad.

"Did the coroner come up with anything last night?" I asked Ben as he looked at slides with a small illuminated viewer.

"Partial thumbprint," he answered, "but it was pretty smudged, so we only got three points. AFIS didn't show any hits."

"AFIS?" Felicity asked.

"Automated Fingerprint Identification System. Ya' see," he retrieved a ballpoint pen from his breast pocket and made marks on his thumb, then showed it to us, "a fingerprint is made up of what they call points. These points come together to make the unique pattern of the print. You or I can have some of the same points on our prints, but when you add them all up, voilà, unique as a snowflake. AFIS is an on-line database that allows us to break down the points that we obtain from a print and convert them into a number. You feed the number in, and the computer checks the database for matches or hits against anyone who has ever been arrested and printed by an AFIS participatin' department. The *quote quote* magic number of points to make a positive ID is eight. With three, we have the possibility of at least narrowin' down the field."

"So," she continued, "since you didn't get any hits, that means he probably has never been arrested, right?"

"At least not by a department hooked up with AFIS." Ben put away his pen and rubbed the ink from his thumb. "Other than the print, the M.E. came up with the fact that the size and shape of the wounds are consistent with those from Ariel Tanner. And also, there was some metallic residue left behind on her ribs."

I replayed last evening's vision in my head, watching carefully. I forced myself to remain detached and clinical. I didn't want to lose my compassion, but I also wanted to keep my breakfast where it belonged.

"From the dirk," I volunteered, "when he cut her open."

"The M.E. said somethin' like that," Ben confirmed.

"Was there anything else?"

"Minor blunt trauma to the head and upper back. Looks like she put up a fight." He read to us from his notes, "And a puncture wound on her arm, just like Ariel Tanner."

"So what I saw was right," I told him. "He's drugging his victims in order to immobilize them. Do you know what he's using yet?"

"M.E.'s still trying to identify it, but the sample from Ariel Tanner came up negative for insulin," he answered. "You bring up an interestin' point, though."

"The killer knows something about drugs and how to use them?" Felicity interjected.

"Bingo," Ben replied. "Which means the killer probably works in a hospital or something."

"Makes sense," I chimed.

"Guess what I found out about your lamp-swingin' buddy?" He looked at me seriously.

"R.J.?" Felicity asked.

"Yeah, R.J.," Ben answered. "Seems he's an orderly at County Hospital, in the emergency room."

"I know that might seem to fit," Felicity stated, "but an orderly? Would he really know that much about the drugs and such?"

"Can't say," he told her, "but if he pays attention and reads a lot, who knows. In any event, he could have access to controlled substances at his job."

"I don't know, Ben," I added. "I agree that something's going on with R.J. that he's not telling us, but do you really think..."

"Hey," he interrupted. "You yourself said that Ariel Tanner thought she knew her killer. Right?"

"She thought she recognized the voice."

"So add it up," he continued. "Friend of Ariel Tanner. He has a key to her apartment. Access to controlled substances and a medical background of sorts." He was counting the points off on his fingers. "Shows up out of the clear blue at the victim's home Saturday, and finally, he shows up here an hour late last night."

Remembering a detail from the day before, I quickly volunteered, "But he said he was out of town on a fishing trip with his father when Ariel was killed."

"Yeah, I know, but I didn't find him all that convincing." Ben brushed away my objection. "So I already had a talk with his dad. They didn't actually leave on that trip 'til later that night, and 'Pops' had no idea where the kid was before that. Based on the approximate time of death from the coroner, he had plenty of time to do it."

"Didn't you upset his parents?" Felicity asked with concern. "I mean, implying that their son is involved in a murder and all..."

"Hey, I just told 'em the truth," he answered. "It's just routine. If they get their shorts in a bunch then that's their problem."

"Why would he have lied?" I mused aloud.

"Maybe he did it."

"I don't believe that."

"Okay, so who knows?" Ben shrugged. "But I intend to find out."

"If knowing the victim is an important factor, then what about Karen Barnes?" I queried. "Is there anything to indicate that he knew her?"

"Not yet," he shot back. "Maybe he picked her because of the color of her hair... Maybe because the opportunity was there... Shit, maybe he didn't have to have a reason."

"Still," Felicity objected, "Rowan or I should have felt something from R.J. if he had killed Karen Barnes just before coming here. We're both Witches you know."

"What's that got to do with it?" Ben turned to her. "Besides, why are you so attached to this kid anyway? You act like you've known him forever or somethin'."

"I just have a major pet-peeve about innocent people being railroaded... And in a way, I DO know him pretty well. When I cast circle last night, he was in it."

"So?" Ben shrugged, obviously not understanding the significance of her comment.

"So a circle is a very intense ritual in The Craft," she explained. "You are joined with your peers, and you share energies. To be able to hide your true feelings during a circle would take more practice than I can even imagine. I don't even know if Rowan or I could do it, and we're both definitely more skilled than he is... No. R.J. was wide open last night. I refuse to believe he did it."

"Tell that to a judge and see how far it gets ya'," Ben replied. "Besides, nobody has convicted the kid yet. I'm just gonna ask him some more questions."

As much as I wanted this to be over, and even with my feelings that R.J. was hiding something, I found the thought hard to comprehend. We hadn't known him long, but I trusted my wife's instincts as well as my own. The morose silence that followed Ben's announcement was abruptly punctuated by Salinger as he leapt to the table and let out a sudden, mournful yowl.

Felicity and I followed Ben, driving in her Jeep. I had imitated his mode of dress by affixing a tie about my neck and wearing a lightweight, tweed sport coat over my jeans. My wife had opted for her no-nonsense look, donning a grey summer suit and black pumps. She also wore glasses instead of her normal contact lenses, which only served to enhance the businesslike appearance she had assumed. The back seat of our vehicle contained a carousel tray loaded with a small selection of slides from the roll I had shot last evening, as well as our slide projector.

"So what do you think about this whole thing with R.J.?" Felicity asked me as she shifted gears and merged with the traffic.

"I don't know," I answered. "Ben makes it sound pretty convincing, and I did have that feeling last night...You said you felt it too."

"Yes, I did," she stated. "But it wasn't that malevolent."

"True," I responded, "you would think that someone evil enough to do what this guy has done would be giving off some seriously bad energies."

"That was my thought."

"What about Salinger and Dickens?" I questioned. "Something about him really turned them off last night. I could maybe understand Salinger, but Dickens? He loves everybody."

"Maybe R.J. has his own cat or something," she speculated. "If they smelled another animal on him, then that might have set them off."

"That's a possibility," I agreed. "I know Ben says he just wants to talk to him," I continued, "and I hate to say this, but I think he's had it in for R.J. since the very beginning."

"It's his nature to be suspicious," she told me. "And I'm sure he's just being thorough. Just doing his job, you know. Don't worry, Ben won't railroad R.J., or let anyone else. You know him better than that."

"I know you're right about Ben," I told her. "But I don't know if he'll be able to control the rest of them. You can bet he's getting pressure from the top on this."

Felicity looked over at me sadly for a moment and then returned her gaze to the road. I knew she didn't want to consider the possibility that Ben could succumb to the public-opinion-guided wishes of his superiors when a young man's life was at stake.

"Shut your window then. The wind is messing up my hair" was all she said.

The command post for the Greater Saint Louis Major Case Squad had been set up in some conference rooms at the Weston city hall, which also housed the small township's police station. Since we lived nearby, the drive was short. According to my watch, it was approaching eleven when we arrived.

"I'm gonna warn ya'," Ben said as we walked with him across the parking lot, "these guys have already seen the paper."

"I suppose they're expecting some kind of weirdo then," I returned, referring to myself.

"I expect you're gonna get some blank stares and snide remarks," he told me. "But if ya' keep the *Twilight Zone* stuff just between us, I think it'll be okay. I'll be there ta' back you up."

"Well, I appreciate that."

Ben led us down a long, tiled hallway and signed us in with a dour-faced desk sergeant, who from all outward appearances, should have retired ten years earlier. He less than enthusiastically provided Felicity and I with visitors badges, and we proceeded on with no interruption. Ben opened the door to a conference room then motioned us in. We were greeted full force by what can only be described as an ordered chaos.

The room was a fissure of activity within an otherwise silent structure. Cafeteria tables were erected against walls, doubling as desks, copier stands, and phone banks. Chipped, blue metal folding chairs clinked as they were being set up. Some squeaked as they were propelled across polished linoleum tiles by the innumerable police officers and support staffers teaming within the confines of the room. The discord of already ringing phones mixed with the murmurs of voices to form a tumultuous racket.

"How many people have you got working on this case?" Felicity asked, taking in the riotous scene.

"Hell, I've lost track," Ben answered. "Other than the core officers assigned to the MCS, all the municipalities involved are giving up whoever they can spare, and then there's the support personnel... Hell, I don't even try to figure it out anymore. What's really scary is, until around midnight last night, this was an empty room."

We advanced farther into the activity, all but ignored by the bustling members of the Major Case Squad. Making our way through the crowded space, we found a place to store the slide tray and projector we had lugged in. Continuing to follow Ben like two strangers brought to an unfamiliar party by a friend, we proceeded to a table set up with coffee and much to my chagrin, doughnuts. We had just begun filling our typical white Styrofoam cups from a large urn, Felicity lamenting about the biodegradability of them, when we were approached by someone known to Ben and me both.

"Hi, Ben. When did you get here?" Detective Carl Deckert approached us and scooped a coffee cup into his hand.

"All of about five minutes ago," Ben replied, then turned toward us. "You remember Rowan Gant, and this is his wife Felicity."

"Nice to meet you," he said with a smile, lightly shaking Felicity's hand, then taking mine firmly. "Hell of a hatchet job they did on you in the paper this morning."

"Well..." I half stuttered, trying to choose my words carefully, "I can't exactly sue them for libel."

"Hell," Deckert returned, "I pretty much figured you were some kinda psychic or something last night anyway. You were comin' up with too many things that nobody else could see."

"Excuse me if I seem surprised," I asked, "but what was said in the paper doesn't bother you?"

"The only thing that bothers me is that the media decided to sensationalize it," he told me as we all took turns doctoring the bitter brew with packets of sugar and powdered creamer. "Truth be told, my mother used to have what she called 'visions'. Everyone in the neighborhood used to call her a Witch, but they listened because her 'visions' always came true. I don't recall her ever being involved in all the stuff you talked about in that interview, but I've seen stranger things. If it helps catch this asshole, I don't really care."

"It's nice to know we have another friend with a badge," I told him. "They're pretty rare."

"Yeah, well, I wouldn't expect many more outta this

group. Ben and I are probably it."

As I looked about the room, I started noticing the cold stares and whispers among the members of the Major Case Squad. I was sorely afraid that what Carl Deckert had just said would soon prove to be true.

At 11:30 we accompanied Ben, as well as the rest of the officers, to an adjoining conference room. Here, the tables were lined in neat rows, and at the head of the room stood a small podium. Felicity deftly set up the slide projector and mounted the tray of transparencies, then seated herself to one side with Ben and I. There remained a dull murmur as detectives took their places at the tables and talked among themselves. Once everyone who belonged in the meeting was seated, Ben stationed himself at the podium and waited. It took only a moment for a quiet hush to fall over the group, broken only by the sharp sounds of ballpoint pens clicking and notebooks being opened to fresh pages.

"First off," Ben began, his voice tired but clear, "for those of you who don't know me, I'm Detective Ben Storm with the city homicide unit. I am the investigating officer on the Tanner case.

"Secondly, let me thank all of you for being here on such short notice. I realize a lot of you came in last night and haven't slept yet. Trust me, I know how ya' feel."

A light, weary chuckle randomly skipped through the room.

"Everyone here should have copies of the case files on Ariel Tanner and Karen Barnes," Ben continued. "If ya' don't, then let me know after the meeting and I'll get them to ya'. I wanted to go over some of my notes with ya' and field any questions you might have. I'd also like to compare notes on the Barnes homicide from last night.

"Look." He paused and let out a deep sigh. "We all know there's a psycho asshole out there, and he's killed two women so far. It's our job to find him and put a stop to it."

I watched on as Ben looked down at the slanted top of the podium and opened a file folder.

"Here's the basic run down," he stated, looking back up at the group. "Ariel Tanner, Caucasian female, twenty-six years of age. Her body was found in 'er apartment last Wednesday evening by her neighbor who noticed her door was propped open. There was no sign of forced entry. Her hands were bound behind her back with duct tape, her throat was cut, and her upper torso had been skinned. This latter procedure was done while she was still alive people... Just so you understand.

"Upon arriving at the scene, we found the words 'All Is Forgiven,' inscribed on the wall with the victim's blood. Also drawn on the wall was a Pagan symbol referred to as a 'Pentacle'. Finally, a wine goblet was found, containing residue of Miz Tanner's blood. All of this leads us to believe that the murderer performed some type of ritual sacrifice.

"There were no witnesses, and the neighbor wasn't home. Coroner's report turned up a puncture wound that is consistent with an injection, so it appears that our bad guy is drugging his victims. Also, there was no evidence of rape. Any questions?" Ben shuffled the papers back into order as he looked out over the seated detectives.

"Did she have a boyfriend?" a voice called out from the back of the room.

"Not as far as we have been able to determine, no."

"Had there been any cult activity in the neighborhood?" someone else asked.

"We checked that out," Ben answered. "All we found were a few high school kids tryin' to put a 'hex' on a teacher. They were harmless, and we scared the hell out of them."

Once again, a mild chuckle rolled through the otherwise

somber room.

"The report indicates," a stone-faced detective near the front of the room spoke up, "that the first victim was involved in the occult. In particular, she was the *priestess* of a Witches coven. What did that turn up?"

"We have, in fact, spoken to her coven. It seems they kicked a member out a few weeks ago, so we're lookin' at the revenge angle, but that doesn't seem likely now that we have a second murder. The ex-member's name is Devon Johnston... So far, we've been unable to track 'im down. I've got the other member's numbers, and we can check them out..."

I was holding my breath, waiting for Ben to say something about R.J. He looked over at me for a moment, then back to the sea of faces.

"...Any more questions?" He scanned the room with a long, silent pause. "Good, then I'll turn you over to Detective Carl Deckert."

Ben stepped away from the podium and took a seat with us once again. Detective Deckert winked at us as he trundled by and filled the void behind the rostrum. He hitched up his pants and cleared his throat, then addressed the gathering.

Deckert's diatribe went much as Ben's had, including a general summation of the facts surrounding Karen Barnes' case, followed by a short question and answer session. When he was finished, he and Ben traded places at the front of the room once more.

"Now that we have that out of the way," Ben told everyone, "I'd like to bring up a consultant that has been working on the Tanner case with me." He turned and gestured toward me. "Rowan, would you like ta' join me up here."

Judging from the stares that suddenly came my way, I

knew immediately that I wouldn't.

I wouldn't *like* it at all.

CHAPTER 9

Ben remained behind and slightly to the right of me as I positioned myself at the stand. I looked out over the numerous detectives seated at the tables, and as I had been warned, they all stared back at me blankly. I noticed a copy of the day's newspaper resting prominently atop the notebook of one of the officers in the front row. The newsprint was neatly folded to display the front page, picture and headline. It may have been coincidence, but it definitely appeared deliberate. My heightened senses easily detected suspicion and disapproval seeping from the group, and from the corner of my eye, I saw Felicity shift nervously in her seat. She could feel it too.

"As Detective Storm told you," I began nervously, "my name is Rowan Gant. I have been consulting with him on the investigation of Ariel Tanner's murder, and more recently..."

"Where's your broom?" a disembodied voice interrupted from the back row.

A grating laugh rippled through the room. Ben started forward, ready to admonish the speaker and anyone else in the room, or so it appeared. I thrust my arm out and stopped him, then looked over and shook my head. He stepped back without a word, though I could feel him seething beneath his silent facade. I took in a deep breath and turned back to the seated officers. Apparently, there was to be no dancing around this problem, and hiding behind Ben definitely wouldn't help. This was something I would have to handle myself if I wanted to gain any respect from them.

"Actually, my broom is at home," I told them sarcastically, indignance replacing the trepidation. "We

came here on my wife's *Hoover Deluxe*... Now, since you
want to act like a room full of school children," I look
around, making eye contact with as many of them as
could, "are there any more smart-ass comments before
continue?"

I remained silent, staring out at them, continuing to m
their eyes and hold them. Some of them looked quick
away. Some fought to hold fast, then folded as the oth
before them.

"Why the hell should we listen to you?" the voice ca
from the back row again.

This time I pinpointed him. He was a young cop
younger than the rest anyway—with dark, styled hair a
the rugged features that often graced print advertiseme
for men's cologne. He fixed his blue eyes on mine and he
my gaze. He was not going to be easily persuaded.

"Could you come up here, please?" I asked hi
motioning him toward the front.

"What the hell are you doin'?" Ben hissed at me.

"Let me handle it," I whispered back over my shoulder

By the time Ben and I had completed our exchange, t
young detective had come to the front and was looking ba
out at his colleagues with a wide grin. He was obviou
quite pleased with himself, and the other detectives we
enjoying the spectacle as well.

"What's your name?" I asked him.

"Bill," he answered, still pleased.

I motioned to the corner of the room. "Detecti
Deckert, could you get the lights please?"

He nodded and switched off the overhead lights. Felic
picked up on the cue and responded by switching on t
slide projector.

"Let's step over here out of the way, Bill," I told t
young detective as I slid the rostrum to one side.

Once we had moved, Felicity tapped a switch on the slide projector's remote control, and the tray advanced, audibly dropping a transparency into the beam of light. The auto-focus kicked in, and a larger than life image of the Pentacle from Karen Barnes' murder scene glowed back at us.

"Can you tell me what we're looking at, Bill?" I asked him.

"It's a star," he told me. "What Detective Storm said, ya know, a Pentacle."

"Very good," I said. "And what does it mean?"

"Whaddaya talkin' about?" he asked, his voice somewhat less confident than before.

"What is the inherent meaning of the symbol, Detective?" I asked again.

"Oh, yeah, that." He shuffled slightly. "Well it means worship the devil and Satan and stuff like that."

"Sorry," I stated apologetically. "Wrong answer."

I motioned to Felicity in the dim light provided by the image reflecting from the screen, and the slide changed. Now the words that had been inscribed on the walls of both murder scenes brightly stared back at us.

"And these words, Detective," I continued, "'All Is Forgiven.' Can you tell me why the killer inscribed them at both scenes?"

"That's easy," he returned. "He's forgiving the victims."

"Hmmm. A little closer but sorry, wrong again. Next slide please."

Suddenly the wall was lit up with the sickening image of Karen Barnes' flayed torso, her glazed eyes gaping back at us.

"Can you tell me why the killer excised the victim's skin, Detective...?" I received no answer. "Detective?"

I turned and saw the young man facing away from the image, breathing heavily and obviously fighting back nausea. I decided that I had made my point and that he was no longer nearly as pleased with himself. I motioned across the room; the lights came back on and the projector shut down.

"Go back to your seat," I told him, then turned and took my place back at the podium.

Ben was grinning at me when I looked up at him, and Detective Deckert flashed me a smile with a surreptitious thumbs up. The rest of the detectives in the room remained quiet as my heckler returned to his seat. A good number of them looked just as green as he did.

"That," I began, "is why you should listen to me. If you want to catch this guy, you need to know *why* he is doing what he is doing. And, that is what I'm here for.

"I'm going to be straight up with you. I really don't give a damn if you like me or not. I don't expect you to believe in my religion or follow its covenants. What I do expect is for you to give me the respect that I deserve and recognize the fact that I just might be able to answer some questions that you can't. I'm here to help you, not entertain you.

"Look, I'll be the first one to admit that I'm not an expert criminal psychologist or anything like that. What I have to say is simply my interpretation of the facts available based on my knowledge of the Wiccan religion. As I said, knowing the whys and wherefores behind what the killer is doing just might prove useful in catching him." I paused to let my words settle. "Now, I'm sorry if I made you look like an ass, Bill, but you seemed rather intent on acting like one even without my help... So, can we get down to business and figure out a way to catch this son-of-a-bitch before he kills again?"

A grumble of assent rolled through the room. I could tell that the majority of them still weren't happy about having me involved in the investigation, but at the same time, I think they realized I might be able to shed some light on certain aspects of the cases.

"Fine," I continued. "I'll begin with telling you something that I am sure you already know. You are dealing with a very unstable individual. The second thing I will tell you is what you aren't dealing with here... What you aren't dealing with is a Witch."

I paused and waited for the chairs to quit shifting and the whispers to subside.

"If you will allow me to explain," I told them. "I am not saying that the person committing these murders is not attempting to practice some type of ritual magick, in fact, I definitely believe that that is exactly what he is doing. I also believe that he thinks the rituals used by a practitioner of The Craft play some part in it. This is very simply not true. An actual practicing Wiccan, or Witch, holds to a very specific covenant within the religion. That covenant is to *Harm None*. Witches do not, I repeat, DO NOT sacrifice people or animals in their rituals. The reason I'm telling you this is that it's going to be very easy for you to point your finger at anyone who might happen to be a Wiccan practitioner, simply because this killer is mimicking one of our rituals. I really would like to avoid that. Not only would it cause undue grief for innocent individuals, it would be extremely counterproductive. For example, just because lemons are yellow and tennis balls are yellow, it doesn't mean you can make lemonade out of tennis balls...What I'm really trying to get at is that just because one mentally unstable individual is using the symbols of the Wiccan religion and committing violent murders, it doesn't mean that all Wiccans are psycho serial killers. Don't put blinders on and follow that kind of distorted logic because it's not going to get us anywhere."

They were looking back at me a bit more attentively than

earlier. I didn't know if I had convinced them, but I hadn't lost them, and at this stage of the game, I had the feeling that this was all I could hope for.

I motioned to Detective Deckert and Felicity once more, and again the room was pitched into darkness. Instantly, the slide projector came to life, clicking rapidly as my wife backed the tray to the beginning.

"This, as we have already established, is a Pentacle. In this position, with a single point at the top, it represents man and life. It is a very common symbol in the Wiccan religion. If this were to be turned one hundred-eighty degrees so that there were two points on top, it would then be referred to as a Pentagram. Some cults have taken it upon themselves to assign a meaning of evil and darkness to the Pentagram, claiming it represents Satan. Notice the horns and the pointed goatee." I indicated the various points on the screen, "Factually, this is inaccurate; however, it has become widely accepted as true over the centuries. That's probably where you got your misinformation, Bill."

I stepped away from the podium and into the path of the slide projector. The image took up a large portion on the wall, and I was able to physically point out aspects without entirely blocking the beam of filtered light.

"In this instance, an upright Pentacle was inscribed as part of a ritual known as an Expiation spell. This spell, or ritual, is particularly Wiccan and is the one that the killer has mimicked with some notable variations. Next slide please..." The projector clicked and chunked as the first image was ejected and the second one dropped in its place. "These words, 'All Is Forgiven,' are also a part of this ritual. The Pentacle and the words were all inscribed at both crime scenes. As Detective Storm already told you, the victim's blood was used to draw the symbol and letters. This would be one of the deviations I mentioned a moment ago. The other would be that instead of using wine or water for the spell, the killer once again used the victim's blood...The fact that this was done, shows that this second ritual was performed after the murder. This correlates with the fact that an Expiation spell is used as something of a 'self-atonement' ritual—similar to penance given in a confessional. This leads me to believe that the killer is feeling remorse for what he's done and is seeking to relieve the guilt.

"Next slide." Once again the projector rotated the tray and displayed the grisly image of Karen Barnes' mutilated corpse. "The method of killing has involved ritual flaying in both cases, followed by cutting the throat in the case of Ariel Tanner and removal of the heart in the case of Karen Barnes."

"What's the point?" a voice asked. "Is he some kind of sadist or something?"

"While that wouldn't surprise me," I answered, "the point behind skinning the victim is to bring them to a heightened sense of pain and fear before their death. From what I have been able to research, our killer appears to be attempting to invoke, or call forth, some spirit or daemon. This, he apparently believes, requires a human sacrifice and requires that the sacrifice be aware of the process. Whatever it is that he desires to call forth apparently feeds on pain and fear."

"I thought you said you Witches didn't do shit like that" another voice came out of the dark.

"We don't," I replied. "Like I said, he isn't a Witch."

"Then where's he coming up with this stuff?" the same voice asked.

"Fiction," I answered. "Horror movies. Novels. Perhaps even any number of texts available on the subject of Black Magick, both accurate and inaccurate. It wouldn't surprise me to find a little of the Spanish Inquisition mixed in as well."

"So," a different voice piped in, "what you're sayin' i
that all this is just a ration of shit, and he's just a sick bastar
goin' around killing people."

"Yes and no," I returned. "I definitely agree with th
'sick bastard' part of your comment, but his rituals aren'
just some 'ration of shit' as you put it. First off, a ritual i
nothing more and nothing less than you make it. It is a wa
of focusing one's energies, and it can be something that yo
make up yourself. It doesn't have to be some pre-prescribe
set of instructions that were written by someone else."

"Hold the phone," another voice chimed in the dark
"You aren't actually suggesting that this wacko is going t
bring some beast or demon here from hell or something ar
you?"

"What I'm suggesting," I told them, "is that a ritual i
used to focus one's energies to make something happen–
like praying or the chants that monks sing. If you're askin
if I personally believe that he's going to invoke something
just let me say that I think there are forces out there that ar
better left alone, and we'll leave it at that."

I waited wordlessly while my last statement soaked ir
There were a few whispers among the group but to m
surprise, no recurrence of the earlier heckling, so
continued.

"Now, I realize I haven't really told you much about th
killer, and unfortunately, I'm not able to do much more tha
speculate based on the existing evidence.

"First, as I said, he's not a Witch, but he appears to b
intimately familiar with The Craft. He might have been
member of a coven at one time or another, but if he actuall
practiced, I would think it more likely that he was solitary
It's possible that his knowledge of Wicca was or is derive
mainly from literature available at almost any bookstore.

"Second. Because of the lack of various components, I have reason to believe that Ariel Tanner's murder was done out of his need to practice his ritual. Karen Barnes' may well have been an actual performance of the sacrifice. I can't be absolutely positive about that because as I told you, he's making up his own ritual here. The basic components of it tell me generally what he's trying to do, but so far, he's left nothing behind that points me to anything specific. Based on what was done to Karen Barnes, my guess would be that it was the real thing for him, but I don't believe he's finished. Until he at least perceives that he has conjured whatever or whomever he seeks, then he will continue to execute the ritual.

"Point three. As depicted in this image, the skin was removed from the victim with notable precision considering we believe that the instrument used to accomplish the task is what's know as a dirk. For those of you unfamiliar with the name, it is a double-edge, European dagger that is about six inches long. Ariel Tanner owned one for use in Wiccan rituals. It was missing from her apartment. Someone able to do this probably has some experience at it and has more than likely skinned an animal or two."

I could hear scribbling in the dark. I may not have reached all of them, but at least some of them were taking notes, and that bolstered my confidence almost immediately.

"Finally. This individual is meticulous about his rituals. The flaying, the inscription, the use of a purification incense. He took his time and made sure he followed a regimen he had set for himself. This is going to indicate someone deeply involved in ritual and ceremony.

"In both instances, he made it a point to prop open the door to the house or building where he committed the murder. This may indicate that he wants the bodies found as quickly as possible. Couple that with the Expiation spell, and I would theorize that he wants to be caught and punished. He is seeking not only atonement from himself but from the world as well."

"If the asshole wants to get caught, why doesn't he just turn himself in?" came another query.

"My guess would be that he would consider that too easy," I replied. "I don't know. Like I said before, I'm not a psychologist, I'm just here to interpret the symbols and ritual for you. The rest is pure speculation. Lights please..."

The lights came up in the room, and I heard Felicity switch off the bulb on the projector, though she left the fan running in order to cool it down. It droned on in the otherwise somber room.

"That's really all that I have for now. I know it's not much," I told them, making my way back to the rostrum. "I will be in contact with Detective Storm and will let him know if I'm able to glean anything else from all of this. Are there any more questions?"

"Yeah," one of the detectives in the center of the room spoke up. "I'm curious about somethin'. Ain't you s'posed to be called a warlock?"

"Big fan of *Bewitched* were you?" I chuckled, feeling the mood in the room lighten at his query. "No, I am a Witch. The definition of warlock is 'liar or breaker of promises'. The word has also been used to describe a practitioner of the *Black Arts*, either of which I am most definitely not. If you want to get right down to it, I'm really just a person like any of you, only I happen to be of a different religion."

"It's heresy. I don't care what you say." The statement was punctuated by a notebook slamming shut and a chair screeching on linoleum.

The voice had issued from a man everyone recognized. Detective Arthur McCann stood up and strode toward the door. He had been a valued member of the county police department for as long as anyone cared to remember. He was the prototypical good guy and esteemed member of his church. I had known him well a few years back when I helped out waiting tables in the small family diner my mother had owned and where he had been a regular customer. These days, he appeared in the paper often, a one-man task force bent on the eradication of the Wiccan religion and occult practices in Saint Louis. It was his belief that anything which didn't include his God was nothing more than a cult and therefore evil. He was not about to listen to anything different.

"If you insist on having a Witch involved in this investigation..." He turned as he reached the door, fixing his gaze on Ben, who was standing next to me. "Then I will have no part of it."

"Arthur," I stated evenly, "how many times have I told you, good is good and bad is bad. I've done nothing bad."

"You speak heresy," he spat back angrily. "You go against the word of God."

"I'm sorry you feel that way," I returned. "And it bothers me that it hasn't been that long ago that you thought I was a pretty good guy...Until you found out my religion that is."

He didn't answer, his face just grew redder, and he stormed out of the room, angrily slamming the door behind him.

While I could still detect a definite lack of enthusiasm for my presence in the investigation by the rest of the members of the Major Case Squad, there had been no more outbursts for the rest of the briefing. We left the frenetic activity behind as Ben escorted us out of the building, dropping off

our visitor's badges with the desk sergeant before exitin
into the bright, sunlit day. The small, nomadic media ci
from the night before had positioned itself in front of Ci
Hall, and local television personalities were vying f
positions from which to do their live reports.

"Looks like a goddammed airhead convention out there
Ben spat as we walked.

The sun was beating down hard on the pavement, an
combined with the moisture from the previous night's rai
we had the makings of a legendary Saint Louis summer da
The humidity was thick in the atmosphere, and the stillne
of the air made the ninety-four degrees on the thermomet
seem less than accurate. Felicity peeled off her light jack
and arranged it over the back of her seat when we arrived
the Jeep.

"I have to tell you," I said to him as I stowed the slie
projector and tray, "it went much better than I expected."

"Yeah, but what was that crap with McCann? I didn
know you two knew each other."

"Awhile ago," I answered. "Back when Mom had th
diner. I helped out waiting tables and got to know him then

"Oh yeah," he said. He had been to the diner many tim
himself. "So I guess he's outta here."

"Looked that way," I said, haphazardly tossing my ow
jacket into the Jeep and getting a stern look from Felicit
"So, why didn't you say anything about R.J.?" Knowing m
wife's expressions, I retrieved the jacket and hung
properly over the back of the passenger seat.

"Pretty much 'cause I'm workin' on a hunch," I
explained. "You see, the way I look at it, everybody star
with ten bricks in their pile. As the investigation progresse
some of the bricks get moved into the suspicious and/
guilty pile, and the rest stay right where they were and don
bother anybody. Right now, I'd say R.J.'s only managed

move a couple'a his bricks over to the suspicious pile."

"When were you planning to talk to him?" I queried.

"I kinda figured on paying him a visit a little later this afternoon."

"What's the plan with Devon?"

"We're sittin' on his house, and I got a basic description from his cousin out on the streets," Ben answered.

"Hey," Felicity interrupted, "in case you two haven't noticed, it's hot and muggy out here, not to mention that I'm the only one standing here in heels."

"Point taken," I told her and then looked back at Ben. "Do you have a little free time to get us in to the Karen Barnes murder scene?"

"Yeah, why?" he asked.

"I'd like to play a hunch of my own," I answered. "I want to make sure I didn't miss something last night."

CHAPTER 10

Leaving the parking lot proved to be much more of a nuisance than I originally expected. We were exiting ahead of Ben, and the moment our Jeep rounded the corner of the building, the drive was blocked by a swarm of reporters and cameramen. Felicity pressed lightly on the accelerator, inching us through the mob as they thrust microphones at our windows and barked questions made unintelligible by the din of them all speaking at once. Viewing the spectacle, it was impossible to miss Brandee Street, short skirt, trendy hair and manicured nails, as she ruthlessly insinuated herself between the others.

"Mister Gant," she shouted over the uproar. "What exactly is your role in this investigation?"

Even with the windows up and the air conditioner cranked as high as it would go, I could still hear her singsong voice. I ignored her and reached over to turn up the radio.

"Mister Gant." She was shuffling along at my window as we inched forward. "Is it true the police have called you in to communicate with the spirits of the victims?"

Suddenly, the crowd parted, and the reason became instantly clear as we saw the flashing red lights and uniformed officers executing much-needed crowd control. With a quick glance in either direction, Felicity shifted gears and gunned the engine, letting out a short squeal from the tires as she propelled us away from the bedlam. I turned and looked out the back window and saw Ben's van behind us, emergency bubble-light flashing on the corner of the roof. Once we merged with traffic, it switched off, and I saw him reach out and pull it inside.

"Awfully determined young lady, wasn't she?" Felicity asked as we came to a stop at a traffic light.

"You could call it that," I answered. "Ben yanked her chain last night, and she threw her microphone at him."

"You're kidding," she stated incredulously.

"Nope. Not kidding. She launched it at him, but she missed."

"What did he do to her to get that kind of response?"

The light changed, and Felicity nudged the Jeep forward into the intersection then hooked into a left turn.

"Apparently there's some kind of long running adversarial relationship between the two of them," I answered. "She follows him around chasing stories, and he won't give her the time of day. Last night he took the microphone out of her hand and unplugged it, then handed it back to her."

"Serves him right then."

"What do you mean?" I questioned.

"Never make a woman angry then be stupid enough to hand her something to throw at you."

The small cinder block building in the back of the park was cordoned off and locked up just as I had expected. We parked our vehicles and followed the same path we had last evening, this time without the rain and organized pandemonium of the crime scene investigation. Ben produced a key and opened up the restroom.

The pungent aroma of the charred sage and rose oil still hung faintly in the air, mixing with the sharp and musty odors of old disinfectant, damp concrete, and the coppery smell of blood. The heavy door swung slowly shut behind us, creaking on hinges badly in need of oil.

"Once the crime scene unit clears this place," Ben told us, "someone is gonna have a hell of a mess to clean up."

Darkening stains smeared the floor where Karen Barnes' body had laid. Spatters of blood spread forth, rusting from bright crimson to dull reddish brown. Smooth surfaces, such as the basin and walls nearby, were greyed by the powders that had been used in the futile attempt to find fresh fingerprints, and all but the smallest shards of the shattered mirror had been removed from the scene.

"It's cold in here," Felicity stated, hugging herself and shivering slightly.

"Whaddaya mean cold?" Ben asked in disbelief. "It's close to a hundred degrees out here."

"Not that kind of cold," she told him. "The cold of death. It's strong enough for me to feel it."

"So you're gonna go all spooky on me too," he said, then turned his attention to me. "What are you lookin' for in here anyway?"

I walked around the interior of the restroom slowly and silently. I had no earthly, or even unearthly, idea what I was looking for. I only knew that something had suddenly begun to gnaw at the back of my brain. A relentless nagging that told me I had missed something that had been staring me straight in the face the night before.

"I don't know," I answered. "But if it's here, I'm going to find it."

I continued to shuffle around the small room, intently inspecting walls and fixtures that had already been perused by eyes more prying than mine. I could feel the same coldness Felicity had mentioned and gave a barely noticeable shiver as it danced subtly up my spine.

"Did I say anything last night when I spaced out?" I asked aloud.

"No." Ben recalled, "You just kinda went blank and stared off. You weren't zoned for long before I decided to snap you out of it... With what Felicity said and all... Ya know..."

"It's all right," I told him. "I understand."

"Why do ya' think ya' might have said somethin'?" he queried.

"Just a thought," I replied, still making my way around the stalls. "I've just got this nagging feeling that I missed something." I glanced over at him. "And for some reason, I think that *something* might be important."

"Well, guys," Felicity spoke up. "My feet are killing me. I'm going to run out to the Jeep and see if my tennis shoes are in my gym bag."

My wife started for the door with a deliberate turn. The gritty shuffle of her shoe soles against the concrete was rapidly followed by a sharp, tinkling sound as she inadvertently kicked a small piece of the broken mirror, sending it skittering across the floor.

"HOLD IT!" I exclaimed. "Don't move."

She froze. Ben froze. I froze.

"What is it?" Felicity finally whispered.

The sound triggered a memory, the memory induced a thought, and the thought congealed in my brain as I closed my eyes and listened to an imaginary pane of glass shatter inside my head. Slowly, I opened my eyes and looked to my wife, then to Ben.

"The mirror," I told them.

"Yeah. You told us why ya' thought he broke it last night," Ben stated. "Somethin' about not wantin' ta' trap whatever he was callin' up, or somethin' like that."

"I know," I returned. "But that's not what I'm talking about."

"Then what?" Felicity asked as she relaxed her stance.

"If Karen Barnes was standing in front of the mirr
when she was attacked," I began.

"Then she might have seen the killer's reflection," s
finished for me, light dawning in her eyes.

"Excuse me," Ben interjected, "but Karen Barnes is r
gonna be givin' any eyewitness descriptions. In case you'
forgotten, she's dead."

"This is true," I told him. "However, I might be able
do the same thing with her that I did with Ariel."

"Channel her?!" Felicity exclaimed. "Don't you thi
that's a little too dangerous?"

"Not if you help me," I replied.

"Whoa," Ben interjected. "This ain't one of those thin
where you could die or somethin' is it?"

"Yes it is." Felicity turned to him quickly. "If it is
done correctly."

"Well I dunno then..."

"Hey," I interrupted them both. "The operative phr
there is 'done correctly'. If you help me," I indicated to
wife, "and we take some precautions, I shouldn't ha
anything to worry about."

"What precautions?" Ben queried.

"An anchor on this plane, for one," I answered. "Gett
me the hell out of there before the moment of death
another."

They both looked at me as if I had totally lost my min
knew it was because they were worried about the possi
consequences, and to be honest, I was too—but I was a
bound and determined to proceed with the idea.

"We have to stop this S.O.B.," I told them. "If doing
could keep him from killing someone else, then I wo
never forgive myself if I didn't go ahead with it. I do
think the two of you could either."

They fell silent, first looking at me, then each other, t

back to me, and finally, to the floor.

"I'm going to go change shoes," Felicity eventually said. "If we're going to do this, I plan on being as comfortable as possible." With that, she pulled the door open and headed for the Jeep.

She had only been gone a few moments when Ben broke his thoughtful silence. He broadcast his current state of mind by smoothing back his hair and letting out a short sigh.

"Ya'know," he spoke, holding his hand at the back of his neck. "Even if you do 'see' somethin', it's inadmissible as evidence. There's no way I can trot you in to the D.A. and say 'here's an eyewitness'... You realize that don't ya'?"

"I know," I answered. "But if I see something, and it gives us a clue or some place to start looking, it's worth the risk."

"I can't ask ya' ta' do this."

"You're not," I told him. "I'm volunteering."

He shuffled about in place. "So, how long is this gonna take?"

"If it all goes as planned, it shouldn't take more than ten minutes or so."

"What can I do ta' help?"

"Make sure no one disturbs us." I paused for a moment, and then added, "And I wouldn't be opposed to you keeping your fingers crossed."

The door once again creaked open, and Felicity reentered minus the pumps and sporting her aerobics sneakers.

"I don't want to hear it," she told us as she came through the door. "I know the shoes don't match the outfit, but they're comfortable. So, how do you want to do this?"

"Ben," I said as I turned back to him, "if you'll just watch the door and take notes if necessary..."

"You got it," he replied, backing up to the door and

taking out his notebook.

I took a position near the washbasin and motioned for Felicity to join me. I selected this point in the room for its obvious proximity to the once-intact mirror. The simple fact was that I wasn't necessarily ecstatic about what I was going to do either. I wanted to be in and out as quickly as possible, so I planned to use every advantage available. If my idea worked, physically positioning myself here would allow me to enter the vision close to the point I wanted to see and then get out quickly, before Karen Barnes took me into death with her.

"Simple cone," I told my wife. "Raise it and project a rope. One end of it should be around my waist, and you should have the other end. I'll try to stay with you, but if necessary, I'm going to let myself fully immerse in the regression, so it's up to you to pull me out if you sense that I'm in trouble...You gonna be able to handle this?"

"Let's do it," she replied, nodding in assent.

We joined hands, left palm up, right palm down. Felicity and I relaxed in unison, our breathing falling easily into sync. We had cast many a circle together, just she and I, and this process had become nothing if not automatic. We both centered ourselves and grounded with the earth, feeling ethereal forces swirl about us in an ever growing, ever tightening, choreographed helix. Energy began flowing from her left arm and into my right. It rushed throughout my body, coursing through muscles, arteries, veins, and nerves, and worked its way around until it completed the circuit, flowing out of my left arm and into Felicity's right. The connection continued, rapidly increasing until the current appeared to us as a solid blur.

I began imagining a rope fixed securely about my waist, the free end anchored here in the physical plane, held fast by my wife. I knew she would be imagining something very similar within her own mind as well. The image solidified, and it was time for me to go.

"Are you ready?" I whispered.

"I'm ready," Felicity answered, her own voice held low.

"Do me a favor and don't let go," I told her, then allowed my inner self to fall backwards into the void.

Colors came and went in a tumultuous blizzard, much as they had when I had done this at Ariel's apartment. Sound slowed and faded, melting into the darkness, then returned as a loud rushing in my ears. Light poured in and the scene before me began to coalesce. It formed in harsh blacks and whites, like a picture on a television screen with the contrast turned to maximum. The brightness slowly dimmed, and color flooded into the apparition until it achieved an appearance of something just the other side of normal.

"Buster, settle down," her voice, my voice, our voice was saying.

A Jack Russell terrier is dancing around our ankles. We're trying to sidestep him as he rings the leash around our legs.

"Buster, sit!" our voice orders the small dog.

He sits and holds one paw up. He whines lightly.

We're turning on the water now. The handle on the faucet squeaks. How many times have we heard that before? It's such a familiar sound. We've been here before. We are washing our hands now; Buster is still whining.

A sound. The door is creaking; someone else is coming in to use the restroom. We hope she doesn't have a dog with her; Buster will freak out. We're turning off the water. Buster is growling. She must have a dog with her.

"Buster, stay!" our voice orders him.

We'll be out of here in just a second. DEAR GOD, what's happening? Let me go! What are you doing? We are

struggling. Someone has grabbed us from behind. Buster
barking. Stop that! There is something over our face now
smells strange. Our ears are ringing. We're weak. The roo
is getting dark.

Look in the mirror, Karen, I told her... or myself...
whatever we had become.

He let go. We have to turn around. We have to run. We
falling. No, push up on the basin. The room is spinni
Ouch, something stuck us on the arm. We're pushing up
the basin. Our knees are weak. We have to stand up. We
looking at the mirror. What is that over our shoulder?
moving. Who is that?

I strained to see through Karen Barnes' eyes
reflection in the mirror. I concentrated and let myself en
into the vision with all my being.

Darkness.
Silence.
My head is killing me, what happened? I can't mo
This bed is hard. Light. I can see. Wait a minute. I've b
here before. This isn't home, it's...I can't remember. I've b
here before though. Where's Buster? Why can't I move?
arms are numb. I wish I could move them. What's going
Who am I?

Did I just see someone move? Who are you? Where
you? Where am I?

What is that smell? It's strange. I've never sme
anything quite like it before. It's like...It's like burning ro
My head is really killing me. Where's Buster?

I'm in the park. I'm in the restroom in the park! N
remember. Someone grabbed me. My God, am I paralyz

Somebody help me.

Who am I? Karen? Yes, that's it. I'm Karen.

That movement again. I can hear something. Something shuffling. What is it? Wait a minute. There's something over my mouth. Why is there something covering my mouth. A rapist. I'm being attacked by a rapist! Please, somebody come in and help me. Somebody stop him.

Where is my husband? He isn't home yet. Somebody help me. Where is Buster? My head is killing me. Please somebody help me. Don't let him rape me.

What is that? Something is on top of me. No, SOMEONE is on top of me. What are you doing? Don't rape me, please don't rape me. Why are you wearing that robe? What is that in your hand? Your eyes, I can see your eyes. I've never seen eyes that grey. They're so cold.

NOooo!

He's cutting me. My skin is on fire.

NOooo!

Pain. Pain beyond all.

Fear.

Darkness.

What is that tugging at me? Who am I? Karen? No, that's not right, Karen's dead...If Karen is dead then who am I? There's that tugging again. It's coming from my waist. A rope. I'm tied to a rope. Who is that? She's pretty. What beautiful red hair she has. What is that she's saying? I can't hear you. Speak louder. Do you know who I am? Are you the one that is pulling on the rope?

Falling.

Darkness.

Light.

He's still on top of me. How long was I passed out? It

*couldn't have been long if he's still here. Dear God I hurt.
My chest is burning. What is that pressure? Why is this
happening? Our Father, who art in heaven, hallowed be Thy
name, Thy kingdom come...NOooo!*
   Pain.

Ouch! What are you doing? It hurts when you pull on
that rope so hard. I've seen you before. You have such pretty
hair. What? You want me to come to you? Why? Do you
know who I am? I thought I was Karen but Karen is dead.
Why are you so upset? I'm very tired. Maybe I should just
go to sleep.
   Darkness.
   Light.

Fear.
Pain.
Terror.
Darkness. Cold, endless darkness.

I was intrigued by the sight before me. I wasn't entirely
sure how I was managing to float above it in mid air, but I
was comfortable, and the mechanics of it were the farthest
thing from my mind. Ben and Felicity were kneeling on the
floor, and my friend was checking the pulse on a body
sprawled between them. They looked very grim and seemed
upset.
   "Rowan, follow my voice."
   I heard my wife call to me, but I never saw her lips
move. I wondered why she couldn't see me; I was floating
right above her.
   "He hasn't got a pulse!" Ben exclaimed. "I'm going to
start CPR."
   "Who hasn't got a pulse?" I thought. I needed to see

whom they were huddled over.

"No!" Felicity told him. "Not yet, this isn't what you think it is."

"Rowan, I know you're there. I'm pulling the rope as hard as I can. Help me! Follow my voice."

Once again, Felicity's melodious voice echoed in my ears, but her lips never parted. I floated a little closer. I had to see who was lying on the floor between them.

"Are you fucking nuts, Felicity?" Ben exclaimed loudly. "He's dying! His fucking heart stopped beating!"

"Dammit Ben," she shot back at him wildly. "I know what I'm doing, and your interruptions aren't helping!"

"Rowan! Help me dammit! Follow my voice!"

Ben jerked back in surprise from my wild-eyed wife. I don't think he had ever truly experienced her temper until now. I looked down between them as the space opened enough for me to see. The body on the floor had a very familiar face. Brown hair. Bearded. A small scar on his forehead. Exactly like a scar I had on my own forehead. It slowly dawned on me that I was looking at myself.

"Rowan!"

There was a sharp tug at my waist.

I began falling.

White noise filled my ears. I felt a sharp burst of pain through my chest, and I began hungrily gasping for air. I opened my eyes and looked up to see Ben and Felicity staring back at me. Ben shook his head as if he had just witnessed a miracle and let out a long sigh. Felicity's lips parted in a slight smile as she stroked my forehead.

"Welcome back," she said.

"Thanks for not letting go," I whispered.

CHAPTER 11

The hot, bright sun flooded the landscape, beating down upon us from the clear sky and broiling the last drops of moisture from the ground. By late afternoon, no one would be able to tell that it had rained the night before. I was sitting on the back of Felicity's Jeep drinking the remains of a lemon-flavored sport drink she had kept in her gym bag. The drink was hot and tasted horrible. Its acidic tang slightly burned the back of my tongue and my throat as I swallowed. I had tried to refuse the beverage; my wife however, insisted I drink it all in order to replenish the electrolytes in my body.

My eyes were still adjusting to the glare as I watched Ben and Felicity in silence. I remembered the entire incident clearly. The two of them were shuffling about nervously, making it a point to avoid one another, not saying a word or even making eye contact. Every now and then one of them would ask me how I was doing, and Ben even asked me several times if he should take me to the hospital. I finished the last of the sport drink with a gulp and screwed the lid tightly back onto the plastic container then tossed it over my shoulder into the rear of the Jeep.

"Are you two going to kiss and make up?" I finally asked.

Ben and Felicity both stopped in their tracks and looked at me suspiciously.

"Yeah," I told them. "I heard you two snap at each other. I may not have been in my body at the time, but I was in the room."

"So look," Ben started, looking down at the ground. "I'm not really used to this kinda stuff, Felicity. I..."

"Aye, you don't have to say it, Ben," Felicity interrupted. "We were both on edge. If we should be mad at anyone, it's him." She motioned to me. "Not each other."

"Wait a minute," I protested. "I wasn't involved in your little spat."

"I beg to differ," my wife informed me. "Just exactly who was laying in there with no pulse? I told you it was dangerous."

"She's right, Rowan," Ben chimed in. "I thought you were dead, and for what?"

"Grey eyes," I told them.

"Excuse me?" Felicity intoned.

"Grey eyes," I repeated. "The killer has got grey eyes. I saw them."

"So you actually did see somethin'?" Ben queried as he flipped out his ever-present notebook.

"Just the eyes," I answered. "He was either very careful about being seen, or he was very lucky."

"That's somethin' I don't quite understand," Ben stated.

"What's that?" Felicity asked.

"Why would he care?" he continued. "It's not like his victims can give an eyewitness description."

"Fear," I stated simply. "I think that might be why he props the doors open too."

They both stared at me blankly as if I had lost them.

"Think about it," I proceeded. "When my body shut down in there, my spirit or soul, whatever you prefer to call it, left. But it didn't go very far, obviously, because I watched you two argue about giving me CPR. That's what turned me on to this idea. I think the killer not only feels remorse but fear as well. He performs the Expiation spell for forgiveness, and he props the door open so his victim's spirit can leave."

"I still don't see the connection with hiding his face from

the victims," Ben puzzled.

"He fears retribution from the spirits of his victims," Felicity interjected, realizing what I was trying to explain. "He keeps his identity hidden so they can't find him."

"You mean ta' tell me he thinks the ghosts of his victims will come after him for revenge?" Ben asked incredulously. "That's nuts. That's just plain nuts."

"It all depends on what you believe, Ben," I told him.

"What about the fact that he killed her out here in the park?" he protested. "It seems like that would fit more with the wantin'-ta'-get-caught theory you mentioned."

"I don't know why he killed her out here," I replied. "I just know what I feel, and what I feel right now is that he's propping the doors open to let the victims' spirits escape."

"This is a pretty secluded section of the park," Felicity interjected as she shaded her eyes and looked around. "You've got the wooded area with the fitness trail, but that's about it. Most of the activity would be taking place closer to the front of the park where the pavilions and ballfields are."

"Jeezus, this is one twisted fuckhead," Ben muttered.

"We knew that already," I told him.

"Does R.J. have grey eyes?" Felicity asked.

"Not that I recall," I replied, "but I can't say that I paid that much attention."

"I still wanna talk to 'im anyway," Ben stated flatly.

Ben's comment was followed by an awkward pause as his suspicion had once again reared its omnipresent head.

"So why don't we head over to the house," Felicity finally suggested, breaking the silence. "It's cooler and there's fresh, herb, sun tea in the fridge."

"Sounds great to me," I intoned. "Besides, that's where my cigars are."

"I'm with you," Ben added.

Felicity rolled her eyes and went around the Jeep to

climb into the driver's seat.

Felicity was changing into shorts and a t-shirt while Ben and I set fire to a pair of cigars out on the back deck. I was just finishing the final adjustments to the patio umbrella when she came out to join us, preceded by our two bounding canines. She set a tray containing glasses and a pitcher of iced tea on the table and then lithely draped herself in a chair to join us.

It was still early afternoon, and the temperature had not yet begun to decline. The air remained thick with humidity, but there was a slight breeze, and as long as we stayed relaxed in the shade, the clime was at least tolerable.

"So I made a coupl'a calls on the way over here," Ben announced, helping himself to the tea. "Seems Deckert managed to dig some info up on Devon Johnston."

"Have they found him?" I asked, taking my turn with the pitcher and pouring a glass for my wife.

"Not yet," he continued, "but we're still lookin'."

"What did Detective Deckert come up with?" Felicity asked, taking a sip of her drink.

"Found Johnston's parents," Ben answered, "or his mother anyway. His dad is deceased."

"Why did it take until today?" I queried. "Not that I'm being critical."

"Illinois license," he replied. "We were just searching the Missouri DMV records initially. His mom lives in Urbana, and apparently, that's where he grew up. He just never switched his driver's license over. But, that's not the interestin' part. It seems that one Mister Devon Johnston was recently dismissed from his position as a medical technician with Mercy Hospital... And accordin' to his records with the DMV, he's got grey eyes."

"So that should take the heat off of R.J.," Felicity stated.

"Not really," Ben told her. "It just gives me another asshole who's moved one of his bricks into the suspicious pile ta' worry about. Granted, his bricks are a little heavier than R.J.'s."

"Seems to me they should be a lot heavier," I interjected.

"Like I said," Ben blew out a stream of smoke, "the information you get from one of your visions doesn't do a damn bit of good in a courtroom. If it gives us a lead, great, but I still hafta come up with hard evidence. Hell, I don't even know why I believe you. This ain't exactly an everyday method of investigation, you know."

"Maybe because you're an open-minded individual," Felicity chimed. "Whether you want to admit it or not."

"Yeah," he agreed. "But sometimes, I still feel like I might be a little nuts to go for some of this stuff."

I knew exactly what Ben meant; I had even been known to be a bit skeptical myself in earlier years. I had been a practitioner of The Craft for all of my adult life, and though I had come to accept the things my otherworldly senses would tell me, I could still be surprised. As someone unfamiliar with the supernatural talents of the mind, this had to be very hard for him. I had to admit, he was holding up better than most.

I took advantage of the momentary silence to watch our dogs at play in the sun-soaked backyard. They tumbled and rolled with one another, tails wagging in a delighted frenzy as they wrestled, oblivious to the horror we three humans were being forced to contemplate. I sometimes wished I could be just as unmindful.

"Any ideas where Devon might be?" I queried, ending the self-imposed reticence.

"Nada," Ben answered with a slight, somewhat animated shrug. "His mother hasn't heard from him in six months, or so she says. We've got somebody sittin' on her place too, just in case. We checked with his former co-workers, and it appears like he's a bit of a loner. None of 'em really got to know 'im that well, and from what was said, they really didn't care to either."

"What about Cally?" Felicity intoned. "He called her once. Do you think he might try to contact her again?"

"We hafta hope that she'll tell us if he does," he returned. "We're watchin' her place, but if he calls 'er or meets 'er somewhere else, we'll prob'ly miss it."

"Can't you follow her?" I asked.

"Not enough evidence at this point." Ben turned his attention to me. "Last thing we need is ta' get nailed for harassment."

Ben paused as he puffed on his cigar and quietly watched the hummingbirds assault a hanging feeder like WWII era airplanes in a spectacular dogfight. Eventually he reached up and began smoothing his hair. Felicity and I looked at each other then back to him, as we were both intimately familiar with the gesture.

"So let me ask you somethin'," he finally spoke.

"Shoot," I returned.

"You said somethin' about this creep taking Karen Barnes' heart with 'im so he could 'finish the ritual'. What was that all about?"

"It's part of the sacrifice," I explained. "And what he does with it is entirely dependent upon what he is trying to accomplish. He might burn it, or he might bury it... Hell, he might eat it."

"I was afraid you were gonna say somethin' like that," he mumbled.

"I wish I could say for sure, but I'm still not entirely

clear on what he's trying to do." I continued with a frustrated sigh. "To be honest, something about his whole ritual is bothering me."

"How so?" Felicity asked.

"The energy at the crime scene."

"What energy?" she queried, confused. "I didn't feel anything except death."

"Exactly," I replied.

"What are you two talkin' about?" Ben interjected his question, coming fully upright in his seat and paying rapt attention.

"Whenever a Witch or practitioner of magick does something, an invocation for example," I explained, "he or she leaves behind residual energy. Kind of a left over that just floats around until it dissipates."

"So what's your point?" he pressed.

"That excess energy wasn't there," Felicity stated. "Neither of us felt it."

"I was at that scene within hours of the murder," I told him. "And we were there again today. That energy should hang around for a good long time, but there's nothing there. Just the energies given off by Karen Barnes. Her fear, pain, and especially her death."

"Okay," Ben replied slowly. "So I'd still appreciate it if ya' could tell me what this is s'posed ta' mean."

"Maybe nothing," I answered. "There could be a few different explanations, like maybe he just went through the physical motions but didn't actually perform the ritual as he should have. It's just something that kind of bothers me."

"So it's not a lead or anything like that."

"No. At least I don't think so."

Ben returned his attention to the cigar held loosely between his fingers then relaxed and leaned back in his seat. It was obvious that he was on edge, and I was certain that a lack of sleep was partially to blame.

"When is the last time you had a decent night's sleep, Ben?" Felicity asked him, following my thoughts as if I had spoken them aloud.

"I think it was sometime during winter 'bout three years ago," he answered facetiously.

"Do you really need to talk to R.J. today?" I questioned. "Couldn't that wait till tomorrow?"

"Probably. Why?"

"You need sleep, Ben," my wife stated matter-of-factly.

"Yeah, chief," I agreed. "No offense intended, but you're all edgy, and you look like someone ran over you with a truck."

"Your health is going to start suffering," Felicity intoned. "You can't keep going like this. You really need to decompress."

"Yeah... I know," he answered with a sigh. "I haven't seen my wife face to face in nearly a week. Shit, she told me this mornin' on the phone that the little guy asked her if Daddy still lived there."

"Go home, Ben," I told him. "Go home and hug your kid, kiss your wife, and have a meal with your family. Then get some sleep."

"I haven't got the time," he objected.

"Unless you have some kind of secret information that you haven't told us about," I admonished, "you aren't going to catch this guy tonight. You need some sleep, man. Besides, it's not just you working this case. The entire Major Case Squad is on it now."

"Yeah, yeah, you're right." He slumped more noticeably in his chair. "But I still wanna talk ta' the kid today. I think I'll sleep better if I do."

"If that's what it takes, do it," I told him. "But get some rest either way because something tells me we haven't seen the end of this yet."

"What a cheerful thought," he mumbled.

Ben eventually left us in search of R.J. Felicity and I spent a quiet afternoon together trying not to think about serial killers and of course, was unable to ponder anything else. In an effort to put the subject out of our minds, we made a quick trip to the store and returned with fresh, yellow fin tuna steaks for the grill. Together with a medley of vegetables from our garden, we made a light meal and after cleaning up the dishes, generally lazed about into the evening hours.

Stories of Ariel Tanner and Karen Barnes' murders flooded the airwaves as the top story during the late evening news on every station. Details about the crimes were convoluted and misconstrued to the point that they were telling a different story on each channel. The two points they all agreed on were the nominative "Satanic Serial Killer" and the practice of flashing the newspaper photo of me on the screen. Touching my thumb to the remote, I rolled back through the channels in the hope they had found something else to talk about. I was giving serious consideration to turning off the chattering box when a familiar face, other than my own, leapt out at me from the screen. I swiftly reversed the direction of my scan and came to rest on that station.

Detective Arthur McCann's worry-lined face stared back at me with concern and determination creasing his brow. Apparently, he had just finished speaking as the picture suddenly cut to a wide-eyed Brandee Street anxiously clutching a microphone. I punched up the volume a notch and settled in.

"Can you explain a little more about the Wiccan religion," she asked him.

"Certainly," Arthur returned authoritatively. "This so-called religion is nothing more than a fancy name for cult activities. The individuals involved undermine the morals of our children and recruit them into these cults. There they become addicted to drugs and often are the victims of sexual abuse."

I had heard his speech before, but each and every time, I was amazed by what he said. I found it hard to believe that an intelligent human being could be so blind to the truth.

"Do you believe that one of these Wiccan cultists is responsible for the bizarre murders that have recently occurred?" Brandee's voice came again.

"Since I'm not involved in the investigation, I cannot directly comment, but I will say that it wouldn't surprise me," he answered.

"You have been one of the leading authorities on cults within the Saint Louis County Police Department for the past few years. Why aren't you involved with the Major Case Squad?"

"I resigned from the MCS this morning due to a shift in caseloads," Arthur succinctly replied.

"Way to go Arthur," I thought as I listened to his reply. "At least you engaged your brain before opening your mouth this time."

"Would your resignation have anything to do with the involvement of Rowan Gant as a consultant to the Major Case Squad?" Brandee persisted.

"I have no comment on that." He continued his guarded, tactful stance.

"Mister Gant is a self-proclaimed Witch and practitioner of the Wiccan religion," she pressed harder. "You yourself stated that this amounts to nothing more than a cult.""

Arthur's face had reddened, and I could tell that he desperately wanted to spill his guts. He was dying to tell the world of the police department's moral decrepitude due to my involvement. He probably even wanted to take a few verbal shots at me personally. But Arthur McCann was only a few short years away from his pension, and whatever his personal beliefs, he was still a dedicated cop.

"No comment," he finally returned.

The picture changed back to the talking heads behind the anchor desk on the stylized set. They began to banter back and forth, making what they believed to be clever quips about me, and Witches in general.

It wasn't long before I was thoroughly disgusted with the entire exposition and switched the television off. Following my wife's example, I went to bed.

A distant scream.
Darkness.
Indigo Darkness.
A point of light far away.
A distant scream.
The light grows brighter. Larger. Closer.
I move toward the light.
The light stays beyond my reach.

A violent chord struck sharply upon an unearthly instrument. Grating tones that seem to last forever, carrying themselves visibly aloft on directionless winds. Sounds that can be seen as well as heard.

A terrified scream.
Grey.
Damp, thick greyness.

It's raining. Not heavily, just a gentle mist. A light sprinkle raining down from a gloomy grey sky.

"Rowan, so nice to see you again."

I turn to the voice and find Ariel clad in white lace. She smiles at me then looks upward. I try to speak but have no voice. She looks up at the sky, the misty rain lightly bathing her innocent smiling face. She looks back to my face, eyes smiling and a strand of hair clinging damply to her cheek.

"It always rains here," she says to me. "I don't know why. It's mostly just a misty rain."

A dark figure rises from the grey nothingness behind her.

A figure black as night.

A figure wrapped in a hooded robe.

"Do you like the rain, Rowan?" Ariel asks me. "I do, but I think it rains too much here. What do you think?"

A flicker of light.

No, a reflection.

There is something in the dark figure's hand.

Once again I try to speak. I try to warn her. I scream a silent scream.

Her eyes grow large in sudden astonishment. Her lithe body jerks upward in a violent spasm. A crimson stain spreads savagely across her breast.

I've seen this before.

I can't make it stop.

I can't look away.

"Why, Rowan?" she mouths wordlessly. "Why?

Indigo darkness.

A distant ceaseless scream.

"Why don't you make it stop, Rowan?"

I turn again. Ariel faces me, her lace gown streaked vermilion. Glassy eyes stare unblinkingly at me. Her lips are frozen in a perpetual scream, yet only silence moves past them.

"How can I make it stop, Ariel? Tell me." My voice halts and jerks, changing in speed and pitch as if haphazardly

pieced together.

"Please make it stop, Rowan?" Her pleading voice meets my ears.

Her lips never move.

Misty rain.

Grey misty rain.

An endless scream.

I don't know when the nightmare started or even how long it lasted. It could have begun mere moments after I closed my eyes or for all I knew, the last slumbering seconds before reopening them. Logically, I knew that the entire sequence couldn't have taken more than a few minutes at the most. Emotionally, I was certain it had lasted for hours.

Felicity was still sleeping soundly when I awoke bathed in sweat and tangled almost irremovably in the sheets. My heart was racing, and I gasped hungrily for air to feed it. Slowly, I withdrew myself from the damp snarl of the bed linens and retrieved my Book of Shadows from the nightstand next to me then made my way to the bathroom and closed the door. I switched on the light in an effort to chase away my sudden irrational fear of the darkness then perched myself on the cool tile ledge surrounding the tub and began the task of relaxing. Fifteen minutes and three cups of water later, my pulse and breathing finally returned to normal.

Pulling the ink pen from its loop in the cover, I opened the Book of Shadows, my diary of dreams and thoughts, and proceeded to record every detail of the vision I could remember while it was still fresh in my mind. Every single thing I saw, no matter how nonsensical. Every little nuance of my emotions, each and every sliver of information, I scribed within the pages of the book until there was nothing left to write.

Senseless fear fought to grip me once again as I doused the light and returned quietly to the bedroom. I mentally beat the emotion down and after returning my Book of Shadows to the nightstand, slid into the bed next to my wife. I cuddled next to her in search of comfort, and she shifted lazily as I slipped my arm around her. I pressed myself to relax and rested my cheek against her soft auburn hair, drinking in its sweet scent. Before long, fatigue won out over irrational panic, and I floated easily into the world of sleep.

The clock on the nightstand read 1:45 A.M. when I rolled over and peered blearily at its glowing face. I was enveloped in a fog of half sleep and struggled to grasp the concept of why I was awake at such an hour. A loud, obnoxious clamor reached my ears and then fell silent. I closed my eyes and decided I must be dreaming, then rolled over. The noise, now more clearly a ringing sound, filtered into my ears again and was followed by Felicity's sharp elbow poking me in the ribs.

"Aye, Rowan, get the phone, then," she mumbled from her own half dream state.

I rolled back to face the nightstand and groped for the receiver. When my fumbling fingers finally located the device, I grasped it and lifted it from the cradle, cutting off the noise mid-ring.

"Hello," I croaked, my voice permeated with sleep.

"Didn't wake you, did I?" Ben's tired voice came rhetorically from the earpiece.

"You're not in my driveway again, are you?" I mumbled.

"No," he replied. "But I can have a squad car there in

about fifteen minutes if you don't feel like driving."

"What's wrong?" I asked, quickly becoming more alert.

"Number three" was his only reply.

CHAPTER 12

I jotted down the address and nudged Felicity into wakefulness. After dragging on a pair of jeans and a button-down shirt, I started a pot of coffee and proceeded to put on my socks and tennis shoes. By the time the coffee was finished brewing, my wife had dressed and was sitting at the breakfast nook with her camera bag slung over her shoulder.

"You want some of this?" I asked her as I filled an oversized travel mug with the hot black liquid.

"Aye, is it decaf?" she asked sleepily.

"No. Sorry."

"I shouldn't then," she said with a slight yawn. "The doctor said I should be avoiding caffeine, what with the baby and all. I've already broken that rule a couple of times this weekend."

"Makes sense," I agreed. "Would you rather skip this and go back to bed? I can go by myself."

"No." She shook her head and stifled another yawn. "I'd rather go along and see if we can catch this guy. That way we can all go back to bed and get some sleep."

I tucked the address into my shirt pocket and snapped the lid onto the travel mug. Upon opening the front door, we were greeted by slightly cooler temperatures than earlier in the day, though the air was still heavy with humidity. Moments later we were on our way, my petite wife behind the wheel.

The clock was just clicking over to 2:30 A.M. when we rolled to a halt on what should have been a quiet side street in the small suburb of Stone Knoll. The scene was similar to the methodic confusion I had experienced just one night before, minus the rain. Felicity was quickly mesmerized by the flickering lights and sat momentarily transfixed until I rescued her from the stupor with a gentle nudge.

News vans were already rolling in on the scene as we made our way past parked patrol cars to the crux of the activity. A uniformed officer executing his duty blocked our path as we neared the yellow tape that cordoned off the house.

"You'll have to move back folks," he stated evenly as he insinuated himself between us and the end of the driveway. "Press isn't allowed in this area."

Apparently, we had been mistaken for members of the media, and I quickly understood why when I remembered the bulky camera bag slung over my wife's shoulder.

"We aren't with the press," I told him. "I'm Rowan Gant, and this is my wife, Felicity. We were called here by Detective Benjamin Storm."

"Hold on just a second," he returned with a nod and then spoke into his radio handset.

A few seconds later, Detective Carl Deckert came out of the front door and trundled down the driveway to the barricade where we stood.

"Rowan, Felicity," he greeted us, nodding at the officer who acknowledged and extended a clipboard for us to sign in. Deckert waited patiently for us to finish then held up the tape so we could duck under and shook our hands quickly as we walked.

"Ben's inside. Sorry no one was out here to meet you," he apologized. "But it's a little on the busy side around here."

"Aye, that's understandable," Felicity told him, her voice laced with a full Celtic lilt.

"So you're pretty sure it's the same guy?" I asked.

"Pretty sure," Deckert answered, pulling out surgical gloves and handing them to us as we neared the door. "But there are some changes in the M.O. That's why you're here."

"What kind of changes?"

Deckert opened his mouth to reply and then paused for a moment before continuing, "I'd better let you see for yourself."

"Do you always carry these things around in your pockets, then?" Felicity queried, indicating the gloves as she drew them over her hands.

"In my line of work..." he shrugged and then added with a grin, "Besides, my brother-in-law owns a medical supply company so I get 'em cheap—as in free. So... if you don't mind me askin', what's with the heavy accent all of a sudden?"

"What accent?" my wife asked, cocking her head to the side.

"She's the real-deal Irish," I interjected, answering for her. "It tends to really bleed through when she gets tired."

"O'Brien, yeah." He nodded. "Makes sense. Just wasn't expectin' it."

"You get used to the linguistic flip-flops after awhile. You should hear her when she's had a couple of drinks."

"Aye, will you two quit talking about me like I'm not even here, then?" Felicity declared.

"Sorry, honey," I told my wife as I turned my attention to her. "Now, when we go in, ground, center, and be careful. You're gonna feel a lot of stuff flying at you, and if you don't watch it, you'll *zone out*. Trust me, I've already been through it. If you feel like you're headed for trouble, get out."

"Okay." She nodded assent, and I literally felt her falling into a slow, rhythmic breathing pattern that mimicked my own. "I'm ready."

We entered and followed Deckert toward the rear of the house, carefully weaving our way around crime scene technicians who were focusing intently on their jobs. The cold aura of death surrounded us as we advanced down a narrow hallway and through the doorway at its end. The frigid atmosphere permeated the room, stabbing me with its sharpness. A quick glance at Felicity showed me she was feeling it as well.

The room was simple, basically rectangular in shape with an antique chest of drawers dominating one corner. Against the wall, a matching dressing table resided. The makeup and perfumes that adorned the top of the table were neatly arranged to the back, and occupying the center were two hardened puddles of candle wax, one white, one black. Next to them, a wine glass was wrapped around its volume of crimson liquid. An ornate, pivoting frame, supported by similarly carved wooden arms, was canted slightly against the wall. The mirror it had once held now lay shattered, spilling like silvery gems across the floor. The once hidden wall behind it now bore the pastel-shaded image of a Pentacle and three familiar words inscribed in a dripping scrawl.

A queen-size bed, stripped of the top layer of linens, jutted out into the middle of the room from the wall opposite the dressing table. Occupying the center of the bed was a long mass covered with a white sheet. Hands protruding from beneath the edge of the fabric and bound to the headboard with duct tape gave clear evidence as to the identity of the mass. The pungent odor of burned sage and rose oil still hung cloyingly in the air.

Ben was talking to the medical examiner when we walked in, and he looked up as we ventured farther into the room. The forensics team had recently finished dusting for fingerprints, and the dark grey powder coated any likely surface they had checked.

"Keep it up and the department is going to have to issue you a badge." A grim-faced Dr. Sanders greeted us as we stopped at the foot of the bed.

"Dr. Sanders," I said and motioned to the medical examiner. "This is my wife, Felicity O'Brien. Felicity, Dr. Christine Sanders. The doc here is the one that stitched up my head."

"O'Brien, huh," Dr. Sanders said as she canted her head in my wife's direction. "Maiden name?"

"Aye," she answered.

"Good for you," the doctor approved. "I kept mine too."

Felicity smiled and then returned her own nod. I'm sure she was relieved at not having to explain the difference in our last names for once.

"Thanks for comin' down, you two," Ben said, once the introductions were over.

"No problem," I replied and then motioned to the covered body. "Same as before?"

"Not entirely," he answered. "That's why I called you."

"What's different?" I queried.

Ben nodded to Dr. Sanders, who skirted around us to the other side of the bed and grasped the corner of the sheet.

"You gonna be okay with this?" He directed the question at my wife. "The real thing's different than pictures, ya'know."

"Aye," Felicity drew in a deep breath and let it out heavily. "I'll be all right, then."

"You must be really tired," he observed aloud.

"Well it IS the middle of the night."

"Yeah, and yer doin' the accent."

"I don't have an accent," she replied. "You do."

"Yeah, right." He nodded then turned. "Go ahead, Doc."

Dr. Sanders threw back the covering to reveal the nude corpse of a young blonde woman. The victim's glassy, dead eyes stared up at the ceiling, frozen for all time in sheer terror. Her torso had been flayed but not completely as with the previous two. This time the killer had removed only patches of her skin, carefully arranged in a geometric pattern that formed a Pentagram.

"The killer removed the heart in a fashion similar to that of the Barnes woman," Dr. Sanders began, "but the removal of the skin was much more precise than the previous cases. I would venture to say he's getting better at it."

"I was wrong," I said, kneeling down to have a closer look. "Karen Barnes was just lesson number two for him."

"Whaddaya mean?" Ben asked.

"He's still practicing," I explained. "Lesson one was Ariel Tanner. He taught himself to skin a living human. Lesson two, Karen Barnes. How to remove a still beating heart... Now, lesson three... He's refining his technique. Making it more complex... More exacting..." My words trailed off as my eyes roamed over the mutilated remains of the young woman. My stomach revolted against the sight, and I forced it back down, fending off the nausea.

"There's another twist to the whole thing," Ben told me then turned his attention to the medical examiner. "Doc?"

"There is trace evidence of semen on the sheets," she explained. "I'll have to check her back at the morgue, but the preliminary exam indicates that she was subject to sexual intercourse very recently."

"Maybe the asshole is startin' to get off on what he's doin' to these women," Ben spat.

"I don't think so," I told him. "The killer is too involved

with the ritual. To defile his sacrifice would make no sense."

"Skinnin' people alive then rippin' their hearts out doesn't make any sense either." Ben was becoming angry with the situation, and it showed in his voice.

"To you and me, no it doesn't," I calmly stated. "To him, I think it does."

"Well, when I find this son-of-a-bitch, it's gonna stop makin' sense to him real quick," Ben returned. "As for the semen, I have to assume he raped her, and that might let us ID his blood type and maybe narrow the field down."

"I know," I answered, "but I don't think that's what happened."

"Who is she?" Felicity, who had been silent until now, asked somberly. "Do you know?"

She was facing the wall, avoiding the hideous display. I could see that the color was just returning to her pale cheeks.

"Ellen Gray, per her driver's license and work ID in her purse," stated Detective Deckert who had been observing quietly. "According to the neighbor, she's separated. Her old man moved out about two weeks ago."

"Does he know yet?" she pressed.

"No. Not yet."

"I take it the door was propped open like the others?" I questioned.

"Yeah," Deckert answered. "Lady across the street works the three-to-eleven and noticed it when she got home. She came over to see if something was wrong and found her. Luckily, she had enough wits left to dial nine-one-one. By the time the paramedics showed up, she was so hysterical they had to sedate 'er and take 'er to the hospital."

"Any ideas about how the killer got in?"

"Sliding doors on the basement," he returned. "Looks like someone popped the latch with a pry bar or something."

"Then she probably didn't know him," I submitted.

"Maybe, maybe not," Ben announced. "She was a nu
at County Hospital."

"Where R.J. works," Felicity almost whispered.

"'Zactly," Ben replied.

"Did you talk to him like you planned?" I queried.

"He wasn't home. And it was his day off, so he wasn'
work."

"That still doesn't prove anything, Ben," Felicity t
him.

"Maybe not, but he sure as hell just moved anot
coupl'a bricks over to the other side of the scale."

"Has anything turned up to indicate that R.J. knew Ka
Barnes, then?" she asked.

"No, not yet," Ben answered, "but we'll be talkin' to
husband and neighbors again in the mornin'."

"Ahem," Dr. Sanders cleared her throat, and we
turned to her. "I hate to interrupt, but if you're finished v
the body, I need to get her to the morgue."

"Sorry 'bout that, Doc," Ben told her. "Go ahead. W
done."

"Any revelations, Mr. Gant?" she said, looking at me.

"Excuse me?"

"You were correct about the fingerprint on the Bar
woman, even if it was smudged," she explained. "I was
wondering if you had any new ideas."

"Not at this point in time," I answered. "Sorry."

"Just checking," she said with a thin smile.

We moved off to the side and allowed Dr. Sanders
her assistant to carefully place the lifeless young wo
into a body bag and zip it shut. They expertly placed he
a gurney and proceeded to wheel her out.

"I guess she's been reading what the papers have ha
say about me," I stated after they left.

"She's okay with it," Ben told me. "She doesn't necessarily believe in it, but she's okay."

Felicity was still looking a bit pale, but she seemed to be holding up well so far. She had retrieved a camera from her bag and was going about the task of photographing the back area of the room where the killer had performed his atonement ritual. We knew the pictures would be redundant, but cameras were like a focal point for her, probably due to her profession. Simply peering through a lens brought an entirely different clarity and dimension to the world around her, and she used it to her advantage.

"When do you think you'll be notifying the husband?" I asked.

"We'll be contacting him as soon as the M.E. gets to the morgue," Deckert told me. "It shouldn't be long. Why?"

"Something just doesn't feel right," I answered.

"You think the old man did it?" he questioned. "Like a copy cat or something, to cover it up?"

"No, that's not it," I replied. "I think it was the same guy, but I've got a really weird feeling. The whole sex thing just doesn't fit with what this guy seems to be up to. Maybe she and the husband got together for a fling, or maybe she's got a boyfriend, and that's why they split up. I just don't believe the killer raped her."

"We'll be checkin' all of that out," Ben agreed. "But remember, we're dealin' with a sicko here."

"You're right," I told him. "But it's too much of a deviation. I think there has to be some other explanation."

"Hey, you two," Felicity's voice came from behind us. "Come over here and have a look at this."

My wife was still holding the camera deftly in her hands but had pulled it away from her eye and was staring at the dressing table with a puzzled expression.

"Aye, is this fingerprint stuff supposed to do this?" she

asked, pointing at the hardened puddle of white wax where
candle had once been.

"Supposed to do what?" Ben responded to her query w
one of his own.

"Glow like that. Don't you see it, then?"

"See what, honey?" I asked. "All I see is what's left o
candle."

"The fingerprint," she pled in exasperation. "Right th
in the wax. Open your eyes."

"There can't be a fingerprint there," Deckert assert
"Forensics already dusted over here, and they said
candles were clean. Besides," he contended, "an imprint
wax would be pretty obvious."

"It's not an imprint on the wax," explained Felicity. "
a fingerprint IN the wax. It's like it's inside it." She step
closer and thrust her index finger at the center of the sm
mound.

Ben and I both leaned closer but still couldn't
anything other than the remains of a candle. Felicity
becoming more agitated each time we told her as much.

"It's glowing, you guys," she volunteered. "It's like
person had something phosphorescent on his fingers
something."

Her last statement gave me the clue I needed. Thoug
was still unable to see what she was seeing—and nei
was Ben nor Detective Deckert, I was sure—I sudde
realized what was happening. My wife was definitely se
the fingerprint in the wax; however, she was *seeing* it
what a Witch calls Second Sight. This ability is
something that can always be turned on or off at will.
the stuff of clairvoyance and psychometry—the talen
witness the future and read the energies and impression
inanimate objects. It was the simple gift of being abl
observe those things that are hidden from earthly eyes.

"Felicity," I posed, "could the fingerprint be on the underside of the candle? Is it possible that you're visualizing it?"

"Aye, I suppose it could," she said as a look of understanding spread across her face. "Yes. Yes, I think that could be it!"

"You'd better get your forensic guys to check the underside of that pile of wax," I told Detective Deckert as I turned. "If they plan on collecting and bagging this stuff for evidence, they might destroy the print if they aren't careful."

Deckert hurriedly left the room and soon returned with a member of the crime scene unit who had been working elsewhere in the house.

"We already dusted this area," he told us as he was led to the melted candle. "There's nothing there."

"Just humor us," Ben told him. "I need ya' ta' check the bottom of the wax."

"The bottom?" the evidence technician echoed.

"Yeah, the bottom," Ben replied.

The young man stared at the hardened puddles with a baffled expression on his face, then shrugged. He knelt on the floor and opened a thick case he had been carrying. After rummaging briefly through its contents, his hands emerged holding a can of compressed air and a tool resembling a putty knife. Using the compressed air, he blew away the residue from the earlier dusting and cleared the area around the piles of wax.

"The white one," Felicity volunteered. "That's where it is."

"Okay," the forensics tech acknowledged in a humorless tone.

After rapidly shaking the can of air, he turned it upside down and aimed it at the remains of the white candle. The propellant in the can that normally expelled as a jet of gas

when held properly upright now streamed from the nozz
as a frigid mist.

"What're you doin' that for?" Detective Deck
questioned.

"If I cool it down enough," the tech explained, "I shou
be able to lift it off the surface in one piece."

The technician quickly moved the spray back and fo
across the wax for a few moments then released the trigg
and set the can aside. Slowly and carefully, he slipped t
thin, knife-like tool under the edge of the now somewl
frosted mass. With great patience and skill, he worked t
blade gently around the edge as we watched on, until fina
the oblong heap of dull white paraffin popped loose in o
complete piece. Setting the bladed tool aside, the technic
gingerly turned the wax over in his gloved hands a
inspected it closely.

"Right there in the middle," Felicity intoned, trying
peer around him.

He remained silent, but from where I stood, I could
his face, and the expression now crossing it was one
disbelief. He placed the wax upside down on the coun
then quickly retrieved a brush and small bottle of pow
from his kit and began gently dusting the mass.

The candle had been a votive type and had apparen
been mass-produced in a factory as was evidenced by a t
metal plate embedded in the center. The piece of metal l
been the anchor used for the wick when it was origina
made, and it was the focus of the evidence technicia
scrutiny at this very moment.

"I don't believe it," he muttered. "There's a print th
big as shit. It's partial, but it's a good one."

"Son-of-a-bitch," Deckert said slowly.

"How in hell did you know that print was there?"
forensics tech asked, turning to Felicity.

"Lucky guess," Ben answered for her. "I want that print lifted and run yesterday," he continued. "And while you're at it, check all the candles from the previous crime scenes."

"That might be a problem," he replied.

"Whaddaya mean 'that might be a problem'?" demanded Ben.

"There were no prints on them." The tech visibly inched away from an angered Ben Storm. "So we just pried them up. They're in quite a few pieces."

"Dammit!" Ben exclaimed, turning in place and rubbing the back of his neck in a physical display of his exasperation. Once again he faced the tech and stabbed his index finger at him purposefully. "As soon as you guys are done here, I want you checkin' out those candles. You understand me?"

"I'll do what I can, Detective," the forensics tech assured him, no longer exhibiting his earlier cockiness.

"And you," Ben continued, turning and hooking his arm around Felicity. "Let me know if you ever need a job."

A younger, but no less stone-faced desk sergeant issued Felicity and I visitor's badges when we entered the police station where the Major Case Squad was currently headquartered. We walked down the long, familiar hallway and entered the room where the core of activity had been occurring when last we were here. At this early hour of the morning, the space was dark and still, entirely devoid of the earlier urgent bustle. Detective Deckert flipped a wall switch as we entered, bringing the stubbornly flickering fluorescent lights to life.

"Go ahead and have a seat," he said. "Anyone besides

me interested in coffee?"

He hung his jacket on the back of a chair and ambled over to the coffeemaker, rolling up his sleeves as he went.

"Me," Ben announced.

"Make that two," I added.

"Would you be havin' any herbal tea?" Felicity queried.

"We got a box of some kinda lemon tea or some odd thing like that," Deckert called out.

"Aye, that'll work," Felicity told him, heading over in his direction. "Here, let me give you a hand, then."

I took a seat at one of the long cafeteria tables that had been set up to serve as a staging and conference area. Ben stripped off his own jacket and loosened his tie then joined me. He rubbed his tightly shut eyes then the back of his neck, shoulders drooping as he let out a long sigh. His hair was unkempt and his shirt stained with sweat. He was obviously still operating on little sleep.

"You didn't take our advice did you?" I asked him.

"I took it," he answered tiredly, head tilted back and eyes closed. "I just didn't get a chance to use it."

"You know, Ben, you can't catch this guy all by yourself. Let some of the other cops do some of the work."

"They are, I just like to know what's goin' on, and there aren't enough hours in the day to keep up."

"Remember how worried you were when you thought I was dying earlier?" I asked.

"Yeah, what about it?" he replied. "That's what bein' a friend is."

"You're right," I told him. "And I'm starting to get worried about you."

He let out another heavy sigh and slowly tilted his head forward, opening his eyes as he did so. His gaze came to meet mine, and we sat there silently for a long moment.

"I know you are. I know the little woman is too. I

appreciate it, I really do," he finally said. "Let's just catch this asshole, then I'm takin' a vacation. True story."

"Here you go," Detective Deckert said as he slid a cup of coffee in front of Ben. "It's still brewing, so this is a bit thick if ya' know what I mean."

A similar cup appeared in front of me, placed there by my wife as she sat down. She clutched a cup of hot water and was rhythmically dipping a tea bag in it.

"How are you feeling?" I asked her.

"Fine, but I'm tired," she replied and leaned against me. "And a little queasy, but I'll be fine."

"Allison had morning sickness for the first six months," Ben offered.

"Morning sickness?" Deckert stated rhetorically. "I didn't know you two were expecting. Congratulations. How far along?"

"Early yet," Felicity told him. "Six weeks."

"Well, it's nice to hear some good news in the middle of all this crap," he said and lifted his coffee cup in an informal toast.

"I hate ta' bring it up," Ben interjected, "but we have to talk about the case. The way I see it, we still have an asshole out there killin' women, and we aren't much closer to knowin' who it is than we were when we started. Now personally, I think R.J.'s pile of bricks is startin' to add up on a side of the scale where he'd rather not be."

"You still need to talk to Devon," I offered.

"True." He continued, "And his pile isn't exactly tiltin' the scale in a positive direction either, but the fact is, R.J. very possibly worked with the latest victim."

"You know," Felicity stated thoughtfully. "It might not be either one of them."

"That's true," Deckert chimed, "but you follow the leads you have."

"What about that partial fingerprint?" I queried. "How soon do you expect to know anything?"

"The lab guys should have somethin' for us in a coupl'a hours," Ben answered. "It's all gonna depend on how soon they get finished at the scene and how much of the print we actually have..."

"And if its owner is in the system," Deckert added. "If he isn't, then it could be weeks before we get any replies from the non-participating municipalities."

"We haven't got weeks," I told them flatly. "This psycho has killed three women in less than ONE week, two of them in as many days."

"You got any better ideas?" Ben asked.

"No," I replied candidly, "and it irritates the hell out of me."

"Welcome to the club," he replied.

They were still processing the fingerprint from the latest murder scene when Felicity and I left to go home. With Detective Deckert's help, we convinced Ben to do the same, as repeated calls to the forensics lab had only served to frustrate him more. It was agreed that we would attack the situation anew after whatever modicum of sleep we could get. I half expected to find Ben at my door for breakfast the next morning.

CHAPTER 13

F elicity was feeling the effects of her first actual bout of morning sickness when the phone rang the next day. As expected, the person at the other end of the line was Ben, however, this time he was calling from the Major Case Squad headquarters instead of my driveway. His voice, though somewhat somber, sounded much less weary than it had only a few hours before.

"So are you free to come down here?" Ben's voice issued from the earpiece.

"Yeah, I don't have any client meetings today, so I can shake loose for a while," I replied. "Felicity's not feeling too well though."

"Get used to it," he told me.

"So what's up?"

"We got the kid down here," he returned, referring to R.J. "Says he doesn't want a lawyer, but he wants you here."

"Did you arrest him?"

"No, one of the local muni's picked 'im up on a DUI about the time we were at the crime scene last night... this mornin'... whatever."

"Driving under the influence, huh," I mused. "How'd you find out about that?"

"Since we decided we wanted to question him," Ben began, "and I couldn't find 'im yesterday, I decided to run his tags this mornin'. Sometimes crap like that pays off, and it did this time 'cause there he was. He looks like he's fightin' a hell of a hangover, but other than that, he's no worse for wear."

"Why does he want me there?" I queried.

"Somethin' to do with the whole Wiccan thing, I guess,"

he replied. "When we said we wanted to ask 'im a few questions about Ariel Tanner and Karen Barnes, he got kinda paranoid on us."

"You didn't mention Ellen Gray at all?"

"Not yet. I still have a few things to check out before I play that card."

"But if he's not under arrest," I puzzled, "can't he just walk out?"

"He got a bit rowdy with the officer that stopped him, so they decided to set an example," Ben explained. "City of Andrew Heights is gonna hold 'im over for arraignment on the DUI and a resisting charge. I just got the muni to let me have custody for a while."

"Okay," I told him. "Better let me grab a shower and all that. I'll be there in about an hour."

"We're not goin' anywhere."

As I was hanging up the phone, Salinger jumped up to the corner of our entertainment center and seated himself. He looked up at me with his bewhiskered face and large eyes forming a caricature of a wizened prophet then let out a doleful meow.

"You don't really think R.J.'s guilty, do you?" I asked him rhetorically as I scratched him behind the ears.

He replied only by closing his eyes and purring loudly.

"Aye, Rowan, was that Ben on the phone?" Felicity asked as she trudged slowly into the room with soda crackers in one hand and a cup of what smelled like ginger tea in the other.

"Yeah, that was him," I told her. "He's at the MCS headquarters. They've got R.J. down there, and he's asking for me."

"Did they arrest him?" she asked with a start.

"Yes and no." I explained, "He was arrested on a Driving-Under-the-Influence charge early this morning. Ben went looking for him again using his license plate number this time, and that's how he found him. He *borrowed* him from the municipality that arrested him, so he could ask him a few questions."

"Why is he asking for you instead of an attorney, then?"

"Who knows?" I shrugged. "Probably because I'm a Witch—at least that's Ben's theory. Apparently, he got pretty antsy when they told him they wanted to ask him about Ariel and Karen."

"Aye, wouldn't you?" Felicity asked.

"I suppose I would."

"So, how long before we have to be there? I don't know if I'm over this nausea yet."

"You don't need to go," I told her. "You can stay here and rest for a while, and I can fill you in later."

"Are you sure?" she queried. "I don't have a photo shoot scheduled until this afternoon, so I've got the morning free."

"I'm sure," I replied. "You need to get some rest. The accent is still a little heavy."

"Oh, stop it, then."

"Seriously though, honey. I can call you if anything happens."

"You're sure?"

"I'm sure."

"Okay then."

I left her lounging on the sofa in our living room, surrounded by three cats displaying curious concern as only they can do.

I parked my truck behind City Hall and checked in at the desk. I was apparently becoming a familiar face, or I was anticipated, as the Sergeant had a visitor's badge in hand as soon as he saw me. After checking in, I continued down the corridor and was met at the door by Ben and Detective Deckert.

"How's Firehair?" Ben inquired, calling Felicity by one of his many nicknames for her.

"She was starting to perk up," I told him as we continued farther into the bowels of the building. "I expect she'll be fine."

"Good, good," his voice trailed off as we descended a flight of stairs, and he fell silent.

Detective Deckert's face wore a somber expression, and his only greeting to me when I arrived had been a stiff nod. He was still silent as we rounded a landing and continued downward. It didn't take the heightened senses of a Witch to feel the tension coming from the two. Tension directed toward me.

"So look, Rowan..." Ben finally broke the silence as we stopped in front of a heavy steel door. "I got somethin' I need ta' tell ya', and I don't think you're gonna like it much."

"I had a feeling," I acknowledged. "It's something about R.J. isn't it?"

"Yeah, you could say that," Deckert intoned.

Ben let out a heavy breath and smoothed his hair back. His brow was creased with apprehension as he wrestled with what he had to tell me.

"So there's no way to sugar coat it," he spoke. "I just got off the phone with the forensics lab a minute or two before you got here..."

"Something about that fingerprint?" I feared I knew what he was about to say.

"Yeah, that print," he answered. "The muni that popped R.J. this morning entered his prints into AFIS, and the lab boys got an immediate hit."

"It matched?" I stared at him in disbelief.

"Like an identical twin."

"Damn," I whispered. "I thought it was a partial print?"

"It was, but there was enough there to make a positive ID."

"What about the wax from the other scenes?"

"They were clean, but that doesn't matter. The one found last night matches. No two ways about it."

"That's not all." Deckert expounded, "The M.E. came up with some long, dark hairs on the body as well as some other fibers."

"And the lab ran a check on the semen found at the scene last night. Blood type O Positive," Ben added. "Same as R.J."

"If I remember correctly, O Positive is fairly common," I protested. "Somewhere near forty percent of the population shares that blood type."

"Yeah, it is," Ben agreed. "But fingerprints ain't. The lab's gonna run a DNA analysis too, but that'll take awhile." He paused. "We got enough for a search warrant, Rowan... I'm sorry man, but I think R.J.'s involved."

"What about his eyes, Ben?" I pleaded, unwilling to believe what I was being told. "What color are his eyes?"

"His eyes are brown," he responded. "But like I told ya', that's inadmissible... Besides, maybe you made a mistake."

"No," I expressed, "I didn't make a mistake."

We stood in silence for a moment, Ben's hand on the doorknob. My mind raced, trying to formulate a logical way to refute the evidence Ben had outlined. Even with my own suspicions about R.J., I was reluctant to believe he was the killer. There had to be an explanation, and it needed to be a good one.

"Are you charging him?" I questioned.

"Not yet," Deckert returned. "We're gonna see wh[at] turns up when we search his place first."

Ben opened the heavy door, and we entered anoth[er] corridor in the basement of the building. Fluorescent lig[ht] fixtures were unevenly spaced along the acoustic dr[op] ceiling, bathing the hallway in a harsh blue-white light. O[ne] of the older tubes would occasionally flicker into darkne[ss] then burn dull orange at each end before snapping back [to] life, if only for a moment. The glossy, painted, cinder blo[ck] walls had aged from the original white to a sickly yellow tone that was deepened at intervals by the orange glow. T[he] walls felt close when combined with the low drop ceili[ng] and I fought back a thin wave of claustrophobia.

We continued down a cracked asphalt tile floor and ca[me] to a halt before a uniformed officer stationed at a large me[tal] desk. Chips and gouges in the grey painted piece [of] furniture testified to its age and use. A green desk blotte[r,] telephone, and a sign-in sheet adorned its sparse surfac[e. I] couldn't help but be somewhat amused by the fact that [the] pen accompanying the sheet was chained to the desk[. A] dilapidated drip coffeemaker, stained from years of u[se,] sizzled and popped in the corner behind the duty officer-[a] careless spill being turned into yet another crusty residue [on] its heating plate.

Ben and Deckert surrendered their sidearms to [the] uniformed man, and he locked them away in the d[esk] drawer. With a wordless grunt, he indicated the sign[-in] sheet, and the three of us added our names to it. With [that] task completed, the voiceless guard led us farther down [the] corridor and unlocked the door to the first interview ro[om.] We stepped in—Ben, Deckert, and finally me. The weig[hty] door swung shut behind us, and the lock dropped back i[n] place with an audible metallic clunk that echoed from [the] bare cement walls. A plain wooden table with two cha[irs] much like one would find in a small kitchen, was positioned near the center of the room. A bedraggled, unshaven R.J. filled one of the chairs. He looked up with a nervous start as we entered. For the second time in less than three days, R.J. was in the custody of the police. His at once depressed and fearful expression showed that he was still no more practiced at it than he had been the first time.

"I wasn't sure you'd come," he ventured, looking at me.

"Why not?" I asked, advancing past Ben and Deckert then pulling out the chair opposite him.

"Because of how I acted Saturday night." He looked at the floor then back at me as I took a seat. "I wasn't exactly Mister Congeniality... Then, when you shook my hand and I blocked you..."

"I would have done the same," I replied soothingly. "Hell, I had no business trying to feel you out like that. It was pretty rude."

"I can understand why you did it," he told me.

He seemed somewhat calmer than when we first entered, but he still looked around the room nervously, shifting back and forth from me to Ben and Deckert. He wrung his hands, and every now and again, his voice would quaver slightly. I could see, feel, hear and even smell the fear coming from him. The emotion that bothered me most though was the sensation of guilt.

"What's going on?" he finally asked me. "Why do they want to talk to me about Ariel and the other lady? Am I a suspect or something?"

By now, Ben and Detective Deckert had moved farther into the room. Ben was standing to my right, and Deckert had propped himself in a corner, behind and to the right of R.J.

"Are you sure you don't want an attorney?" Ben interjected.

"What do I need a lawyer for?" R.J. demanded fearfully

As he spoke, I felt a sharp, piercing pain in the pit of m stomach. Ben didn't reply. To an observer such as myself, was obvious that he was using R.J.'s own fear as levera against him. It was a wholly unpleasant and ugly side of m friend that I knew was a necessary evil for his line of wor It was a side, however, that I truly didn't wish to see.

"You knew Ariel Tanner pretty good, didn't you?" Be continued.

"Yeah," R.J. answered, "you know that."

"Uh-huh," Ben grunted. "How 'bout Karen Barnes? Y friends with her too?"

"I told you already," R.J.'s voice implored, "I nev heard of her until you asked me about her. Was she the la that was killed Saturday?"

A ripping sensation tore painfully through my low abdomen once again.

Ben still refused to answer him. "What were you doin' Ariel's flat Saturday morning?"

"What're they doing, Rowan?" R.J. begged. "They thi I killed her? They think I'm the killer?!"

His voice went up in pitch and grew wilder with eve word. He was stricken with absolute disbelief at what he f Ben was implying.

"Were you there to pick somethin' up, R.J.?" B continued. "Maybe something you forgot?"

"Like I said before," R.J. explained almost angrily, was there to water the plants."

"Saturday was a little soon, wasn't it? I mean, you sa she was s'posed ta' leave Friday night. You don't think s might have watered them before she left?"

"She asked me to keep an eye on her place!" R screamed, jumping up from the chair. "I didn't know needed your fucking permission!"

"Now, R.J.," Deckert's calm voice expressed feigned concern. "Take it easy. They're just questions." He had left his position in the corner and was now resting a comforting hand on R.J.'s shoulder. "Detective Storm just gets a little carried away sometimes."

Good cop, bad cop. I couldn't believe Ben and Deckert were playing that tired game. Anyone who had ever seen a cop show on television, good or bad, knew the routine. I could only assume that being in the hot seat made R.J. vulnerable enough to fall for it.

Pain shot through my stomach once again, more intense than before. Extreme enough to make me wince as it hit. I assumed I was simply feeling empathy for R.J., and I took a moment to focus my concentration on blocking the spasms as he slowly lowered himself back into his seat.

"You showed up late at our meeting Saturday night." Ben began hammering at him again. "Where were you?"

"My mom's cat got hit by a car," he explained. "I had to bury it for her and get cleaned up before I could come over."

Suddenly Dickens' and Salinger's reactions to him made sense. A cat's heightened sense of smell would have detected not only the scent of the other animal but any blood he might have gotten on himself, even if he washed. The cats HAD smelled death, just not the death of a human.

"I assume that can be verified," Ben retorted.

"You can ask my mom," R.J. shot back. "And you can dig up the cat if you don't believe her."

"We just might."

Ben scribbled purposefully in his notebook. The scratch of the pen against the paper was the only sound in the room, and it was earsplitting in the silence.

Ben interrupted the quiet. "You mind lettin' us in on why you were drivin' around shitfaced early this morning?"

"I dunno."

"Come on, man." Ben's voice took on an accusato edge. "You've gotta have a reason for getting' hammered a Sunday night."

"Sunday's just like a Saturday to me," R.J. rebutte maintaining a modicum of nerve. "Sunday and Monday a my days off."

"Good for you." Ben's words were sheathed in sarcas "That still doesn't tell me why you blew close to the leg limit and had an open beer in your hand when you we stopped."

"I had a fight with my girlfriend," R.J. returned. "I gue I just lost it for a little while."

"What time would that have been?"

"I dunno. Around five I guess."

"What's your girlfriend's name?"

"I wanna leave her out of it."

"C'mon, R.J.," Deckert's soothing voice issued fro behind him once again. "I'm sure she'd be happy to he you out. We can't verify your story unless you give us l name."

The discomfort struck my abdomen again, penetrati the mental defenses I had erected to stop it. A du throbbing ache followed and refused my attempts to ev it—so much for mind over matter.

R.J. remained steadfastly silent, displaying a harden resolve. Even I was curious as to why he was so adam about concealing the identity of his girlfriend.

Deckert spoke again. "Don't you think she's probal worried about you? You never know, she might have call to try and make up."

"Why're you guys so worried about who my girlfrie is?" R.J. spat. "What's she got to do with anything?"

"Why are you tryin' so hard to keep her a secret?" B retorted. "I would think you'd be happy to have an alibi."

"An alibi for what?" R.J.'s confused voice squeaked slightly. "We had the fight yesterday."

"Exactly."

"Whaddaya mean, 'exactly'?"

"Another young lady was murdered last night," Deckert filled in the blank.

"I'm gonna tell ya' a story, R.J." Ben pressed on, slowly pacing three steps past him and three steps back. "It's a story about a sick asshole that likes to torture young women and kill them. Ya' see, this psycho thinks he has a purpose for doin' this, but it's all just somethin' he dreamed up in his twisted little mind." He punctuated his statement by pausing and poking his index finger at R.J.'s forehead. "So, every time he kills one of these young ladies, he feels really bad..."

Ben was obviously telling his tale in order to force him to crack. I knew that it wouldn't be long before he started plugging R.J.'s name into the story here and there to turn the screws.

"So when Mister Sicko feels bad, he hides behind a little religious ritual he learned," Ben continued, "and whaddaya know, BAM! He forgives himself, and everything's okay again. You know that little ritual, don't you, R.J.?"

"I didn't kill anyone" was his measured reply.

"Now, it all starts out when our asshole gets himself a crush on a young lady who, shall we say, attends the same church. Let's call this young lady, Ariel, just for the sake of argument. Now, Ariel doesn't like Mister Asshole the same way he likes her, you see... Just a second... You had a crush on a young lady named Ariel, didn't you? What a coincidence."

"I didn't kill Ariel," R.J. insisted, raising his voice. "How many times do I have to tell you, I didn't kill anyone?"

Ben paused and engaged himself in a tremulous staring

contest with R.J. When the young man finally shifted
gaze downward, Ben looked quietly from Deckert's face
mine. I managed to find a small bit of solace in the fact t
my friend's expression showed me without a doubt that
wasn't enjoying what he was doing to the young man.

"Let's skip the rest of the story," Ben finally said. "H
about if we get back to a few questions." He pulled out
small notebook again and began leafing through
eventually stopping at a page and tucking the others ba
"So, are you familiar with a Miz Ellen Gray?"

R. J. bolted upward from the chair, his red-rimmed e
widened and wild. I could physically see his muscles te
throughout his body as he fought to bring himself un
control.

"Why are you asking about her?" he demanded. "W
happened?"

Deckert rested his hands on R.J.'s shoulders once ag
and gently but firmly guided him to his seat.

"Tell me!" he appealed.

"She was the girlfriend you were trying to protect, wa
she?" I broke my self-imposed silence, as the reason for
feelings of guilt became instantly clear. "You two w
having an affair, weren't you?"

He never answered me. I could feel his anguish
confusion as he silently held his head in his hands. I
wasn't obvious to Ben and Deckert, it was at the very le
obvious to me. R.J. was not the killer. Of this, I
completely sure.

"She's dead, isn't she?" R.J. finally asked, lifting
head slowly. I didn't have the heart to tell him that E
Gray had been the third victim, but the tone of his voice
me that he had already figured that out. I could only l
away as he stared sullenly into space.

"Now I want a lawyer," he stated flatly.

The solemn atmosphere of the room was disturbed suddenly as a key audibly turned in a lock, and the heavy steel door was pushed open, revealing the hardened face of the guard.

"Detective Storm," he stated with businesslike brevity. "Phone call."

Ben excused himself and left the room. Detective Deckert and I remained behind, locked in with a stubbornly silent R.J. His gaze remained fixed upon an invisible spot on the wall behind me. Deckert and I simply stared at one another.

Only a few brief moments passed before Ben returned to the interview room. His jaw was set grimly, and his eyes held more than just slight concern.

"Carl," he addressed Deckert. "Can you see that our friend here gets his phone call? I've got somethin' ta' take care of."

"Sure," Deckert replied coming instantly more alert. "Is everything okay?"

"I'll let ya' know," Ben told him, then turned his attention to me. "C'mon, Rowan, I need you ta' come with me."

I was perplexed at first, then morbidly hopeful as the thought that another murder might have occurred crossed my mind. I disdained the concept of such a thing happening, but it would go a long way in clearing R.J. of the crimes.

"What's up," I asked as Ben and I hurried up the hallway. "Has there been another murder?"

"No," he replied as he signed us out and slipped his weapon back into its holster. "Not another murder."

"Then what?" I pressed. "What was that call about?"

"Let's just get goin'," he ordered, grabbing my shoulder and nudging me forward.

"What the hell?!" I exclaimed. "What's going on Ben?"

He let out a heavy breath, and his hand shot up to smooth his hair back and then came to rest massaging his neck.

"That call was Allison," he finally said.

"Yeah," I urged, instantly feeling concern for him and his family. "Is everything okay? Is the little guy all right?"

"They're fine," he answered without concern. "They're just fine."

"Then what's going on?" I demanded.

"Allison's on duty today," he finally told me. "She called because an ambulance just brought Felicity in to the E.R. at her hospital."

CHAPTER 14

I never knew that Ben had an actual siren in his van, that is, until now. He had wasted no time, quickly attaching his red magnetic bubble light to the roof of the vehicle and plugging it into the cigarette lighter as we flew from the parking lot. Soon, we were careening down the highway, siren screaming from behind the grill. Ben pushed the van to its limit, as if the sooner we arrived at the hospital, the quicker we could make everything better. As if simply by being there, we could magically prevent whatever had happened, even after the fact.

"What did Allison say?" I appealed still struggling with my safety belt.

"Just that an ambulance came in, and Felicity was in it," he answered, still keeping his attention on the road.

"Did she have any idea what was wrong with her?" The metal finger on the seatbelt finally slipped in with a satisfying click.

"No," he replied as he hooked the van around the slower traffic. "You sons-of-bitches! Can't you hear the siren!" he screamed at the other drivers and then turned back to me. "No, she didn't. She said she was conscious when they brought her in though."

The pains in my stomach were growing more intense with each passing moment. I began to realize that it wasn't R.J. that I was feeling empathy for. It was my wife.

"She was fine when I left her," I volunteered. "Just a little morning sickness. Hell, I've only been gone for a couple of hours. What could have happened?"

"I dunno," Ben offered, "but like I said, Allison told me she was awake when they brought her in, so that's a good sign at least."

"It has to be something to do with the baby," I asserted

"You don't know that. I'm sure everything's fine."

"No. It's not." I held fast as another burst of pain sh
through my abdomen. "I've been having pains in
stomach for about an hour now."

"So?"

"So, it's called empathy," I told him. "At first I though
was getting it from R.J. because he was nervous and all th
but now I know better. I'm feeling Felicity's pain."

"Like some kinda psychic thing or somethin'?" Ben h
asked, half remarked. "Jeezus, you guys are unbelievable.

The siren continued warbling loudly as he quick
cranked the steering wheel to the right, sending us into
cloverleaf from Interstate 64 to exit onto Kingshighway. T
hospital was within sight now, only the sluggish traf
barring our way. Ben drove the van halfway up onto
inside shoulder in order to skirt around the cars that we
slowly moving out of our way, and the engine groaned
protest at the abuse it was taking. The vehicle buffe
wildly and rocked on worn suspension when the tires fina
leapt from the curb and once again contacted le
pavement. Moments later, we broke through the lethar
traffic, and Ben propelled us forward without heed to
signal lights and signs.

We quickly traveled the two short blocks runni
alongside the hospital, whereupon we hooked right, slidi
at first then accelerating out of the turn. At the end of
short sprint, Ben jammed on the brakes, forcing the Che
to screech to a halt before the entrance to the emerger
room.

"Go. GO!" he urged as I wrestled my way out of
seatbelt and flung my door open.

I jumped from the van and ran the short distance to

entrance. The automatic doors instantly began to open, though not fast enough in my mind, so I turned sideways, forcing my way through as the gap widened. The cold, conditioned air, reeking of antiseptic, slapped me hard in the face as I pushed my way through a second set of doors and stumbled to a stop at the admitting desk.

"O'Brien," I insisted. "Felicity O'Brien. Where is she?"

A blank-faced nurse quietly stared back at me and seated herself at a computer terminal behind the desk. Reaching up, she slid a clipboard and pen toward me.

"Fill this out and return it to the desk," she stated mechanically and without emotion.

"Dammit, I don't need treatment!" I pushed the clipboard hard across the counter, and it slid off onto the floor with a raucous clatter. "I'm looking for my wife, Felicity O'Brien. She was brought in here a little while ago!"

By now, Ben had joined me, leaving the haphazardly parked van where it was, red light still flickering wildly. He had at least taken the time to turn off the clamoring siren.

"And your name is?" the nurse questioned like an automaton.

"Rowan. Rowan Gant," I returned impatiently.

"Relation?"

"I told you already!" I shouted. "She's my wife!"

"Ben, Rowan!" The exclamation came from our immediate right.

We both turned quickly to face the direction from which the voice had issued and were presented with the somber face of Allison Storm, Ben's wife. Her white uniform was obviously rumpled more than usual. A long strand of her fine brown hair hung wildly across her face, and she gently brushed it away with the back of her hand.

"Where's Felicity?" I asked roughly. "What happened?"

"Calm down, Rowan," she told me. "She's okay. She's

going to be fine."

"The baby?"

She just looked down at the floor then back at me. "I'm sorry."

"What happened?" I appealed, fighting back the emotion that was continuing to well inside me.

"Why don't you come with me," Allison soothed. "I'm on a break right now. We'll go see Felicity, and we can talk."

I desperately wanted to know what had happened to my wife, but at the same time I knew Allison was right, I needed to calm down. I knew she wouldn't give me the run around, so I simply nodded and forced myself to remain quiet. Ben and I followed her down the long hallway, twisting and turning until we reached a bank of elevators. The three of us waited in silence and once the polished metal doors slid open, stepped inside and rode upward. I was too preoccupied with my concern for Felicity to even notice which floor we finally arrived at. A few short stretches of corridor mixed with a couple of quick turns, and we entered a private room.

The first thing to catch my eye was my petite wife, innocent and childlike as she peacefully slept in the hospital bed. An IV bag hung from a stand nearby with the long plastic tube leading from its base to the back of her hand where it was neatly and firmly taped in place. I quietly made my way farther into the room to the side of the bed and gently caressed her cheek.

"She's sedated," Allison volunteered. "She needs to rest for a while."

"I won't wake her," I whispered and then turned to face Allison. "Now, can somebody please tell me what happened?"

"It's my fault," a slightly familiar voice quietly admitted

from behind me. "I'm sorry, Mister Gant."

I turned to see the owner of the voice, and my eyes fell on Cally's face. She had been seated in the corner of the room the entire time, unnoticed, and now stood, uncertainly staring at me. Her face wore the expression of a school child that had just disappointed a respected teacher.

"What do you mean it's your fault, Cally?" I asked, turning fully to face her.

"I couldn't reach Detective Storm." She began gushing, tears welling in her eyes and rolling across her flushed cheeks. "They said he was in a meeting and couldn't be disturbed. I tried calling you, but Felicity said you were with the detective, so I told her and she came over. I never should have called."

She was crying harder now, burying her face in her hands, shoulders beginning to heave.

"Told her what?" I prodded anxiously. "Come over where?"

"To my house," she whimpered. "I told her Devon was on his way over and that I couldn't reach Detective Storm, so she came over to my house."

Ben, ever the cop, immediately pulled out his notebook and flipped to a fresh page in preparation for taking notes. I strode the few steps between Cally and myself and then took her gently by the shoulders.

"Easy Cally, calm down." I slowly guided her back into the chair then retrieved a small packet of tissues from the table and knelt beside her. "Now, take a deep breath, ground and center. I know you can do it."

A hot, tingling sensation washed over me, and I instantly realized that I needed to heed my own advice. I placed my hand on hers and continued to soothe her with calm encouragement, easing her—and myself—into a relaxed breath. When her shuddering stopped, and she dabbed the last of the tears away with a tissue, I continued. "Now, tell me what happened."

"Like I said," she outlined, watching my face studiously, "I couldn't reach Detective Storm, so I tried to call you. I wanted to tell someone that Devon called me and said he was on his way over. He knew the police were looking for him because of his neighbor or something. Felicity said you were with Detective Storm, so I told her about it. She took down my address and told me to just stay put. She said she would be over in a few minutes and not to worry about anything."

Ben was scribbling rapidly when I looked over at him. Allison, having already heard the story, was dutifully tending to Felicity, checking her IV and pulse.

"Go on," I urged.

"Well, Devon got there before Felicity did," Cally continued. "He was acting pretty wired, like he was scared and all. He kept asking me if the police had talked to me."

"What did you tell 'im?" Ben questioned.

"I told him no," she turned her face to him, "but I don't think he believed me. He kept asking if I was lying." She turned back to me. "Anyway, when Felicity got there, she rang the doorbell, and Devon went crazy."

"How do you mean?" I demanded. "What did he do?"

"Just spastic, you know," she went on. "He accused me of calling the cops and started yelling a lot. He wouldn't let me answer the door."

Ben's voice came from behind me. "Did he attack you?"

"No," Cally told him. "Not really. He just stayed between me and the door and kept yelling about the cops and the ASPCA, and all."

"So, I'm still not clear on what happened to Felicity," I expressed, biting back my growing impatience.

"I guess she could hear Devon yelling and got worried or

something," she ventured, "because all of a sudden she came through the door. I guess it was unlocked, and she just decided to try and help me, you know. Devon thought she was a cop, and I guess he was trying to get away because he just took off for the door. He ran right into her and slammed her into the wall real hard." She started slowly weeping again, sniffling as she spoke, "It's my fault. If I hadn't called her, this never would have happened."

"No, Cally." I forced my voice to remain calm. "It wasn't your fault. You did the right thing by calling."

Ben's practiced voice came again. "Did anyone else show up? Any cops?"

"Yes," she answered. "They chased after Devon. I don't know why they came. I guess Felicity called them."

By now she had returned to fully involved sobbing, and no amount of reassurance from me was going to convince her that she was not to blame. I glanced back at Allison and motioned for her to trade places with me, which she did assiduously. This done, Ben and I quietly retreated from the room.

"I thought Felicity knew we had the place covered," Ben stated low-voiced once we were in the hall. "Why the hell did she go over there?"

"I don't know," I puzzled. "Maybe she forgot? Maybe she just wanted to help Cally. Only she can answer that. Do you think they caught the bastard?"

"I'll call in and find out," he replied. "He couldn't get far if he was on foot. Whaddaya make of that bit about the ASPCA?"

"Yeah, I noticed that. The ASPCA," I echoed, "like maybe he thought the police were after him because of the whole incident with sacrificing the dog."

"My thoughts exactly."

"If he committed the murders, it seems like that would be

the furthest thing from his mind," I ventured.

"Yeah, I think you're right," Ben agreed. "We'll still t
to him though."

"You still think R.J. did it, don't you?"

"I think I've got a lot of evidence that points straigh
'im. A lot of it is circumstantial I admit, but there's
fingerprint on the candle, the blood type, and the hairs. D
test'll show for sure if he was with Ellen Gray."

"But that's just on the latest victim, and we know he v
having an affair with her," I maintained.

"He never admitted to that."

"Come on, Ben. You saw how he acted when
mentioned her name," I pointed out.

"What I saw him do was clam up and ask for a lawyer

"I would have too," I contended. "Besides, you still c
connect him with Karen Barnes."

"I can connect him with Ariel Tanner," he shot b
angrily. "Shit, we're obviously dealin' with a psycho, ma
the kid's got a fuckin' split personality or somethin'!"

I stared back silently, stunned by his sudden outbur
knew this case was wearing on him, but something else v
there too. His hand went up to his neck, and he let o
heavy sigh.

"Listen," Ben's voice was much calmer. "I'm sorry, m
I shouldn't be snappin' at ya'. It's just that..."

Ben was unceremoniously interrupted by the shrill t
of his beeper as it demanded his attention. He automatic
pulled it from his belt and quickly perused its liquid cry
face.

"It's a call from the coppers I had sittin' on Cal
house," he told me. "I'd better get in touch with 'em."

"Go ahead," I urged. "I'll be with Felicity."

"Look, Rowan..." Ben struggled with the words as
wagged his finger back and forth between us. "Are you

me okay?"

"Yeah," I reassured him. "We're fine. Go make your call."

Allison had managed to calm Cally down once again and had taken her to get a cup of coffee in the hospital cafeteria while I quietly watched over my sleeping wife. I was positioned in a chair that I had pulled next to the bed, and my almost unblinking eyes stayed focused on her serene face. The seconds ticked by on the wall clock, folding themselves into minutes, which in turn, folded themselves into a quarter-hour and eventually, a half-hour. I don't know if the sedative simply began to wear off or if my intense stare acted as an ethereal catalyst, but Felicity's eyes finally began to flutter open. Gently she returned to the realm of the conscious.

"How're you feeling?" I whispered as I leaned forward and brushed the hair from her face.

"Aye, tired," she murmured, "and sore."

I returned a half-hearted smile. "I'll bet."

"Rowan…Has anyone told you…About, you know…"

"Yeah, I know about it. Allison told me. I'm sorry."

A small teardrop glistened in the corner of her eye and slowly rolled across her cheek to wet the pillow.

"I'm the one who should apologize, then," she returned. "I never should have gone over there. Cally just sounded so frightened…"

"Shhhh." I brushed away the next tear as it began to journey down her face. "It's all right. You did exactly what I would have done. It's okay."

She blinked rapidly then took in a deep breath and let it

out slowly. She lay there in silence, just looking back at me for a few short moments as she regained her composure.

"Is Cally okay, then?" she finally asked.

"Physically, she's fine. He never laid a hand on her," I answered. "Mentally. About as well as can be expected. She blames herself for what happened to you. Allison took her down for coffee a little while ago."

"It wasn't her fault."

"I know," I assured her. "I know."

"Aye, what about Devon? Did they catch him?"

"Ben went to check on that. The officers that were watching Cally's place just beeped him."

Watching her face, I could see that the tranquilizer had not worn off and was creeping up on her once again. Her breathing became easier, and she began sliding backward into relaxation.

"I've got a shoot to do this afternoon," Felicity told me groggily.

"No you don't. I'll call them and re-schedule for you."

"Are you sure?"

"Yes, I'm sure."

"I love you" was the last thing she whispered before drifting into the arms of sleep.

"I love you, too," I returned and kissed her lightly on the forehead.

I waited a few more minutes before deciding to go in search of Ben. I attempted to retrace our steps in coming to this room and as I had not paid attention, quickly became lost. As I rounded a corner, I came upon what resembled a small break room and was almost immediately bowled over as a red-faced Allison Storm rushed angrily past me. I looked after her then peered into the open doorway, only to find Ben, hands in his pockets and hangdog expression creasing his face. Something was definitely wrong between the two of them. I assumed it was the amount of time he was spending on this case and that I had just witnessed the tail end of an argument it had caused.

"You okay?" I queried as I stepped through the doorway.

"What? Yeah." He looked up and noticed me. "Yeah, I'm fine. How's the squaw?"

"She woke up for a minute or two," I replied. "She's doing okay, considering. Oh, and I guessed right. She went over there because she wanted to help Cally."

"Sounds like her."

"You sure you're okay?" I asked again and hooked my thumb over my shoulder. "You seem a little preoccupied, and Allison looked kind of irritated..."

"Yeah, I'm good." He pulled his hands from his pockets and straightened from where he had been leaning against the wall. "She's okay. It's just been a rough day for 'er. Hell, for all of us."

I decided not to push any further out of respect for my friend. If he and his wife were having problems, it was none of my business unless he chose to tell me. If he made that choice, I would be there to listen, no questions asked.

"So," I changed the subject, "that phone call get you anywhere? Did you find anything out?"

"Oh yeah." He brightened noticeably. "They were in the lobby. Seems the son-of-a-bitch is in surgery right this minute, in this very hospital."

"Surgery?" I puzzled. "What happened, did they shoot him?"

"Nope." Ben explained, "Seems the idiot went over a fence when they were chasin' 'im and landed smack in the middle of a dog pen. Apparently, the pit bull livin' in it at the time was not pleased."

"How bad?" I grimaced.

"Sounds REAL bad," he answered. "It took 'em awhile

ta' get the dog off 'im. Unfortunately, they ended up havin' ta' drop the hammer on it."

"Is he going to live?"

"Don't know. Benson—that's the copper that I talked to—told me the doc said he'd lost a lot of blood. It's pretty much touch and go right now."

"The threefold return," I muttered under my breath.

"What was that?" Ben asked.

"The threefold return," I pronounced more clearly. "It's a belief we Witches have, that everything we do will return to us threefold. Good or Bad."

"Yeah. What goes around comes around. You've said that before. So?"

"So Devon sacrificed a dog," I explained.

Ben looked at me, and his eyes widened as the irony behind what I had just said sunk in. When he finally opened his mouth, all he could say was "Oh."

CHAPTER 15

While Felicity slept, Ben and I executed a roughly choreographed shuffle of vehicles: first, driving my wife's Jeep from Cally's house back to where it belonged then retrieving my truck from behind the police station. He remained silent and distant as we drove about, completing the tasks, keeping his eyes glued to the road before him and saying only as much as necessary. I didn't like seeing him like this, but I knew I could only wait until he was ready to talk, for anything else would only drive him further into his world of introspection. I mutely reassured myself that everything would work out between Ben and Allison and that all would return to normalcy soon. Besides, I had my own pain to contend with.

"So, what's the plan?" I asked him.

We were standing next to my vehicle on the parking lot of the police station. It was still early afternoon, and the bright sun had only recently begun the downward portion of its arc through the sky. A light breeze blew in, tousling Ben's already disheveled hair as he looked back at me wearily.

"I'll see if the search warrant has been issued for R.J.'s place," he sighed. "And we'll be waitin' to hear from the hospital about Devon. Other than that, it's business as usual."

"I know we've been down this road before, Ben," I ventured, "but I really believe R.J. is innocent. You aren't going to find anything at his place."

"For his sake, I hope you're right," he acknowledged. "But, I still have a job to do, and I wouldn't be much of a cop if I didn't follow all the leads. Look, Row, I'd like ta' agree with you, but even you hafta admit the fingerprint on the bottom of that candle is pretty incriminatin'."

"Yeah. It is," I agreed, "but I'm sure there's an explanation for it."

"Lemme know if ya' think of a reasonable one," Ben returned.

We stood a little longer, silently staring at one another. Tension still radiated from my friend, and I felt there was something he wished to say but couldn't find the words. The sounds of sirens being tested filled the wordless void around us as shifts changed and squad cars entered and left the lot.

Finally, I broke the speechless interlude. "So, you'll call me if anything turns up?"

"Yeah, I'll let ya' know," he told me with a nod then added, "Give Felicity my best and... Tell 'er... Tell 'er I'm sorry."

"I'll do that."

Ben had already disappeared into the door of the police station by the time I backed out of my parking space and shifted into forward motion. I reached over and turned up the radio as I pulled out of the lot. I hung a quick right and melded with the traffic then pointed myself in the direction of home. Before returning to the hospital, I still needed to call Felicity's client to re-schedule as well as put together an overnight bag for her, just in case.

The last few nondescript chords of a song I didn't recognize filtered to my ears, and a DJ's voice blended in behind them. Before she had a chance to tell me the name of the song I had just ignored, I punched a preset and switched to the local *National Public Radio* affiliate. I was looking for something other than the events of this day to occupy my mind—even if only for a few moments.

The afternoon faded slowly into evening, and the end of visiting hours approached at an ever-quickening pace. Once Felicity had returned to wakefulness, I spent the evening filling her in on the events that had occurred with R.J. This did little to improve her demeanor, so I elected to leave out the incident with Ben and Allison for the time being. As if my news weren't enough, the doctor assigned to her case chose to keep her overnight for observation despite her vehement and very animated protestations. The rest of my evening was spent listening to her grumble.

When the nurse finally decided to eject me from the room, I kissed my still fuming wife goodbye and promised to return bright and early the next morning.

I arrived home to a sedate household—the dogs moping about listlessly, and the wide-eyed cats lined up along the windowsill, ears twisting like radar dishes searching for even the most remote sign of Felicity. Anyone who tells you that animals don't sense when something is wrong, or that they can't show concern, has definitely never owned a pet.

I tended to their various needs of being let out and in, food, water, and generous amounts of attention before locking up for the night. The house felt empty and hollow without Felicity. We had been separated before but never under circumstances such as these. Never, at a time when among my greatest fears was that of going to sleep—going to sleep and facing another nightmare.

I put on a pot of coffee and stubbornly decided that I would wait out the night. I would read, play solitaire, watch old movies, but under no circumstances would I allow myself to re-live Ariel's death in my dreams. Of course, everyone knows about the best-laid plans of mice and men.

My first mistake was choosing to sit on the couch while waiting for the coffee to finish brewing. My second mistake was allowing my eyelids to close as exhaustion crept up on me.

Darkness.

Darkness without shape or form.

Cold, bone chilling darkness from the heart of nowhere.

I was floating.

I was falling.

I was screaming.

"Rowan." Ariel, once again in a white lace gown, smiled brightly at me. "Have a seat. It's been so long since I've read for you."

I was sitting. It was sudden. The movement disjointed. I didn't recall moving to the chair.

I was sitting.

Ariel smiled at me across the table. A table that until moments before had never existed. Her face was vibrant, her eyes bright and alive. Her strawberry-blonde hair lofted gently on a cool breeze. In her dainty hands, she held an oversized deck of cards. A deck of tarot cards. I watched as she shuffled them quickly. Or did she? Her hands never moved.

"This represents him," she said aloud, looking down at the center of the table.

The Knight of Cups.

"No, Ariel. The Knight of Cups is not my significator," I *try to tell her. "It doesn't represent me."*

My words fall soundlessly to the floor like a grotesque parody of a children's cartoon.

"This covers him." She continues to look only at the table.

The Devil.

She's not reading for me.

She's reading for the killer.

"This crosses him," she continues.

The Tower.

I watch the cards intently.

"Rowan, how nice to see you," a lilting voice comes from behind me.

I turn.

Ariel is smiling at me. A dark shape, hooded and malevolent, moves behind her. I want to warn her, but I know that I can't.

Crimson spreads across the white lace.

"Why, Rowan? Why?" her gurgling voice calls to me.

Darkness.

Dull black void.

"Hey, Mister," a tiny voice asserts itself.

I turn and look down.

A young girl. Silky, strawberry-blonde hair tied back with white bows. A white lace dress encases her. She looks up at me with large, sad eyes. A familiar deck of cards is clutched tightly in her tiny hand. She holds it out, offering them to me. I take the cards.

"Why don't you stop the bad man?" the child asks.

Before I can reply, she is gone.

I spin about in search of her and find only darkness. I look back to the deck of tarot cards in my hand. They seem so tiny. I turn over the top card.

The Seven of Pentacles.

Pain rips through my back and into my chest. Out reflex I look down. The gilt end of a beveled blade protruding from my chest.

Blood.

Scarlet, thick blood runs down my shirt.

"All...Is...Forgiven." A dark voice laughs from behind me. The knife juts farther from my solar plexus.

I look down at the tarot cards in my hand. Slowly the spill into space, fluttering then fading away. I fight to focus on them as they quickly flash their faces to me before the disappear.

They are all the same card.

They are all the Seven of Pentacles.

Darkness.

An endless tortured scream.

I awoke to the sound of my own voice. Maybe *voice* isn the right word as it was more the sound of my own bloodcurdling and tortured scream. The dogs were alert stationed before me, growling and barking as if an intrude had burst into the house, invading their territory. The ca were nowhere to be seen, and I can't say that I blamed then

Once again, I was bathed in a cold sweat, breathin heavily as though I had just finished running a marathon This was becoming ridiculous. I had only managed on decent night's sleep out of the past four, and it wa beginning to take its toll. This time the nightmare had take on even more intensity. It was obvious that Ariel was tryin to tell me something; I was certain of it. Doubtless, she ha been trying to do the same in the last dream as well.

After calming the dogs, I immediately retrieved my Boo of Shadows and recorded the still vivid details of this late nightmare. By the time I finished, fatigue once agai overtook me, knocking the second wind from my sails and leading me into a restless sleep.

The next morning, Felicity was dressed and waiting for me when I arrived at the hospital. Her doctor had released her earlier, and she was more than ready to remove herself from the premises. She had been fortunate in some respects as her injuries could have been far worse. Other than the miscarriage, she sustained only two cracked ribs and some minor bruises.

My fiery-tressed wife demonstrated her stubbornness and resolve in her refusal to be pushed out of the hospital in a wheelchair, though she did allow me to carry her overnight bag for her. I left Felicity sitting on a bench at the main entrance while I rode up in the elevator and then brought my truck down through the spiraling corkscrew of the parking garage. Moments after I left her, I exited the concrete structure, quickly zipped around the block, and brought the truck to a halt directly in front of the bench.

"I should have known you would be ready to leave," I told her after I turned onto the street.

"I hate hospitals," she answered. "You know that."

"Well, you must have at least gotten some rest."

"What makes you say that?"

"No heavy accent this morning."

"I don't have an accent."

"Exactly."

"Oh, leave me alone," she returned with a slightly annoyed tone then returned to the original subject. "I didn't need to stay overnight. I feel fine."

I pushed the truck forward and turned left onto

Kingshighway. "I'm glad you feel fine, but what did the doctor say?"

"He said I was okay," she acknowledged. "I just need to take an iron supplement for a while."

"What about the ribs?"

"He told me they'd be sore for a week or so," she went on. "But they'll heal up okay."

I veered right toward the on-ramp and sped up, merging with the highway traffic. We rode along in silence for a few moments, Felicity staring out the side window.

"How are you with the whole miscarriage thing," I gently queried. "I mean mentally."

"I honestly don't know," she replied, her voice flat. "I'm kind of in shock I guess. I'm not sure if it's really sunk in yet." She let out a long sigh and continued staring out the window. A few moments passed, and she turned to me once again. "I don't know that I really felt all that pregnant."

"What do you mean?"

"Well, I mean, I know I had the morning sickness and all…" She fumbled as she searched for the words to explain her feelings. "But that was only once. I don't think I was pregnant long enough for it to really sink in. I don't know. I hope I don't sound callous. I'm sure I'm not making any sense to you."

"You don't sound callous," I reassured her. "And I think I understand."

"I'm depressed about it," she announced after another long pause. "I just don't think I'm going to go off the deep end or anything. What about you? How do you feel about all of this?"

"I'm disappointed," I told her, "and a bit depressed. Mainly, I'm pissed at Devon."

"Did you ever hear how his surgery went?"

I changed lanes then glanced over at her. "Haven't heard

a thing."

"Have you talked to Ben?"

"Not since he dropped me off at my truck yesterday afternoon," I outlined. "Something's going on with him and Allison. He was real quiet."

"Like what?"

I explained the incident I had only partially witnessed as well as Ben's abnormally introspective demeanor that followed. Felicity agreed with my theory that Ben's dedication to his job, combined with the extra hours he had been working, might be putting a strain on his relationship with Allison. Since she knew Ben as well as I did, she also agreed that we would have to wait for him to come to us.

We exited the highway and continued up the tree-lined streets toward our home.

"They're going to charge R.J. with the murders," Felicity finally announced in a depressed tone.

"We don't know that," I responded. "Like I told you last night, a lot depends on what they find in his apartment."

"No. I can feel it," she insisted. "They're going to charge him, and he's not the one."

"I know," I told her. "But the police can't make their decisions based on the ethereal feelings and gut reactions of a couple of *Witches*."

"Then we need to find something that they CAN base their decisions on."

I looked over at her. She wore a determined expression combined with a creased brow, which told me the wheels were already turning beneath her auburn mane. I had kept the second nightmare a secret from her, as I didn't want her to worry. Now that the third one had forced its way into my life, I suspected it might be time to fill her in. I thought maybe, if we worked on it together, we could decipher the clues I felt Ariel was attempting to give me.

"So, I think I could use your help with..." I looked bac
to the road as I turned down our street and quickly change
my train of thought. "What the hell?!"

The street in front of our home had become a sma
circus of news vans and media personalities. Ta
telescoping booms extended from the vehicles, pushing di:
antennas skyward in competition for the best angle ar
location. Camera-toting video technicians, burdened wi'
battery belts and miles of cable, lounged against the vans
a state of detached boredom while nearly half a dozen on-a
talents milled about expectantly.

"We really don't need this," I expressed my thoug
aloud as we approached.

"Tell me about it," Felicity agreed. "You think they'll g
away if we just ignore them?"

"I doubt it," I mused sardonically. "They're televisi
reporters. They don't pick up on things as fast as yo
average household pets do."

Intent on not being driven from my home by tl
tenacious reporters, I swung the truck into our driveway a
sped past them around to our garage in back of the hous
They sprang immediately into frenetic activity, adjusti
neckties or primping coiffed hair, as they motioned testi
for their apathetic cameramen to follow them.

"So what do we do now?" Felicity asked as the gara
door automatically slid shut behind us. "We can't sit in he
forever."

"No, we can't," I agreed. "Why don't you go in and c
Ben. Let him know what's going on. While you're doi
that, I'll go out front and ask them to leave."

"Ask them to leave?" she echoed. "You don't really thi
that's going to do any good do you?"

"Of course not, but it can't hurt."

She answered me with a familiar roll of her eyes bef

opening her door and stepping out of the cab. "Whatever."

The throng of TV journalists was shuffling about in my driveway like a directionless herd of cattle. Some of them focused their attention on the front of the house while others craned their necks in an attempt to see where Felicity and I might have disappeared. When I rounded the corner however, the division of observation ended and all eyes, including cameras, were brought to bear on me.

"Mister Gant, can I ask you a few questions?"

"Dirk White, Channel Four News, Mister Gant, has there been any progress in the investigation?"

"Rumor has it that a suspect is in custody. Is that true, Mister Gant?"

"Mister Gant, Mister Gant. Brandee Street, Eyewitness News. Is it true that your wife was directly involved in the capture of a suspect?"

They shouted their questions, assaulting me from all sides as they attempted to make themselves heard over their rivals. I remained calm and continued to amble easily up the drive toward them, making it a point to be in no particular hurry. Inevitably, I reached the small crowd and came to a halt a few feet away.

Brandee Street burst forth, her honey-blonde mane moussed into immobility. "Mister Gant, sources close to the investigation say that your wife was injured while aiding in the apprehension of a suspect in the Satanic Serial Killer case. Would you like to comment?"

Ignoring the question, I held up my hands in a quieting gesture and waited for the huddled group to settle down. Much to my surprise, it didn't take long for them to comply. Apparently, they assumed I was about to make some type of statement as they all held their microphones forward and stared at me expectantly. What I did tell them, however, was not what they wanted to hear.

"I just came out here to let you know that you're wasting your time," I announced. "My wife and I have no intention of making any statements about the case or answering any questions. So, we would appreciate it greatly if you would please leave us alone."

Brandee Street was the first to ignore my speech. "Was that your wife with you in the truck, Mister Gant?"

"Was her injury serious?" another reporter interposed.

As I mutely waved off the questions, I noticed a dark grey station wagon as it slipped up next to the curb on the side street across from my house. The thought of another reporter joining the crowd that was currently assaulting me was less than pleasant.

"I told you we aren't going to answer any questions," I repeated. "Now can you please leave us alone?"

I cast a glance in the direction of the station wagon and noticed that the driver was still positioned behind the wheel. The sun visor blocked the upper half of his face, and his hand obscured the lower half, as he appeared to be speaking into what I assumed to be a hand-held tape recorder. I wondered to myself if Felicity had managed to contact Ben.

"Mister Gant, is there any truth to the rumor that there is a suspect in custody?" Another reporter, Dirk White, quickly rattled off the question then pushed his microphone at me.

"Are you people deaf?" I appealed. "How many times do I have to tell you we aren't going to answer any questions?"

I was only seconds away from throwing my hands up in utter exasperation and retreating to the interior of my home. Now, more than ever, I understood why Ben always referred to the media as vultures. Mere moments before I sought an escape, a patrol car from the Briarwood police department rolled to a halt on the opposite side of the street. The light bar adorning the top of the marked sedan flickered to life, and a thick, uniformed officer complete with mirrored aviators emerged, citation book in hand. With a sly grin, the cop nodded and gave me a silent wave. He opened his trunk and rummaged around for a moment, then finding what he was after, set about the task at hand. I almost couldn't contain my amusement when I noticed that he was adeptly attaching boots to the front tires of the news vans, rendering them immobile, presumably until a towing service arrived.

"Do your stations cover towing expenses?" I asked the swarm of reporters.

"Excuse me?" one of them returned.

"I was just curious," I continued. "Getting a vehicle out of the impound lot can be a little pricey, especially when you add in the towing costs."

One by one at first, then almost as a collective, realization set in, and they turned in their tracks. Various muttered expletives filtered to my ears, and I noticed that Brandee Street let out a small, angry shriek and stamped her foot as I had seen her do two nights before. I was momentarily forgotten as they all began to stride purposefully to their vans. A cameraman I recognized as Ed, the collector of Brandee's temper tantrums, hung back from the group. He grinned widely and flashed me a quick thumbs up.

"Good one" was all he said before sauntering off to join the rest.

I was certain that the officer had his hands full with the crowd of whining prima donnas and was hesitant to bother him, but I wanted to be sure he was aware of the grey station wagon parked at the corner. As I debated how to get this information to him, I looked over to see if the car was still there. I was greeted with the sight of the vehicle's occupant as he strolled across the street toward me, gingerly balancing a baking dish in his hands. Instead of another reporter as I had suspected, I was surprised and relieved to

see Detective Carl Deckert, grey hair flying on a lig
breeze.

"I thought you were another reporter when you pulled
over there," I admitted, motioning to the bickering throng
he trundled up my driveway.

"I'll bet," he responded. "Sorry I didn't get here soone

"No problem. Seemed pretty quick to me."

"How's Felicity doing?" he asked as he reached me.
heard what happened from Ben."

"Doctor gave her a clean bill of health. I'd expect sh
going to be a little sore though." I fell into stride with hi
and we continued up the flagstone walk. "Mentally,
seems okay. She's a pretty strong individual. I'm sure sh
be fine."

"Good. Good. Glad to hear it."

We climbed the stairs, and I opened the front door
him.

"Honey, where are you?" I called out as we entered
living room, and I shut the door. We were greeted only
the cool air and calm atmosphere. "We have a visitor."

"I'm in the kitchen. Who is it?" she called back. She
us halfway as we proceeded through the dining room in
direction. "Detective Deckert," she smiled, "this is
surprise."

"Carl, please. Just call me Carl." He offered the bak
dish to her. "I hope this doesn't seem silly, but I told
wife about what happened and all...Anyway, she m
lasagna and insisted I bring it over to you two."

"It's not silly at all." Felicity took the dish from him
motioned for us to follow her. "Come on in. Tell your v
thank you very much. It's very nice of her."

"No offense intended, Carl," I showed him farther
the kitchen and offered him a seat at our breakfast n
while Felicity stored the dish in the refrigerator, "but I

expecting Ben."

"None taken. He asked if I would handle it," he explained as he sat down, absently brushing his disheveled grey hairs back into place. "I wanted to come by and deliver the lasagna anyway."

Felicity was working at preparing a pitcher of herb tea, and I interposed myself between her and the cabinet as she strained to reach an upper shelf. "Why don't you sit down, and I'll finish this up."

"I'm fine," she objected.

"I'm sure you are," I rejoined. "But I've got this really intense desire to make tea, so why don't you let me do it?"

I'm sure she would have argued more had Detective Deckert not been there. Since he was, however, she quietly resigned herself to the fact that I was going to coddle her for a while and joined him at the table. I had scarcely managed to begin transferring the sun-brewed liquid into the ice-filled pitcher when our guest spoke up.

"This is probably none of my business," he blurted hesitantly. "But you two are pretty close with Ben and his wife, aren't you?"

"Definitely," I answered. "Ben was my Best Man. We've known the two of them forever."

"Why do you ask?" Felicity looked over at me as she spoke, then back to Detective Deckert. "Is something wrong?"

I continued what I was doing but kept my attention on the conversation.

"You could say that," he sighed. "Like I said, it's probably none of my business, but I couldn't help overhearing him on the phone last night... Then he asked me to come over here when you called a little while ago." He nodded his head at Felicity.

"I noticed that he was a little distant," she agreed. "What

did you overhear?"

"Well," he explained, "I only heard one side of t[...]
conversation, but I got the gist of it."

"He and Allison are having problems because of t[...]
hours he's been putting in, right?" I volunteered.

"They've got a problem all right," he told us. "But [...]
work schedule isn't it. Near as I can figure, Ben's w[...]
blames him for Felicity's miscarriage."

"She what?!" I exclaimed.

"Why would Allison do that?!" Felicity appealed.

"Hey," Deckert held up his hands defensively, "fr[...]
what I overheard, he agrees with her."

CHAPTER 16

"It's not his fault," Felicity voiced adamantly. "I'm the one that made the choice to walk through that door. He had nothing to do with it."

"You know that, and I know that," Deckert nodded, "but he still feels responsible. He seems to think that if he never got you two involved in this investigation, you never would have gotten hurt."

"That's just plain ridiculous," I stated. "All he did was ask me the difference between a Pentacle and a Pentagram because he'd seen this hanging around my neck." I hooked a finger beneath the silver chain and lifted the small pendant from behind my shirt. "Other than that, I volunteered. Hell, he was against the idea of me getting involved in the first place. I had to talk him into it."

Deckert shrugged and echoed my sentiments, "I know, I know, but he's your friend, and he feels responsible for you." He let out a long sigh. "Shit, it's part of being a cop. You feel responsible for everyone."

At that moment, Detective Carl Deckert looked far older than his years. It was clear that he and Benjamin Storm had been cut from the same cloth when it came to loyalty to their friends and loved ones—when it came to loyalty to their careers as well. In a way, I felt I was seeing my best friend's future being played out before me by the man seated at my kitchen table.

"We need to have a talk with those two," Felicity ventured. "We've got to get this straightened out."

I had finished preparing the mint tea and placed the full pitcher along with glasses on the table then slid in next to my wife. "Any ideas on how we should do that?"

"We need to speak to them when they're together, one," she posed.

"Sure, but that's going to be a little hard to accomp with this investigation going on. Ben's hours are a l unpredictable right now."

Detective Deckert cleared his throat, and we both tur our attention to him. "I doubt that'll be a problem. should be home at a decent hour tonight."

"Why's that?" I queried.

"That's another piece of news I need to give you." looked distantly out the window of the atrium then bacl us. The deep furrow in his brow revealed the fact that was struggling with exactly how to go about it.

"R.J. is being charged with the murders, isn't h Felicity intoned flatly.

"Not yet, but don't be surprised if it happens within next day or so," he echoed. "For the murder of Ellen Gra least. We got the warrant and searched his place early morning."

"What did you find?" I wasn't sure I wanted hin answer the question.

"Black and white candles. A lot of 'em," he detai "And a set of artists pastels among other things."

"There has to be some kind of logical explanation shook my head. "What about the dirk, Ariel's athamè. you find that?"

"The knife?" he echoed, shaking his head. "No. Not but we're still looking."

"You've got the wrong person, Carl," Felicity implo "I can't give you tangible proof, but I just know R.J. i guilty."

"I know you two think he's innocent, but so far, evidence points to the opposite. I think you might backing the wrong horse."

"The candles don't mean a thing," I declared. "If you searched our house, you'd find a ton of candles. Witches use them for everything, so we have a tendency to buy them in bulk."

"Especially if you find them on sale," Felicity added. "And as far as the pastels go, maybe he's an artist."

"Since you mention it," Deckert returned, "he did take a few art classes at the community college, and guess who his instructor was...one Karen Lewis, better known to us by her married name, Karen Barnes."

"He knows all three victims," I muttered to myself.

"Looks that way," he continued. "So if you add that in with the candles, the pastels, and his familiarity with your religion..."

Neither of us had a convincing argument to offer. We sat glumly, firm in our belief that the young man was innocent of the crimes but completely unable to prove it.

"Well, what did HE have to say?" Felicity almost demanded.

"We haven't talked to him about it yet."

"Well then, he might have a logical explanation for some of the things you found," I expressed. "You won't know until you ask."

"Look," Deckert intoned after a long pause. "I'm sorry I had to be the one to tell you all this, but to be honest, I don't understand why you two are so sure this kid's innocent. Hell, from what I understand, you just met him a few days ago."

"That's true, but at the risk of sounding cliché," I explained, "it's a Witch thing. It's just a gut feeling."

"What about Devon Johnston?" My wife was on a mission, and she wasn't about to give up. "We haven't heard anything yet. Isn't he still a suspect?"

"He pulled through, but he's gonna be laid up for a good

long time," he answered. "We talked to him this mornir
and Ben checked out his alibi. Except for killing a dog, t
assault on you, and a couple of trespassing charges, he's
the clear." Once again he stared past the small jungle
potted plants and out through the atrium window. Afte
short pause, he let out a sigh of resignation and th
continued in a fatherly tone, "Trust me, I'd like to belie
you guys, but like I said, there's a lot of evidence, even if
is circumstantial. It's the fingerprint you found on the can
that really clinches it."

"I wish I'd never seen it," Felicity muttered in a deject
tone.

"And if R.J. really is guilty?" Deckert asked
rhetorically. "How would you feel then? Look, I don't wa
to see an innocent kid go down either, but I'm not so si
that's what's happening here. The shrink says it looks li
the kid got himself a crush on these women and then g
rejected. It just kept building, and he finally snapped a
carved 'em up. Got himself a vicious circle going. Kil
woman then feel guilty. Fix it, in his mind anyway, with tl
expulsion thing of yours and then do it all over again."

"Expiation spell," I corrected. "And as pat and logical
that all sounds, it doesn't feel right." The hair rose on
back of my neck, and a tingle ran down my spine as I voic
my next thought, "R.J. being unjustly accused isn't
biggest worry right now though."

"What is then?" he questioned.

"If we ARE right, and he IS innocent," I express
grimly, "then the real killer is still out there, and that mea
another young woman is going to die."

The waxing moon was creeping steadily toward fullness and had just begun its trek across the cloudless, early evening sky as we parked in front of Ben and Allison's home. Nestled snugly within the confines of the historic district of the city, the stone structure rose upward two stories from the well-kept lot to a steeply pitched, slate tile roof. The two of them had spent the first few years of their marriage restoring this house, and Felicity and I had been there to help them put it all together. Now, the two of us felt as if we were, in a figurative sense, responsible for tearing it apart. We weren't about to let that happen.

After Detective Deckert left earlier in the day, I called Ben at the MCS command post. He had remained distant and guarded during the conversation, much as he had the day before, but I was determined in my desire to resolve the situation and effectively invited Felicity and myself over for a visit. Before he could object, I said goodbye and hung up.

Allison met us at the front door wearing a thin, disconcerted smile and kept silent as we entered. Ben was wearily lounging on the sofa, tie undone, and fingers twined around the neck of a full bottle of beer.

"Can I get you something to drink?" Allison offered mechanically.

"No thanks," I responded, "I'm fine at the moment."

Felicity just shook her head. Allison fidgeted nervously, reminiscent of a trapped animal. It was as if our declining her offer had somehow cut off an avenue of escape, leaving her no choice but to face that which she was working so hard to avoid. After spending a tense moment recalculating her options, she hesitantly positioned herself on the couch. She took a seat noticeably distant from Ben but close enough to give the outward appearance that nothing was wrong. Still, the strain with which this was done would have been palpable to even the most oblivious stranger. The fact that we knew them as well as we did turned the small sign into a lighted billboard.

"Where's the little guy?" I asked as Felicity and I found chairs opposite them.

"He's sleeping over with his friend across the street," Allison replied, seeming to ease somewhat at the benign question.

"I guess Deckert told you 'bout R.J.," Ben interjected, unceremoniously changing the subject.

"He did," I answered, "and while we have our own views on the subject, that's not the first thing on our agenda."

"Agenda?" Ben repeated. "Are we havin' a meetin'?"

"You could say that."

The two of them simply stared back at us sullenly. We sat and allowed the thick silence to envelope the room and the four of us with it. Felicity and I had troubled over this conversation the entire afternoon, and though we had discussed and rehearsed everything we wanted to say, when it came down to the wire, the memorized script was forgotten.

"Look, Felicity, I'm sorry," Ben suddenly gushed. "If there was anything I could do, I would. I wish I had never mentioned this case to you guys."

"So Deckert was right," I asserted. "You really do blame yourself for what happened."

"If the shoe fits," Allison muttered.

"Are you serious?" I faced her. "You actually believe Ben is at fault?"

"What the hell is wrong with you two?" my wife blurted, unabashedly taking the bull by the horns.

"Whaddaya mean?" Ben's expression changed from guilt to shock at Felicity's candor.

"What I mean is, what gives you the right to feel responsible for my miscarriage?"

"If Ben hadn't..." Allison started.

"*Cac capaill!*" My wife spat a Gaelic profanity. The gates were open, and Felicity was living up to the stories about redheads and their tempers. "Ben had nothing to do with it!"

"I got you involved in this whole mess," Ben insisted. "If I'd never asked Rowan to help, you never would've lost the baby."

"You didn't ask, Ben," I expressed evenly. "I volunteered. So did Felicity."

"She didn't volunteer to have some asshole slam 'er into a wall," he shot back.

"I went over to Cally's house of my own accord," my wife interjected slowly and with more than a hint of anger. "You can't possibly be responsible for my actions. And you, Allison." She shifted her blazing stare. "How can you possibly blame Ben for something he had no control over?"

"Maybe he didn't cause it directly," Allison returned. "But he never should have brought you into this."

"She's right," Ben added. "You guys aren't cops. I never should have exposed you to the risks."

"*Damnú ort!*" Felicity stood as the expletive burst from her lips. "How dare you! How can you two be so selfish?!"

"Selfish?"

"Yes, selfish!" she shouted. "This is MY pain, not yours! It's MY fault!"

I joined Ben and Allison in their stunned expressions as I turned to my wife. We had discussed at length the fact that Ben was not to blame for the accident, but at no point had she ever affixed that blame to herself.

Until now.

Felicity remained standing, her auburn hair draping forward as she dropped her chin, murmuring through choked whimpers. "It's my fault. I'm the one to blame."

I was caught completely by surprise. I inwardly dam
myself for not recognizing the fragility of her mental st
Even with the heightened senses I had developed thro
years of practice and meditation, I had completely mis
this possibility. I shouldn't have even needed those sense
know that something like this could happen. I felt horr
fallible. I had let her down.

"No, Felicity." Allison was up from her seat insta
maternal instincts in overdrive. "No it isn't."

I stood and placed a comforting hand on my sobl
wife's shoulder. "It's not your fault, honey. It's nobo
fault. It was an accident."

She turned quickly and buried her face against my ch
shoulders heaving as she let out the pent up emotio
wrapped my arms about her gently, holding her close
trying to avoid putting pressure on her cracked and bru
ribs. Ben was on his feet now. Both he and Allison lo
back at me in astonishment. It was obvious from
expressions that they hadn't foreseen this eventuality eit

I continued to hold this woman I loved more than
very life, crooning softly to her and allowing her to rel
the torrent of tears she had been silently gathering for
past day. We all stood wordlessly in the living room
Felicity's weeping ebbed. Eventually, she began to c
The shaking slowly faded away, and the sobs were repl
by muted sniffles. She looked up at me with reddened
and brushed a tangle of hair from her face.

"I'm sorry," she whispered.

"It's okay," I told her. "You don't have anything t
sorry about."

She released her grip on me then stepped back unstea
and shot Allison an embarrassed glance. "You woul
have a tissue then, would you?"

"Sure I do," Allison soothed and slipped an arm a

her shoulders. "Come with me."

Ben and I stared after them as Allison led Felicity down the hallway adjoining the living room. Considering the circumstances, I figured they would be gone for a while.

"Jeezus, Rowan, I'm sorry," Ben sympathized as he rubbed the back of his neck. "I never thought..."

"Neither did I," I echoed as his words trailed off. "Neither did I."

The blame and self-accusation had finally completed its rounds, starting with Cally and ending with Felicity. Of everyone involved, she understandably took it the hardest. It was nearing midnight before we finally left Ben and Allison. All four of us were emotionally drained and physically exhausted, but the two of them were getting along much better than they had been when we first arrived. The cathartic episode left Felicity red-eyed and fighting a sinus headache, but in a somewhat selfish way, I was relieved that it was now over. Whether the police wanted to believe it or not, there was still a psycho out there, and I was certain he was preparing to kill again. I needed to be able to apply all of my attention to figuring out who he was before that happened.

"So I guess I managed to make a complete fool of myself this evening," Felicity lamented, eyes shut, head tilted back on the headrest and rubbing the bridge of her nose.

"I wouldn't say that," I consoled. "You just did what anyone else in your position would have. I wouldn't worry about it."

She took in a deep breath and let it out slowly. "At least Allison and Ben are straightened out."

"Yeah. I think they're pretty clear on the subject now."

We continued on quietly, and I hooked a cautious left through the flashing yellow light at the intersection, speeding onto the highway in the direction of home.

"I guess I owe you an apology," I finally announced.

"For what?" She was still massaging her sinuses, head back and eyes closed.

"For not being prepared," I explained. "For not knowing how it was that you really felt."

"How could you have known?" she half asked, half stated. "I told you I was fine. You aren't a mind reader."

"I'm a Witch. I should have sensed that something was wrong."

"You've been preoccupied lately," she admonished. "You can't expect to be able to do everything."

"I can at least expect to be sensitive to you and your feelings," I expressed, glancing over at her.

"Don't beat yourself up over this, Rowan." She opened her eyes and looked at me. "Take it from someone who's been doing just that. It won't accomplish anything."

I paused for a moment, pondering the wisdom of what she had just said. "I just wanted you to know I love you," I whispered.

"I never doubted it."

CHAPTER 17

Darkness.
Cold, lifeless, complete darkness.
Falling.
Screaming.
Silence.
Light.
I'm standing somewhere. I'm standing nowhere.

There is something in my hand. I look down and notice that I am holding a cane. My hand is encased in a white glove. I am dressed in white.

Formal.

A white tuxedo with tails.

"Hello, Mister," a small voice calls from the void.

I turn to find a small child. A young girl with silky, strawberry-blonde hair tied up with perfect, white satin bows. She is dressed in a lacy, white, party dress and Mary Janes. She's looking up at me with large, curious eyes. She holds out her tiny, gloved hand to me and then waits.

I take her hand.

A scream.

Silence.

The young girl is tugging on my coattail.

"Give him the tickets, Mister," she tells me.

"What?" I ask. "Who? What tickets?"

"Tickets, please." There is a faceless man standing before me.

In my hand, I hold two smooth rectangles. I turn them over in my hand. I don't know where they came from or why I have them. I can only assume that they are the tickets the man wants.

At first glance, they appear blank.
At second glance, they appear patterned.
At third glance, they appear familiar.
I look at them closer.
The Seven of Pentacles.
"Mister, give him the tickets, or we'll miss the show."
The young girl continues to tug on my coattail in frustrati
"Hurry."
I give the faceless man the tickets. I don't know why.
We are sitting.
We are in a theatre.

Seats seem to extend forever into the shadows. They
all empty. The young girl and I are the only audience.

There is a program in my hands. It is printed on a sin
sheet of fancy paper and folded in the center. The sym
adorning the front of the page is the Seven of Pentacle
begin to peel open the crisp parchment.

"They're starting." The girl nudges me and points to
stage before us.

I look up. The tall vermilion curtain is swinging op
slowly. A grey mist is beginning to spill from the slit form
in the center.

The curtains are open wide, suddenly, as if they
never been closed.

A faceless woman with strawberry-blonde hair, dres
in elegant white lace is standing center stage. She is flan
on her left by a faceless brunette and on her right b
faceless blonde. They are all dressed alike.

The grey mist spills over the edge of the stage and
filling the theatre. It hangs wetly around my ankles, creep
incessantly up my legs.

A scream.

A splash of red spreads across the breast of the woma
center stage, and her body heaves violently as a gurg

voice calls out, "Why, Rowan, Why?"

I try to get up. I can't. The cold grey mist has crept up over my knees and into my lap. It is holding me in the seat. I can't move.

I look over at the young girl. She is staring intently at the stage.

A scream.

I look back to the stage. I don't want to, but I can't help myself. A crimson stain bursts forth on the chest of the faceless brunette woman. She begins crumpling to the floor, shrouded in the mist. A new voice gurgles, "Our Father who art in heaven, hallowed be Thy name..."

The mist has made its way farther up my body now. It floats about me mid-chest. I look over to the young girl. I expect her to be completely covered in the paralyzing fog.

She isn't.

She looks back at me curiously as the fog licks at her but never touches. I open my mouth, but I can't make a sound. She turns back to the stage.

A scream.

Blood, thick and red, flows from the chest of the blonde, quickly forming a Pentagram, then blending into a formless blotch. She begins to slip downward into the fog, her gurgling voice reaches my ears, "Who are you? Why are you doing this to me?"

The woman center stage is still standing. She continues to shake violently, her head rolls forward, and a face forms where there had only been void. Her eyes open, and she looks directly at me. She begins to slide away into the grey mist, and her mouth begins to move, "Why don't you stop him, Rowan?"

Her body disappears. Standing in place behind her is a hooded, robed figure, a bloody dirk held firmly in his grip. He looks at me, then to the young girl, then back to me again. He appears faceless, but even at this distance, I ‹ see his eyes.

Cold.

Cold, grey eyes.

The thick fog erupts before him. A plume rises quic then dissipates, falling back to the floor almost as quickl it had risen, leaving behind the lace clad form of yet anot young woman. She screams.

The scream echoes forever throughout the shadows. ‹ robed figure raises the dirk, then plunges it downward.

Blood.

Dark crimson, thick with the young woman's life. The that flows out of her in time with her waning scream. ‹ hooded figure thrusts his hand into her chest, then wrenc it back as her dying body crumples to the floor.

The mist is just below my chin. I'm completely unabl move now, and I'm finding it hard to breathe. I look ove the young girl next to me.

"This is just the dress rehearsal," she tells me matter factly, looking up at my face with large bright eyes. "‹ got to go now, Mister."

I try to speak as the girl slides off her seat and beg skipping up the aisle, a fogless void enveloping her. Noth comes out. She disappears.

"All...Is...Forgiven," a deep, demonic voice filters ‹ my ears.

I look back to the stage. The hooded figure holds hand aloft, vermilion streaks dripping down his bare arm his hand there is grasped a still-beating heart.

The fog has reached my face. I try to hold my breath, it slides in anyway. It creeps into my nostrils and into mouth. It tastes foul.

It continues to rise and now covers my head.

I can hold my breath no longer.

Darkness.
An endless scream.

Once again, I awoke to the sound of my own tortured scream. As Felicity had suspected days ago, the nightmares weren't going to end until this was over. Not until the real killer was found and stopped.

As neither of us had foreseen, the episodes were growing more intense. Each nightmare was more disturbing than its predecessor—more vivid, more maddening. Each dream was drawing me closer to what could only be an inexorable convergence with the cancerous insanity eating away at the mind of the murderer.

My wife straddled me in the bed, gripping my shoulders and shaking me violently. I continued to scream.

"Rowan!" Her mouth formed the word, my name, but her voice couldn't penetrate the banshee wail that filled my ears. "ROWAN!"

A stinging sensation suddenly radiated through the side of my face as my head wrenched to the side, and silence faded quickly into the room. It had taken the shock of Felicity's hand impacting my cheek to awaken me from the pain of the nightmare.

"I'm sorry," I heard her say, rapt concern flooding her voice.

I pulled her close.

It was my turn to cry.

"How many?" she asked softly after my sobs had waned. "How many of these nightmares have you had?"

"Four," I choked, pulling back from her and pressing the heels of my palms against my eyes.

"They're getting worse, aren't they?"

"Yes," I affirmed, "they're getting worse."

My wife rolled to the side and fluidly got out of bed. She

continued to stare at me as she slipped into her bathrobe
expression rapidly beginning to show irritation on top o
concern.

"Why haven't you told me about this?" she demar
angrily as she knotted the belt.

"I started to this morning." I swung my legs over the
of the bed and hauled myself up. "But that media circus
waiting for us, and then everything else..." I let my v
trail off.

"Well, *everything else* is over," she flatly rebutted
objection. "We're going to talk about it now."

"I'll be all right," I protested. "We can talk in
morning."

She glared back. "Now."

The tone of her voice told me in no uncertain terms
shouldn't argue. I finished pulling myself from the bec
stood shakily, still rubbing my eyes.

"Can I take a shower first?" I queried.

"I'll be in the kitchen," she answered.

I felt somewhat better after standing under the cool
of the shower for a few minutes. At the very least, I w
longer drenched in sweat, and I had stopped shaking fe
most part. Felicity was seated at the breakfast nook, cra
a mug of freshly brewed coffee in her hands when I ent
Salinger, Dickens, and Emily lined the wide window
staring back at me through slit eyes, ears cocked out
sides of their heads as if they were three wise, albeit
and furry, prophets.

I pulled down a mug from the cabinet and poured n
a measure of the black caffeine-laden brew.

"Feeling better?" Felicity asked as I poured.

"A little," I replied and then slid in across from her. I had quickly recorded my latest nightmare in my Book of Shadows before showering, and it was now tucked beneath my arm. I pulled it out and dropped it to the table with an audible smack. The trio of felines followed its course in unison, from my hand to the table, and then looked back at me expectantly. "I'm still feeling rattled though."

"So you want to fill me in, then?" My wife peered at me over the rim of her cup before taking a sip.

I tapped the bound sheaf of papers that was my dream diary. "I've written them all down. The first one was Saturday when I fell asleep on the couch."

"I remember," she confirmed.

"I didn't have one that night though," I continued. "I guess I was too exhausted."

"So, is it a recurring nightmare?"

"In some ways I guess it is, but not really." I thoughtfully fingered the rim of my coffee cup. "Ariel is always in them. She's always dressed in white lace, and by the end of the nightmare, she's always dead."

"That's pretty straightforward," Felicity told me, analyzing my words carefully. "Just think about what you've seen."

"It's bad enough seeing her die over and over," I outlined. "But she always says something like, 'Why don't you stop him?'"

"Subconscious reaction to a feeling of helplessness?" she proffered. "You want to be able to save her, but you can't. It's probably your own psyche saying it."

"That's what I thought at first too," I partially agreed. "But there's too much detail, and the variations in the dreams seem to form a pattern. It's as if Ariel is trying to tell me something. Like she's trying to give me clues to the identity of her killer."

"So you don't think these are just nightmares then?"

"Not since the third one," I answered. "They're just too damn real...And they keep getting more intense."

"What kind of clues do you think she's giving you?"

"I'm not exactly sure. One of the things that has recurred in the past two nightmares was the Seven of Pentacles."

"The tarot card?"

"Yeah. In the third dream anyway." I flipped through the pages of the Book of Shadows halfway hoping an answer would leap out at me. "Ariel always was fascinated with tarot."

"What do you think it means?" Felicity queried.

"The inherent meaning of the card is something like *hard work and patience brings growth...* and something to do with money, if I'm remembering correctly. I was never that interested in the cards."

"Neither was I," she echoed then paused. "You said it was a tarot card in the third dream. What was it this time?"

I scribed in the air with my finger while taking a sip of my coffee. "The symbol, from a card, only it was on a pair of tickets and a program."

"What, like concert tickets or something?"

"Tickets to a play. Or I guess it was a play."

"What do you mean?"

"Well," I sighed. "In this nightmare, I went to what appeared to be a play, but there was this little girl with me. I'm pretty sure she's Ariel as a child," I explained. "Anyway, she told me that it was just a dress rehearsal."

"What was the play about?"

"The murders," I answered flatly. "The curtain opens up and there are three faceless women on the stage. A strawberry-blonde in the center, a brunette on her left, and a blonde on her right."

"Ariel, Karen, and Ellen."

"That's what I'm figuring," I agreed. "Anyhow, all three of them are dressed in white lace gowns, and there is this grey mist that keeps spilling off the stage. It creeps across the floor like some kind of fog and just keeps getting deeper. It paralyzes me and holds me in the seat, so I have to sit there and watch as this shadowy figure kills them one by one. Ariel, then Karen, and then Ellen."

"What does the little girl do?"

"She just sits there and watches. For some reason, the fog never touches her."

"And she told you it was just a dress rehearsal?"

"Yeah. After the shadowy figure kills all three women, this plume of mist rises up, and then as it dissipates, there is this other woman..." I stopped mid-sentence as the portion of the nightmare I had just described replayed itself in my mind like an endless loop of film. The realization suddenly struck me like a fist between the eyes. "DAMMIT! How could I have missed it!" I exclaimed.

I leapt from the table, sending the heretofore-quiescent cats into a frenzied rush to escape. They bolted in three separate directions and in the same direction all at once, sending saltshakers and other table adornments to the floor. Coffee sloshed from my cup, and my wide-eyed wife shot upward from her seat.

"Rowan! What's wrong?!"

"Another woman appeared on the stage, and the bastard killed her too," I spoke quickly, advancing across the room and snatching the telephone from its cradle. "He killed again! The son-of-a-bitch has killed again!"

I punched the lighted buttons, frantically dialing Ben's home number.

"Aye, are you sure?" Felicity appealed as she tended to the spilled coffee.

"It has to be," I answered confidently and then began impatiently urging the phone. "Come on, come on, pick up!"

I pressed the handset tightly to my ear, listening to the electronic vibrato of the ring at the other end of the line. If nothing else, this portion of the nightmare was suddenly clear to me. Ariel was telling me that there was either going to be another murder or that another had already occurred. A gnawing hollowness in the pit of my stomach insisted that it was the latter.

"Rowan, don't you think..." Felicity started.

I brought my hand up sharply and waved to cut her off as on the fifth ring, the receiver at the other end was picked up.

"Hello," a rough, hazy voice, still thick with sleep issued from the earpiece.

"Ben, it's Rowan," I blurted into the handset. "There's been another murder."

"Do what?" Ben's voice came back to me. "What are ya' talkin' about?"

"The killer, Ben. He's still out there, and he's killed again," I insisted urgently.

"Slow down, man. Where are ya'?"

"I'm at home."

"The killer murdered someone at your house?"

"No, no. Nobody at my house. Listen to me, R.J. isn't the killer. The bastard is still out there, and he's killed someone else."

"Who, Rowan? Who's dead?"

"Another young woman. I don't know her name."

"How do you know this?" Ben's voice sounded much more alert now.

"You wouldn't believe me if I told you," I expressed. "Just trust me on this."

"Well, where did this murder take place?" I could hear him shuffling paper, preparing to take notes.

My mind had been working so fast I had rushed ahead of not only the rest of the world, but myself as well. I motioned to Felicity to hand me my Book of Shadows and began leafing through the last few pages, scanning them as fast as I could. As I had feared, there was nothing to indicate where the murder might have taken place.

"Rowan? You still there?" Ben's voice crackled from the earpiece.

"Yeah. Yeah, I'm here."

"Well? Where'd this happen?"

What I was about to say was sure to portray me as a lunatic. I only wished I had another choice. "I don't know."

"You don't know?" Ben's incredulous voice issued again. "Whaddaya mean, you don't know?"

"I mean I don't know where it happened, I just know that it has," I answered in a pleading tone, knowing full well that my words now sounded hollow and empty.

"Lemme get this straight." He ran down the high points. "The killer is still out there, and he's killed another young lady. You don't know who, and you don't know where, but you just know it happened. So, you decided to call me at..." He paused, I assume to check the clock. "At quarter of four in the morning ta' tell me all this?"

"Yeah," I muttered.

"And how you know this, I wouldn't believe, even if you told me?"

"Yeah." I couldn't think of anything else to say.

"Try me."

I was dejected. I was frustrated. I was angry that I had no way to make him believe me. I did the only thing I could think of to do. I told him the truth.

"A vision. Okay?" Discontent permeated my voice. "It's something I saw in a vision when I went to sleep tonight."

"Jeezus, Fuck, Rowan!" The earpiece buzzed as he

shouted. "Are you kiddin' me?! You called me at alm•
four in the mornin' because of a goddamned nightmare?!"

"It's not just a nightmare, Ben," I plead. "It's more th
that. You don't understand..."

"Hell yes I understand!" he cut me off. "You got so•
kinda bug up your ass about R.J. not bein' the killer, and
can't leave it alone. Now you're havin' nightmares about

"No, Ben, that's not it," I insisted. "I know it sounds t•
way, but trust me..."

"Look, Rowan," he spoke slowly. It was obvious he v
trying to hold back anger. "You're just gonna have ta' acc
it. The D.A. is filin' charges against R.J. tomorrow morni•
and that's the end of it. Now drink some warm milk
somethin', and go back to bed. We'll talk about this in
mornin'. Goodbye."

"No, wait, Ben? Ben?"

I was talking to dead air.

I slowly settled the receiver back into its base and sta•
at it, silently cursing myself for being unable to convi•
him.

"He hung up," I finally said.

"Aye... I got that feeling. I'm sorry Ben didn't beli•
you," Felicity told me in a mild voice. "I was trying to s•
you before you called him."

"I should have listened," I granted. "He's been pr•
understanding about everything so far, but this...I kno•
must have sounded like I was nuts."

She slipped her arms around me and nuzzled in cl•
slowly rubbing my back in a comforting manner. "•
sounded concerned, and convinced."

"I sounded nuts," I repeated. "You don't have to su•
coat it. I've just never had involuntary visions this inte•
before. I'm not quite sure how to handle it."

"I don't know if I would either."

"If I just had something tangible," I mused. "Some kind of concrete proof."

"Maybe it hasn't happened yet," Felicity returned. "Maybe there is still time to convince him, then."

"Maybe, but I really doubt it. I've got a bad feeling that I'm a day late and a dollar short."

The relative stillness of the room was broken by the clamor of the phone as it began to ring. Without releasing my grip on my wife, I reached for it just as STORM, BENJAMIN and a number played across the liquid crystal face of the caller ID box.

"Hello," I answered, fully expecting to be chewed out by my friend or even his wife.

"Good, you're still up." The earlier anger in Ben's voice had been replaced by something resembling horrific awe. "Better get dressed. I'll be there to pick ya' up in a half hour."

"Someone found a body," I ventured, already knowing it to be true.

"I'm just glad you're on our side," he muttered, "'cause you ain't natural, paleface. You just ain't natural."

CHAPTER 18

"**D**arla Anne Radcliffe," Carl Deckert was telling me as we stood in the bedroom of the Westview area apartment. "Twenty-five years old, flight attendant." He was reading mechanically from his small notebook. His grey hair was disheveled, angling up in the back where his head had only recently been in contact with a pillow. "The redhead out front is her roommate. They both work for the same airline, and she just got in from a flight at two A.M." He motioned to the scene before us. "When she got home, this is what was waiting for her."

"Door propped open?" I queried as I knelt to inspect the gory spectacle.

"Yeah," he answered tiredly. "It was open."

The other victims, Ariel, Karen, and Ellen had been splayed out like rag dolls, little care taken as to their appearance once the ritual was complete. This was different. The young woman before me lay like an adornment. Her nude body stretched out upon the bed as if she were a decoration. As if she were being offered.

Her shoulder length brown hair fanned out in a silky halo around her head, perfectly arranged. Her arms were at her sides, unbound, palms upward. Glassy, green eyes stared unblinking from a slackened face, forever intent upon the textured ceiling above.

A Pentagram was carefully excised from the skin of her chest and stomach, even more precisely than it had been in the case of Ellen Gray. The pentagon created by the convergence of the lines at the center of the symbol was positioned centrally and just below her ribcage. At this point, muscle and flesh had been removed to leave a gaping five-sided hole. Reaching out, I held my glove-encased fist above the opening, making a visual measurement.

"That's where he pulled her heart out," I ventured bluntly. "Directly through the center of the Pentagram." I hated the fact that I had become so clinically detached from these horrors. It was beginning to make me feel almost inhuman.

"You think this might be some kind of copycat deal or something?" Deckert asked. "This one's not bound up like the other three."

"No," I expressed positively. "It's the same guy. The pattern of flaying is too much like it was on Ellen Gray. That detail never made it to the media, so it wouldn't be able to be copied."

Deckert grunted agreement. I could tell that he hadn't really believed we were dealing with an imposter, but someone had to ask the question.

"Does it smell different in here to you?" Ben asked. He had been quietly scrutinizing the scene ever since we arrived. "Sweeter than before. Kinda reminds me of some opium I took off a dealer I popped a couple'a years back."

"That's exactly what it is," I answered, still kneeling next to the corpse. "Hallucinogenics were sometimes used by ritual magicians in days gone by. I expect you'll find that some was added to the incense he burned."

"I still don't get why she isn't restrained like the others," Deckert asserted. "Shit, she looks like she just laid there and let him do it. No fight, no struggle."

"She probably couldn't," a new but familiar voice issued from behind us.

I turned to see Doctor Sanders peering over the rim of her glasses at us. She looked back down at the clipboard she was holding and finished signing whatever document was attached to its face and then handed it to her assistant.

"You mind expanding on that a bit, Doc?" Ben asked.

"D-Tubocurarine chloride," she stated matter-of-factly as she stepped past him.

"Dee Tube of what?" Deckert voiced in a confused tone.

"D-Tubocurarine chloride," she repeated. "It's a curarine derivative."

"English," Ben urged.

"Curare," she returned seeming somewhat annoyed. "You know, poison darts, all that jazz. Tubocurarine is commonly used as a paralytic agent for patients experiencing violent and uncontrollable seizures. The tox reports came back on the Tanner and Barnes cases. They both had it in their systems. I'm willing to bet we'll find it in the Gray case, and this one as well."

"Would the individual still be able to feel pain?" I asked.

"Absolutely," she answered with a nod, "The patient would remain conscious and fully aware. Totally capable of feeling pain, just unable to move. The effects are usually short lived but drastic."

"That would fit with what this S.O.B. is trying to accomplish." I offered.

"But that still doesn't explain why the other three victims were restrained, and this one isn't," Deckert observed. "If he shot the others up, why didn't they just lay there too?"

"I can shed some light on that for you. May I?" Doctor Sanders looked at me and motioned to the body.

I stood and moved back as she leaned over and turned the young woman's lifeless arm slightly to allow a better view. Expertly, she ran the index finger of her gloved hand across the cooling skin and brought it to rest. "Right here," she announced. "He injected her intravenously. The other three were intramuscularly." She left her finger where it was until we had all inspected the puncture wound then gently rolled the arm back against the body. "Tubocurarine chloride is some pretty wicked stuff, but it's unpredictable when injected into muscle. Dosages are pretty tricky as well because just a little too much can cause respiratory arrest."

"So it's possible that the other victims weren't completely paralyzed," I thought aloud.

"Precisely," Doctor Sanders affirmed. "Based on the differing amounts between the Tanner and Barnes cases, I'd venture to say that the killer was experimenting. It can also depend on how long it was in their system because it can metabolize in as little as thirty minutes."

"What about the fact that the killer ingested blood from the victims?" I queried. "Wouldn't the drug affect him then?"

"Doubtful." She shook her head. "He would have to ingest much more than he has for it to have an effect on him, and even then it's unlikely."

I continued to stare quietly at the lifeless body so neatly arranged upon the bed. The killer had been more precise with his movements, more exacting. Nothing was wasted. After a few moments, I realized I was holding my breath. I let it out in a long sigh. The cloying odor of the opium made my nostrils tingle as I drew in a fresh breath. Something was rattling around in the back of my brain. Something recent. Something I should know.

"I guess this clears the kid," Deckert was speaking to Ben. "Maybe," Ben answered, "maybe not. His fingerprint was still on that candle. Maybe there's an accomplice. Like a cult thing or somethin'."

"No," I volunteered over my shoulder without taking my eyes off the corpse. "There's only one killer. I would have felt it if there were more."

"Hey, Doc." Ben turned his attention to Doctor Sanders. "Have you established a time of death yet?"

"I'd place it around eleven last night, give or take an

hour," she replied. "I can be more specific once I get a liver temp, but between ten and midnight is your ballpark."

The sigh that Ben Storm let out was barely audible. I suppose I heard it simply because I could also feel the tension as it drained from him. I could sense him relaxing as if an unbearable weight had just been lifted from his shoulders. I felt all this because I had been aware of his thoughts. I had known what he was thinking ever since I had climbed into his van less than an hour ago.

"Feel better now," I asked without turning.

"Huh?" he grunted.

"Do you feel better now that you know I didn't commit this murder?" I turned to face my friend.

"How did..." His voice trailed off as he looked at me, obviously both surprised and embarrassed.

"What are you talking about?" Deckert inserted, genuinely befuddled.

"I had a vision tonight," I explained. "Something of a nightmare I suppose. In it I saw that this murder had occurred, so I called Ben and told him." I didn't go into the details of his not believing me. "Of course, being the good cop that he is, when the body was found, he immediately considered me a suspect. That is, until the doctor here established that it probably all happened while he and I were sitting in his living room drinking a beer."

"Rowan... Look, I'm sorry man... I..." Ben stuttered.

"Forget it," I told him sincerely. "You didn't have any choice. I know I sounded like a lunatic when I called you..."

"Yeah, but you're my friend," he protested. "And after everything that's happened... Well, I shouldn't have doubted you."

"Really, Ben. It's okay. I would have done the same thing if I were in your position. Let's just figure out who it is, so we can stop him."

"How did you know anyway?"

"Like you said. I just *ain't natural*." I smiled.

He nodded and returned the smile, and I knew that the matter was settled.

I turned back to the neatly arranged sacrifice. The earlier thought was clawing its way forward from the back of my head, tearing painfully at my brain. I knew for certain that the answer was right in front of me. I just didn't know why I couldn't see it.

Her arms were at her sides, palms upward—an act of supplication. Her hair was fanned out like a diaphanous halo floating around her head. The flaying was precise and clean.

Deckert and Ben were still talking behind me, discussing the question of whether or not this event actually did clear R.J. of the crimes. I pressed myself to tune them out and listen only to the rhythmic patterns of my measured breathing. I wasn't about to try channeling this young woman, especially without Felicity here to anchor me on this plane. I simply wanted to read the room with something other than my eyes. I wanted to know what the killer was up to. What he was trying to accomplish.

I stretched my senses outward, closed my eyes, and concentrated on the sound of my own heart. I raked my senses through the ethereal atmosphere only I could see. I let every molecule of residual energy run through my otherworldly fingers like ghostly grains of sand. To be inspected. Scrutinized. Discarded.

Nothing.

I could feel nothing but darkness and death. It was just like the other crime scenes. It was as if no ritual or ceremony had ever been performed in this room.

"This is just the dress rehearsal," a child's tiny voice echoes in my brain.

"This is just a dress rehearsal," I whispered aloud as my

eyes opened wide.

"What was that, Mister Gant?" Doctor Sanders looked up from her work.

"A dress rehearsal." I made the comment louder now as the thought scratched its way up through my brain to reside clearly and positively in the front. "Look at the way she's arranged." Ben and Deckert had broken off their conversation to listen to me. "Her hair. Her hands, palms upward in supplication or offering. The detail of the flaying. The opium in the incense." By now I had moved around the bed motioning to each of the points I had mentioned. "The whole ritual has gotten more complicated each time. The first three were for practice, and this one was the final dress rehearsal."

"Dress rehearsal for what?" Ben appealed.

"For the invocation," I answered quickly. "For the actual ceremony."

"No offense, but so what?" Deckert interjected.

"So it's something that has bothered me ever since the second murder, but I could never really put my finger on it." I continued, "I've never felt any residual energy from the crime scenes. I know that means nothing to you, but to me it's important. I've just been assuming that I was missing something, and now I'm sure that I was."

"I still don't follow."

"The refinement in the ceremony with each murder. This has all been one big rehearsal for the final ceremony. This was the *dress rehearsal*. The next time it's going to be for real."

"That still doesn't tell us anything," Deckert returned. "It just means that the asshole is going to kill again. That is, unless you're trying to tell us you actually believe he's going to summon up a demon or something."

"That's entirely beside the point," I returned. "I'd rather

he never get a chance to even try. All of this DOES mean something though. It tells us WHEN, and in a certain respect, WHO he's going to kill next. That's what I've been missing."

"How's that?"

"Based on some of the things I dug up when I researched ritual sacrifices." I continued, "If I'm on the same page he is, and I'm pretty sure I am, he'll plan to perform the ritual on a full moon."

"Anyone got a calendar?" Ben called out. "When is the next full moon?"

"This Friday," I told them before anyone else could respond.

"Okay, so that's the when." Ben looked at me expectantly. "What about the who?"

I bit back a rush of bile in my throat at the thought, then quietly uttered the answer, "He'll believe he needs a virgin."

"A virgin?" Deckert posed, "How the hell is he going to know if the victim is a virgin?"

"A kid," Ben answered him flatly, still holding my gaze.

"A kid?!" Deckert exclaimed. "Holy fucking shit, you can't be serious!"

"Tell me I misunderstood, Rowan," Ben appealed, eyes still fixed on mine. "Please."

I couldn't.

I just looked away.

There was a note waiting for me when Ben dropped me back at home later that morning. Felicity had already left for a photo shoot she had scheduled, and she was letting me know that she would be home later in the afternoon. I showered and changed clothes while the coffeepot performed its prescribed duty. After grabbing a cup and filling a thermal carafe with the resulting brew, I settled in at my desk upstairs.

I hoped that doing some work would take my mind off the events of the past days and allow me at least some small period of rest. Much to my chagrin, I found the reason behind why the previous week had been so grueling. I was entirely caught up. No unanswered support calls. No clients needing upgrades or modifications. I had nothing to do.

I was just preparing to call it quits when I noticed the yellow pickup slip in my box. It had been lying there since Saturday afternoon, completely forgotten. The odds were that the package was a software backup from a client needing a minor modification or a database recovery; either of which would only amount to an hour or so worth of work. In any event, it was better than nothing, so I snatched up the canary ticket and made the short drive to the post office and back.

As expected, the small package contained a tape cartridge full of data. The included trouble sheet indicated that the database was corrupt and needed to be recovered, which was one of the contract services I provided to my clients. I quickly scanned over the trouble sheet to see if there was any more information and noted that this particular client was located in Seattle, Washington. I was just preparing to slip the cartridge into my computer's tape drive when the hair rose on the back of my neck.

"It always rains here," Ariel's voice rings through my head. "It's mostly just a misty rain."

Rain.

Constant misty rain.

Seattle, Washington.

The second of my nightmares suddenly made sense as

the electrochemical reaction within my brain generated the connection. It almost always rained in Seattle. I remembered that from a magazine photo layout Felicity had done about the *Seattle Bumbershoot Festival*. A festival to celebrate the rain. Work was once again forgotten as I seized the phone and stabbed out Ben's cellular number on the keypad.

His voice came after the second ring, "Hello?"

"Ben, it's Rowan."

"Hey," he replied, "I was just gonna call you. You'll be happy to know that the D.A. decided to hold off on filin' charges against R.J. pendin' further investigation."

"That's great," I answered quickly, "but that's not why I called."

"What's up?"

"I know I'm going to sound crazy again," I started. "But I'm calling about another vision I had."

"When? Just now?" he asked.

"No, a couple of nights ago," I continued. "I've been having them almost every night since I got involved in this whole thing. They just haven't necessarily made sense until now."

"So what is it?" he pressed anxiously. "Did you see another murder? The kid?"

"No, not yet." I hoped we could make that *yet* into a never. "I'm pretty sure this one is a clue about the killer's identity, but I don't quite know what to make of it."

"Well spit it out man," he urged. "What is it?"

"Seattle," I told him. "Seattle or the Pacific Northwest. I think that's where he's from or something."

I could hear him scribbling notes in his book. Less than half a dozen hours ago, he had considered me a lunatic and possibly even a murderer. Now he was accepting what I said on blind faith. He wasn't taking any chances.

"What makes you think Seattle?" he asked.

"Rain," I told him simply and then explained it. "It almost always rains in Seattle. In the vision, I saw Ariel and she told me that it was always raining. I think she's trying to tell me who the killer is or where he's from at least."

"Okay. I'll check NCIC and call Seattle PD to see if they have any cases similar to ours, open or closed. You got anything else I should know about?"

"I've had two other visions, but nothing has clicked yet... except maybe money."

"Money?" he asked in a perplexed tone.

"It doesn't make sense to me either but then neither did the rain until just a few minutes ago."

"No problem. I'll start makin' some calls, and I'll get in touch with ya' as soon as I know somethin'. If anything else falls into place for ya', call me right away."

"I will. Talk to you later. Bye."

"Bye."

I gently settled the handset back into its holder, silently grateful that Ben had been willing to believe me this time. I only wished that a young woman hadn't had to die in order to open his eyes. But then, that wasn't his fault.

I really didn't feel like working anymore, but my clients weren't paying me to track down serial killers; they were paying me to fix their computer software. I turned back to the small tape cartridge and spent the next hour and forty-five minutes earning my living.

It was almost three hours before I heard anything from Ben, and instead of calling, he and Detective Deckert simply appeared at my house. The pendulum clock had just issued an audible announcement of the time, telling me that it was

1:00 in the afternoon when I answered the doorbell.

"What's for lunch?" Ben said to me as I swung open the front door.

"I was just nuking some lasagna," I answered.

"That'll work."

The dogs scrambled about, nosing one another out of the way in a contest for the attentions of the two visitors. I sent them out the back door as Ben and Deckert seated themselves at the kitchen table.

"Where's Firehair?" Ben asked, lounging back in his chair.

"Working. She had a shoot for some department store scheduled today."

"Shouldn't she be restin' or somethin'?"

"How long have you know Felicity, Ben?" I returned.

"Yeah. You're right. Forget I ever asked that."

"So, I'm assuming you didn't just come by for lunch," I told them while preparing the dish of pasta.

"You assume correctly," Ben returned, "but I still wanna eat."

"I'm working on that," I answered and looked over at Deckert who gave me an animated shrug.

"Well, it appears that you're two for two on this nightmare thing," Ben started. "We hit paydirt with the Seattle PD. They've got an open case that bears a striking resemblance to our four. Especially Ariel Tanner."

"Coed at the *University of Washington*, Seattle." Deckert picked up the thread. "Found dead in her dorm room. She had been skinned in a similar fashion to the Tanner woman, but the autopsy revealed that she was probably already dead due to respiratory arrest."

"He overdosed her on the curare," I mused.

"Kinda," he replied. "Toxicology showed the dose to be too low to have caused respiratory arrest in your average person. Seems this young lady was unlucky enough to be a member of the small percentage of people who are hypersensitive to the drug."

"Considering what she would have had to endure otherwise," I observed, "I'm not sure I would call her unlucky in that respect."

"Yeah," he grunted, "I see what you mean."

"The mirror in the room was shattered, and there was a Pentacle inscribed on the wall along with the words 'All Is Forgiven,'" Ben added. "Not to mention that the door was propped open. Sound familiar?"

"More than just a little," I answered. "But shouldn't it have shown up earlier? I thought this was what things like NCIC and VICAP were all about."

"They are," he affirmed. "Clerical error. The case was never entered into the database."

"Lovely... Well, did they turn up any leads?" I queried. "Fingerprints? Anything?"

"No prints," Deckert answered. "According to their forensics lab, the size and shape of the incisions were consistent with those of a scalpel or a similar cutting implement."

"There's a medical school at the *University of Washington*," I voiced. "A friend of mine attended it. That would tie in with the curare and the theory about the killer having some kind of medical background as well. When did this happen?"

"A little less than a year ago," Ben answered this time. "And nothin' else came up on the NCIC database, so to our knowledge, he hasn't killed anywhere besides here and Seattle."

The timer on the microwave beeped, so I stepped over to pull out the tray of lasagna. I moved through the task of dishing it onto plates automatically, still pondering everything that had been said.

"So our killer moved from Seattle to Saint Louis sometime within the last year," I ventured, "and might have been a medical student at the *University of Washington*."

"That's how it looks," Deckert acknowledged. "The Seattle PD is compiling a list of the med students they interviewed right now."

"How soon do you think you'll hear something?" I placed steaming plates before the two men and absently offered them silverware.

"Hopefully sometime this afternoon," Ben answered, cutting into the lasagna with his fork. "They're as anxious to find this asshole as we are."

"Yeah," Deckert added. "As if it wasn't enough that this shithead maimed and killed this girl, it turns out she was the daughter of some big cheese out there. The family posted some obnoxious amount as a reward." He glanced up from his plate and noticed me leaning against the counter lost in thought. "So are you gonna eat or what?"

For all intents and purposes, I had switched to automatic pilot when the two of them began filling me in on the latest news, and the fact that I was hungry was all but forgotten. Before I could answer, the dogs began yelping loudly, raising their general, happy, canine ruckus at the back gate. A moment later, the reason became obvious when we heard the front door open, followed by Felicity noisily entering.

"Ben, your van is in my parking spot," her voice came from the other room.

I turned to Detective Deckert. "I guess I'll get that chance after I heat some up for her." I jerked my thumb in the direction of the living room and then waved my index finger at the both of them. "I'll let you two get her caught up with what's been going on."

CHAPTER 19

"So what's with this theory about the next victim being a child?" Felicity was mechanically sorting film canisters. "I mean, is there something that can be done?"

While she was eating, Ben and Deckert had brought her up to date on the days events, from the latest murder to the discovery of the connection with Seattle. We had now moved to the dining room table where she could do some work while we talked.

"It took some doin' since we don't have any hard evidence," Ben answered, "but I managed to convince the chief of the possibility of a child abduction. We've got coppers stationed at all of the area schools, but the truth is, we really don't know what we're lookin' for. This asshole hasn't established any kind of pattern or anything.

"And what with school just starting in some districts, the effort has been hard to coordinate."

"Not to mention that it's quite a bit of ground to cover," Deckert added. "He could try to grab a kid outside of the metro area for all we know."

"What about the police in those areas?" she posed. "Can't they help out?"

"They are," Deckert explained, "but you're talking about some real small departments. They can only spread themselves so thin, and like Ben said, he hasn't exactly been sticking to a particular stereotype...and now we're guessing that he'll go after a kid..."

I had been listening quietly, pondering the facts as they were reiterated for my wife's benefit and trying each of them out on the mental jigsaw puzzle I had created. Each of my nightmares provided another piece, and I felt that my recent revelations had begun putting them together. The border was completed, I was certain of that, and something told me that I had most of the pieces necessary to fill in the center but for some reason, still lacked the dexterity to do it.

I was troubled as much as the rest of them by the paradox the killer had created. It was obvious that he was practicing, preparing himself for the rite of invocation I believed he intended to perform. With each victim, he had grown progressively more intense, displaying increasingly greater skill at his grotesque art. Each of his steps seemed carefully planned out, but at the same time, the selection of his victims appeared random.

Ariel Tanner, Karen Barnes, Ellen Gray, and now Darla Radcliffe. Other than the fact that three of them knew R.J., they had little in common. There was nothing to indicate that they knew one another. The fact that R.J. was still in custody at the time of the fourth murder tended to rule him out as a suspect and in my mind, as the common thread I was searching for. The women lived in different parts of the city and county. They had different professions, different hair colors, different eye colors, sizes, weights, shapes, birth dates, this, that, and the other thing. They appeared to have nothing more in common than being adult, mid-to-late twenties, and female. Now I believed that the killer's next victim would be a child, so even that pattern, minute as it was, instantly began to unravel.

"Rowan?"

I plunged back toward reality at the sound of Felicity's voice sharply prodding me. "Wha...What?"

"You were starin' off into space for a minute there," Ben interjected. "Somethin' we should know? You weren't goin' all *Twilight Zone* on us were you?"

"No. Nothing like that," I answered, still dragging myself out of my introspective trance. "I was just thinking about the victims. There's got to be some kind of connection that we're missing. He had to pick them for a reason. There has to be a common thread."

"I'll buy that, but I got no idea what it is," he returned. "We talked to friends, relatives, and neighbors of all four of 'em. We've been over the crime scenes dozens of times. Personal effects as well. Nothin'."

"Why does it matter?" Deckert interjected. "If you think he's gonna go for a kid this time then all bets are off."

"I don't know." I stood up and began slowly pacing about the room. "Maybe it would give us a better idea of who we're looking for. Maybe it's something the four of them could have in common with a child...I don't know." I began to mutter, "It just bothers me..."

"You're thinking that if we knew the connection," Felicity ventured, "that we might have a better idea of the type of child he might abduct?"

"In general, yes. That is, of course, assuming that he hasn't grabbed a child already."

"We thought of that," Deckert expressed. "There haven't been any unresolved child abductions in the area within the past two years."

"What about Seattle?"

"Nothing," Ben added. "If he already grabbed a kid, either it hasn't been reported, or it happened somewhere in between here and Seattle. I've got a coupl'a guys workin' on compilin' a list right now, but that's gonna take some time."

"Dammit! There has to be something." My pace was quickening as my patience began showing wear. "There's something there, and I'm too blind to see it."

"You can't blame yourself, Rowan," Felicity chimed.

"Why not?" I shot back as I came to a halt and motioned to Ben and Deckert. "They're taking me at my word on all of this. They've got cops all over the place watching schools all day. What if I'm wrong? What if this bastard doesn't try to grab a kid after all? What if he kills a waitress from the local pancake house? Or a secretary? Or anyone else for that matter...Then it's MY fault because I was wrong."

The room fell hushed as my diatribe ended, and the three of them watched me in concerned silence. After a long moment, the quiet was ushered from the room by the raspy sound of Detective Deckert clearing his throat.

"Do you think you're wrong?" he asked simply.

I allowed his words to fade softly away before bringing my gaze up to meet their faces. "No. No, I don't."

"Then stop kickin' yourself in the ass," Ben ordered. "It's not gonna help us figure out who this sicko is."

"I'm beginning to wonder if anything is," I whispered.

"If it weren't for you, we'd have never made the Seattle connection," he continued. "It's not like this asshole has been leavin' behind a lot of clues. Trust me, even I don't believe I'm about to say this, but right now your dreams or nightmares, or whatever the hell you call 'em, are the best leads we've got. So far, you're two for two, and that's a damned good average in my book."

"But the dreams aren't just 'Bam, here's the answer', Ben," I objected. "The clues are obscure and symbolic. Like the Seattle thing. I had that dream days ago, and it was about rain. I didn't make the connection until I got a package from a client that's based in Seattle, and it triggered the thought. I still don't know what the other ones mean."

"So maybe you just need to relax," Deckert volunteered.

"Could be." I leaned against the doorframe and let out a long sigh. "That would probably help."

"I don't mean to push, especially on that note, but you mentioned somethin' about money on the phone earlier," Ben queried. "Any idea what it means yet?"

"No, not yet... And there's a perfect example of what I

mean about the clues being obscure. What I saw in the dream wasn't actually money, it was a tarot card."

"You mean like those fortune teller cards," Deckert intoned.

"Exactly." I pushed away from the doorway and retrieved a tarot deck from the top drawer of the buffet then seated myself back at the table. "This deck belonged to my mother," I told them as I unwrapped the square of white silk that encompassed them. "Neither Felicity nor I have ever been really into tarot, so I had to look some of this up. Ariel, on the other hand, was fascinated with it. In my dream, we were sitting at a table, and she was reading the cards for me...but not really FOR me, more like TO me."

"I don't believe I'm asking this," Ben spoke this time, "but what did she tell you?"

"Nothing really." I fanned the deck of seventy-two oversized cards before us and began carefully choosing those that had appeared in the dream. "I think this one represents the killer."

As they watched, I placed the Knight of Cups face up in the center of the table.

"Why's that?" Deckert asked.

"Whenever Ariel read tarot," I explained, "she used a method know as the Celtic Cross. The variation of the style she followed requires that the reader choose a card called a *significator* to represent the person being read for. This was the card she chose in the dream."

"So what does that tell us?"

"If you follow the assigned, or divinatory as it's called, meaning of the card, then it would represent a young man with light hair and eyes."

"Not exactly a specific description is it," Ben ventured rhetorically.

"She continued with this card." I reached out and placed

The Devil over the significator card. "As you would expect, this card can signify violence and black magick. In this position of the Celtic Cross, the card represents the general atmosphere surrounding the subject." I placed The Tower across the two cards. "Next, the sixteenth card of the Major Arcana, representing an overthrow of existing ways of life, imprisonment, even death. This position shows the forces that oppose the subject of the reading."

"It represents us," Felicity whispered softly.

"That's my guess," I agreed. "Anyway, that's where the reading stopped. Suddenly everything changed, and I witnessed her being murdered by a shadowy figure once again."

"Excuse me if I appear stupid," Ben puzzled, "but where in the hell did ya' get money outta that?"

"From this card," I answered and tossed the Seven of Pentacles face up onto the pile. "Seventh card of the suit of Pentacles, sometimes called coins. The money card. A little girl appeared in the dream and handed it to me... It recurred several times in the next nightmare as well. That's why I think it's important."

"You still just don't know why," Deckert volunteered.

"Exactly."

At that moment, the wall clock executed its assigned task and announced the time with a loud bong. The singularity of the tone signified that it was half past the hour. The black metal hands imperceptibly rotated around its ornamental face and showed the time to be 4:30 P.M.

"Sheesh, I didn't realize it was gettin' this late," Ben announced after glancing over his shoulder at the timepiece. "I still have to get by the bank and hit the ATM."

The bank.

Mentally, I turned the piece of the imaginary jigsaw puzzle in my ethereal hands. Its curved, interlocking fingers instantly took on a familiar shape, matching obviously with its mate. I pressed the fragment downward and watched it slip snugly in where it belonged.

"That's it," I whispered.

"What's it?" Felicity asked. "Are you okay, Rowan?"

"The bank," I spoke more audibly. "Money. The bank. The killer works at a bank." I turned quickly to Ben and Deckert. "The four victims. Did they go to the same bank?"

"I don't know," Ben answered. "But I doubt it. They all lived in different parts of the city."

"I don't know either," Deckert admitted. "But we can find out. Ben's probably right though. Even if they did use the same bank, that doesn't mean they used the same branch."

"Let's check it anyway," I told them adamantly. "It has to be the connection. It just has to be."

Material leftovers from the lives of the four women resided within catalogued and labeled plastic bags—purses and wallets that, until the deaths of these women, had been sacred repositories of their ordinary, extraordinary, and personal items. Purses that husbands and boyfriends refused to violate, taking them instead to their loved one held at arms length and waiting patiently for her to pull that which he sought from its depths. Purses, the contents of which had now been heartlessly fondled, inspected, dusted, and inventoried by the hands of complete strangers.

These tangible remnants, once owned by the four women, now lay neatly upon the surface of the conference table at the Major Case Squad command post. "Bagged and tagged" as Ben would often say. Dispassionately "bagged and tagged" and now waiting for Ben, Deckert, and myself to join the ranks of the prying strangers.

"I wouldn't bother with any credit cards," I volunteered as they began rummaging through the contents of the clear plastic bags. "It's going to be a checking or savings account. Something that would get them into the bank where he could see them."

"Here's one," Deckert announced and tossed a worn, blue leather checkbook on the table in front of me. "It's Ariel Tanner's."

I reached for the checkbook and hesitated noticeably when he volunteered the identity of its former owner. I don't think either of them noticed, as Ben was still searching through a bag, and Deckert had turned his attention to the next one in line. I took a deep breath in through my nose and then let it out slowly through my mouth, forcing myself to relax. Only then did I pick up the checkbook and flip open the cover.

The checks were a simple mottled tan, a line of text boasting the fact that they had been printed on recycled paper. Across the upper left corner, ARIEL R. TANNER was imprinted in bold black letters, her address and phone number followed beneath in slightly smaller type. Just above the memo line was a shadowy, stylized logo of a domed building bisected by a line of sturdy type.

"Capitol Bank of Missouri," I read aloud.

"Same here," Ben echoed, peering up from the checkbook he was holding, then added, "Ellen Gray."

My heart started to race. Thus far, two of the four women had used the same bank. While there were several branch offices throughout the metropolitan area, it was easily possible they had both visited the same one at some point in time. My theory with regard to the last two nightmares was being proven true.

"This is it," I exclaimed. "I was right. This is the connection."

"Don't get too excited," Deckert interrupted, a sagging frown tugging at the corners of his mouth. "Community Bank of Overmoor." He waved the grey vinyl-covered checkbook at me. "Karen Barnes."

"Westview Federal Savings," Ben recited in a dejected tone. "Darla Radcliffe... Sorry, Rowan... It was a hell of a try though."

My rising bubble of elation had been abruptly punctured by Detective Deckert, and as I began dropping back toward earth, Ben ripped a mile wide tear in the fabric that sent me crashing. There were three different banks between the four victims. I didn't understand. That piece of the puzzle had fit in so perfectly. I couldn't be wrong.

"Can I see those?" I asked tonelessly as I dropped into a chair.

The two solemn detectives quietly slid the checkbooks across the table to me. I reached out and picked up the first one. I opened the pebbly-surfaced grey vinyl to reveal the happily colored pastel checks imprinted with the names RICHARD H. BARNES and KAREN L. BARNES. The dark black logo for the Community Bank of Overmoor stood out in hard contrast against the dusty blue background, wordlessly telling me I was wrong.

I sat holding the rectangular booklet of smooth paper and grainy plastic. Something simply didn't feel right. I ran my fingers over the checks, tracing the lines imprinted on their faces. They were crisp and clean. The cover felt stiff and new, unsullied by repeated use. I could even detect a faint chemical odor, like that of vinyl upholstery. On a hunch, I flipped open the register occupying the other half of the checkbook and pored over the first line.

"This is a new account," I voiced immediately, turning

the register to them. "Look at this. According to the starting balance, it was opened less than a month ago."

"Son-of-a-bitch," Deckert muttered as he stared at the date.

"I'm willing to bet they had an account at Capitol Bank," I volunteered.

"I'll call the husband," he stated, taking the checkbook from my outstretched hand.

The call was short and bittersweet. While I was glad that I didn't have to be the one charged with calling the dead woman's husband, at the same time, I felt for him.

"You were right," Deckert affirmed as he dropped the handset back into its cradle. "They closed their account at Capitol earlier this month."

"I hate to rain on your parade, guys, but this account isn't new." Ben had been reviewing Darla Radcliffe's checkbook once again and now waved it at us as we turned our attention to him. "Look at the date code next to 'er name. She opened this account over four years ago."

I wasn't going to give up. Three of the victims had used the same bank, and it had to be the connection. This was the clue that was going to identify the killer; I was sure of it. The fact that the fourth victim had conducted her business with a different bank couldn't be allowed to dispel my theory.

My mind raced, briefly touching upon each of the catalogued facts it held and lingering momentarily on the ones that triggered a thought. Two of the victims were single, one separated, and one married. Ariel Tanner was single, and she was killed in her apartment. Karen Barnes was married, and she was killed in the park. Ellen Gray was separated, living alone. She was killed in her home. Darla Radcliffe was single, and she was killed in her apartment.

"He didn't want to chance a confrontation," I muttered

thoughtfully to myself.

"What's that?" Deckert looked up at the sound of my voice.

"Just thinking out loud," I told him. "One of the victims was married, one separated, and the other two were single, right?"

"Yeah," Ben chimed. "So?"

"So Karen Barnes was killed outside of her home where she would most likely be away from her husband," I continued. I wasn't even sure what I was driving at myself, but voicing it seemed to be helping my thoughts take on a recognizable shape. "The other three were killed in their homes."

"Go on," Deckert seemed intrigued.

"Well, if I'm right, and the killer does work at a bank, then he would have access to information about the victims, and he would know their marital status."

"So you figure he used that info to avoid being interrupted by someone who could kick his ass," Deckert submitted.

"Yeah, I guess something like that."

"While that makes sense," Ben agreed, "it still doesn't wash, 'cause we just established that Darla Radcliffe didn't use the same bank as the other three."

A fact, at the same time both obvious and insignificant passed quickly through my mind. Mentally, I stopped and flipped backwards through the imaginary file. "Darla Radcliffe had a roommate, didn't she?"

"Yeah," Ben answered, absently snapping open his notebook and paging through it. "Butler. Wendy Butler. They both worked for the same airline. She wasn't home though. She was fillin' in on a flight for..." His words trailed off as the pieces started falling into place.

"...Her roommate," I completed the sentence. "Wendy

Butler has an account at Capitol Bank. *She* was supposed to be victim number four." I tossed the last comment out on the table and waited silently for a reaction.

"She's stayin' with her parents," Ben stated, as Deckert dialed the phone, glancing over at the proffered notebook for the number.

No other words had been spoken since my remark, and in the stillness of the room, I could hear the faint buzz from the handset as the phone rang at the other end. After a few brief seconds that pretended to encompass lifetimes, I detected a click followed by a distant voice.

"Miz Butler, this is Detective Carl Deckert with the Major Case Squad..." He spoke into the mouthpiece while Ben and I listened patiently, "...I'm fine, thank you...Listen, I'm terribly sorry to bother you, but I need to ask you a question..."

Just as he had done earlier in the call to Karen Barnes' husband, Detective Deckert came quickly to the point. A repeated apology and a "goodbye" later, he settled the handset back on its base. His gaze had remained on me from the moment he had asked the woman where she did her banking. It still hadn't wavered.

"Bingo," he affirmed. "Wendy Butler has had an account with Capitol Bank for about two years."

"See if you can find out who we need ta' contact for employee records," Ben told him hurriedly. "I'll see about a warrant just in case we need it."

Deckert nodded and reached for the phone once again. His hand stopped midway in the air, and we all turned with a start as the door to the small conference room swung open and another detective poked his head in.

"Storm, Deckert," he spoke urgently, "we just got a call from the Sherman police chief. They've got a seven-year-old girl that never made it home from school."

CHAPTER 20

"How the hell did this happen?!" Ben was saying. "Did they have their heads up their asses or somethin'?!"

We were no longer cloistered away in the small conference room, and his angry voice pierced through the veil of noisy activity going on around us. It was a certainty that the other members of the Major Case Squad heard him, but they continued about their assigned duties with no perceptible hesitation.

Deckert, somewhat calmer than Ben, pressed the other detective, "Did anyone actually see the kid get snatched?"

"No," he answered. "At least no one that they've talked to. They're searching the area right now, but it doesn't look very promising...They found her book bag, but that's about it."

"Dammit, they shoulda been expecting somethin' like this! We told them..." Ben continued his semi-contained explosion, "What did they give us on the kid? What's 'er name?"

"You're not gonna believe it when I tell you," the other officer returned. "It's kind of a strange coincidence."

"Ariel," I announced flatly from behind them. "The little girl's name is Ariel."

"Yeah, weird isn't it? He looked past Ben and Deckert at me. "How'd you know?"

"Lucky guess."

"Anyway," he continued, "she's seven years old, just started the second grade. Shoulder-length brown hair, blue eyes, and she was last seen wearing a blue dress. Denim, the mother said."

"Just a second." Ben looked quickly at his watch. "You said she never made it home from school. When was she reported missin'?"

"According to the call, she got out of school at around three-forty and should have been home by four. The mother went looking and couldn't find her, so she called it in at a quarter after."

"Jeezus!" This time the explosion was a little less controlled. "It's after six and they just called! What the fuck were they waitin' for? An engraved invitation?"

The other officer took a noticeable step back from the seething mountain that was Detective Benjamin Storm. Of the things that could set him off, anything he perceived as incompetence was the most likely to do it. Combining it with the fact that a child's life was now most likely perched perilously close to the edge of nothingness only served to feed his growing temper.

"We still have time," I stated calmly.

"What?!" he turned on me quickly, responding only to the sound of my voice. His demeanor softened slightly when he realized whom he was facing.

"I said, we still have time. Not much, but it's better than nothing. He'll keep her alive until the time arrives for the ritual. He might keep her drugged, but I don't think he'll harm her at this point."

"Why's that?" Deckert queried.

"He has to keep her pristine," I explained. "No rape, no torture. He's not going to hurt her... Not yet anyway."

"He picked 'er out, didn't he?" Ben demanded. "This wasn't just some random grab, was it?"

"I'm sure he did. The fact that her name is Ariel is probably just a coincidence. I doubt that it had anything to do with his selection." The little girl in my visions flashed before my eyes. "I should have recognized it sooner though."

"Recognize what?"

"The little girl in my visions." I spelled out my thoughts for them, "She appeared as a young, childlike version of Ariel Tanner. I was being told that THIS Ariel had already been chosen, but I didn't understand. I just assumed he would grab any child he could."

"So, if he had her picked out in advance, then the bank must still be the connection," Deckert volunteered. "She must have a trustee account or something."

I nodded in assent. "I'd be willing to bet on it. That's how he was able to see her and pick her out... For all the good that does us now."

"We might not have stopped 'im from grabbin' this kid," Ben declared indignantly, "but we're on the right track now... We're close, and I'll be damned if he's gonna get a chance to hurt 'er. You got anything else from these dreams of yours we should know about?"

"No, not off the top of my head," I answered, "but I have them written down in my Book of Shadows at home. I guess I should probably go over them again and see if there's something I missed."

"Why don't you take Rowan home and do that, Ben." Deckert patted him on the shoulder. "I'll get on that employee list and warrant."

"You sure?"

"Yeah. I'll get Benson and Jonesey here to give me a hand." He motioned to the detective that had informed us about the kidnapping. "You check out anything else Rowan might have, and with a little luck, we'll be going over that list by the time you get back."

"Yeah, okay," Ben grudgingly agreed then added," I don't care if he had 'er picked out already or not, I still think they had their heads up their asses."

I hadn't expected Cally's van to be in the driveway when Ben and I arrived at my house. As unexpected as that was, I was even more surprised to find R.J. seated in my living room with her and Felicity. Having had some rest and a shower, he looked much better than the last time we met. The image of him in the interview room was one I hoped I would soon forget.

R.J. stood as we came through the door. He shuffled nervously, looking from us to Cally and back. It was obvious that he hadn't expected Ben, and his presence brought a fleeting look of anxiety to his face. The expression quickly melted away and was replaced by a thin, sheepish smile.

"I hope we're not bothering you," he began uneasily. "Felicity said you were helping Detective Storm."

"No bother at all." I extended my hand. "You're looking much better than you did a couple of days ago."

His smile widened slightly at my comment. He took my hand and shook it firmly. "I just wanted to say thanks to you and Felicity for sticking up for me. You don't really know me that well and all...well, you know...I just really appreciate it."

"I was happy to," I replied. "I just didn't believe you were guilty. Problem was, I didn't have any proof, and unfortunately, the police had a lot of evidence to the contrary."

"You mean me and Ellen," he submitted.

"That, among other things."

"I guess you already know that you were right. We were seeing each other. She and her husband had been having trouble for a while, and, well, I guess I was just there to listen when she needed it."

"That's pretty much what I thought," I nodded. "But the thing that really bothered me was finding your fingerprint on the candle."

"I brought some candles over to Ellen's place," he returned. "We were burning one when we got together that afternoon."

"Forensics determined that there were two separate white candles in that pile of wax," Ben added impatiently. "One right on top of the other. We missed it at first. I just found out this afternoon and haven't had a chance to tell ya' about it."

I nodded thoughtfully at his comment and then turned back to R.J.

"Anyway," R.J. continued, "Ellen and I had this huge fight about..."

"Listen," Ben interrupted coolly, "no offense kid, but can you two talk about this a little later? We're runnin' against the clock here, and I really need Rowan to stay focused right now."

R.J.'s expression hardened at his comment, and I could see a sarcastic reply forming on his lips. Fortunately, Felicity sensed something was amiss and broke in before he could expel the venomous comment.

"What happened?" her voice began strongly then trailed off in an almost fearful tone, "He didn't..."

"Yeah," Ben spat. "Seven years old. She disappeared on her way home from school."

"What are you talking about?" Cally spoke up. "Are you saying he's killed a child?"

"Not yet." I motioned for R.J. to have a seat and then positioned myself on the arm of the nearby loveseat. "But he abducted one, and it's only a matter of time before he does kill her."

"I don't get it." R.J.'s earlier irritated scowl had been replaced by a look of confusion and concern. "What does he need a kid for?"

"The sacrifice."

"I thought he'd already been performing sacrifices," Cally expressed.

I looked over at Ben questioningly. Throughout this investigation, Felicity and I had been privy to information that no other civilian had. I wanted to be sure I didn't betray the confidence that had been placed in us by saying too much.

"Go ahead," he told me with a shrug, fully understanding the look I had given him.

"From what we've been able to ascertain, he's just been practicing," I explained after receiving my friend's blessing. "He's never actually performed the ritual."

"What makes you think that?" Cally pressed.

"The increased precision displayed at each murder. He's getting progressively better at what he's doing. Also, the additions he makes each time, like incense and arranging the body." I recited the major points. "In addition to all that, neither Felicity nor I have been able to feel any residual energies left behind at the scenes. If he had actually performed a ritual, then something like that should be overwhelming to someone sensitive to it."

They both nodded in agreement.

"The fourth victim was the real kicker," I continued. "The perfect dress rehearsal, but with two exceptions."

"What're those?" R.J. questioned.

"There wasn't a full moon." I paused. "And the victim most likely wasn't a virgin."

"So that's why he took a kid," he mused aloud and then glanced over at Ben. "And the full moon is Friday, so that's why you're running out of time."

Ben nodded. "Give the man a cigar."

"Do you have any leads? Any clues at all?" Cally interjected.

"A few. Not many though." I stood and moved across the room as I spoke. Earlier in the day, I had placed my "Dream Diary" on the bookshelf, and I now retrieved it. "That's why we're here right now, to have a look at this."

"What is that?" R.J. asked.

"My Book of Shadows. I've been having nightmares ever since I got involved with this case, and I've been recording them here. Apparently, they contain clues about the killer, or it seems that way so far. They predicted the death of the fourth victim and the abduction of the little girl... Unfortunately, I just didn't interpret the meanings soon enough to prevent either of those things from happening."

"Maybe there's something we can do to help," Cally volunteered, focusing her attention on me. "We used to discuss dreams with Ariel all the time."

"Yeah," R.J. agreed with her. "Ariel was real good at figuring out the weird stuff."

"That would explain some of the things in here then." I waved the notebook. "She's been appearing in my nightmares, and the clues have definitely been obscure."

The atmosphere around Cally and R.J. had grown tight with bristling energy. I could almost feel an electrical surge flowing from the two of them as they relaxed and attuned themselves with their surroundings. Even with the weight of the current situation, I was hard pressed not to feel a sense of pride in how well Ariel had taught them about The Craft. It was obvious to me that they truly wanted to help.

"You mean you think Ariel might be directing your visions?" Cally posed.

"I'm sure of it."

"Whoa, that's pretty intense, man," R.J. exclaimed.

I glanced over at Ben who was quietly observing the scene before him with professional detachment. Even though he had recently come to accept my visions as true precursors to future events, what we Witches were now viewing as a normal conversation certainly had to appear outlandish to him. His exposure to our way of life over the past week appeared to have opened his eyes however, as he seemed to be taking it all in stride.

"What kinds of things has she been throwing at you?" Cally prodded.

"A good example would be the Seven of Pentacles showing up all over the place."

"The suit of coins," she recited mechanically. "The money card."

"You read?" Felicity inquired.

"Yeah. I learned from Ariel," she acknowledged. "She was really into tarot."

"Unfortunately, we aren't," I outlined. "So I had to do a little research on the meanings. Even so, it still didn't make any sense until today."

"I almost forgot to ask," Felicity expressed. "Was your idea about that right?"

"He was on the nose," Ben spoke up. "All of the victims had accounts at the same bank except the Radcliffe woman. So *Svengali* here says, 'What about her roommate?' And bingo! There it is. Her roommate's bank account matched up with the other three."

"More than likely she was the intended victim," I finished the story. "But they were both flight attendants, and they just happened to trade flights that day."

"Talk about bad luck," R.J. whistled. "But what about the little girl?"

"Her name's Ariel, believe it or not, but I don't think that's her connection. They're checking, but the guess is that she has a trustee account or something at the same bank."

"Well, that would make sense," Cally mused. "Money, bank accounts, and all that." She shifted slightly in her seat. "But you're right. It's pretty obscure."

"So you figure that the killer works at the bank they all used or something?" R.J. ventured thoughtfully.

"Capitol Bank to be exact," Ben responded. "And yeah, that's the theory right now."

"Capitol Bank?" Cally echoed. "Wow, that's weird."

Ben shifted his gaze over to her. "Whaddaya mean?"

"Roger." She turned to me. "You know, the guy we told you about that was just a poser? Well, he works at Capitol Bank. That's where he met Ariel." She gave a visible shudder. "To think he might be working with this sicko. It gives me the creeps."

"By any chance," Ben reached into his jacket and pulled out the familiar, worn black notebook that never seemed to leave his side. "Would either of you know if he happened to move here recently, like say, within the past year?"

"Yeah, I think he did," R.J. nodded thoughtfully. "He was from somewhere out West or someplace like that."

"I seem to remember him saying something about Washington state," Cally added. "Why?"

"Because another one of the clues in the dream was constant rain," I explained. "When I finally managed to connect that with Seattle, we found out that a murder just like these happened out there about a year ago."

"Do you really think it could be Roger?" Cally's eyes had widened almost instantly.

"I don't know," Ben announced, "but I plan ta' find out."

"What does Roger look like?" I queried.

"Oh, late twenties, early thirties," Cally described. "Kind of stocky, about five-eight with sandy hair."

"What color are his eyes?" I pressed.

"Bright blue."

"No they aren't," R.J. interjected. "Those are contacts. Remember, he lost one at a coven meeting once, and he looked like one of those malamutes or something. He's got grey eyes."

"Yeah, you're right. I forgot about that," she agreed and then turned to me. "Is that important?"

I didn't answer her directly. I looked over at my friend who was now holding his pen frozen in space inches from his notebook, staring back in amazement. "I saw grey eyes when I channeled Karen Barnes. The killer has grey eyes."

We all stared around the room at one another silently for a moment. The pieces of the puzzle had fallen completely into place, making a fully formed image—the image of a young man with light hair and light eyes.

Ben was the first to break the stunned hush. "I'm gonna use your phone."

CHAPTER 21

"Tell 'im that's not my problem, and yes we do have a warrant," Ben roared into the telephone. "Now I want the employee file on Roger Henderson yesterday!" He covered the mouthpiece with his hand and glanced over at me. "President of the bank is throwin' some kinda black tie thing at his house tonight. He seems ta' think that it's more important than... Hell No!" Someone apparently spoke at the other end as he abruptly ended his comment and returned his attention to the handset. "Why don't ya' ask 'im how he'd feel about havin' a sobriety checkpoint right outside his front door?" The pause was brief while the person at the other end assumedly relayed Ben's intimidating rhetoric. "Yeah, I thought so. Have a patrol in the area pick it up and tell 'em to ignore the stop signs... Yeah, Uh-huh. Thanks... Yeah, is Deckert still there? Yeah, put 'im on..."

Cally, R.J., Felicity, and I watched wordlessly as Ben continued directing the efforts of the Major Case Squad via the telephone. The device had been cradled between his ear and shoulder for over fifteen minutes while he relentlessly barked questions and orders into it. He stopped only momentarily to quickly shift the handset to the other shoulder and turn to a fresh page in his notebook.

The atmosphere in the room had stiffened with morbid tension the moment Roger's name became associated with the murders. The original response had been one of sympathetic horror at the prospect of him working side by side with the killer. That feeling was almost instantly replaced by disbelief, followed by disgust the moment the light of suspicion fell directly upon him. Stunned as I was by the revelation that a member of Ariel's coven, poser or not, might in fact be the killer, I could only imagine how Cally and R.J. were feeling. They had stood in circle with him, and if I were either of them, it would be making me sick.

"...Tell me we actually do have a warrant, Deck," Ben was continuing his conversation with Detective Deckert now. His query didn't surprise me, as there had been no such document when we left the MCS Command Post, and this was the first contact he had had with them since. "Good, good. Better get the prosecutor on the phone, and have Benson tell the judge not ta' get too comfortable, 'cause I'm bettin' we're gonna need another one."

Ben proceeded to outline the events of the last hour that had caused the few remaining pieces of the puzzle to slip easily into their respective places. The picture was becoming clearer every moment, and I had the distinct feeling that my friend was preparing to frame it and hang it on the wall.

"...Okay, so you get everyone back in. Let's see..." Ben glanced at his watch. "It's seven-ten now, so I should be back no later than seven-thirty... Yeah, I know. Yeah. Yeah. Just tell 'em ya' can't find me or somethin'... Yeah, see ya' in a few."

"If you don't mind my asking," I queried as he settled the handset back onto its cradle, "what was that last bit about not being able to find you?"

He looked around the room letting his gaze flicker uneasily past Cally and R.J. before once again locking with mine. "I guess it doesn't matter who knows. The media'll be all over it soon enough. Seems that since there's an abduction involved, the Feds are all over this thing."

"Is that good or bad?"

"Don't know yet, but I can tell ya' one thing for certain..." He let out a frustrated sigh and directed his index finger at me. "They ain't gonna be real excited about you."

"Have they taken over the investigation or something?"

"Not yet, but they've apparently been callin' every ten minutes lookin' for me. Hell, I've been expectin' it since the beginning. I'm surprised they waited this long."

"How do you plan on handling it?"

"Right now?" Ben reached up to smooth his hair in his distant manner that bespoke of intense thought. "Right now I need ta' get back and help Carl take care of all this shit with warrants. As for the FBI, I'll just hafta cross that bridge when I get to it."

"What do you want us to do?" Felicity interjected.

"At the moment, I doubt there's anything that ya' CAN do," he answered. "Since no one here knows where this guy lives, and accordin' to the DMV, he never got a license in the state of Missouri, we hafta wait until we get that employee file."

"How soon do you think that'll be?" R.J. posed.

"All depends on *El Presidente*," he sarcastically referred to the bank official. "He wasn't too excited about leavin' his little shindig. If he doesn't screw around, then we should have it within the hour."

"What'll you do once you get it?" I queried, though I was pretty sure I already knew the answer.

"Check his work schedule against the presumed time of the abduction," he detailed. "Plus, see if anything matches up with the info from the Seattle PD. If he's got half a brain though, I'm sure he's usin' an alias."

"And if it looks like he's the one?" I pressed.

"Then we get the warrant and go kick his fuckin' door down."

"I'm going with you," I declared flatly.

"Wait a minute, I don't know about that..."

Coming quickly up from the couch, Felicity joined his protest, "What do you mean you're going with him?"

"I mean exactly what I said. I'm going along."

Our two guests fidgeted nervously in their seats but remained silent. If either of them had an opinion on the subject, it appeared that it wasn't going to be voiced in the immediate future. Having anticipated the objection, I steadfastly held Ben's gaze and allowed myself to relax. I knew it was going to take more than just words to convince him.

"Listen, Row," Ben put on his best sympathetic cop voice and began his explanation. "I realize you've been involved in this thing almost from the beginning, and without you, I don't know if we'd have gotten as far as we have—at least not this fast—but, servin' a warrant is a lot different than goin' over a crime scene. Besides, I still hafta figure out how I'm gonna explain you to the Feebs."

"Listen to Ben, Rowan," Felicity agreed. "It's too dangerous."

"She's right man," he added. "What if this asshole has a gun or somethin'? I don't need to worry about you gettin' hurt."

While the two of them were pleading their case, I was focusing my internal energies. My unwavering stare never left Ben's own, and as they remained locked, I set mystical wheels into motion.

"I don't need to worry about you either," I told him in a tranquil, even voice.

"Whaddaya mean?" Ben blinked and looked over at my wife with a questioning glance. "What's he talkin' about, Felicity?" His gaze almost immediately returned to mine, drawn back by an unseen force. "It's my job. I'm trained for it, you ain't."

"You're trained to deal with normal criminals," I maintained in the same even tone. "This one definitely isn't normal. We still don't know what he's capable of."

"We know he's capable of torturin' and killin' four women—maybe five if you count Seattle. Plus kidnapping." He shot back, but his eyes stayed locked with mine. "So I think we pretty much have the bases covered there."

"That's not what I mean, Ben. I'm talking about The Craft, or even more likely, ritual magick. He hasn't played any of those cards yet. Not for real."

I felt Felicity ease away from me as she realized what I was doing. To her, and anyone in the room other than Ben Storm for that matter, my speech probably sounded like a dull monotone. To my protesting friend, nothing would have changed. In his mind, we were simply carrying on a conversation through which he would explain to me the reasons I wouldn't be joining him. He had no idea that in a way, he was being hypnotized. He was experiencing the true meaning of being bewitched.

"That stuff again?" he asked. "Look, you've made a believer outta me with some of this... You know, like the dreams and all that, but gimme a break. What's he gonna do? Shoot fire out of his eyes or somethin'?" He chuckled lightly. "Even better, turn us all into frogs and make his getaway? Come on Rowan, get serious..."

"I never said anything like that," I returned. "And I am serious."

"What then?" he demanded. "What's he gonna do?"

"I can't say for sure, but I know there are any number of things that he might be able to do. I doubt you'd believe me if I told you what they were."

We had been down this path before. I knew for a fact he wouldn't believe me. The only way I was going to prove my point was with a demonstration, and as much as I hated to do so, that was exactly what I had been preparing. Through the practiced use of both my voice and my eyes, in the past few moments I had set the stage. I had transfixed him on an ethereal level. Within the next few seconds, I would use the power of suggestion coupled with just a dash of the supernatural to put on the show.

"Yeah, I thought so. Look, I appreciate your concern and all, but I gotta draw the line somewhere. Since I'm the one with the badge, I'm goin' and you're stayin'."

Ben moved past me as he made the declaration. I waited until he reached the front door before I released the compact ball of energy I had formed inside my mind. It sailed invisibly along a crackling ethereal arc and enveloped my friend with a light aura of static. Its earthly manifestation came with a familiar electric snap when he reached for the doorknob. The only thing that remained for me to do was make a suggestion.

"If that's the way you feel, okay," I called after him. "By the way, what's that crawling on your arm?"

Ben looked down at his sleeve absently, and his eyes suddenly grew wide in horror. His face began to pale as he slapped at his arm and let out a surprised yelp. The rest of us in the room saw nothing. Only I knew what he was witnessing, and that was only because I had been the one to create the illusion. An illusion that took advantage of my friend's irrational fear of spiders and was done in the name of making my point.

"Jeezus!" he shouted aloud as he whipped about, quickly slipping himself out of his sport coat and shaking it violently. "Holy fuckin' shit! How the hell did that goddamn thing get on me?!"

"Calm down, Ben," Felicity told him. "It's gone."

She was correct. In truth, it had never actually been there. What he had seen had only been in his head, and that spectre could last no more than a few brief seconds. It was definitely gone.

"Whaddaya mean gone?" he shouted, still slapping his

jacket against the door. "Did you see that fuckin' thing? It was huge! It was a goddamn tarantula!"

"She's right, Ben, it was never even there," I expounded. "It was just a glamour."

"There's nothin' glamorous about it!" he shot back, still visibly shaken but starting to calm. "It's a friggin' spider."

"No, Ben," Felicity corrected, "a glamour, not glamorous. It was an illusion. A phantom image. All courtesy of your best friend here."

"Whoa, cool," R.J.'s voice came from behind us, followed by Cally sternly shushing him.

"You mean like it was a spell or somethin'?" he asked as he gingerly inspected his jacket, holding it at arms length.

"You could call it something like that," I explained. "It's really just some basic hypnosis, the power of suggestion, and admittedly a little psychic energy thrown in for good measure. Sorry, but I figured you'd be a little more receptive to the idea if you experienced it first hand."

"You're tryin' to tell me that this asshole might be able to do somethin' like that?" He was carefully slipping his sport coat back onto his large frame, still appearing somewhat uneasy and keeping an eye out for the imagined spider.

"Maybe. Maybe not. I just don't know."

"So what if he can? What're you gonna do about it?" he queried.

"Catch it before it happens. Try to block it. Warn you," I outlined. "I don't know. In any event, I'll be much better prepared to recognize a glamour than you will."

"Well, as long as I ignore spiders crawling on me, I should be okay," he protested.

"He would most likely do something worse. Remember, I just scared the hell out of you, and I'm your best friend. Like I said, I used only a small"—I laid heavy emphasis on the word small—"amount of the psychic energy I could muster. I doubt he'll be anywhere near as nice."

"Is he shittin' me?" Ben asked Felicity seriously.

"As much as I wish he was," she frowned, "no. He's telling you the truth."

"Lovely. You know I oughta kick your ass for that stunt," Ben told me with a slight grin then glanced back to my wife as if for approval.

"Hey, it's between you two." She held up her hands in a mock leave-me-out-of-it gesture and then suddenly grew earnest. "Do me a favor, Ben. If you're going to take him with you, this time don't bring him home with any stitches."

"Count on it."

"Thanks for the vote of confidence," I mumbled.

"She just knows your track record, white man," he turned back to me. "Just one question. Why'd you hafta pick spiders? You know I can't stand the things."

"Actually, I didn't, you did. All I said was 'what's that crawling on your arm?' Your own fears and imagination did the rest of the work for me."

He shook his head. "Just what I needed ta' hear."

I was still clipping my visitor's badge onto my pocket when Carl Deckert met the two of us at the door to the MCS command post. His normally laid back demeanor had been replaced by one of frantic urgency as he held the door open and hustled us into the room.

"I've got something you might want to have a look at," he told us as he excitedly waved a sheaf of papers at us. "You're not gonna believe it."

"What?" Ben queried, following him to a nearby desk. "Whaddaya have?"

Shadows fell darkly across the corner area from the flickering fluorescent tubes in the ceiling lights as they dimly sputtered away towards uselessness. Deckert reached out and craned the flexible neck of a small lamp forward and switched it on, effectively illuminating at least part of the desk's scarred surface.

"I just got this right after you hung up," he spoke rapidly as he shuffled through the papers and slid an eight-by-ten photo beneath the puddle of light. "The lab lifted this from the little girl's vinyl book bag."

The black-and-white-toned image depicted a curving pattern of lines arcing around into what might have been a tight whorl. Might have been, because they abruptly ended in a blank, smeary looking splotch.

"This one is from the Barnes woman," he continued and slid a similar grey-toned image in next to the original.

"Son-of-a-bitch," Ben slowly enunciated the words as he leaned forward to inspect the fingerprint photos more closely.

Not being familiar with fingerprint analysis, I appealed, "Somebody want to fill me in?"

"It's a partial right thumbprint," Detective Deckert explained. "The one you turned us on to with your *vision* or whatever you call it."

"Yeah, I kinda caught on to that," I acknowledged. "But I thought it was too smudged to do anything with."

"That's what we thought," he continued. "But that was before we got the second print which just happened to be quite a bit clearer."

"They both look smudged to me."

"It's a scar," Ben volunteered, completing the explanation for me, then turned to Deckert. "Any hits from AFIS?"

"Not yet," he returned. "It's been scanned, and they're

trying to do a digital image match, but that takes a little longer. The first one didn't hit, but this one is clearer, so maybe..."

"One of you Detective Storm?" a voice issued from behind us.

We turned to find a uniformed officer peering at us expectantly, a manila envelope tucked under his arm.

"That's me," Ben answered.

"Got something here from Capitol Bank for you." The officer held out a clipboard and pen. "I need ya to sign for it."

Ben quickly scribbled his signature on the paperwork then exchanged the clipboard for the envelope and muttered a quick "thanks." He was already ripping it open before the officer was out the door.

"Hey Storm!" another voice called from across the room. "Got a cellular call from a Special Agent Mandalay on line two. Wants to talk to you."

"Tell 'im I'm not here," he shouted back as he rifled through the contents of the envelope.

"He's a she," the voice returned.

"Then fuckin' tell HER I'm not here," he shouted back angrily.

"What are you looking for?" I queried as I watched him quickly shuffling through the papers.

"Ten print card," he answered. "All bank employees are printed for security and exclusionary purposes."

"Exclusionary purposes?"

"Like if the bank gets broken into or robbed," Deckert explained. "Employees' prints are going to be all over the place, so we need copies in order to exclude them from any of the prints lifted during the investigation."

"Here it is," Ben intoned urgently and tossed the heavy stock card face up on the desk.

Each of the outlined squares contained a neatly inked copy of Roger Henderson's fingerprints. The black and white study of irrefutable personal identification stared back up as the three of us brought our eyes to bear on the right thumbprint.

What met our triple-barreled gaze was a curving pattern of lines arcing around into what might have been a tight whorl. Might have been, because the lines ended abruptly in a blank, smeary looking splotch.

"It's him," I whispered.

"Get the prosecuting attorney on the horn," Ben ordered Deckert calmly as he handed the rest of Roger Henderson's employee file to him. "Then call Benson. I want a warrant yesterday."

"I'm on it," Deckert was already dialing the phone.

"Detective Benjamin Storm?" a demanding, almost angry, female voice came from behind us.

We turned once again and were greeted by an attractive brunette woman who appeared to be in her late twenties. She was dressed in a nicely fitted grey suit that scarcely managed to conceal the forty-caliber bulge at her right hip.

"Yeah," Ben answered.

She thrust her hand forward. In it was a large leather case, held deftly open with her index finger as she prominently displayed her badge and FBI identification.

"Special Agent Constance Mandalay," she announced indignantly. "I thought you weren't here?"

Ben looked her coolly in the eyes without blinking and answered her accusation head on. "I lied."

CHAPTER 22

The two of them engaged in a short-lived staring contest as Agent Mandalay slipped her identification back into her jacket and folded her arms across her chest. Petite-framed and standing no taller than five-foot-six, she was forced to look up at Ben, but that wasn't unusual as most everyone else had to do the same.

Ben stood with his hands on his hips, eyes tightly locked with hers. To the outside observer, they seemed to form a brief living caricature of David and Goliath. Had the urgency and gravity of the current situation been of a lesser degree, I am certain the standoff would have elicited a number of laughs.

"Well, at least you're honest about that." Agent Mandalay maintained her resentful demeanor as she spat the comment. "How long did you plan to keep ducking my calls? You had to know I'd show up here eventually."

"For as long as I needed to," Ben retorted, continuing with the precedent he had set for truthfulness. "And unfortunately, yes, I knew some Feeb would come walkin' through the door at some point. Hell, I'm surprised ya' waited this long."

"Had it been up to me, we wouldn't have," she shot back. "I was ready to come down here when you made your queries through VICAP. You should have called the Bureau for help with the first homicide. We have a lot more experience in this field than you do. We have experts on occult practices that..."

Ben cut her off mid-sentence, "I got my own expert, thank you."

"Who? Him?" she stated incredulously as she waved her

hand in my direction. I assumed she recognized me from the media coverage. "He claims he's a Witch, for Chrissake! I'm talking about people with PhD's, not some flake you picked up off the street."

I was mildly insulted, but then, I was also quite used to the ridicule and demeaning commentaries from uninformed, closed-minded individuals. The fact that I made no secret of my religion forced me to deal with it on a daily basis. Fortunately, witch burning was no longer an accepted practice, so verbal debasement and occasional graffiti were pretty much the worst I had to face. Because I had become so jaded to it, her comment was easily and quickly disregarded.

Ben, on the other hand, was furious. Ever since I had known him, he had been very protective of his family and friends. Even though he had wallowed in his own disbelief until just recently, he had never passed judgment upon my religion or me. The look that suddenly crossed his face was testimony to the fact that he was not about to allow someone else to do so.

"You wait just one goddamn minute!" he asserted, angrily thrusting his index finger at her. "Don't come in here with your holier-than-thou attitude and start insultin' people you don't even know. Whether you like it or not, Rowan Gant is part of this investigation. A VERY IMPORTANT part."

"Yes he is. He should be a suspect."

"Don't even go there! If it weren't for him, we'd all still be scratchin' our asses tryin' to figure out what's goin' on. I'll put him up against your PhD's any day of the week."

"Is that why you have four homicides and a kidnapping to deal with?" Thick, bitter sarcasm dripped from her comment.

"I've got four homicides and a kidnappin' to deal with

because there appears to be a bumper crop of sick assholes this year," he echoed. "Now, in case you haven't noticed, I'm busy. Because of Rowan, we know who the sonofabitch is, and I'm tryin' ta' get a warrant, so we can stop him from killin' this little girl. If you wanna help, fine. If you wanna cop an attitude and cause me a lotta grief, then you can take your fuckin' Ivy-league-piled-high-and-deeps and shove them up your..."

"Ben!" Carl Deckert's voice sliced surgically through the air as if on cue, preventing Ben from completing his verbal instructions to Special Agent Mandalay. "The warrant's signed. Benson's on the phone."

"Tell 'im to get his ass back here now," Ben turned and barked over his shoulder. "I want everyone in the conference room in fifteen. And have somebody get a map of the streets around this shithead's house."

Detective Deckert acknowledged and immediately relayed Ben's message into the phone before hurrying off to set up the meeting. Ben turned his attention back to the thin-lipped, staunchly staring face of Agent Mandalay.

"Like I said, Special Agent, I'm busy. If you're still interested in helpin', the tactical meeting is in fifteen minutes."

Her expression never changed as she hissed venomously, "I'll be there."

"How in the hell can you stand wearing one of these things?" I whispered my question to Ben through the darkness behind his van.

I was trying to force myself to ignore the itching sensation that was erupting over the majority of my torso as we took our positions in the shadows. The air was unmoving and viscous with humidity, and though it was already after ten in the evening, the mercury had only dipped into the mid-eighties.

Rivulets of sweat brought on by the tenseness of the situation, as well as the heat, were tickling my chest and back as the force of gravity inched them slowly downward. Mid-chest, a particularly sensitive bundle of nerves began to complain. The more I tried to keep my mind off it, the more intense it became, until finally, a violent itch burst forth. Instinctively, my hand shot up to relieve the prickling sensation with what promised to be an ecstatic scratch. Unfortunately, instead of giving me the relief I sought, my fingers impacted with a dull thud against the object of my earlier vocal disdain—a *Kevlar* flak vest.

"Ya' just do," Ben whispered back. "Besides, I promised Felicity I wouldn't let ya' get hurt."

The tactical meeting had gone quickly as the veteran members of the MCS had studied the enlarged street map in order to plan the best avenue of assault. From the moment the warrant was signed, the machine that was the Greater Saint Louis Major Case Squad shifted into high gear—each individual doing whatever was necessary to ensure the success of the operation. The local police department had been immediately notified and the house placed under surveillance. That had been just over an hour ago. Thus far, the only activity in the residence had been the lights going off.

We had stationed ourselves on a side street diagonally across from the address while the rest of the force had fanned out around the home. The houses directly behind and to either side had been surreptitiously evacuated in order to keep the occupants out of harm's way. To someone such as myself who had witnessed such things only on television cop shows, the entire process seemed oddly surreal.

Every member of the Major Case Squad and more than a handful of officers from the local municipality, uniformed and not, were spread in a tight circle around the small brick house. Here and there, if you knew exactly where to look, you could occasionally catch a fleeting glimpse of one of them through the shadows. A flash of eyes peering out the gap of a full-face-hugging balaclava. A quick instant where the stenciled yellow POLICE on someone's flak vest came into view or even the glint of the streetlights from the barrel of a gun.

"Are you sure you need this many people?" I whispered nervously once again. "I mean, I'm not trying to tell you your job or anything, but, you know..."

If Ben noticed my anxiety, which I'm sure he did, he didn't mention it. "I'm a great believer in excessive force," he quipped softly. "'Specially when it comes ta' assholes like this one."

The streets were barricaded for two blocks in either direction, and there had been no vehicular traffic for the past ten minutes. The only sound to be heard was the almost mechanical on-again off-again warbling of nature's chitin-covered orchestra in the trees. Even the city had fallen quiet, or so it seemed.

The sound of a car coasting quietly to a stop behind us violated the hush. I started nervously, and Ben simply turned, still tactfully ignoring my jitters.

Detective Deckert had switched off the headlights and killed the engine farther up the street then allowed the stored momentum to roll the vehicle smoothly up to us. As soundlessly as they could manage, he and Special Agent Mandalay climbed out of the station wagon and gently pushed the doors shut. Our position was fairly obscured by a tall evergreen hedgerow, so they were able to duck down and remain unseen as they made their way forward. The moon had stationed itself behind a shadowy wall of clouds, and we were parked as far away from the streetlights as possible. However, there was still enough of a dim glow for me to see that Deckert had squeezed himself into a vest as well. Over hers, Agent Mandalay had donned a dark blue windbreaker bearing the stenciled logo "FBI" across the left breast.

"What the hell is he doing here?!" Special Agent Mandalay hissed at Ben as she drew up next to us.

"Observin'," he returned evenly.

"What do you mean 'observing'?" she declared. "This is a law enforcement operation. He's a civilian."

"Raise your right hand, Rowan," Ben ordered without taking his gaze from her.

"Do what?" I voiced my confusion.

He glanced over at me quickly. "Raise your right hand." When I had done so, he returned his cold stare to Agent Mandalay. "Do you, Rowan Gant," he began, "Swear to love your wife, pet your dog, and uphold truth, justice, and the American way, so help you whatever deity it is you Witches worship?"

"You can't deputize him!" she hissed once again. "This isn't a cowboy movie!"

"Well, Rowan? Do ya'?" he pressed.

"Sure," I replied, not knowing what else to say.

"I'm going to have your badge, Storm!" she pronounced angrily through clenched teeth.

"Jeezus Christ," Deckert interjected in a harsh murmur. "Will you two give it a rest!? We've got a psycho to stop. If you're that desperate to have a battle of egos, I'll be more than happy to ring the freakin' bell for ya'... AFTER we catch this guy."

The combative stares lingered between the two of them a

moment longer, then Ben turned his head and reached up to the microphone clipped on the shoulder of his vest and depressed the talk button.

"All positions report in," he whispered.

The radio on his belt, set to low volume, crackled slightly as each of the pre-designated teams reported in one by one. When all had answered their readiness, Ben slipped his pistol from its shoulder holster and hefted it slightly. Deckert and Mandalay followed suit, the latter still frowning intensely as she quietly filled her hand with a government issue *Sig Sauer P226*.

"You do only what I tell ya' ta' do, when I tell ya' ta' do it," Ben directed the command to me. "Stay behind me at all times, and if I tell ya' to stay put, then don't even fuckin' breathe. Got it?"

"Yeah," I nodded. "I got it."

With another quick glance at Agent Mandalay, he thumbed the microphone switch once again and whispered, "All right, we're goin' in."

I had all but forgotten the earlier itching of the flak vest. Now, as we stealthily advanced across the street and up the steps to the porch of the old brick house, the unpleasant chafing had returned with a vengeance. I was certain that a large part of my discomfort was psychological, directly related to the fact that I was unable to scratch.

I fought to relax and push the sensation from my mind, but the tenseness of the situation had opened the valve on my adrenal gland to full. Energy was crackling riotously through my body like a downed power line in a storm and I noticed much to my chagrin that my hands were shaking.

Ben flattened himself against the wall to the left of the door and silently motioned with his empty hand. His signals made it clear that I was to remain with him while Deckert and Agent Mandalay were to take a similar position on the right. Following his instruction, I pressed myself into the brick, attempting to disappear into its face. Looking out over the front yard we had just crossed, I could see various figures that had advanced behind us, cutting off any avenue of escape for the occupant of the house. I was greatly impressed by the precision with which the entire operation was being executed.

After a few more wordless signals, Ben reached over and slowly depressed the latch on the screen door until it released with an audible metallic click. The noise was something that wouldn't even be noticed on a normal day, but to us, it sounded as loud as a gunshot. He waited for an eternity, then just a few moments more. No lights came on. No sound issued from the house. The silence was broken only by the raspy cadence of our own shallow breathing. I couldn't speak for the other three, but my heart was racing at a madman's pace, threatening to burst from my chest and be contained only by the *Kevlar* body armor.

Ben began pulling the screen door open at a laboriously slow speed. All the while, his eyes remained locked with those of another cop who had crept up the stairs and was now crouched on the top step. I could only see the man's eyes as his face was obscured by the tight fabric of a full-face mask. Still, I recognized him as Bill, the young detective that had given me so much grief at the Major Case Squad briefing. He glanced over at me briefly as a flicker of recognition ran through his eyes then gave me a slight nod. From the manner in which the fabric covering the lower half of his face momentarily stretched, I almost believed he smiled.

The screen door was halfway open now, and Ben kept a steady pressure on it, easing it wider by the second. The aluminum frame pivoted almost soundlessly on the evenly spaced hinges, making only a slight whispering sound of mild friction. It was when the door reached three-fourths its open arc that my heart stopped.

Maybe the frame was bent slightly, maybe there was rust deep in the hinges, or maybe any of a countless number of other reasons. Whatever the exact *maybe* was, the point was moot. The door emitted a sudden small groan of protest, followed instantly by a piercing creak that echoed across the empty street. In the split second following the end of the harsh metallic wail, the porch light snapped on.

Time slowed for me. I don't know if it was a supernatural effect or just a psychological aberration due to the newness and intensity of the situation. Whatever it was, it made the next few moments appear to me in what I can only describe as Hollywood slow motion. Ben was nodding vigorously as he yanked the door fully open, sending another series of loud groans resounding through the night. As I turned, I saw Bill come up from his crouch like a sprinter at the sound of a starting pistol. Two long strides later, his shoulder met the wooden door, followed by his full weight in motion, causing the frame to buckle and splinters to fly in several directions.

The Hollywood slow motion continued with a decelerated soundtrack meeting my ears. The frenzied crash of the shattering doorframe was drawn out into a banshee wail resembling fingernails on a chalkboard mixed with marble-sized hail hitting a tin roof. Bill's voice joined the raucous clamor with a commanding, stretched out *"Pollleeeeeeccccce!"*

Detective Deckert and Special Agent Mandalay had turned their heads to shield themselves from the storm of fracturing splinters and were now slowly turning back as they stepped out from the brick wall. Fluidly, they aimed their bodies at the newly created opening, pistols held at the ready, and rushed forward, echoing Bill's cry.

A deep, rushing chord filled my ears, and at its finish, I

plunged into chaotic real time. By now, several other cops had rushed up the stairs and were filing quickly in through the now fully open door, their flashlights sketching comet trails in the darkness. Ben was screaming "go, Go, GO!" as he waved them onward, still holding the traitorous screen door wide open.

"You stay here!" he shouted at me as the last of them passed us, and he whipped around the aluminum frame, rushing headlong into the pandemonium.

A few short moments later, the clamor began to subside, and I started hearing muffled shouts of "Clear!" from several different voices. The interior lights snapped to life one by one, casting a dim incandescent glow. Soon afterwards, Ben returned to the front porch wearing a crestfallen face. He looked at me sadly and motioned with his head for me to come inside as he holstered his sidearm and snapped the quick-release shut.

"The son-of-a-bitch isn't here," he pronounced dully. "He's gone."

"What about the little girl?" I pressed.

"He must have her with him."

"But the porch light," I protested. "It came on when the door creaked."

"Coincidence. It was on a timer." He reached up and angrily wiped the sweat from his forehead. "They were all on a fucking timer."

CHAPTER 23

A queer, pulsing static encompassed me as I stepped across the threshold of the front door. I could feel the individual hairs on my body as they hastily rose to attention, generating a painful prickling sensation throughout. For the third time in the last half hour, the insistent itching returned, appearing and disappearing in mobile patches across my chest. Since the immediate physical danger was well out of the way, I reached around and ripped apart the Velcro tabs on the flak vest with an audible swoosh. I didn't remove it but loosening allowed breathing room for my sweat-drenched skin and more importantly, enough space to slip my hand in for a quick, blissful scratch.

"Don't touch anything yet," Ben told me as we advanced farther into the sparsely decorated living room. "Evidence Unit'll be here in a few minutes."

"Yeah. No problem." I nodded assent and continued to glance about the room.

My hair follicles were still stinging with strained discomfort, making my skin seem to crawl, while an arc of intense energy played up and down my spine. It felt pretty much as though I was holding on to a frayed extension cord while standing in a puddle of water. Slowly, my scalp began to tighten and my temples to throb. I had one hell of a headache coming on.

None of these sensations were new to me. I had felt them a handful of times in the past, though not often, thankfully. They were warnings—the physical manifestations of a "supernatural burglar alarm." Roger, like any Witch, or practitioner of ritual magick, had shielded his boundaries. He had cast protective energy about his home as a way of marking territory to let others who were aware know that they shouldn't intrude. In the physical world, I had simply stepped across the threshold. However, being an uninvited guest, in the realm of the ethereal, I had done the equivalent of breaking a trip wire on a hypersensitive home security system.

Two things immediately occurred. First, the walls of protective energy enveloped me with urgent warnings in an attempt to make me leave. Second, wherever Roger Henderson was hiding, he was made aware of my intrusion. Of course, as I said, these warnings were for others who are aware, so being the only Witch in the room, I was forced to endure the increasingly painful attempts at expulsion in tortured solitude.

The one feeling that wasn't a direct descendant of the ethereal burglar alarm was the searing arc of energy playing xylophone on my vertebrae. Red hot, intense, and angry, it was the blatant otherworldly signature of the home's occupant. The unmasked, undisguised essence of Roger Henderson's immortal soul. Vile, putrid, and swelling with evil. I had to engage my own defenses in order to keep from becoming violently ill. It was obvious, at least to me, that though he wasn't here now, he had been here very recently. We couldn't have missed him by more than a few hours.

I was only superficially aware of muttered apologies and "excuse me's" as officers pushed past me to go in and out the door. Several moments passed before I realized I was standing frozen, one step over the threshold, partially blocking the entrance of the house. Slowly, I shuffled around the room and as Ben had ordered, was careful not to touch anything—physically, anyway. As I moved farther inward, a new feeling joined the jamboree of sensations that were clawing at me for equal time. The feeling was fear. It was small and feminine but very intense. It was the fear projected by a little girl named Ariel. I pushed the feeling back and placed it on mental "hold" as I realized my breathing had quickened. I fought to maintain a grip in the physical realm, and closing my eyes, I willed myself to relax. When my respirations came back under control, I allowed my eyelids to flutter open and focused on the scene before me.

The walls in the small square room were washed with a thin coat of light blue paint, applied lethargically with what had apparently been a worn roller. Several swaths were severely lacking in coverage, unabashedly exposing the original antique white that lay beneath. The floor, at one time smooth, finished hardwood, was scuffed and gouged, with wear patterns criss-crossing the surface in a well-beaten path. A lone, straight-backed chair sat against a sagging card table—the only two pieces of furniture in the room.

The stained tabletop was littered with cigarette butts from an overflowing ashtray and a paper plate containing a half-eaten sandwich. The curl of the drying bread, a browning crust of mustard, and the unidentifiability of the luncheon meat gave evidence that the sandwich was several days old.

"Can't say a helluva lot for his taste in decorating." Deckert was standing next to me. I hadn't noticed him until he spoke.

"I know what you mean," I answered with a small sigh and began massaging my temples. My head was killing me, and I knew it was only going to get worse before getting any better.

"You okay?" Concern crept into his voice as he rested a hand on my shoulder.

"Yeah, I'll be okay. Just a headache." I didn't feel like trying to explain the concept of protection spells and ethereal burglar alarms at the moment. From what I had come to know about Carl Deckert over the past week, I was sure he wouldn't cast a jaundiced eye upon me, but I wasn't exactly certain he'd believe me either. It really didn't matter anyway. I was the only one who had to deal with it.

"Probably all the excitement," he volunteered in a fatherly tone. "I got some aspirin out in my car, if you want some."

"Thanks," I smiled weakly, "I might take you up on that later." All I really needed to do was get out of this house, but I knew that wasn't an option at the moment.

"Looks like you got a fan club," Ben called to me from a few feet away.

When I looked over, he was motioning to a bizarre collage. The section of wall directly above the card table was haphazardly peppered with newspaper clippings regarding the murders. Upon closer inspection, several yellow marks could be seen streaking the newsprint, and each of them was highlighting my name.

"He knows I'm helping with the investigation," I offered. "He's just trying to..."

"Great intel, Storm," Special Agent Mandalay's sardonic tone pierced the even murmur of the other voices in the room to cut me off. "Did your expert get it from his crystal ball or something?"

"We didn't have just a hell of a lotta time, ya'know," Ben spit back. "Surveillance showed lights goin' off, so we had ta' assume he was in here. We had no way of knowin' they were on timers."

"Well I'm not impressed," she returned.

"And what would you have done? Tapped his phone and sat around with your thumb up your ass?" His voice increased in volume by a notch.

"I would have made sure he was here," Agent Mandalay

raised her voice as well. "This place looks like it's been empty for days."

"No it hasn't," I interrupted calmly. "He's only been gone a few hours."

She turned and looked at me as if I were a small child butting in to an adult conversation. "The expert speaks!" she exclaimed cynically. "Why don't you let the rest of us in on it. How do you know he was here a few hours ago?"

"I can feel him," I answered her barbed question simply. "He had the little girl with him."

In an exaggerated motion, she tossed her head back, rolled her eyes, and then let out a loud, frustrated breath, "I suppose you can *feel her* too?"

"As a matter of fact, yes. I can feel her fear."

"You ARE kidding. Right? This place is abandoned. Just look around you."

Before I could answer, a surge of blinding pain bit viciously into my skull like a white-hot poker. As long as I was inside this house, my foothold in this plane of physical realities was shaky at best, and the sudden stabbing affectation was all it took to knock me over the precipice. I winced internally as the pain struck again, and I tumbled backward into the darkened abyss of the recent past.

Fear.
Confusion.
Pure, unbounded terror.
The terror of a small child.
A dark figure. Stocky and thick. Brimming with exaggerated excitement. I can smell a mixture of emotions in his profuse, oily sweat.
His excitement.
Her fear.
His anger.

Her terror.

He enters the room hurriedly. He's holding a loosely wrapped bundle. A tattered blanket, stained and filthy with abuse and neglect. It encompasses a limp mass. Apparently, there is some weight to the bundle as he struggles to shift it while he wrestles with the door. Using his knee, he pushes the door shut then turns and backs against it, forcing the latch to pop into place. He jerks slightly, and a tiny hand falls into view from beneath the unclean shroud. The tiny hand of a frightened little girl.

It doesn't matter. He's inside now. He's certain no one saw him carry the bundle in. They are all at work. All of them. Even the prying old bitch across the street is gone. He made sure of that before getting the bundle from his trunk.

Maybe he should have killed her, he thought. The old nosy bitch.

No.

No. She was too close to home. The police would have been crawling all over the place, and that might have disrupted the Ritual. His chance to sacrifice The One. *Besides, she was too old. Her age-spotted skin hung loosely from her skinny frame. He could see it in his mind.*

Whenever she waved at him from her yard, it would flop and flap like a banner waving in the breeze. No. Her skin was definitely too loose. He couldn't practice on someone with loose skin. That would never properly prepare him for The One.

The One *would be young. Her skin elastic and unblemished. Not wrinkled and flaccid.*

The One.

She was resting in his arms right now. This very moment. He was so very pleased to have found The One.

Bright, glaring lights flared suddenly, burning like flash powder ignited in direct contact with my eyes.

Mommy!
Where is my mommy?!
I'm so scared.

It's very dark. My eyes still sting from the flare of light. There seems to be a dim glow coming from just behind my head, but I'm not sure. It may only be a phantom image.

I can feel the little girl's presence in the room. Her fear. Her mental cries for her mother. Still, I can't see her.

My eyes are beginning to slowly adjust to the murky light. I'm in the basement. I can barely make out a shape across from me. It appears to be moving.

My eyes adjust some more.

I can tell that the shape is the stocky man I had seen upstairs. He is huddled over something on a long plywood and two-by-four workbench. The dirt floor is uneven and littered with trash. My legs feel like heavy, metal fence posts set securely in cement.

I try to move.

The man stops suddenly as if he hears something. He cocks his head to the side and turns it slightly. I stop my struggle to move.

He waits, listening intently.

I hold my breath.

Finally, slowly he turns back to his task. Once again, I try to move forward.

Mommy!
Daddy!
I'm so scared.

I'm standing directly behind him now. I can clearly see what he is huddled over. The nude, bound body of the little girl.

He pulls a tourniquet tight on her upper arm and then uses two fingers to slap the tender inner flesh in search of a vein. In his other hand, he expertly holds a full syringe. The needle glistens in the dim light.

Carefully he slips the needle into the vein. I can feel the stinging pinprick in my own arm.

Mommy!
Daddy!

A tiny plume of blood spurts into the syringe, mixing in a milky cloud with the other fluid. He drives the plunger forward. Slowly. Evenly.

"You can't stop me, you know," he says without turning.

I know that he is talking to me.

He moves quietly to the end of the bench and tosses the used syringe into a bucket already overflowing with trash.

"She's The One," he tells me. "This is her destiny."

The little girl's nude body is stretched out, loosely bound on the table, her denim dress wadded next to her. He reaches out and grasps it, crushing it into an even tighter ball. With an angry toss, he flings the faded blue fabric projectile across the room. It smacks against the wall with a muffled thump then slides raspily downward, slipping behind a pile of paint cans, and disappears.

"You're too late, Rowan Gant," he says, turning to me. "You weren't there to save Ariel Tanner, and you won't be there to save The One."

The last things I saw were his cold grey eyes.

"He said he had a headache a few minutes ago," Detective Deckert's voice began distantly and grew quickly closer.

"Rowan? Hey, Rowan? You all right?" Ben was looking

at me questioningly.

I felt myself grab firmly back onto the physical plane and cling for dear life. My head was still throbbing, and the angry burn of Roger's ethereal signature was maintaining its hold on my spine.

"Some expert," Special Agent Mandalay's voice reached my ears. "You ask him a question, and he passes out on you."

"Shut up," Ben barked at her without turning. "Rowan. You okay, man?"

"Yeah," I returned weakly. "Sorry about that."

"You went all *Twilight Zone*, didn't you?" He didn't wait for me to answer. "What did you see?"

"Downstairs. In the basement," I recited. "There's a workbench. That's where he kept her when he was here this afternoon. He's keeping her drugged. You'll find her dress behind some paint cans. Her blue denim dress."

"Give me a break," our resident FBI skeptic declared in exasperation. "He sounds like a tabloid psychic."

Ben ignored her spiteful comment and instead, turned to one of the other officers. "Ackman. Check it out."

We stood waiting quietly as the man carried out the order, disappearing down the hallway, then the basement stairs. After a few protracted moments, we heard him coming back up the wooden stairway.

"Hey, Storm," he called as he poked his head through the doorway. "Better come have a look down here. There's a wad of blue denim behind some paint cans, just like Gant said. Could be the kid's dress."

Ben turned to Agent Mandalay, and a smug grin spread across his face. "Show me one of your PhD's that can do that."

"So, don't take this the wrong way or anything," Ben began. "But there's somethin' I'm havin' trouble understandin'..."

I was relaxing in my seat, eyes closed. Without opening them, I prodded him forward, "And that is?"

We were belted into his van and in motion toward my house, having only just left the scene. The evidence technicians had arrived soon after the discovery of the little girl's discarded dress. They were still photographing, dusting, and bagging everything in sight when we finally chose to abandon hope of any immediate clues to her current whereabouts. A palpable sense of urgency surrounded them, and it was spreading like a rampant contagion through every member of the Major Case Squad. Even Agent Mandalay fell victim to its almost ubiquitous virulence. She had elected to remain behind at the scene with Detective Deckert while Ben provided my transportation home. Considering the volatility of one part Mandalay mixed with one part Storm, it was probably a good idea for them to be separated for a while.

After a full two hours inside Roger's house, I had begun to feel as if there were nothing left of me to give. A verse from an old *Blue Oyster Cult* song kept running through my head in an endless loop—*You see me now a veteran of a thousand psychic wars. My energy is spent at last, and my armor is destroyed...* Funny how things like that seem to drift in from nowhere.

Even at that, none of them was in any bigger hurry to stop Roger and save this little girl than I was. I would have gladly stayed longer, no matter how I felt, but the final decision hadn't been left to me. Ben ordered me to go home, and since I had come with him, he was seeing to it personally that I was returned safely. Deckert had seconded the motion, and Agent Mandalay took no convincing whatsoever. She was happy to see me go, though after the incident with the child's dress, I had caught her looking curiously at me across the room from time to time. But, of course, only when she thought I couldn't see her.

"What I don't get is this," Ben continued. "If you could sense, or feel—or whatever the hell you do—all that bad *ju-ju* comin' off just the house and stuff, then why couldn't Ariel Tanner and the rest of her group pick it up from him? I mean he was right there in the flesh and all? Shouldn't they have noticed somethin'?"

I wasn't surprised by the question, and I was glad that he had waited until we were alone before he asked it. Knowing him as I did, that shouldn't have surprised me either.

"Theoretically, yes."

"And what's that supposed to mean?"

"Well, if I'm right, there are a couple of reasons why they might not have picked up anything from him," I paused.

"Whaddaya want, a signed invitation? Spit it out."

"Number one is the Expiation spell," I continued, finally opening my eyes and sitting up a little straighter as he merged us onto the highway. "My guess is that he feels pretty good about himself once he's absolved himself of the guilt. That would make him give off some positive *vibes*, so to speak. The positive energies would tend to cancel out the negative ones. You know, yin and yang, the great cosmic balance and all that."

"Yeah, okay." He nodded his head thoughtfully. "I can see that. Basically, it just tells me he's a crazy fuck, and what he did to these women just doesn't matter to 'im."

"That's one way of looking at it."

"But why can you pick it up now?"

"He's escalating," I offered. "He's cycling through the absolution and anger quicker as the time for the sacrifice draws nearer."

"Have you figured out why he's doin' this yet?"

"No, unfortunately. I'm not sure that he even knows."

We continued in silence while Ben digested my answers. Finally, he looked over at me and spoke, "So what's number two?"

I was already regretting that I had told him there was more than one reason. The second was the one that I was still wrestling with myself. Still, I had already opened my mouth, so there was no turning back. Whether I had come to grips with it or not, I needed to tell Ben.

"Number two," I said with a tired sigh, "is that he was probably able to mask over his energies because he's a lot better than I expected him to be."

"Whaddaya mean 'better than ya' expected 'im ta' be'?" he appealed. "Ya mean like better at the hocus-pocus stuff?"

"Yeah. The 'hocus-pocus' stuff." I didn't feel up to arguing over his choice of terminology.

"But not better'n you, right?"

I didn't answer him.

"Aww, Jeez, white man," he grumbled, "I hate when you clam up like that... Tell me he's not better than you."

"I don't know yet" was all I could say.

CHAPTER 24

Cally's van was gone from my driveway, and the lights were out when Ben dropped me off. I had called Felicity from his cell phone shortly after the evidence technicians arrived on the scene and let her know that I was still in one piece. While that fact had been a relief to her, the news was still clouded by bitter disappointment at our having arrived too late to rescue the little girl and apprehend Roger. Before saying goodbye, I reminded her that there was still time before the full moon and that we weren't giving up. When I pressed the glowing END button on the face of the phone, I lingered, momentarily lost in thought as I wondered to myself if that small amount of time was going to be enough.

The dogs stirred instantly when I entered the house, doing exactly what they perceived as their canine duty by checking to be sure I wasn't some unfamiliar intruder. As soon as they had satisfied themselves as to my identity via cold-nosed, doggish snuffling, they both wandered sleepily back to their beds, wagging their tails with lazy contentment.

Two of our three feline residents, Dickens and Salinger, were in the middle of one of their many nocturnal wrestling matches. My intrusion into what they had declared to be their ring served as sufficient enough surprise to bring them instantly apart. Looking for all the world like two furry, mismatched bookends, they absently licked their paws and peered up at me as if to say "What? We weren't doing anything."

I kicked off my shoes then made my way softly into the bedroom. My wife was sound asleep, curled in the center of our bed, tightly hugging my pillow. I thought of crawling in as well, but she looked too peaceful, and I feared I would wake her. Besides, even though it was rapidly approaching two in the morning, I wasn't actually sleepy. I had far too much on my mind to relax at the moment, and my earlier headache still plagued me in the form of a dull throb running down the back of my neck. Gently, I pulled the sheets up over her shoulders then quietly padded back through the house.

The wall clock rang out its familiar double chime in proclamation of the hour as I stretched out on the couch. If I were ever going to relax, I would have to clear away some of the annoying debris that had collected in my mind over the past few days. Of course, after the infusion of adrenalin I had received earlier this evening, my guess was that such a task would be next to impossible, at least for the time being.

Dickens jumped stealthily up to the arm of the couch nearest my head and announced himself with a throaty feline trill before crawling determinedly around me. After a false start or two, he stretched across my chest and proceeded to purr himself to sleep. He remained there undisturbed, even when I slowly stretched and yawned. My eyes seemed to almost itch, and my eyelids felt oddly heavy as I let out a long-winded sigh. As they slowly closed, I reminded myself that I wasn't sleepy. I wasn't sleepy at all.

"Hey, Mister." A little strawberry-blonde girl, wrapped in a white lace dress, was tugging at me. *"Hey, mister, wake up."*

Falling.

Darkness.

Light.

Darkness.

"Wake up, Mister!" her tiny voice more urgent now. *"It's*

almost time. We're going to miss it."

"Miss what?" I try to ask.

I can see my words, but I can't hear them. They visibly leave my mouth in a rush and shoot skyward like helium-filled balloons. I watch them as they disappear into the darkness. When I turn my gaze back downward, the little girl is staring up at me urgently.

"We have to go now!" she exclaims, pulling on my hand. "Now!"

I'm running.

I can hear my footfalls on thin carpeting. My heart is pounding behind my ribs. My breaths are deep and labored, and the cold air stings my throat and lungs. I don't know if I'm running from or running to. The little strawberry-blonde girl is nowhere to be seen.

I'm running.

I'm sitting.

"I told you," the little girl says to me. "We almost missed it."

I turn to face her. I don't know where she came from. I vaguely remember that she was gone, but I don't know why. I feel that she has been there all along.

"I have to go soon," she says and points at a spot far above my head. "My turn is next."

I look up and see a large round disk, mottled white and grey. The moon. It lacks fullness by only a thin sliver along the edge. I lower my eyes back to her.

The little girl is no longer little. She is a full-grown woman. She is Ariel Tanner, dressed in white lace and surrounded by a dimly glowing aura of milky light. She is kneeling next to me, holding my hand and smiling.

"She doesn't understand," Ariel tells me. "You will have to explain it to her."

"Explain what?" I ask. My own words meet my ears as a

mirror image of themselves, echoing softly "?tahw nialpxe."

She places two fingers across my lips to hush me and shakes her head. Her soft hair billows weightlessly, the aura dancing in perfect unison with each individual strand. "You have to stop him, Rowan. It's all up to you now. Only you can save her."

She lowers her fingers from my lips and stretches forward then lightly kisses my cheek. As she pulls away, she smiles shyly at me.

Her eyes widen with surprise, and the shy smile drains away. Her lips form a mute frown as a glossy patch of vermilion appears on her bosom, spreading like oil across the white lace.

"Why, Rowan, why?" she mouths as she falls away from me into nothingness.

I reach for her, but she is gone.

Darkness.

Light.

Darkness.

Falling.

Falling upward into the light.

Another nightmare?" Felicity was sitting next to me on the edge of the sofa when I awoke from the fitful slumber.

"Yeah," I answered, "like that's a surprise, huh?"

"Anything in it that might help?"

"I dunno," I returned lethargically as I pulled myself upright. "It mainly just told me that we were running out of time, as if I needed a reminder."

She moved out of my way as I swung my legs around and allowed my feet to drop to the floor.

"Want some coffee?" she asked.

"Yeah, sure. What time is it anyway?"

"Almost noon," she called over her shoulder as she

headed for the kitchen. "I figured you didn't get in till late, so I let you sleep."

"Thanks. I appreciate that. I think."

"Ben called earlier." She returned with a mug of hot coffee and handed it to me. "He said to tell you thanks."

"For what?" I queried and took a sip of the hot liquid, letting it burn the sleep from my throat.

"For all your help," she answered. "They caught Roger early this morning. He came back to the house, and they were waiting for him."

I stared back at her incredulously, almost dropping the steaming mug. "He what? What about the little girl?"

"She's fine. Not a scratch on her. She's already been reunited with her parents."

I couldn't believe it. After everything we had been through, Roger had walked right back into the hands of the police. I suppose I should have been thankful, but I just couldn't shake the feeling that something was out of sync. A sense of foreboding that made me believe that something was terribly wrong.

"I need to go talk to Ben," I announced and began searching about for my shoes.

"Slow down," Felicity insisted. "Don't you think you'd better take a shower first? No offense, but you look pretty rough."

She was right. The activities of the night before, combined with eight hours on our living room sofa, had to have taken their toll on my appearance.

"Yeah, okay," I agreed. "But do me a favor will'ya? Call Ben and tell him I'm coming down to see him."

"Sure. No problem." She pecked me quickly on the cheek. "Now go get cleaned up."

I left her dialing the phone and tossed my clothes haphazardly into the hamper as I stripped. The sun was coming in brightly through the window, eliminating the need for artificial light, so I just kicked on the exhaust fan and climbed into the shower.

With a quick turn of the porcelain handles, I started the water flowing and adjusted the temperature to my liking. I turned to allow it to flow down my back and held my eyes closed, willing away the remaining tension in hopes of at least a few moments relaxation. It was then that something Felicity had just said struck me as odd. She asked me if the nightmare had contained anything that might help, yet she already knew that Ben had called. She knew that Roger had already been captured. I started to call out to her in search of an explanation.

When I opened my eyes, I was looking directly at the back wall. Across the normally pristine white tiles, dark crimson strokes inscribed—

ALL   IS   FORGIVEN

—A sour, cackling laugh filled my ears, and the water against my back suddenly felt oddly thick. I looked down at my chest where it splashed across my shoulders and saw blood, viscid and hot, dripping from my skin.

I tried to escape the horror, only to find the shower curtain had become solid and unyielding. I began to pound on it wildly, screaming for my wife, as the enclosure quickly began to fill with the sticky, crimson liquid. My cries remained unheeded as the level reached my chest, then my chin, until finally, I was submerged. My throat and lungs began to burn, and I was starting to black out. No longer able to hold my breath, I was about to face my own innermost fear. I was drowning.

I awoke screaming.

Felicity was over me, firmly grasping my shoulders and

shaking me into consciousness. "Rowan, wake up! Rowan!"

I bolted upright on the couch, steeped in my own sweat. The cool breeze from a nearby register sent a shiver up my spine as the air conditioner followed orders from the thermostat and worked to maintain the temperature.

Soft morning light was beginning to filter in between the slats of the mini blinds covering our windows, bringing a murky pallor to my surroundings. My wife, clad in an oversized t-shirt, was staring back at me with the same gentle concern I had seen in her eyes just one night before.

"Another nightmare?" she asked rhetorically, sitting back on the edge of the sofa.

"Yeah," I sighed, "a weird one. Whatever you do, don't tell me it's almost noon, and Ben called to tell me thanks."

"Why would I?"

I heard a muffled series of barks, telling me that the dogs wanted to be let back in. For some reason, that familiar noise, added to my wife's puzzled expression and my overall feeling as if I had been beaten severely with a two-by-four, was the evidence I needed to tell me I was actually, truly awake this time.

"It's a long story," I told her.

After a shower that began hesitantly, I relinquished the remaining hot water to Felicity and prepared a quick breakfast. Over eggs scrambled with broccoli and Swiss cheese, a side of turkey bacon, and coffee, she and I discussed the events of the past evening. For the most part, the discussion was one-sided, with me doing the talking and her doing the listening as I filled her in on the details of the assault on Roger's house, followed by those of the doubly bizarre nightmare. The latter accounting, I recorded in my Book of Shadows as I went.

"I got a call from a client last night," Felicity announced while we put away the freshly washed dishes. "Apparently, they lined up a last minute product shoot with some model that's only available today."

"Go ahead. I'll be fine," I answered her unspoken question.

"Are you sure, then?" she posed. "I can refer it over to Hartley. He owes me one anyway."

"Really. I'll be fine," I assured her. "There's no need in both of us sitting around here staring at the walls. I don't know if there's much more either of us can do to help Ben right now anyway. Besides, like I said, Agent Mandalay isn't exactly my number one fan."

"Okay. If you're sure."

"I'm sure."

I helped her load the Jeep and waved goodbye as she backed out slowly and went on her way. The landscape around me was growing brighter as the sun crept higher in the morning sky, chasing away the dimly shimmering globe of the moon—the moon that was less than twenty-four hours from full.

I called Ben shortly after Felicity left and was told that he was following up leads in the field. After leaving a message for him, I resigned myself to performing what had become the more mundane tasks in my life—support calls, returning email, and even some minor house cleaning. Don't get me wrong, I was actually looking forward to returning to the everyday normalcy, but not until this whole thing was over and done with.

It was approaching three in the afternoon when the phone rang. Ben was on the other end, returning my call.

"So, any good news?" I queried into the handset.

"No," he told me, "not really. The parents made a positive ID on the little girl's dress. And they found a spot where the floor had been dug up in the corner, but that's about it."

"That's where he buried the hearts he took from the victims," I stated mechanically.

"Yeah... It wasn't pleasant... Oh, and that tip ya' gave us on the syringe. We found it right where ya' said it would be. Lab showed traces of a sedative called Diazepam."

"Not the curare?"

"No," he returned. "Seemed off to me too, so I asked the doc about it. Apparently, that stuff paralyzes the blink response, and he would have to use some kinda artificial lubricant to keep her eyes from dryin' out. Also, repeated doses could build up in 'er system and cause respiratory failure. Sounded kinda high maintenance for someone tryin' ta' duck the cops."

"But it makes sense," I volunteered. "He doesn't want her injured. I'm convinced of that. In my vision, he kept referring to her as *The One*. As odd as it may sound, he holds her in very high reverence. She has to be pristine for the ritual, but he also has to keep her under wraps until the full moon."

"Yeah, it sounds odd all right, 'specially when ya' consider what he plans to do to 'er in this ritual thing." There was a lengthy pause at his end. I could almost see him trying to form his words. "So listen, Row. About that whole hocus-pocus thing last night. What did'ya mean when ya' said ya' don't know if he's better than you or not?"

"I meant exactly that. I don't know."

"But I thought you were some kinda *Master Witch* or somethin'," he appealed. "Like a Black Belt of Witch stuff. Ya'know what I mean?"

"There's no such thing, Ben. The Craft is a continual learning process."

"That still doesn't tell me why ya' think he's better'n you."

"Something happened during that vision that took me by surprise. I've never experienced anything like it before, and to be honest, it bothered me quite a bit."

"Wanna talk about it? After everything I've seen lately, I'm willin' ta' listen."

"Okay." I took a deep breath and let it puff out my cheeks as I exhaled. "But you might not want to hear it. If I'm right, I could be the reason he knew we were coming."

"How so?"

"Well," I continued, "you understand that when I've had these visions at the crime scenes, they were recreations of the recent past, right?"

"Yeah, go on."

"That's the kind of vision I had at Roger's house but with a major exception. He talked to me."

"I'm not sure I follow."

"In the vision," I explained, "Roger spoke directly to me. He told me that I hadn't been there to save Ariel Tanner, and there was no way I'd be able to save *The One*. He looked right at me. Called me by name."

There was a long pause at the other end of the line as he mulled over my latest revelations. "So lemme get this straight..." His words were measured carefully. "Ya'think that when you had that vision, you like went back in time or somethin'? And he saw ya' there and knew you were comin'?"

"No, not at all," I corrected. "I had a vision of something

that happened in the recent past. I think Roger knew we were close because of me. Because of the energies I've been giving off."

"So, what about this bit where he was talkin' to ya'? I still don't get it. Where does that fit in?"

"I think that since he knew we would be coming, and he knew that I would be there, in a sense, he was waiting for me. He insinuated himself into the vision."

"You mean he was there?!" Ben's voice became instantly more animated.

"Not in the physical sense," I expressed, "but I wouldn't be surprised if he was nearby."

"Shit! That's all I needed to hear." The animation in his voice was replaced by calm dejection. "So the fact that you think he somehow got 'imself into your vision is what's got ya' thinkin' you somehow tipped him off."

"That's my theory."

"Well, don't let the ice princess hear that," he expressed, referring to Special Agent Mandalay. "She's still givin' me a royal pain in the ass about your involvement in this case. She doesn't need any more ammunition."

"How are you two getting along today?" I queried out of a mild curiosity.

"Like oil and water. Ya didn't expect any different did'ya?" he admitted.

"You know, Ben, she's just doing her job. You took a lot of convincing about The Craft as I recall."

"Yeah, yeah, I know," he conceded. "I just don't have time for it right now... What? Hold on a sec..." I heard him stave off a muted voice in the background. "Listen, I gotta go. You'll call me if you have another vision or somethin'?"

"You'll be the first."

"Okay. I'll check back in with ya' as soon as we know somethin'. Later."

"Bye."

I lied. Sort of.

If anything relevant came into my mind via any means, conscious thought or ethereal vision, I would certainly call Ben immediately. However, I had carefully avoided telling him about my most recent dream. If my theory about Roger entering my vision was correct, then I was firmly convinced that he had entered my nightmare as well. It was my belief that he was responsible for the bizarre secondary sequence. He was trying to frighten me, and that was the chink in his armor. He was just as unsure about me as I was about him.

I didn't tell Ben about it. I hadn't even told Felicity the entire story. I was the only one that knew because it was something I was going to have to face on my own.

CHAPTER 25

Iexpected Ben to have someone watching Roger's house, and I had no idea whatsoever how I was going to handle the situation; therefore, I was somewhat surprised when the neighborhood seemed devoid of surveillance. Of course, that was just how it appeared on the surface.

The digital clock on the in-dash stereo had just flicked over to seven P.M. when I pulled down the Overmoor side street. Felicity had called me earlier to say the photo shoot was running late and that she probably wouldn't be home until after nine. I didn't tell her as much, but I was actually glad she'd be out late. I was certain that had she been present, she would have done everything in her power to talk me out of what I was about to do.

She can be very persuasive.

After a couple of slow passes through the subdivision, I rolled my truck to a stop behind the evergreen hedgerow we had used for cover the night before and switched off the engine. I waited in silence, my view of the house slightly obscured, and fought to gather the courage I desperately needed.

I had come here for a purpose. Roger had invaded both my vision and my nightmare. In the vision, he had demonstrated his overconfidence by taunting me and issuing a challenge. In my nightmare, he hedged his bet, playing on my fears in order to frighten me away. It might have worked had it not been for three haunting words—"Why, Rowan, why?" In every nightmare, Ariel Tanner appeared before me and asked that question. I had come to fear that most of all each time I drifted off to sleep, simply because I didn't have the answer. I couldn't tell her, "Why." I couldn't even tell myself because I wasn't even sure what she was asking. As nonsensical as it seemed, something deep inside kept telling me that if this little girl died, it would be my fault. My fault because I hadn't tried hard enough to find the answer to "Why?"

I was so deeply lost in my thoughts that my heart skipped a full beat when I heard the sudden tapping on my window. I snapped back from my distant stare with a startled jump and quickly turned. Carl Deckert was standing outside my window, hand raised as he prepared to rap his knuckles on the glass once again.

"Hey. How's it going?" I asked with a smile as I rolled the window downward.

"Okay, if you like sitting around watching an empty house while a lonely old lady talks your ear off," he replied. "If you don't mind my asking, what're you doin' here?"

His answer told me why I hadn't spotted the surveillance. They must have set up shop in the house across the street. The one whose occupant Roger had thought of as the "nosy old bitch."

"Ben asked me to come out here and have another look at the place," I spoke quickly, hoping he wouldn't see through to the truth. "He wanted me to see if I could pick up anything else that might help."

"Why didn't he come with you?" he asked suspiciously.

I said the first thing that popped into my mind, and it actually sounded pretty good. "He said something about keeping that FBI agent busy, so she wouldn't get in the way."

"Yeah, those two are a piece of work," he grunted. "She was there waiting for him this morning. They still hadn't stopped chewing on each other when I left. I guess he probably just forgot to tell me you were coming."

"Could be," I said aloud, while inside my head I was

saying, "Don't call him. Don't call him."

He grinned and nodded, "Yeah, that's probably it. Hell, this guy's not gonna show up here anyway. You want me to go in with you?"

I breathed an inner sigh of relief. "No. That's okay. I'll be all right by myself."

Detective Deckert gave me a slight shrug as I climbed out of the truck's cab and shut the door. "Suit yourself. I'll be right here across the street if you need me."

I nodded my head as I reassured him, "I'll be fine."

The interior of the house was much as it had been the night before with the exception of the dark grey fingerprinting dust coating various surfaces. The lights were off, and the few shafts of the setting sun that managed to filter in between gaps in the heavy drapes harshly illuminated small slices of the room, casting the rest in hard-edged oblique shadows. I pushed the door shut behind me, cutting off even more of the external light and symbolically sealing myself into the eerie dwelling.

The expected pain augered itself up my spine and into my skull the moment I set foot in the house. I stumbled for a moment and then steeled myself against further onset of the agonizing sensations as I moved farther into the room. I wouldn't be able to stop the pains from coming, but at least I could be ready for them.

A burning fire like molten lead filled my body, and my skin felt stretched and tortured by countless pinpricks as my hair seemed to come to life, stiffening to create endless waves of gooseflesh. My eyes were watering, and thin streams of tears began flowing down my face. I staggered against the blinding pain, peering through clouded eyes, and forcing myself to move farther down the hallway.

Unearthly screaming filled my ears as I pressed forward.

The amplified sound of jagged metal against a rapidly spinning grinder.

The mournful whistle of a teakettle.

The wail of a chainsaw.

Everything and nothing.

The piercing noise penetrated my bones, making me vibrate like a human tuning fork, and grew impossibly louder when I reached out for the basement door.

I grasped the tarnished handle tightly, refusing to let go even though it seemed to glow red hot, threatening to sear the flesh from my hand. Quickly, I jerked my wrist and flung the door wide, only to be engulfed in writhing ethereal flames.

Summoning my wits, I beat back the flames, denying their existence both with my mind and my voice. The imaginary fire vanished with a choked sputter, and I stepped forward through the open doorway, clinging desperately to the wooden railing until my feet finally met the dirt floor at the bottom of the stairs.

I stood staring into the darkness, concentrating on pushing away the violent spasms of pain while I waited for my eyes to adjust. There was a salty taste in my mouth, and my nose was starting to burn. I brought my hand up, and the lower half of my face felt wet and sticky. Slowly, I stretched my hand out into a thin shaft of light that angled purposefully down the stairwell, forming a focused stripe across the darkened floor. I could see that my fingers were covered in blood. My nose was bleeding.

A cleaver of pain buried itself between my eyes, insisting that it be allowed to split my skull and let my brains spill out. I was beginning to regret that I had come here without someone to back me up. My grasp on the physical world was weakening. The last thing I recall was that I'd told Carl Deckert I would be fine.

Fear.
Anger.
Fear.
Anger.
Surprise.
"I didn't expect you to come back." Roger is speaking to me.

We are surrounded by darkness, yet we are awash in an eerie light. The little girl, clad in white lace, levitates near him. Floating weightless in the air. There is no visible means of support.

"Sorry to disappoint you," I return, and this time my words echo through the air instead of disappearing into nothingness.

He is standing no more than twenty feet away from me, dressed in a dark ceremonial robe. The hood is pushed back to reveal his face, and it lay limply across his shoulders.

"I'm not disappointed," he says. "Just surprised. I don't know what you think you're going to do."

The little girl's body is drifting about on a gentle breeze, bobbing up and down slightly, but never straying far from him.

"Stop you," I tell him evenly.

"You can't stop me," he says. "I told you, she's The One."

"Why are you doing this?" I ask.

His only response is a sour, demonic laugh.

Falling.
Screaming.
Silence.

"Rowan, so nice to see you." Ariel is standing before me. Beside her is the little strawberry-blonde girl, holding tightly to her hand.

"Mister, why don't you stop the bad man?" The little girl looks up at me with wide, sad eyes and then turns her gaze to the right.

I follow her eyes, looking far off into the distance. There is a grove of trees surrounding a small clearing. Centered in the clearing is a hooded, robed figure standing with hands raised high. Moonlight glints from an object held in those hands. Moonlight glints from an athamè.

A small figure lies prone before the cloaked one. A small figure clad in white lace. Preened and arranged. Unblemished and virginal.

The scene begins to grow increasingly distant as trees erupt from the landscape, obscuring the view as they continued to appear, closer and closer.

Immediately before us, the earth trembles and begins to sink. Almost as quickly as the depression is formed, it is filled with water. The glossy surface ripples in the slight breeze, moonlight reflecting from it in a shimmering stripe. The ground continues to shake, and another stand of trees erupt skyward. The tall pines form a line before us, now completely obscuring the clearing and all but the smallest glimpses of the shallow lake.

I turn to the little girl. She is pointing at the sign. "What does it say, Mister."

I look downward, following along her finger to the small white sign. Bold black capital letters spell out PLEASE DO NOT FEED GEESE.

"Only you can save her now, Rowan," Ariel's lilting voice gently touches my ears.

I turn to her, and she holds forth her hand. In it, a tarot card. A tarot card known as The Moon.

She stiffens and the card flutters from her hand. Her eyes go wide and blood streaks down her dress.

"Hey, mister, what time is it?" The little girl is talking to me. "What time is it? Hey, mister!"

I look up to the glowing, marbled disk of the full moon high above. Spinning around its face are the hands of a clock. I watch as the minute hand chases rapidly after the hour hand, overtakes it, then begins the race anew.

"Hey, mister!" the tiny voice demands. "What time is it?"

Darkness.

A deafening, demonic chord.

The sound of water splashing violently.

I can't breathe. My lungs are on fire, and the flames are licking up my throat. My chest feels heavy, and there is something tightening about my neck. The atmosphere feels thick and fluid around me. I want to gasp for air, but something is telling me I shouldn't. My thoughts are beginning to cloud; my mind is turning murky and dark.

I open my eyes, flailing my arms in front of me. I so desperately need air. I need to breathe. The air is thick and murky. It stings. I catch a distorted glimpse, rippling and blurry, of the full moon above. It is all that I can see. All except for one thing—a pair of murderous grey eyes.

My world begins to fade.

Twilight.

An endless scream, "Why, Rowan, why?"

Darkness.

Falling.

Impact.

I refused to go to the hospital. My head was still throbbing, and I needed to clean myself up, but I was firmly convinced that there was nothing wrong with me that couldn't be fixed by getting away from this house and drinking a cup of willow bark tea. I had to voice my protestations several times, each with increasing fervor, but eventually Deckert, the paramedics, and the uniformed officer resigned themselves to the fact that I had made up my mind.

From what Detective Deckert told me, he had started growing concerned after I had been inside the house for little more than an hour and had come over to have a look. He searched the rooms on the ground level and finding them empty, assumed I had gone into the basement. I'll never forget the look on his face as he came to this point in the story and announced, "This is where it starts ta' get kinda weird."

Acting on his assumption, he headed for the basement stairs, only to find the door jammed tightly shut. The handle seemed almost frozen in place, and he couldn't turn it no matter how hard he tried. He said he called out to me several times but never received an answer. Thankfully, growing even more concerned, he went to his car to obtain a tire tool with which to pry the stubborn door open.

"So this really cold wind came rushing up the freakin' stairs the minute I got the door open," he told me, eyes wide as he continued his story. "And I woulda' swore I heard someone laughing. Y'know, evil, like from one of those horror flicks."

He found me lying unconscious at the bottom of the steps, face down in the dirt and streaked with blood. He immediately called the paramedics, and I had regained consciousness around the time they arrived at the house.

It was already after eleven in the evening when we

walked into the Major Case Squad command post. The last thing I remembered before having the latest vision was discovering that my nose was bleeding, followed by a pain resembling a *Louisville Slugger* being stopped by my face. The nightmare still resided somewhere in my grey matter but for some reason, had become only a ghost of itself, lacking in the crisp details of my other visions. I hoped that the dullness was only the result of the pounding headache that was still threatening to break free of my skull and that the specifics would come back into sharper focus once it subsided. One thing I knew for certain was that I had witnessed something very important on that ethereal journey. Now I just needed to remember what it was.

Ben gave me a few moments to wash my face and down a handful of aspirin, in lieu of willow bark tea, before he hustled me into one of the smaller conference rooms. The look on his face was more than enough to tell me that the meeting wasn't going to be a good one.

"Goddammit, Rowan!" No longer able to contain his anger, Ben ruptured. "What the hell were you thinkin'?!"

He had barely closed the door behind Deckert and Special Agent Mandalay. I doubted that it mattered whether or not he waited, since his voice surely carried through most of the police station anyway.

"I was looking for answers," I returned meekly.

"Answers to what?"

"Why. The answer to why. In every nightmare, Ariel asks me why."

"You mean why is this asshole killin' people?" His voice had lowered in volume, but my answer only served to raise it again. "Who knows? Maybe he walked in on his parents screwin' when he was a kid. Maybe his high school prom date stood him up. They've got a million excuses these days. Why's it fuckin' matter now? We know who he is."

"It might not matter at all." I dabbed at my nostrils with a tissue. The bleeding had long since stopped, but the phantom tingling remained, making me feel as though it was starting all over again. "That might not even be the 'why' she is asking... I don't know... It could just be her way of keeping me from giving up."

"Let me get this straight." Agent Mandalay was still leaning against the wall, arms folded across her chest. Her studious gaze hadn't left me since we entered the room. "You jeopardized this investigation because you think a dead woman is talking to you in your dreams?"

"I didn't jeopardize anything," I told her matter-of-factly, avoiding a direct answer to her question. "Roger Henderson isn't going to return to that house and we all know it."

"You really do." She stared back incredulously, reading between the lines of my non-answer. "You think you're communicating with a ghost or something!" She turned to Ben and gesticulated at me as if I were on display. "That's it! Now I'm officially convinced that he needs a psychiatrist. I want him off this investigation now."

Ben started to protest angrily, "Hold on a minute, I..."

"NO! You hold on a minute, Storm," she insisted vehemently, "I want him out of here."

"This is still my investigation, and I say he stays."

"Not anymore. Pursuant to the federal kidnapping statute of nineteen thirty-two, this case falls under the Bureau's jurisdiction. It's my investigation now."

"C'mon," Detective Deckert tried to interject, "Rowan's right. This fruitcake wasn't comin' back to the house. It was a long shot and we knew it. I tell ya', something real strange was happening in that place."

She wheeled quickly around to face him. "Maybe you need an appointment with a shrink, too!"

"You weren't there," he shot back, "besides, whattabout

last night? Rowan told us where ta' find the little girl's dress and all that."

"Lucky guess," she stated flatly and turned back to Ben. "I'm calling in to the field office to let them know I'm taking over this investigation. I want him out of here by the time I'm off the phone."

None of us spoke for a long minute after Agent Mandalay stomped out of the room, slamming the door hard behind her. I winced slightly as the noise pierced my still aching head.

"Well," Ben puffed out his cheeks as he sighed, "I guess that's that."

"I'm sorry, Ben," I looked up from the floor. "For what it's worth, I was just trying to help."

"Hell, ya' just gave her somethin' else ta' flex her muscles about," he grunted. "She pretty much took over the investigation this afternoon anyway. Now she's just makin' it official."

"I just wish I could remember the vision I had. I'm sure it means something."

"Have you been able to remember any of it?" Deckert queried.

"Not really," I answered. "Just something about not being able to breathe, but that could've been my own anxiety. I don't know. If this headache would just go away..."

"Maybe if ya' get some rest," Ben volunteered. "You can always call me if you remember somethin'. You got my cell phone number."

"Yeah, I can do that. I'm still sorry for causing all the trouble though."

"Hey, no prob, white man," he returned as he gazed through the thick window that was the top half of the door. "The dragon lady's got nothin' on what's waitin' out there for you."

"Huh?" I gave him a confused grunt.

In answer, he simply pointed into the distance outside the window. I slipped my glasses back onto my face and stepped over next to him. Peering in the direction he indicated, I immediately saw what he was referring to.

Red hair tousled about, green eyes glowing harshly, and Irish temper fully aflame, Felicity was striding across the room.

CHAPTER 26

"I told you I've already gone through this with Ben," I explained to Felicity as she viciously up-shifted the Jeep and sped onto Highway 170, aiming north toward where my truck was still parked.

She had begun reading me the riot act from the moment we left the MCS command post. While we were still inside, I had been subjected to the patented Felicity O'Brien silent treatment. It was shaping up to be a very long night.

"Aye, but you haven't gone through it with me!" she shot back angrily. "I come home to an empty house, no note or anything. The next thing I know, Ben is on the phone telling me that Carl is bringing you in to the station bleeding. What was I supposed to think?! What were YOU thinking?!"

"I told you already. I was looking for an answer."

"You could have told me what you wanted to do when I called this afternoon."

"Would you have agreed to it?"

"Maybe."

"Be serious, dear."

"That's not the point!" she burst forth once again. "Whether or not I would have agreed to it has absolutely nothing to do with what you did. You lied to Carl and you lied to me."

"I didn't lie to you," I told her. "I just didn't tell you what I had planned."

"Don't split hairs. You know exactly what I meant!"

"You'll want to exit up here at Page and hang a left," I told her, as much to change the subject as to provide her with directions. It didn't work.

"So what did you accomplish?" she demanded stonily.

With a downshift and quick spin of the wheel, she arced the Jeep through the green light at the bottom of the exit ramp and merged into the right lane.

"I had another vision," I answered her. "At least, I think I did."

"What do you mean 'you think you did'?"

Open mouth, insert foot, I thought to myself. I didn't really intend for the last part of that sentence to come out, but I guess my own personal doubts were starting to take hold. It didn't matter much now because I knew my wife, and she wasn't going to let it drop. I had no choice but to explain it.

"I haven't been able to remember much of anything," I began outlining. "I feel like I had a vision, but everything is all foggy. I seem to remember the little girl, and I keep flashing on not being able to breathe, but that's about it. The rest is all just a blur."

"Why do you think that is?" She cautiously pushed the vehicle onward through an intersection guarded by a winking yellow traffic signal. "Do you think it might have something to do with what Carl was saying then?"

Detective Deckert had detailed to her his story about the basement door and the events that followed. Every time he reiterated the tale, his eyes grew wide, and he would shake his greying head while repeating, "It's just kinda weird, y'know?" I almost wished that Agent Mandalay had been the one to have his experience. Then maybe she would be slightly less skeptical.

"It's possible. Roger spoke to me in the vision last night, and then there was the nightmare..." I mused aloud. "I was expecting some kind of presence from him. That's why I went there in the first place."

We were both silent for a short while as Felicity pressed the Jeep along, occasionally shifting gears up and down to adjust speed for the various intersections we crossed. The pulsing yellow and red signals gave warning at each junction, serving also to punctuate my realization that the hour had grown later than I realized.

"How's your head?" Felicity finally asked.

"Still hurts—hang a right up here on Ashby—but not as bad as before." I settled back in the seat and closed my eyes for a moment. "I took a handful of aspirin earlier, and they're starting to kick in. Not quite as fast as willow bark tea, but they don't leave an aftertaste."

"I know what you mean."

I could feel the Jeep sway to the left, centrifugal force acting in opposition to the right-hand turn. My eyes were still closed, and I heard the smooth, metallic click of the stick shift as the gears were shifted down then back up. The hum of the tires against pavement was pinpricked by a low, quick, electronic beep as Felicity's watch announced the half-hour.

"What time is it anyway?" I asked, still resting limply in the seat. Before she could answer, I began a wildly disorienting carnival ride between realities.

"Hey, mister, what time is it?" A little, strawberry-blonde girl is talking to me. She is dressed in white lace and is tugging franticly at my sleeve. "What time is it? Hey, mister!"

"It's twelve-thirty," she answered.

"Hey, mister, what time is it?" The little girl is pointing above the horizon. The pregnant globe of the moon is lifting itself heavily, casting its reflected light down upon her upturned face. The hands of a clock spin urgently about the mottled silvery-white surface. "What time is it? Hey,

mister?"

"Rowan? Rowan? Are you okay?"

There is a grove of trees surrounding a small clearing. Centered in the clearing is a hooded, robed figure standing with hands raised high. Moonlight glints from an object held in those hands. Moonlight glints from an athamè.

A small figure lies prone before the cloaked one. A small figure clad in white lace. Preened and arranged. Unblemished and virginal.

"Rowan! Answer me!"

Trees begin to erupt from the landscape, and the earth begins to tremble and sink. The depression fills with dark water and ripples in the slight breeze. The moonlight reflects in a shimmering stripe.

Another stand of trees erupt skyward. The tall pines form a line before us, completely obscuring the view except for a few small glimpses of the shallow lake.

"What does it say, mister?" The little girl is pointing at a small sign. Bold letters spell out PLEASE DO NOT FEED GEESE.

"Rowan! Breathe, dammit!"

I can't breathe. My lungs are on fire, and the flames are licking up my throat. My chest feels heavy, and there is something tightening about my neck. The atmosphere feels thick and fluid around me. I want to gasp for air, but something is telling me I shouldn't. My thoughts are beginning to cloud; my mind is turning murky and dark.

"ROWAN!"

I snapped fully back into conscious reality when Felicity combined her urgent voice with even more urgent one-handed jostling. We had just rolled to a halt in a bus turnout near the off-ramp onto Midland. The Jeep made a jarring lurch as she frantically switched off the engine and in her haste, released the clutch pedal a second too soon. At almost the same instant, I gasped, ravenously sucking in the cool air.

"Rowan! Answer me! Are you all right?"

I choked and sputtered on the intoxicating oxygen and wheezed in more as I began to catch my breath. The dull ache that had been residing in the back of my head for the majority of the evening was now making an all out assault on my skull, pounding rhythmically through my scalp. The faint tickle of oncoming nausea started down the back of my throat, and my mouth began to water slightly. I fought it back, concentrating on my breathing and forcing myself to at least try to relax.

"Okay," I sputtered between breaths, "I'm okay."

"What happened?" Concern permeated Felicity's voice. "You stopped breathing."

"The vision." I was no longer gulping air, and my respirations were beginning to slow. "The vision came back."

"What did you see?"

"The little girl. A small clearing and some trees. The full moon," I described slowly, reviewing the brilliant Technicolor playback of the memories in my mind. "The moon had hands on it. Like a clock. They were spinning around, and the little girl kept asking me what time it was." My speech started coming quicker as the vision flooded in. "There was a lake too. And a row of pine trees that hid the clearing. The little girl was pointing at a sign."

"What did it say?"

"Please do not feed geese, in bold letters." I painted the image for her. "It was black on white. Like a road sign."

"A park sign maybe?" she ventured.

"That would explain what it said," I agreed. "And the lake and trees too. Do you have your cell phone with you?"

"Sure." She pulled it from a pocket on the side of her purse and offered it to me. "Who are you going to call? Ben?"

"Yeah. I promised I'd let him know if I remembered any of the vision. This whole park thing might be important."

Thumbing the power switch, I began stabbing out Ben's number on the lighted buttons. The amber, segmented digits advanced across the small display, and a second later there was a brief, mechanical trill from the earpiece as the phone rang at the other end.

"Storm," Ben answered with a sharp, frenetic tenor to his voice.

"Ben, it's Rowan. I remembered some of the vision."

"Hold on a second..."

I could hear him exchanging words with someone in the background. Various noises were issuing from the small speaker in the handset. Those sounds, coupled with his tone of voice, led me to believe that all hell had broken loose, and the MCS command post was at ground zero.

"What's the story?" Felicity queried, noticing my expectant silence.

"He's got me on hold," I answered. "It sounds like everything's hitting the fan over there. I guess we can go ahead and get moving. No use in just sitting here."

She nodded and reached for the ignition. There was a muffled plastic rattle on the other end of the phone and the clunk of a door being shut, followed by a relative hush.

"Sorry 'bout that," Ben's voice issued forth again. "It's a

fuckin' circus down here."

"What's going on?"

"Aww, the parents made an appeal to the kidnapper on the ten o'clock news. We've been gettin' crank calls ever since you and Felicity cut out. Forget about that, whaddaya got?"

The engine on the Jeep had sparked to life and was now idling smoothly. Felicity popped the vehicle into gear and started rolling forward.

"I remembered the vision," I expressed. "I'm not sure what all of it means, but I've got some ideas."

"Shoot."

"Well, I'm pretty sure he's going to do the ritual outdoors where he can see the moon. I think he might be planning to do it in a park or something."

"Any idea which one?"

Felicity gunned the engine slightly and eased from the bus turnout onto the off-ramp leading into the city limits of the small Saint Louis suburb of Overmoor.

"Not for sure. In the vision, I saw trees and a small lake," I explained further. "The only specific thing about it I can remember is a sign that said 'please do not feed geese'."

"No offense, white man, but do ya' know how many parks with lakes and geese we have in the metro area alone? Not to mention the state."

"Too many."

We continued down the small incline, past a wide opening in the chain link fence that ran alongside the ramp. I watched out my window as the obese moon lumbered across the night sky, arcing high above the trees. Apparently, a slight breeze was blowing, as I noticed the boughs of a stand of pine trees were gently waving. A line of tall pines obscuring all but the smallest glimpses of the lake behind them.

"Stop," I almost whispered at first and then spoke louder. "STOP!"

Felicity immediately cranked the steering wheel to the right, pulling us onto the shoulder. The tires ground coarsely against the loose gravel when she jammed on the brakes and brought us to a sliding halt.

"What? What's wrong?" she appealed.

Similar questions, only spoken by Ben's voice, were issuing raspily from the cell phone as I handed it to her and opened my door. Slowly, I covered the short distance between the Jeep and the fence, staring out across the moonlit landscape. I twined my fingers through the links and pressed my face against the warm, galvanized metal, intently studying the scene.

A line of tall pine trees reached upward to the star-speckled night. Between them, I could see the occasional shimmer of moonlight reflecting from rippling water. At the head of what appeared to be a trail, a small white and black rectangle was affixed vertically to a short post. It was too far away to read with the unaided eye, but I didn't have to make out the words to know that it simply said, PLEASE DO NOT FEED GEESE.

I turned my gaze upward at the almost perfectly round disk floating in the sky. Marbled grey and white, its luminescence cast the view in an eerie glow. In my mind, I could see the minute hand relentlessly chasing its smaller and slower rival about the surface. Overtaking it and repeating. Overtaking it and repeating.

A familiar, searing fire sprinted suddenly up my spine, bringing with it a dark foreboding. The hair stood out from the back of my neck, and my body felt like a living pincushion in a vat of alcohol as every other follicle stiffened to attention. Crackling static danced across my skin, setting its already tortured surface ablaze.

"Hey, mister, what time is it?" The little girl tugs on my sleeve. *"I have to go soon. What time is it? Hey, mister!"*

The hardened steel wedge of realization buried itself soundly between the hemispheres of my brain and drove relentlessly inward. I scrambled back to the Jeep in a frenzy, awkwardly slipping and falling on the loose gravel twice before making it. Felicity had the cell phone pressed to her ear and was apparently filling Ben in on my sudden, inexplicable behavior. Sensing what I was after, she handed me the device before I could snatch it away from her.

"It's happening now, Ben!" I fired into the phone with absolute certainty.

He began protesting immediately, "Wait a minute, you said the full moon would be on Friday."

"It's after midnight, Ben," I appealed, fighting to keep from shouting. "It IS Friday. Look at a calendar or a newspaper or something. What is the exact time the moon will be full?"

"Hold on..."

I could hear the door swing open and his distant voice as he called out for a calendar. Quickly, he returned, joined by the sound of rustling papers and other voices.

"It's not on here, Rowan," he responded in exasperation. "It's got the phases but not the times. Wait a minute... what's that?" One of the muted voices interrupted him, and he left me hanging for a thirty-second eternity. I could hear frantic muttering in the background before he returned. "Benson's kid is an astronomy student. He got her on the horn and she says that in our time zone, it'll be one-thirty-seven A.M."

"What time is it now?" I appealed to my wide-eyed wife.

"Ten till one," she answered.

"Less than an hour, Ben," I told him insistently. "He's going to kill her in less than an hour."

"But where? He could be at almost any park in the state.

Shit, he might not even be IN Missouri anymore."

I realized that in my rush to convince him of our severe deficit for time, I had not yet voiced my other revelation. "No Ben, he's still in Missouri. In fact, he's right here. Right now. I can feel him."

"Right where?"

"Wild Woods Park, just inside the city limits of Overmoor." I turned to face the gently waving pine trees once again. "I'm standing right outside the fence."

"Are you sure about..." He cut himself off before he could finish the question. "Forget I said that. Stay right where you are, Rowan. You understand me? I'm callin' Overmoor and gettin' some squad cars over there right now. We can be there in fifteen minutes, twenty tops. Don't go in until we get there, Rowan. You hear me? Don't go in the fuckin' park."

CHAPTER 27

True to what Ben had said, two Overmoor squad cars descended upon us at almost the same instant I switched off the cell phone. At my urging, we moved the three vehicles farther down the shoulder in order to remain out of the line of sight of anyone in the park. Seventeen lethargically oozing minutes later, Ben and Detective Deckert arrived, followed hotly by a dark sedan bearing U.S. government plates.

Special Agent Constance Mandalay looked far more intimidating than attractive in the muted glare of the distant streetlamp. The strict angular shadows that sliced through the sodium vapor glow painted her slight figure in an almost violently imposing likeness as she fixed her angry gaze on me.

"Did I not make myself clear, Mister Gant?" she javelined the query tersely. "You are no longer a part of this investigation. Period. Now, since Detective Storm seems intent on following you blindly about, you've not only bought yourself a world of trouble, you've managed to jeopardize his career as well."

My head was still being relentlessly hammered from the inside, and fire danced up and down my spine, making me painfully aware of Roger's presence in the moonlit park. The seemingly endless misery coupled with our race against time had begun deeply affecting my overall disposition. I was walking nothing other than the paper-thin edge between steady calm and explosive anger. The instant Agent Mandalay inserted herself into the grotesque equation, I lost all semblance of balance.

"Go fuck yourself," I told her drily.

"EXCUSE ME?" she demanded incredulously, visibly taken aback by my uncharacteristic and graphic instruction.

The low chatter among the uniformed officers came to an abrupt halt, and everyone present turned their eyes upon the close-quartered standoff that had materialized between us.

"I shouldn't have said that," I apologized for my rudeness but still maintained my umbraged tone, "but you've had it in for me from the very beginning, and I have no idea why. To be honest, I don't care that you don't like me. Whether you want to believe it or not, Roger Henderson is in this park." I stole a quick glance at my watch and then displayed it to her. "And in less than twenty-five minutes, the sonofabitch is going to stick his hand into a little girl's chest and rip her heart out. Now, if arresting me makes you happy, then be my guest. Just do that little girl a favor and wait until after we've stopped this asshole from killing her."

Agent Mandalay stared back at me with a slackened expression. A retort half formed, her lips parted suddenly then almost immediately closed without revealing the substance of the comment. The only sound to escape her was a reluctantly acquiescent sigh. "Okay. Fine. We'll search the park, but rest assured, Mister Gant, I am not through with you."

"Fine." Still unflinching, I held her contemptuous stare. "All I want to do is save the little girl."

She all but ignored my comment and turned her attention to the uniformed officers who had been observing our sharp exchange. "It looks like we're in the middle of a residential area. How big is this park anyway?"

"We are, ma'am, and it's pretty small," a sergeant replied. "Just a few acres. It used to be the grounds of a seminary."

"Doesn't sound like a very secluded place for a ritual murder." She directed her sarcasm toward me.

"Actually, it is fairly obscured. The idea was to leave it as natural as possible," he offered. "With the exception of the trail, it's pretty heavily wooded on the opposite side of the lake."

He began stumbling over his words near the end of the sentence. I could tell by his expression that if looks could kill, she had just stared him into an early grave.

"All right, Mister Gant." She turned back to face me once again. "Any suggestions as to WHERE in the park we'll find him?"

The details of my vision had become clearer and more precise with each painful recurrence. They were now so sharply in focus as to seem almost unreal.

"About thirty yards up the hill on the other side of the lake." I described in words what my mind was replaying in overblown, pixilated color. "There's a small clearing. It's surrounded on all sides by trees and bushes. There's an indirect entrance from the back."

She looked back to the uniformed officers and raised a questioning eyebrow.

"Yeah, he's right," one of the patrolmen spoke up. "There's a clearing there. We've caught a few teenagers hiding out in there, partying in the middle of the night."

"Deckert," she dictated as she unbuttoned her jacket and slipped her sidearm from its holster. "You're with me. You four," she directed herself to the uniformed officers. "Spread out and flank the clearing. Storm, you stay here with Mister Gant and his wife, and keep an eye on the entrance."

"But..." I started to protest.

"Save it!" she shot back. "You're staying here."

Ben grabbed my arm and shook his head as I started forward. I could feel Felicity's hand resting on my other shoulder, leaching her own mixture of fear, anger, and desperation into me.

"Look, Mandalay," Ben lashed out. "If you want my badge then come and get it. But until it's in your hot little hand, get off your power pony and give it a rest. I'm goin' in and Rowan's comin' with me."

"Suit yourself," she remarked flatly. "But be aware that you're kissing what's left of your career goodbye and getting your friend charged with interfering in a federal investigation in the process."

"O'Brien. That's spelled capital O apostrophe capital B, r-i-e-n," Felicity broke her self-imposed muteness.

"Excuse me?" Agent Mandalay demanded.

"I just wanted to make sure you spelled my name right when you filed the charges," my wife told her flatly. "I'm going in too."

Special Agent Mandalay simply turned and stalked off into the night, waving for the others to follow. Ben, Felicity, and I brought up the rear, quickly and quietly covering the forty odd yards along the shoulder to the park entrance. As a group, we advanced across the small paved parking area to the trailhead and proceeded up the short path to the starting marker. There, low to the ground, a white metal rectangle was bolted securely to an earthbound wooden post. PLEASE DO NOT FEED GEESE was embossed on its surface in bold black letters.

The group fanned out, following the trail in opposite directions, skirting around the lake on both sides. Everyone moved as quietly as possible, and I was fighting to contain several pained groans that threatened to seek release as the white-hot intensity of Roger's presence burned up my spinal cord and into my brain.

A bright stripe of cold moonlight traced a ribbon of white across the rippling surface of the dark water. The night was silent save for the occasional light breeze through the upper reaches of the trees. Even the crickets were refusing to sing their songs. We continued to creep along the path, moving as hastily as discretion would allow.

Ahead of me were Agent Mandalay and Detective Deckert; to my left, Felicity; and behind, Ben. The other officers were no longer visible, having slipped around to the other end of the lake and into the thickening woods. I cast a quick glance to my right and captured an instant flash of movement near the rocky shoreline. There immediately followed a loud plop as something hit the water.

Like sharply honed combat veterans, Mandalay and Deckert dropped to one knee, pistols directed at the fading sound. Ben did the same, dragging Felicity and I downward with him. Taking aim, he instantly snapped on a small but powerful flashlight, sighting it alongside his weapon. A muted glow diffused eerily through the water from the tightly focused beam.

The forced hush was thick around us, and I swallowed hard to evict my heart from my throat. The five of us stared almost unblinking into the murky water seeking out any and all movement. More than a few of our precious seconds expired before we pinpointed the source of the sound. Centered in the ribbon of moonlight, a rounded stub protruded upward from the water, followed by an ovalish dark hump, roughly the size of a dinner plate. Slowly, the large turtle began to paddle away.

After releasing soft relieved sighs, we regained our upright stances and proceeded deeper into the park. As we rounded the easternmost end of the shallow lake and made our way around to the backside, Ben quietly solicited Felicity's and my attention and motioned for us to stop.

"I want you two ta' wait right here," he whispered.

"But Ben," I objected, "what about..."

He didn't let me finish. "Right here!" he insisted, whispering through clenched teeth.

I had no choice but to stand silently watching as he moved past us along the path with Agent Mandalay and Detective Deckert. In mere moments, the three of them shrank to small blue-black silhouettes on the dimly washed landscape then disappeared as they seemed to melt and join with the shadows.

The antimony-veined disk of the moon jeered down at me when I allowed my gaze to drift upward. Though imperceptible to the naked eye, I knew only a thin thread-like arc of darkness remained along its edge. Looking back down, I pressed the side of my watch, and a dim blue-green glow illuminated its face. In less than twelve minutes, even that dark wisp of a thread would be gone.

We stood alone in the uneven shadows, mutely straining to glean whatever details we could from the silent landscape. I kept watch on the opposite end of the lake, expecting to catch a glimpse of the uniformed officers through some of the thinner sections of the trees. They had a slightly farther distance to travel, as the trailhead had started closer to our end. However, our momentary diversion, courtesy of the lake inhabitant, should have evened out the time.

Should have, but for some reason the four patrolmen still hadn't appeared, and a gnawing worry was starting to brew deep in my stomach.

"Something's wrong," I whispered to Felicity.

"You feel it too?" she half asked. "I'm freezing."

Felicity always sensed ethereal presences as coldness, no matter what the temperature truly was. The less pleasant the energy she sensed, the colder she got. She was shivering as she leaned against me.

"The other cops. They should have come around the end of the lake by now, but I don't see them."

"What do you think happened?" she questioned through

chattering teeth. "Where are they?"

"I don't know, but I'm willing to bet that..."

I wasn't afforded the opportunity to complete the sentence. A sixteen-pound sledgehammer, swung at full force, impacted squarely with the back of my head, shattering my skull and spilling its contents onto the path. At least I can only imagine that to be the closest example to the unbearable pain that suddenly stole away my breath, my sight, and even my very thoughts.

I doubled forward involuntarily.

Voluntarily.

With extreme prejudice.

I was willing to do almost anything to make it stop. The ripping spasm escaped down my spine and out through every nerve ending I possessed. My knees buckled, and I pitched to the ground. I don't know if I was screaming; I might have tried, but my hearing had fled with my other senses. Pure indigo darkness tugged at my soul, insisting that I enter into marriage with it.

"Why, Rowan, why?" Ariel Tanner stood before me shrouded in white lace, wisps of her strawberry-blonde hair floating gently on the breeze.

"I don't know, Ariel. I don't understand," I groaned.

"Yes, you do," her melodious voice sang. "You have always known. Tell me again, what does Rowan mean?"

I choked the answer out from behind blinding pain, "Strength...Security...Protector."

Ariel smiled knowingly. I began to feel energy flowing from her and into my body, chasing away the ravaging spasms. It was then I realized that the question had not been hers, but my own all along, "Why me? Why was it I who had been chosen to pursue this killer?"

The answer was as simple as my name.

I returned to reality curled into a ball on the mossy ground, breathing in the loamy odor of the soil. Roger's telltale fire still licked viciously up and down my back, but gone was the unbearable agony that had recently occupied the space where my head should have been. Clarity and focus had crept up from behind and ousted it from power.

"Rowan! Rowan, what's wrong?!" Felicity was insistently shaking me as she whispered.

I emulated her hushed tone as I climbed to my feet. "How long? How long was I out?"

"A few minutes. You just fell to the ground and curled up into a fetal position. What happened?"

"I'll tell you about it later. Did the other cops ever come out of the woods?"

"Not that I saw," she shook her head. "I was a little preoccupied with you, so I wasn't really watching."

The night grew suddenly still and impossibly, even more silent. I looked up into the inky sky at the moon bursting into fullness then down to my wide-eyed wife. Less than forty yards away, up the hill and to the right, the fragile pane of silence was shattered into innumerable glistening shards by a woman's terrified scream.

My heart double-skipped then settled into a steadily increasing rhythm as the adrenalin injected itself into my system. I had no idea what I was going to do. I only knew that before the piercing, horrified sound even began to fade, my legs were pistoning, pushing me up the hill toward its point of origin. Stealth was no longer an issue, and my feet were thudding loudly against the carpet of thick vegetation. I thrust my hands outward, warding off low hanging branches, which sought to assault my face with stinging, leafy slaps as I weaved through the increasingly thick woods.

Somewhat lighter, but no less frantic, footfalls echoed

behind my own. I knew them to belong to Felicity as she followed me on my insane headlong rush into whatever peril awaited.

A second shattering scream pierced the air, easily overcoming the manic kettledrum my heart was creating in my ears. Thickly foliaged bushes and young trees had continued to grow more numerous as I pushed farther away from the marked path, and they now presented themselves as an almost unbroken barrier before me. Yellow flickers of light I knew to be burning candles teased me through small bare spots in the oncoming brush. A third scream followed weakly on the heels of the second, telling me I had no time to search for the clearing's entrance.

Still clueless as to what I was going to do, I tucked my face behind the protection of my arms and plunged forward into the thicket. Burrs and needle-like spines tore and stabbed at my flesh while ground-hugging vines attached themselves ropelike around my ankles. My progress slowed as the sinewy ground cover seemed to pull against me in an attempt to drag me downward. Deep sobbing reached my ears, and I pumped my legs harder, tearing free and bursting scratched and bleeding through to the other side.

When I pulled my wildly lacerated arms from my face, the scene before me was much as I had witnessed in my vision. The young girl was laying on her back near the center of the small clearing, clad in silky white lace. Her glassy eyes stared upward through the dark green canopy of the trees, unblinking. Candles burned, red, yellow, blue, green, and white about the perimeter, black near her head. I had only a split second in which to take in the details of the display as my attention was immediately diverted by yet another fearful scream ice-picking my eardrums.

Special Agent Constance Mandalay stood transfixed on the opposite side of the clearing, her unfired sidearm tossed carelessly to the ground out of reach. Her eyes were wide in absolute terror, and her mouth trembled as thin tears wetted her cheeks. In the dimness of the shadows, I could see a sparkling halo of energy surrounding her. My eyes instinctively followed the crackling ethereal tether that whipped snakelike through the air, ending unsurprisingly at Roger Henderson's black-cloaked form.

Once again, Agent Mandalay's lips parted, emitting a high-pitched, unearthly sound. I wondered at why more attention hadn't been attracted to the small clearing by her night-breaking shrieks. At the same time, I could only fear what might have happened to Ben, Deckert, and the others.

The spidery lightning bolt remained connected between the two of them, pulsing outward from Roger in a quickening pace and snapping violently against her spasmodically jerking body. Visible sparks leapt from each point of contact, hissing through the air and quickly extinguishing before reaching the ground.

She had begun to slap and claw at herself as if something were trying to rend the flesh from her bones. I don't know what horror she was seeing; it was something meant solely for her. I only knew that whatever innermost personal fear she had kept locked away in the depths of her subconscious was now loose and ravaging her in ways unthinkable. Roger had been the one to release the obscenity, and by continuing to feed its illusory presence, he was going to kill her.

I was airborne for less than a second. I barely remembered the decision to launch myself at Agent Mandalay's tormentor—it had been that close to automatic. So intent was his focus on her, he hadn't even noticed my presence until we collided. My shoulder met hard with his midsection as I flung my full weight into his stationary form. A guttural huff exploded from his surprised mouth as the impact drove the breath from his lungs, sending the two of us on a collision course with the spiny thicket surrounding the clearing.

The primary objective of my less than thoroughly thought out plan was to sever the supernormal connection between Roger and Agent Mandalay, effectively ending the deadly glamour. My secondary ambition was to subdue him until he could be turned over to someone more qualified to make a proper arrest. Fortunately, the first part went exactly as I hoped. It was the second idea that immediately presented itself as a problem.

His initial shock rapidly fading to nothing more than a memory, Roger regained his breath and twisted wildly from my grip as we slammed into the thorny hedges. He scrambled upward from the tangled heap, fighting to break free as he regained his feet. From my prone position, I pitched myself forward, stretching my arm until I believed I could feel tendons tearing away from bone—then I reached even farther. Claw like, my hand hooked around his ankle as he fought the scrub for freedom, and with an agonized jerk, I knocked him off balance, casting him once more to the ground.

The two of us dragged ourselves to our feet almost simultaneously, first into a crouch then fully upright, slightly more than an arms length apart. Roger wheeled around to face me and we both froze. His hood had fallen back across his shoulders, and his face was exposed to the night. Hatred smoked in the grey-ashed cinders of his eyes as he locked his glare on me, and the sinewy tendons in his neck bulged angrily as he tensed.

"I warned you, Gant," he seethed. "You can't stop me."

"I already have. Look at the moon," I choked between somewhat labored breaths. Internally, I was regretting what my desk bound choice of professions had detracted from my physical condition. "Give it up Roger."

Slowly, he looked up through the shadowy foliage to the swollen globe. Absolute fullness was only a handful of heartbeats away, and he knew it the moment his eyes were filled with the silvery visage. With an almost calm intent, he just as slowly lowered his gaze back to mine. His smoldering grey irises started to crumble away like ash from a burning coal, revealing a savage red-orange glow.

The fire that had earlier danced up my spine now seared like a blowtorch across my body, slathering its malignant excrement upon me. Bracing myself against the supernatural attack, I pressed my own energies outward, deflecting his rage and forming an ethereal barrier between us. The blaze of pain was immediately doused, and my tortured skin quickly cooled.

Roger was unprepared for the backlash of his own energy and almost didn't catch it in time. The stream of malice-driven power exploded against his own hastily erected defenses in a roiling shower of crimson lightning. He stumbled backward from the shockwave and fought to maintain his balance. To the average spectator, we would have appeared to be doing something on the order of shadow boxing. To a crowd of Witches, one hell of a fireworks presentation was taking place. However, the exhibition was cut short as my opponent realized his chances of defeating me in such an arena were almost non-existent.

I caught only a vanishing glimpse of Agent Mandalay from the corner of my eye as she crawled forward reaching for her gun. My ears were filled thickly with a demonic banshee wail from Roger as he propelled himself low into my stomach and drove me through the ripping thorns of the thick brush. He bear-hugged me as I fought to maintain my balance, backpedaling into the foliage. I hammered my fist downward and felt it glance across his ribs, a sensation that was immediately followed by jellied numbness chased with glass shards of pain as the blow reverberated up my arm.

My stability faltered as we exploded through the wall of scrub and ricocheted off a solid tree trunk. A crush of agony ripped through me as my attacker's shoulder dug inward, and I heard the sickening sound of my own ribs as they cracked. We lurched to the ground, glancing from a tree stump, and began to roll. I fought to keep my arm hooked around his neck as our momentum increased. Rocks and small trees insinuated themselves into our wild path, exacting what revenge they could as we rolled over them. I reached with my free arm to grab at the tough saplings, trying to halt our progress down the ever-steepening hill, but to no avail. My grasp was too slow and our inertia too great. I ended up with nothing more than damp fistfuls of leaves and a raw, bleeding gash across my palm.

Our chaotic journey down the hillside ended almost as abruptly as it began. In a tangle of flailing limbs, we were catapulted from a low earthen ledge at the bottom of the hill.

With a dull thud, Roger and I impressed ourselves into the muddy shoreline of the small lake. I laid there gasping as the shock of the sudden stop began to subside. My right arm was still curled tightly around my assailant's neck, locked firm and unyielding. My heart was racing as I stared upward at the night sky, listening to shouting voices in the near distance.

Roger hadn't moved since we stopped rolling. I had maintained a desperate hold on him for the entire journey down the hill, and his head now seemed oddly cocked to the side. Resting against him in the mud, I listened for any sound from his limp body and not only heard nothing but felt nothing. Wearily, I disentangled myself from his still form and extricated my arm from about his neck. The voices were drawing closer and were joined by the sounds of running footsteps against soft ground. I hauled myself up to my knees, then shakily, to my feet.

Sharp, blinding pain surged up my thighs then down my calves, and my kneecaps felt as though they had been detonated like small explosive charges. My legs buckled, and I pitched backward, slapping the surface of the water with a stinging smack, and then I slipped under. Most of my breath had been forced from my chest with the surprised yelp elicited by the sharp pains in my legs, and the murky water rushed in to fill my nostrils. I knew I was in no more than two feet of water, so I clamped my eyes shut and started to sit up. Unfortunately, I felt a sudden weight on my chest and an angry hand firmly encircling my throat.

I began flailing my arms in front of me, pounding against the weight and trying to force it off my chest. My lungs burned from lack of oxygen, and the violent physical exertion only added fuel to their blaze. The bonfire in my chest crackled desperately up my throat, singeing it like a blowtorch. My body begged me to gasp for air; my mind forcefully told it not to.

I opened my eyes in the murky shallows and blinked rapidly as silt tried to settle in them. My vision, distorted as it was, started to darken and tunnel as my brain screamed helplessly for oxygen. I knew I was on the verge of passing out, and I fought even harder in the face of my greatest fear. Drowning.

My water-filled ears picked up the thick sounds of splashing as I flailed against Roger, his hand ever tightening around my neck. He pushed me hard into the spongy lake bottom, forcing me another inch farther from the cool, fresh air. Through the rippling surface of the silty water, I could see the glowing moon, which had moved past full, and although undetectable to the naked eye, into its waning phase. Its cold blue light glinted sharply from an all too familiar double-edged dagger held poised above me by the madman.

Murderous grey eyes bore down on me through the murky surroundings, smoking with the same fire they had displayed earlier. Ariel's athamè flashed once again as my attacker prepared to plunge it downward. My vision continued to stretch forth in a tunnel-like fashion then slowly began to fade.

Before I could close my eyes, the blade jerked out of its killing arc and followed a harmless trajectory away from me. At the same instant, the dull thrashing of water distantly entered my ears and was joined by a muffled explosion.

A dark rain spattered the surface of the water above my face and mixed lazily into milky spirals—cloudy helixes of vermilion in the dim moonlight. A second blunted thump sounded, followed quickly by a third, then a fourth. Three more showers of the thick crimson rain sprinkled wildly across the water's surface. The hand around my throat spasmed twice then fell limp. The weight pressing down on my chest shifted heavily and slid sideways.

Cool air rushed forcefully into my lungs, flowing down my throat in a thick gulp as I suddenly broke the surface. I gasped gratefully, sputtering and choking on the lake water I had sucked in, and blinked rapidly to clear the debris from my eyes. I began flailing angrily as I felt a large meaty hand entwine itself with the front of my shirt in a viselike grip then relaxed when I realized I was being pulled out instead of being pushed back in.

Felicity, Deckert, Mandalay, and two of the officers gathered in a loose semicircle around me as I laid gasping on the bank. Ben's large hand was still tightly gripping my waterlogged shirt, shaking me.

"Rowan?! Rowan?! Are you all right?" his concern-laden voice urgently met my ears.

I looked around the worried faces of the group then back to his. "Little girl?" I croaked.

"She's fine. The other coppers are with her," he smiled down at me. "There's an ambulance on the way."

Telltale distant warbling was growing louder as emergency vehicles raced to converge on us. I struggled to sit up, only to find they weren't going to allow it. Ben and Felicity both pressed me back down gently.

"Stay put," my wife ordered softly. "They're coming for you too."

I didn't protest, I just continued biting off large chunks of the night air and swallowing them hungrily. Again, I focused on Ben's face.

"Hey, Tonto," I choked out between breaths, "you shoot the bad guy?"

"Yeah, Kemosabe," he grinned. "Yeah, I shot the bastard."

"Next time," I wheezed, "don't take so damn long."

CHAPTER 28

"**B**en was telling me you got a call from that muckity-muck up in Seattle," Deckert posed and then took a hearty sip of beer. "What'd he have to say?"

He, Ben, and I were seated around the patio table on the back deck of my house. A little more than a week had passed since that night at Wild Woods Park, and I had coaxed them over for a day of barbecue and relaxation. We all desperately needed the chance to decompress from the pressure of the maniacally whirlwind investigation, as well as the intensity of its abrupt ending.

"He wanted to give me the reward he'd been offering," I answered, carefully trimming the end from a *Cruz Real #19*. "Everyone's firmly convinced that Roger was responsible for his daughter's murder, so he wanted to pay up. How he got my name, he wouldn't say."

"What did you tell him?"

"I gave him a list of charities. *Environmental Defense Fund, Nature Conservancy, World Wildlife Fund* and the like." I set a wooden match alight and touched the fire to the end of my cigar. "I told him if he really wanted to do something for me, that he should split the reward between them in the names of his daughter and the other victims."

"In other words," Ben interjected, waving his own cigar in my direction, "ya' turned it down."

"I like to think of it as redirected," I expressed.

Allison, Felicity, and Mona, Detective Deckert's wife, were leisurely roaming the perimeter of our large backyard. Every now and then they would pause to admire the last fitful colors of summer that still bloomed in our various wildflower gardens.

Benjamin Storm Junior was giggling with the unencumbered innocence of youth as he tumbled and rolled in the center of the yard. Our dogs let out excited, puppyish yelps, tails wagging and ears perked, as he chased them about in a wild game of tag.

The domestic Saturday afternoon scene was kind and familiar. I longed to lose myself to the relaxed feeling of security but knew deep down that it was a place I could only visit. I would never again be allowed to live there.

Ariel Tanner's death had forced me to deal with a question I had denied without even knowing it. The question of what my purpose within this lifetime was to be. The answer was one that I had only now begun to come to terms with.

It was only a matter of time before something evil would knock upon my door again, and I knew it. I hoped I would be prepared to face whatever it turned out to be.

"I still can't get over that glamour thing." Carl leaned back in his chair, cradling his beer bottle. "I mean I was lost! I couldn't find anybody, and the woods just kept getting darker and thicker no matter which direction I went. Seemed like it went on forever. Next thing I know, everything clears up, and I'm on the other side of the freakin' park hearin' all this screamin'. It was weird. Just plain weird."

From the descriptions provided by Ben, Carl, Agent Mandalay, and the other officers, I had come to the conclusion that they were all most likely affected by a *Spell of Misdirection*—a glamour of sorts. The closer they had come to the small clearing, the more disoriented and confused they became. The illusion of the thickening woods obscured the clearing and led them farther away with each step. Agent Mandalay had simply stumbled into the ritual circle entirely by accident. The amount of energy and concentration Roger Henderson had to have expended in order to affect and maintain such a massive phantasm was almost certainly the reason he had not detected my presence in the park until it was too late.

"Mandalay is the one who caught the worst of it," I volunteered. "Whatever she was seeing, it definitely wasn't pretty."

"That reminds me," Ben spoke up. "I meant ta' ask you... If he could do all that shit, then why was he botherin' ta' drug his victims? Why didn't he just *eenee meenee hocus pocus* 'em?"

"It's just a guess, but there are a couple of reasons I can think of off-hand." I drained the last of my own beer before outlining the ideas. "One would be the unpredictability. An aware mind isn't fooled by illusions and wouldn't fall into a trance. Another would be that even if he were able to hypnotize his victims, so to speak, the sharp physical pain of the flaying would have snapped them out of it. Drugging them was his safest bet to keep them quiet and immobile."

They both thoughtfully nodded acceptance of my explanation. Moving my chair back, I stood and checked the burning coals in the fire pit. A fine coating of whitish-grey ash had formed across half the surfaces of the briquettes. Randomly, the ash had fallen away to reveal a fiery red-orange glow. A small tremor ran the length of my spine as my mind fleetingly focused on the memory of the cancerous grey-red combination of Roger Henderson's violent eyes. I must have stood staring into the pit a moment too long as I was snapped back to reality by the sound of my friend's voice.

"Hey, white man. You okay?"

"Huh?"

"You're kinda starin' off into space, guy," Deckert intoned. "Something bothering you?"

"No. No, just daydreaming." I shrugged off their mildly concerned queries and then changed the subject. "The fire needs a few more minutes. I'm dry, anyone else need a beer?"

"Yeah," Ben answered, then drained the last remnants from his bottle.

"Count me in," Deckert added.

I gathered the empty bottles and disposed of them in the recycle bin before opening the door of the plant-filled atrium and proceeding into the kitchen. Allison, Felicity, and Mona had chased me out of this area earlier and between the three of them, had quickly prepared the food that was to be grilled. Fresh herb scents filled the kitchen and helped me to ease back into the pleasant reality at hand.

I was just opening the refrigerator when the front chime demanded attention. Momentarily placing the beverages on hold, I carefully picked my way through rapidly scattering felines and tugged open the heavy oak door.

"I hope I'm not intruding." An apologetic statement issued from a somewhat casually dressed Special Agent Constance Mandalay. "I noticed Deckert's car and Storm's van in the driveway."

"Not at all," I said, holding the door open wide and motioning to her. "Please come in."

She entered hesitantly and waited in silence while I shut the door. When I turned around, what faced me was a much-subdued version of the hard-nosed femme fatale that had originally confronted me at the Major Case Squad command post. She shuffled nervously and studied the pattern of the hardwood floor between quick glances at me with schoolgirl eyes.

"Listen, Mister Gant," she finally sputtered, racing to get the words out before they could flee, "I just wanted to apologize for my attitude toward you during the investigation."

"Rowan, please," I appealed calmly. "My friends call me Rowan. And there's no apology necessary, Agent Mandalay."

"Constance," she echoed my sentiments. "My friends call me Constance... And I still want to say I'm sorry... I treated you poorly, and I've no excuse... Except maybe for ignorance." She stumbled over the words, and her large eyes glistened as she choked back what might have been a tear. "What... What I saw that night... I... I don't know if I could ever tell anyone... I don't know if I could face it again. I... I just feel that if it weren't for you, I would be dead... If not dead then insane at the very least. I owe you for that, and I just wanted to tell you all this in person... I just needed to say... Thank you."

"You're more than welcome," I granted. "I'm just glad that you're all right."

"I'm getting there," she expressed with a nervous sigh. "The nightmares were bad at first, but I've been okay the past couple of nights. I'm not afraid to go to sleep any more. With a little luck, I should be off administrative leave by the end of next week."

"Just don't push yourself," I advised. "Go back when you're ready. Not before."

"I know."

Timid silence filled the room around us, broken only by the sound of Salinger as he leapt heavily onto the coffee table and studied the new human in the room.

"So, how do you like your steak?" I posed, adding my words to the void.

"Excuse me?"

"How do you like your steak?" I repeated. "They'll be going on the grill in just a few minutes, and I'll need to know how you want it cooked."

"No. I couldn't stay," she protested. "I'm sure Deckert and Storm would just as soon I fall off the face of the earth after the way I acted. Especially Storm."

"I don't know about that. I've known Ben for..."

"Hey, paleface!" We heard Ben's jovial voice booming from the kitchen and growing closer as he ambled through the house in our direction. "What happened to those beers?"

Ben came to a sudden halt as he rounded the corner into the dining room and noticed Agent Mandalay standing across from me. Their eyes locked for a moment, and I could easily sense the fluid apprehension that flowed between them. The only sounds to be heard were the distant voices of Allison and Felicity drifting in from the kitchen.

"I was just asking Constance how she wanted her steak done," I expressed calmly.

Their gazes remained fixed a moment longer, faces expressionless. As if on cue, the heavy tension whirlpooled down an unseen drain, and Ben's face spread into a welcoming smile.

"Hey, Allison," he called over his shoulder, "better wrap up another one of those potatoes." He turned his gaze back to us before continuing. "Another friend just showed up."

Agent Mandalay's face broke into a relieved grin, and she glanced back to me. "Medium rare," she answered in an easy, comfortable tone. "I like my steak medium rare."

EPILOGUE

Eight robed figures stood somberly in the large clearing, bluish light illuminating them from the rotund globe of the full moon. Surrounding the small circle were five freshly planted trees, straight and carefully spaced. Even to a casual onlooker, it was obvious that great care had been taken in the placement and rooting of the saplings. To a brother or sister of The Craft, it would be readily apparent that walking a particular, familiar path between the five trees would form a large Pentacle.

An auburn-tressed woman, long hair spiraling in a brilliant cascade down her back, moved lithely about the group carefully touching a flame to colorful candles appointed at four stations of the circle—yellow to the East, red to the South, blue to the West, and green to the North. She moved as if floating, adding her low, solemn voice to the rest as each of the four towers was hailed.

The woman moved fluidly back to the center of the small gathering, taking a position next to a bearded man, his own long, brown hair flowing loosely about his shoulders. The man lifted a brightly polished athamè to the sky and scribed a perfect Pentacle in the still air. As he lowered the ceremonial knife, the coven members joined in a thrice-repeated chant.

The red-haired priestess once again touched flame to a candle—this time white—in the center of the circle then turned and placed a gentle kiss on the lips of the priest. As they parted, a young man with long, dark hair raised a small horn to his own lips and blew hard into the end, sending a single wailing note to resound from the hillsides. As the note faded on the still, night air, the young man lowered the horn and announced to the gathering, "The horn is sounded for Ariel."

The other members answered him in unison, "So be it."

The priestess looked about the solemn group and closed her bright green eyes. "That today, Ariel is not with us, here in the Circle, saddens us all. Yet, we should try not to feel sadness but joy, for is this not a sign that she has fulfilled this life's work? She is now free to move on, and we should not fear, for we shall meet again. That will be our time for further celebration."

"Let us send forth our love and good wishes to bear her across The Bridge," the priest proceeded on from the last words of the priestess. "May she return at any time she wishes and be here with us. May she also guide the unfortunate victims who shared her death as they move along their new paths. I ask the God and Goddess to bless these five trees we have planted in honor of the lives that have ended and the new lives that will begin. Blessed Be!"

"So mote it be!" The chorus rang out from the coven members, sedate but strong.

In the shadows, unnoticed by choice, a translucent glimmer of a young strawberry-blonde woman clad in a white lace gown stood watching the group. Her hair wafted gently about on an ethereal breeze, a sparkling halo hovering around her petite figure. She smiled as she felt their energy join and rise into a powerful cone. Still, a small teardrop escaped her eye. The coven's mellifluous chant filled her ears as she turned and crossed over The Bridge.

<u>Never Burn A Witch</u>
A Rowan Gant Investigation

Book #2 in the Rowan Gant Investigations Series
ISBN 0967822114 / $8.95 US

THE RETURN OF THE BURNING TIMES

In 1484, then Pope Innocent VIII issued a papal bull-- A decree giving the endorsement of the church to the inquisitors of the day who hunted, tortured, tried and ultimately murdered those accused of heresy-- especially the practice of WitchCraft. Modern day Witches refer to this dark period of history as "The Burning Times."

Rowan Gant returns to face a nightmare long thought to be a distant memory. A killer armed with gross misinterpretations of the Holy Bible and a 15th century Witch Hunting Manual known as the Malleus Maleficarum has resurrected the Inquisition and the members of the Pagan community of St. Louis are his prey.

With the unspeakable horrors of "The Burning Times" being played out across the metropolitan area, Rowan is again enlisted by Homicide Detective Benjamin Storm and the Major Case Squad to help solve the crimes-- All the while knowing full well that his religion makes him a potential target.

Perfect Trust
A Rowan Gant Investigation

Book #3 in the Rowan Gant Investigations Series
ISBN 096782219X / $8.95 US

PICTURE PERFECT

Rowan Gant is a Witch.
His bane is to see things that others cannot.
To feel things he wishes he could not.
To experience events through the eyes of another...
Through the eyes of victims...
Sometimes, the things he sees are evil...
Criminal...
Because of this, in the span of less than two years, Rowan has come face to face with not one, but two sadistic serial killers...
In both cases he was lucky to survive.
Still, he abides the basic rule of The Craft-- Harm None.

This predator could make Rowan forget that rule…

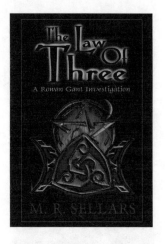

The Law Of Three
A Rowan Gant Investigation

Book #4 in the Rowan Gant Investigations Series
ISBN 0967822181 / $12.95 US

LET THE BURNINGS BEGIN...

In February of 2001, serial killer Eldon Andrew Porter set about creating a modern day version of the 15th century inquisition and Witch trials. Following the tenets of the *Malleus Maleficarum* and his own insane interpretation of the Holy Bible, he tortured and subsequently murdered several innocent people.

During a showdown on the old Chain of Rocks Bridge, he narrowly escaped apprehension by the Greater St. Louis Major Case Squad.

In the process, his left arm was severely crippled by a gunshot fired at close range.

A gunshot fired by a man he was trying to kill. A man who embraced the mystical arts. A Witch. Rowan Gant.

In December of the same year, Eldon Porter's fingerprints were found at the scene of a horrific murder in Cape Girardeau, Missouri, just south of St. Louis. An eyewitness who later spotted the victim's stolen vehicle reported that it was headed north...

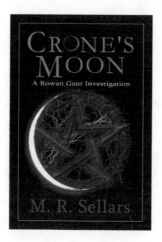

Crone's Moon
A Rowan Gant Investigation

Book #5 in the Rowan Gant Investigations Series
ISBN 0967822149 / $12.95 US

**WHEN THE DEAD SPEAK,
ROWAN GANT HEARS THEIR WHISPERS**

A missing school teacher, decomposed remains in a shallow grave, and a sadistic serial killer prowling Saint Louis by the semi-darkness of the waning moon-- exactly the kind of thing Rowan Gant has no choice but to face. But, this time his bane, the uncontrolled channeling of murder victims, isn't helping; for the dead are speaking but not necessarily to him. Rowan once again must skirt the prejudices of police Lieutenant Barbara Albright as he and his best friend, homicide detective Ben Storm, race to save a friend... and perhaps someone even closer.

Photo Copyright © K. J. Epps

ABOUT THE AUTHOR

Author of the best selling *Rowan Gant Investigations* series of suspense-thrillers, M. R. Sellars began reading at age four, and writing shortly thereafter—he hasn't stopped since. The product of a liberal family, from an early age Sellars was exposed to many different religions and belief systems, both mainstream and obscure. To this day he remains an avid student of the religious diversity that surrounds us. Not one for remaining "in the broom closet," Sellars often gives group lectures on request in order to help dispel the many myths and misconceptions that surround the practice of witchcraft, paganism, and the Wiccan religion.

A self-described "long-haired hippie activist tree-hugger," Sellars studied Journalism and Literature as well as Computer Science throughout high school and college, winning many prestigious awards for writing during his academic course. Although his first love was the written word, fate quickly led him to his vocation of more than twenty years as a Senior Level Electronics Technician and Internet Systems Administrator. Even with his hectic dual career, Sellars finds time to indulge in his hobbies of hiking, camping, nature photography, and cooking. A classically trained, accomplished gourmet chef, he can often be found "playing" in his favorite room—the kitchen.

M. R. Sellars has been an honored guest and speaker at numerous public libraries, community organizations (both Pagan and Non-pagan), and at national events such as the annual *Real Witches Ball* in Columbus, Ohio; the *S.P.I.R.A.L. Pagan Unity Festival* in Burns, Tennessee; *Gathering of the Tribes* in Virginia; *Festival of Souls* in Memphis, Tennessee; *Florida Pagan Gathering*; and the annual *Heartland Pagan Festival* and *Pagan Pride Day Celebration* in Kansas among numerous others.

An avid member of numerous environmental stewardship organizations, Sellars resides in the Midwest with his family where their home is known to be a safe haven for neglected and abused animals. The novels in the *Rowan Gant Investigation* series: *Harm None (2000)*, *Never Burn A Witch (2001)*, *Perfect Trust (2002)*, and *The Law Of Three (2003)* have all spent numerous weeks on various bookstore bestseller lists, and *The Law Of Three* garnered the St. Louis RFT People's Choice Award soon after its debut.

At the time of this writing, Sellars is working on several projects, as well as traveling on promotional tour.

For more information about M. R. Sellars and his work, visit him on the World Wide Web at www.mrsellars.com.